GW00455993

From a young age, James always dreamed of writing a book. With his love of fantasy, a prolific imagination and characters he created as a teenager, he has now finished his first book, *Path of the Gods.*

James graduated from ArtsEd, London with a degree in acting, as well as a higher diploma in guitar playing from the ACM, Guildford.

With Volume II, *Disciple of the Gods,* in the final stages, he is currently working on the completion of the trilogy and has no plans to stop writing.

For Anna

Thank you
for getting
my proverbial
in gear!

James Val'Rose

PATH OF THE GODS

VOLUME I
THE THEURGY
REVOLUTION

To Pauline & Adrian

In darkest Marxton!

James Val'Rose

May 2014

AUSTIN MACAULEY
P U B L I S H E R S   L T D.

A CIP catalogue record for this title is available from the British Library.

ISBN 978 184963 527 1

www.austinmacauley.com

First Published (2014)
Austin Macauley Publishers Ltd.
25 Canada Square
Canary Wharf
London
E14 5LB

Printed and bound in Great Britain

Acknowledgments

Thank you to all the phenomenal authors who have silently inspired me to pursue my dreams. I can only hope that I have chipped off but a fragment of your genius.

Big, big, *big* love and thanks to my family for getting as used to the back of my head as the front, whilst I was away, walking the halls of kings, fighting fiends, journeying to the far reaches of Aramyth and following on my characters' adventures. Your love, no, your support, no, your *tolerance* knows no bounds!

Thank you to everyone who took the time out of their busy lives to read excerpts, chapters and parts, as well as those intrepid few who read the whole thing! Thank you for seeing what I could not, for helping to whittle out all those cheeky mistakes and for your encouragement. At times, it was much needed!

Many thanks to my editor, Hayley Knight, for your initial faith and, most importantly, for making it all make sense; to Rose Northwood and Neil Burrows for such legendary artwork and vision; and to Vinh Tran for bringing it together. Thank you all for giving it life.

And thank you to you, Cherished Reader, for having this, for holding this. I can't thank you enough for your support. So, whether bought, borrowed, begged or stolen – the latter would truly flatter me! – I hope this will find a place in your heart as well as just your bookshelf.

Contents

The War of Unity

Furious thunder rained down from the sky, as wave after wave of fire-tipped arrows ran veins of chaos through the weary defenders. Those quick enough to raise their shields in time may have been protected from the falling assault, but could not be spared the misery of watching their comrades fall from the endlessness, war's irrevocable haze. Few were spared its persecution; as every second drudgingly elapsed into the next, it was made clearer that their paths to heroism were to be well-earned.

The battle had raged for two full days, and by the morning of the third, the defenders were haemorrhaging life. But the fear that lingered inside wasn't that of fatigue; it was what they were pitted against – strange beasts shrouded in darkness, coming at them through the dimensions of a different time and space. It was as though the light twisted and shied away from a demon beneath.

And amidst this phantasm horde were legions of corporeal beings, whose pernicious manifestation, though not illusory, equally delivered the same unrest.

No one even knew how the war had started. It was as mysterious and unexplained as the monsters they were fighting.

This evil uprising, right on the cusp of the Barrens, outside the city of Gatelock, in the direction of the Burning Bluffs, was the first, last and final line of defence for all of Aramyth.

Warriors from every walk of life, of every skill, age and race, gathered in unity for the saviour of their land. An epic congregation of men and women, both magi and not, and green-skins, both short and tall, found themselves in a desperate race to put aside their differences and stand together.

The glimmering stars bowed out to a new wave of burning arrows, the sky turning to fire, bathing the disorientated faces beneath.

As the fiery deluge began, horror played its sadistic game once more. But one face was not afflicted by the same dread, and was instead detached, devoid of all fear and reason.

A young boy of twelve found himself crushed between two men, their shields raised, ready for the impending descent.

Fortunately, the man to his left took a moment and looked down to see the boy's exhaustion, grabbing his shielded arm and driving it firmly into the air.

An indiscernible moment later, the arrows pounded down, so vigorously that the boy was thrust onto his back. The force of this, as well as the quick consecutive thuds on his shield, made his ears ring; and to add, the saturated, churned-up mud beneath began to soak through his smock and trousers – ice to the touch.

The ringing ceased only to be replaced with the clatter of fighting.

"Boy! Boy!" he heard someone say, but the faint was still passing. "Boy! Are you hurt?"

He gave his head a shake and looked to the man at his left. He mustered a 'what?' in response – his head still rang – but the man replied before much more could be said.

"We haven't the time for introductions. Stay close to me, the charge is coming soon."

"The charge?" he managed.

"We can't go on for much longer like this. Most of us have been awake for over two days now, and with little respite. We need to make a final push now or there won't be anyone left standing to fight. I'm amazed you've come this far."

With the sun's ascent above the Burning Bluffs, the dawn's fog was beginning to blanket down, bringing with it a lingering silence.

Every gentle stir of movement flicked the mist up and off the ground, making it dance a little whirlwind.

The silence was abruptly broken by a strong voice coming from a deeper part of the lines.

"Stand ready!" it shouted. "Face the enemy! Ready to charge!"

The boy could now feel the tension between all who were caught up in the vile mist. His earlier saviour placed a hand on his shoulder and leant in. "Stay close to me, remember."

"Yes," the boy muttered.

The voice from afar shouted the final command and each and every soul caught within the mist's clasps broke free and began the final charge towards the enemy...

Part I
The Calling

Aramyth was a land of simple beauty, where the nightly sky above always glistened with a sea of stars, illuminating the snowy Peaks of Paladain below, upon which the Ocean Melos could be heard washing new hopes into the hearts of dreamers.

All seemed dormant.

In Olakwin, between the city of Cearan and the western port city of Nardil, was the Edolan Valley. Nestled in the shadows at the base of the vale, lay a small hamlet by the name of Melfall.

Although home to a scant handful of people, the Vale Inn was always full to the brim with travellers, merchants and adventurers, the road to Cearan bringing its harvest each day.

Though night was upon Melfall and quiet resounded for the most part, a light shone brightly through a window...

***

The newborn child lay nuzzled tightly in his mother's arms, possessing only the knowledge that where he lay was his world, and that he was safe.

With his head tenderly supported in the crook of her arm, Driana glanced at the two others in the room, her friend Melissa, who had been her main support through the pregnancy, and the local wise woman, yet all she was aware of was this tiny, pure, new soul – her son.

The baby's soft susurrus sequestered Driana's attention – attention she was incapable of not lavishing. It drew her hard into the baby's eyes, to a flicker of wisdom departed, and a clean slate left for the world around to leave its impression.

But there was so much he had no idea of – could *not* have any idea of; so much he had to learn. She knew as much as anyone that the world could be an unforgiving teacher, being a learned scholar of its unfairness herself. She prayed that he learn of the bad, but discover the good, be entwined with it, let it suffuse his soul with hope...

With the backs her fingers, she stroked his cheek, desperate to supply him with every nonstop ounce of love that she could. His youthful curiosity swished around the room, but her touch stilled his focus, just as his murmurs stilled hers. Locked together in hush, his eyes strikingly ablaze, she placed the first kiss to his forehead – an invisible mark to the creator's realm saying that he was hers, but a promise to *him* that it was *always and forever*...

She kissed his forehead, and then kissed the bridge of his nose. Her lips sat perfectly either side, almost like that place was designed for kissing.

The two ladies excused themselves from the room, and Driana moved herself to the corner chair, so that she and her son could share their first sunrise together.

Despite her tiredness, she walked with him through Melfall that morning. The day was as young as the child in her arms, which seemed as fitting a time as any to introduce him to the world: for both to meet.

The sun had yet to work its heat into the chilly atmosphere, but the new light in her heart – in her arms – kept her warm. It was a revitalising gift bestowed upon her, and she cherished it. He was a love seconded by nothing. Before him, it was the medallion she treasured and was seen to be wearing always. But now, everything had changed, and residents of the hamlet, and even weary travellers, congratulated her into motherhood.

Unfortunately though, an overwhelming sorrow marred the tapestry of her happiness, impishly unpicking the weaves of her delight.

Only a few weeks after the child's conception, the father, Jerome Davian, had disappeared, vanished without a trace, or a word. She remembered the deep suffering – still felt it – and the hole that it had left in her riven heart, and the scar that remained to remind her.

Melissa had been with her then, supported her in her anguish. Yet, despite her encouragement to let him go – so that she could move on – she still *stupidly* prayed for his return, that no harm had befallen him. She clung to the idea that maybe it had been an urgent summons from the high king, for whom he was a soldier – or so he had told her.

The fact remained that, although she had never considered their relationship serious, she had only been lying to herself. She could not, and had never been able to, for any second that they were together, help loving him. And now that he was gone, she felt punished to love him more; it was like an all-consuming illness, infecting every bit that it touched. To her, their brief time together had seemed a flight with the angels – a carefree vastness of pleasure – and now, it was the slow, painful descent back to the unwelcoming ground, a fall from grace, to live life as a mortal, after having been enwrapped in the folds of heaven.

The time seemed to pass slowly, as she mulled over the endless questions rumbling through her mind, like a snowball rolling its inexorable course down a hill. *Would she see him again? Did she* want *to see him again...?*

Of course she did, but admitting it only pained her more.

It had been a long morning, a morning of triumph and promise, of wishful thinking and dreams. But in her mentally and physically weakened state, she made her retreat back home to her small house.

Cradling the baby, rocking him slowly to slumber, she was ineffably stung by a myriad of feelings. Her body could not contain the tempest and she released her tears, varying streams and undercurrents immersed with thrill and torment.

It was the start of a day she would never forget. All that was left was the child's name. It was her finishing thought before the tears carried her to her own sleep.

The idea blossomed within the stillness without any sign of warning. She would call him after his father; his name would be Jerome.

Chapter I
The Desire

Driana was a lady of forbidden beauty. It was as though she had stolen her looks from Heaven's angels, seized her radiance from Heaven's celestial sphere and purloined the colour in her eyes from the depths of Heaven's ocean.

But she was no thief.

That said though, if stealing the breaths and hearts of men were a crime then she would be the finest of *all* thieves.

Gazing upon her red lips was like sailing on a carmine sea of roses, and her blue eyes, while they occasionally sang with green, hinted at something mystic. Her deep black hair and equally dark eyebrows gleamed with a solar essence.

She was blessed with seraph splendour and it mirrored the soul beneath. Yes, rarely was she without attention, but rarely was it anything else, anything more – something to look at, to adore and go *crazy* over, but ultimately, only ever left for the imaginarium.

There had only been one true love for her, and that was now over and she lived with that solemn acceptance.

***

The years ticked by, as Driana watched Jerome grow. As she sat down each evening she enjoyed watching his life, and the events that marked it: the first time he stood up, the first step he succeeded in making, his first word.

These were the moments that happiness was made of, that made everything so understandable, for as much as she loved Jerome, he could be a handful at times. But that phase soon passed as he grew to be a toddler, then a child and then a teenager.

Fourteen years had raced on, but it left no one with any doubt that Driana had done a remarkable job in raising him.

He was a helpful young soul, and never dithered at the chance to assist, or just be there should she ever ask.

For the most part he didn't take after his mother's looks. His hair was brown, which when coupled with the sunlight often gleamed blond. And even though it lacked in length, Jerome was still able to find a way of making it messy – a talent only a boy could possess, Driana often mused. His eyebrows were very prominent and, like his mother, he also had wonderful, rich blue eyes. His face was well defined and his skin was tanned from the amount of hours spent outside.

Jerome's only knowledge of his father was through stories his mother had told, and they were few and far between. Although it had occurred to him that while his mother often wept at the stories, he could not find it in him to do the same.

Of course he was sad that he had not known him, but to him, his father was just a story: a something that had never been, and therefore nothing that he could never lose.

But the way she told those stories – a gifted storyteller – he was sure that he would have loved him.

Sometimes he would sit and think about it. Painless as it was to him, to Driana it was obviously quite the reverse, and that *did* make him sad.

To ease it though, he had a friend by the name of Peter, who always gave him time, mainly because they were the closest of friends, but also because of their shared situation.

Peter had light fair hair – equally as messy as Jerome's – and green eyes. He lived under the care of a quiet couple, Melissa, Driana's closest friend, and her husband Dreyton.

They had come into guardianship of him when he was just a baby. He had been abandoned outside their front door, with little more than a note nestled upon the cradle in which he lay. Nonetheless, they took him in and raised him as their own.

Jerome and Peter had known each other for as long as they could remember. They had both been told the stories of their lineage, and how both were missing vital parts from each. It was a sour bitterness that they had both experienced, but to two young boys, that sour taste made the joy of company, the heat of the sun and the fresh cool breeze that much sweeter.

In their early years, they accomplished much together. They had often taken walks into the woods of Banneth Fell, known to locals as The Fell, and within, found the most astonishing place to create their own *haven of tranquillity.*

That was how they pictured it anyway, but they were boys, with the call of the wild – the call for adventure – limning their hearts. Dreams of grandeur, tinted by the glamorous hue of treading the hero's path, halted any chance of *tranquillity*.

More often than not, they could be found wielding sticks at each other, scrapping, scuffling, climbing trees and terrorising the wildlife.

And as the years saw them grow, so, too, did everything else. The trees they climbed got higher, the animals they chased got bigger, the fights they had became rougher and picking *swords* became more of a deadly science. But it was their freedom, and they had no incentive of exploring anything else. Moreover, they had never been exposed to anything beyond that life. Their parents, for similar reasons, blanketed them. And consequently, even at the ages of sixteen and fourteen, Peter and Jerome behaved like that of younger boys, but life was about to shatter down upon them faster than they would have liked…

…And it all stemmed from the simplest of things.

Their *haven of tranquillity* really was a remarkable place. Although, ostensibly just a clearing within The Fell, it had all the right ingredients to make it perfect. Just inside the treeline was a big, turfed heath, excellent for hiding behind, spying from, or lazing on… On the other side was a small lake that shrivelled into a stream, which eventually would run its course into the depths of The Fell and onwards to the sea. Over the years, they had both learnt the mastery of staying afloat and even to swim, but from incidents – where play had gone too far – they had also learnt the necessary veneration for it, as well.

***

Jerome had his back to a tree, while Peter perched, looking over the heath. Jerome had spied the rabbit, and the game was to catch it. They had never actually succeeded in doing that, so the game had become a whoever-gets-nearest-to-it-wins sort of game. And, from the rareness of seeing a rabbit, so ready for the taking, this game took precedence over all others.

The only real rule was *no sabotage*. If the other were to make a noise, throw something, or scare the prey away then the other would automatically win. But this rule was never broken, not anymore at least, since they were now both aching to catch one.

Jerome went first, as was his right being the one who spotted it – *spotter's honour*. He slowly crept out, controlling the placement of his feet on the springy woodland floor.

It was close, maybe closer than one had ever been – maybe it just seemed that way, maybe it always did – and he took each step with deadly seriousness. He could virtually *hear* it nibbling, its snappy movements and com*pletely* ridiculous, stigmatic, fluffy-tail bobbing.

He felt close, but he reassessed and, at the current rate of his approach, the rabbit would die of old age before it would be in catching distance. He was about to take another step and then … *gone.*

He and Peter had learnt not to try and sprint after them, make a last-ditch dive to nab it. Not only because it was futile, but also because it would surely scare it away for good, and it was important that the other got a turn.

His head dropped and then he looked over to Peter, who was smug, ducked behind the heath, with only his eyes peeping over the top.

His turn now…

A defiant and churlish part of Jerome hoped that the rabbit was gone … but it wasn't, and Peter crept out from behind the grassy cover.

Jerome watched as a he sneaked up with determination, and he was quiet.

And he was *close … really* close.

He was actually going to do it.

And then, as if some sort of mystic, leporine spirit was watching over and protecting its kith, like a fluffy-floppy-eared guardian angel, a hopping messenger of truth, the rabbit got wind of it and scarpered.

Of course, it was inevitable. And besides, that wasn't the game. It was whoever was closest, and to the frustrating truth, it was Peter.

"Fine," Jerome accepted. "Anyway, it's not like sneaking up on rabbits is a valuable life skill."

"No one ever said it was, and besides, *you* were the one who spotted it!" Peter scoffed.

"Well I've had enough of this whole rabbit chasing nonsense. We're never going to catch one, you know."

Peter chuckled. "You're probably right, but you know we'll always keep trying."

"Not me," Jerome said. "No more. I'm *done* with all that."

"All right… What do you want to do then?" Peter said, after a moment of consideration.

Jerome thought. It was a hard truth, but there was very little that he could do better than Peter, and the things he *could* do better unfortunately weren't the games they played: more the tailoring he had picked up from his mother. A cross-stitch, a chain stitch, a darning stitch, Jerome could list them all *and* recognise them as well. Give them a competition about *that* and Jerome would win, hands down.

However, it wasn't about stitching or hemming or darning or embroidering. It never was, and, in a way, Jerome was fine about that. But the time for thinking was over, and then the words simply spilled out. "Sword fight?"

Why, in the name of God and all His angels, did he say that? *And* he knew Peter was better than him. *Stupid, stupid, stupid!* Of course, he couldn't back down now.

Peter sounded a little snigger, as he picked up two similar-length pieces of wood. One he kept in his hand and the other he threw with disdain upon the floor in front of Jerome.

Tapping his lightly on the floor in a cordial manner, he said, "Your sword."

To add to this jocular formality, a subtle grin marked his face, which he made absolutely sure Jerome could see.

Bending down to pick up that stick took what felt like an age, as he churned over the thought of Peter beating him. But he wouldn't let it happen, he thought. He couldn't. He mustn't.

The weapon was in place and Peter, poised and composed, readied his stance to match.

There was a pause. All became still and quiet for a short period of time... Then the attacks started flying. Wood chip flew left, right and centre, as miscalculated hits from both landed on bare flesh, but the fight continued on and Jerome didn't surrender either. On the contrary the more times Peter landed a successful attack, the more Jerome kept swinging his sword until he felt nothing but determination. However, what made this occasion unlike any of its predecessors was that Jerome's attacks became more precise and accurate, despite his anger and frustration.

Peter was only just managing to defend himself, let alone trying to take the offensive. He could see that Jerome wasn't going to stop. It was too late for that. Peter had to stop the fight the only way he knew how, dropping his sword and taking a few steps back.

For a few moments after the fight was over, Jerome was still flinging his piece of wood around. When he realised it was all over – he'd *won!* – he quickly composed himself and, as he did, looked over to Peter with confusion upon his face.

"What was that?" Peter muttered.

"What was what?"

"That style of fighting? It was deadly."

"I didn't know it was different to anything before. I was just ... swinging a piece of wood around."

"Well, if you say so. Anyway it's getting late and I have to get home. And you should, too."

Peter beckoned his friend to come and they started the long trip home.

Idly they chatted, as they walked, talking of things they had done, of things to come and many other topics, and it was during such a conversation that Peter mentioned to Jerome about training in Cearan.

Jerome dismissed the idea initially, but a seed had been planted in his mind. It was something he had thought of before, but no one had ever recommended it.

His mother had always wanted him to be a tailor, but that was never something that had interested him. Yet she still talked to him about it as though it were absolute, and no degree of argument was ever enough to persuade her otherwise.

He wanted to be something his father would be proud of, even though he had no idea of what that might be. He had great visions of himself running through a war-torn, blood-stained battlefield, slaying men to his left and right, blood flying in all directions, shouts of pain and death, as one man would fall after another, until finally reaching his nemesis.

In his thoughts, his final foe would be dressed in bulky, black armour; and there he would stand face to face with him before bringing him down. Cheers would be heard all over; shouting his name aloud, for Jerome would be the victor!

But these, among others, were only thoughts of a boy lost in his swaying imagination.

They couldn't have been more than ten minutes from home, and they had already been travelling for a good while, when Jerome suddenly stopped and flushed a whiter shade of unwell.

Turning quickly to Peter, he said, "My bag! I left it behind. Peter, I have to go back and get it."

"Jerome, it's almost dark. You can't."

"I have to. It's got my mother's medallion in it. She'll *kill* me."

"What are you doing with her medallion?"

Completely caught up in the plume of worry, he ignored Peter and resaid, "I *have* to go back and get it."

"She'll never let you go out again if you get home much later than this."

"And she'll never let me out if she finds out I've taken her medallion, so either way it doesn't matter … but I'd rather be alive."

Peter, torn between helping his friend and being told off himself, thought for a second, and then said, "…Look, do you want me to go back with you?"

"No point the both of us being late. You head back, I'll be fine."

"Suit yourself, but you'd better run."

Which Jerome did.

"What shall I say if your mother calls round and asks where you are?" Peter shouted back to his friend.

"Anything!"

Peter shrugged his shoulders and continued the last leg of the journey on his own.

***

That night, Banneth Fell was not the only wood to have a lone figure rattling through. Far on the other side of Aramyth, in Dewdrop Wood, out-skirting the south of Toryn, was a young girl. She had been in those woods for just over a day now.

Slung over her shoulder was a bag, which contained food, water and a rumpled blanket. Her clothes were shabby, complete with tears and rips. Most, if all, of the colour that they had originally possessed had long since faded from age and lack of care. Moreover, any colour that may still have lingered on was coated in a layer of mud and grime, and undetectable either way.

Her hair was wild and frayed, held up and together by dead leaves and some very fine bits of kindling, all this adding to its frizzy and dishevelled look.

Her face was also not without additions. It was mostly just filth and grime, but hiding beneath that were a couple of cuts and grazes where she had tripped and fallen into the bracken.

She was in a very sorry state. But she had been on the run for more than just a day and wasn't about to give up now.

She stopped moving, looked around and, seeing that the night was well in session, unhooked her shoulder bag and placed it on the ground next to her.

It had been a long day, she reflected, as she bit off a chunk of stale bread and took a swig of water.

It wasn't quite the evening meal she was used to, but it was enough to keep her in health until she got to safety.

Finally, she removed her blanket from the bag and placed it next to her. Curling up inside it as well as she could, she took one last bite of bread and one final swig of water before putting them away and closing her eyes for the night.

***

Just shy of the treeline, in a clearing at the south of Dewdrop Wood, was a rundown, wooden shack. The world around it seemed huge in comparison, as if a small breeze might cause it to come tumbling down. It was a shack most would feel totally useless on a howling night like this, but some were finding use for it.

Dull candlelight poured out over the wooden table, at which two places had been taken. Both the men were sitting just outside the glow of the candle and were engaged in a low conversation.

From an adjoining room there came mutters and whimpers. Occasionally, the wind picked up outside and howled, pushing the odd draught through the cracks in the shabby framework, thus rippling the gentle constancy of the candle's flame.

Tension arose between the two men until one finally slammed his fist down hard on the table, almost extinguishing the candle, but it bubbled back to stability.

"How much longer are we to wait?"

"...You need to calm yourself, Baylin."

"Calm myself? *Calm* myself? *How* can you say that?" His response edged him downward into the glow, causing his dull, dead eyes to illuminate.

Baylin was a slight individual. His face was gaunt; though white and seemingly untouched by the sun, it wasn't that ... it seemed simply under-coloured and insipid, as if illness stayed with him, lived *in* him. His long brown hair was ruffled and matted with great clumps of grit engrained within.

"You'll either calm yourself or *I*'ll calm you," the other man threatened, as he leant in, resting a hand on his crossbow; it was only a subtle move away.

Unlike Baylin, this man had a much healthier complexion. He had short dark hair and no beard. A scar ran down from the centre of his forehead and just peeked over his left eye that had obviously been damaged from whatever had caused it. He had a strong jaw line and nose and gave off a scent of danger and uncertainty. Both men wore black heavy leather clothes with no truly outstanding features.

Baylin looked up with ferocity. He clenched his teeth and grumbled, but the anger soon subsided, as he conceded against his obvious leader.

No words crossed the lips of either. No words needed to, as both returned back to their positions.

"So what do we do now then?" Baylin asked, obviously concerned, but obviously trying to be as calm as an ill-looking, crossbow-threatened man can.

"We wait."

"What about our friend? What…"

"Shh," the man whispered, as he lowered his head.

Baylin knew not to ask questions and so he kept his mouth shut.

Even though the wind outside was still raging, a silence swept over the room. Something wasn't right – maybe the out of place snapping of a twig or an unexpected, over-enthusiastic rustling of leaves – but both men had their hands on their respective weapons, just in case.

Baylin had only to move his hands slowly towards his belt to which two loaded scabbards had been fastened, while the other man simply took a firmer grip of his crossbow.

Almost ready for the inevitable, the door suddenly burst open and Baylin quickly heaved the table over towards the door, allowing some small cover against any ballistics that may have entered.

The second the candle smashed against the floor it died and all that was left was the weak ambient light provided by the moon.

They stayed quiet behind the table for a few moments until Baylin was given the nod. He slowly sneaked his head out from behind the table to catch a glimpse of the open door. It was clear and Baylin returned to report this.

With a quick nod to each other they both pounced out from their hiding place, taking a foothold either side of the entrance.

They could do no more in preparation, as they had no information on what or how many they were up against, so they both remained still.

Moments later an arrow shot through the open door and stuck in the table with a *thud!* Their enemies were just trying to force them out, but neither flinched – neither one stirred.

Minutes passed, as they both stood motionless. They could do nothing but listen to the howling outside.

Abruptly, Baylin heard the collision of a heavy object, maybe a person – *probably* a person – on the other side of the wall. Then the other man also heard the same thing on his side.

And slowly, those figures began sliding across towards the door. It was difficult to listen to, over the howl of the wind, but both men had their ears firmly pressed against the walls, the grinding and scraping of material over wood very detectable, very obvious.

The figures outside had both stopped in very much the same lateral places. Baylin looked over to his boss who had unsheathed his heavy bastard sword and had taken note of where he last heard the position of the person outside.

Lowering his crossbow to the ground, he took up a line facing the wall. Slowly he raised his sword high above his head and, with extreme force, thrust it straight through the eye of a panel of wood.

A massive yelp, followed by the sound of a collapsing body, came from outside giving him the allotted time to pick up his crossbow and take aim at the door.

A bellow then came crying out from Baylin's side, as a character charged into view, sword in hand, about to advance through the open doorway.

With a click, the crossbow was fired; and a thud, the arrow was shot straight into him, the momentum stopping him dead in his tracks.

He grabbed franticly at his chest, trying to pull the arrow out, but the strength was not there to muster. Instead, he crumpled to the floor. He wasn't dead just yet though, and Baylin dragged the mortally wounded man inside. He moaned in pain, as his dying almost-carcass was carelessly tugged back.

"How many more are there?" Baylin questioned.

Amidst the moaning and gargling, very little was discernible. However, the man was trying to say something. His head turned from Baylin to the other man who was by his sword.

"You!" He took a deep breath and then coughed. "I know you."

"A lot of people know me."

"You are … Garrick."

"Yes." He revelled in the fame – the infamy, as it surely was. "What of it?" Garrick continued, as he wiggled, loosened and removed his sword from the wall.

"More will," – he coughed, gurgled, spluttered, a bulge of clotted blood spewing from his mouth – "come and find you."

"I'm sure they will. And if they are as competent as you were then I doubt I will have very much to worry about."

His words were cold and emotionless, as he walked over to the murdered man.

"More people will … find you."

"I'm sure they will. Why, I even hope they do."

"I … I'm not afraid of you. Y-you—" He coughed.

Garrick knelt down, got in close and personal to the man, enough to feel his rancid breath condensing on his neck.

"You know, for a man about to die, you're taking it all very well. I am impressed," he softly spoke, as he wiped the blood off his sword onto his man's clothes.

"I'm … I'm—"

"Yes?" Garrick said, taking to his feet. He looked at his sword, as if to say, *why did I just clean this?*

Garrick placed his foot firmly on the arrow shaft protruding from the man's body and began to wobble. The moans the dying man tried so hard to hold back turned to wails, as he squirmed uselessly on the floor, coughing up fountains of blood beneath the foot of his torturer; his pain something he related to Hell's fury.

Tears began to glisten and bulge within the corner of his eyes, until gently rolling down his cheeks and then teetering, and finally dropping off the edge of his face.

'Pathetic' was the final word the dying man heard above his own yelps, as Garrick plunged his freshly cleaned sword down and through the man's ribcage, straight into his heart.

The door to the adjoining room creaked open.

"What was that all about?"

"Nothing unexpected, I suppose. Anyway, what have you discovered, Mythos?" Garrick asked, as he glanced beyond to the next room to where a woman was sitting tied to a chair.

Mythos and Baylin both shared similar physical attributes in accordance to their build, but Mythos was slightly taller and looked generally weaker.

He, too, wore black, but it was not as heavy as the other two's attire. It hung freer over his body.

"Not as much as I would have liked. She has been very stubborn. However, I *did* manage to discover somethi—" He stopped, because a figure silhouetted in the doorway caught his attention, and he yelled, "Look out!"

Garrick dived to the side as Mythos tuned his attention…

***

Jerome had never been this late out, he realised, as he stood on the Melfall-Banneth Fell treeline, watching the raucous crowds pouring in and out of the Vale Inn, few of which would have been locals; most being travellers taking shelter for the evening before continuing on their journey either to Cearan or onto Nardil, through the Path of Mante, the only safe passage between Nardil and Melfall and onwards.

Exhausted, hot and sweaty – but *with* the bag – Jerome strode onto the firm well-trodden road running through Melfall and wasted no time in dusting himself down before scampering over to his front door, which he knocked.

Sudden, busied clattering struck up and, shortly after, the door was flung open to a very unrelenting Driana, glowering down over him.

Jerome's head drooped, as he shuffled his way in.

Driana took a quick peep either side of the door to see if anyone else was present. Satisfied there was not, she shut it carefully after. Jerome had already tried sneaking upstairs to avoid his mother's wrath, but his attempt was halted by the sound of his name bellowing towards him.

He turned.

"And *what* time do you call this?" Driana exclaimed.

"I'm sorry, mother."

"Sorry! You're *sorry?* People are strolling out of the tavern with who-knows-*what* on their minds and you're *sorry? Lucky* is what I would call you. You have no i*dea* what kind of people there are around at this time of night."

Jerome could do or say nothing, but even though, he beseeched a 'sorry', which she seemed to dismiss. No words were going to relinquish her anger. All he could do was to turn away and shuffle upstairs to bed, but not before quickly returning the medallion to her bedroom dresser, hoping she would be none the wiser.

Later that night, tucked up in the throws of his cover, he heard footsteps approaching his room. Sleep had been out of the question, and the ruffled sheets were surely testament to it, but he didn't want to face her right now. He felt too ashamed of himself, so he closed his eyes and tried to relax his breath, feigning sleep.

The door slowly opened and Driana entered. Traversing his room like a mother not wanting to wake her child – nothing was quieter – she perched herself at the foot of the bed before slowly sitting, sinking the mattress a touch.

He listened to her breath rocking the midnight air; he heard her sighs full of upset and he almost opened his eyes.

Almost.

He wanted to, to ease her, to tell that he was sorry, that it was *he* who had been wrong, that he loved her, but he kept his eyes buttoned.

She stood up, and tiptoed back to the door, which she opened, taking as many extra seconds as she needed to make sure it opened quietly – the quietest of all kinds.

"Good night, Jerome," she whispered to him.

He couldn't help himself and, to her, he whispered back, "Good night."

She didn't come back though, but her smile graced the air and Jerome felt it as a warm, soothing flow in the midnight air. The argument they had had earlier had been put to sleep, to a place where Jerome also settled.

***

I am standing on the battlefield. My father is next to me. I've never seen him before, and even though he looks at me, and I look back, I can't put a face to the head, yet I know that it's him. It feels good that we are standing together, father and son.

He draws his sword and it spurs me on to do the same. The sword feels light and easily wieldable. We run together down the battlefield...

***

The high tree branches of Dewdrop Wood rippled pleasantly to the invisible breeze, making occasional openings for the sun to beam down onto her weary face.

She blinked awake in a slow wistful mood, wishing the night were not over. But it seemed a pleasant day and so she rolled out of her blanket and got to her feet.

After a satisfying stretch and a big yawn up to the gods, she dug out her water flask and tore off a small chunk of bread.

An unforgiving wisp of wind gusted through the trees and hit her square in the face. Her eyes closed a fraction and she exhaled with the shock.

She had always liked the elements' unpredictability. There was never a correct time or place for it to show off. It just did as it pleased. Free as the wind, she wondered. Well there was the proof, she accepted, as she chomped the last mouthful and guzzled another swig.

The weather gave another display of its might. The wind might be free, but *she* certainly wasn't, and with that reminder she rolled up her blanket, placed it in her bag along with the beaker of water and slung it over her shoulder.

She had only been walking a few hours and she was already outside of Dewdrop Wood. It was a good sign; Toryn, she hoped, would only be another half a day away.

The sun had reached its meridian when she sighted a brook, a good place for a break, *the last break*, she thought, as she glimpsed at the crumbs of bread rolling around lonely in her bag and giving her water flask a shake.

Toryn couldn't be that far away, she thought. *May even get there before sun down*.

She stopped herself from taking that thought any further. This was not the time to hope or be hopeful.

A few clouds had begun to cross over the sun's path, as she watched the huge shadow cover the bright grassland and leave it looking dreary and unwelcoming. The wind had also picked up and, before long, outside the warmth of the sun she was very cold. Fortunately, the clouds blew over and the wind stopped, allowing the chill she felt to quickly depart. Her final leg of the journey had begun.

The sun had just sunk its head behind the horizon, as she saw the high walls of Toryn sticking out in the distance.

Over the past hour the weather had got progressively worse and when she reached Toryn, the heavens had fully opened and a thunderstorm raged.

A huge, stone wall surrounded the whole city. There were many entrances that she knew of, but the one at which she arrived was just on the edge of a small wooded area – a small woodland twinned with Dewdrop.

Two braziers either side of the gate shone brightly and one guard stood on duty wearing full plated armour.

She approached carefully although, because of the rushing rain, the guard didn't notice her until the last minute.

"Halt! Who goes there?" he bellowed, as he lowered his halberd to a menacing, head-height level.

His brash response startled her, but she begged, "Please, let me in."

The guard had been caught entirely unawares. In truth, he wasn't expecting *anyone* to be arriving in such conditions. He quickly recognised her to be a young girl and, although he knew it *should*n't make a difference, he was a kind man and wasn't going to let protocol keep her out here.

"All right, miss," he said, opening the gates and shuffling her into safety. "I'm putting my neck out for you, so don't you be getting yourself into trouble now."

She rushed in, thanking him profusely – and promising him that she would be no trouble – and the door closed behind her.

She may have been inside the walls of the city, but the weather wasn't any easier to bear, as she stumbled and fumbled her way through the muddy slums.

Shops that would normally be open and flourishing were shut and not a trace of a life was to be found anywhere. Even the rats and mice, she thought, would be tucked away in their hidey-holes.

Hours seemed to pass as she searched high and low for a place to rest.

All sense of time and direction was lost as she fought hard against the weather, until eventually she found herself peering over a hedge, surrounding what seemed like a regal edifice and courtyard; and what lifted the weight off her shoulders was a light, glimmering and spilling out onto the stone paving outside.

Not another moment did she wait, as she threw herself over the hedge and scrambled across the courtyard to the heavy ornamental door, which she knocked with the remaining drops of energy she still possessed. The handle began to rattle, and as it did she sank down softy to the ground and let her eyes close.

Chapter II
Partners and Companions

A couple of days had passed since the argument and it had slipped idly from their minds.

However, Jerome's desires were something he was finding harder to contain, and the pressure bubbled away inside him.

He was at an age of excitement and adventure, where simple village life could do nothing other than to fuel the furnace of his passion.

He was going to speak to his mother – he'd decided; he would wait until she returned home and then ask her. Just the decision alone had already relieved some of the built-up pressure, but then it came tumbling back, as he took an instant to think about what he was going to say. What *was* he going to say?

Then a rattle came from the door and Jerome looked up.

Driana strolled in, carrying a loaded satchel, probably full of clothes that needed work done. She caught his purposeful look and stopped.

Putting the satchel down, she said, "Jerome. I didn't expect to see you. Are you not out with Peter?"

"We went out this morning." His response, although a good enough answer to her question, was infused by a curtness … that she unavoidably picked up on.

"But it's still warm," she said, not giving rise to it. "If you hurry, you'll have the evening sun."

Jerome took a deep breath. "Mother, I need to speak to you about something."

'Need' was a big word and Driana couldn't help but hold her hitched breath. "Yes?"

"Well, I've been thinking… I've been thinking about this for some time now."

Breath still held, she said, "And what's that?"

Here goes. "...I've been thinking about ... going to Cearan."

"Cearan? *Why* would you want to go there?" She struggled – *failed* – mask the surprise.

"I've been putting some thought into what I want to do..."

She didn't know if a response was what he was looking for, but it wasn't what he got.

"...And ... I want to go to the city and ... become a soldier."

"A *soldier*?" Pause. "Are you *sure* you want to be a soldier? It's a very dangerous li—"

"Yes. I really do. I've thought about it and ... I want to be like my father, there—"

She gasped and Jerome stopped, realising what he had just said. His face flushed red. She felt mortified. Tears jabbed at her eyes, and she turned away from him, walking over to the nearest chair. She sat, trying her best to conceal her turmoil, but it was no good. She could not contain the knot swelling in her throat, as little weeps began echoing into the lingering quiet.

Jerome did not know what to do. His mind hounded him on what he could do or say, but he just stood still.

"Mother ... I-I ... I'm..."

His stuttering words weren't enough.

They were feeble against the palpability of his mother's grievance. He gave up. Even if he *could* think of something to say, she would be completely unresponsive.

Jerome took the long walk of shame to the front door. Everything sounded exaggerated: the handle, as it rotated, the door, as it creaked open, his footsteps crunching against the rough ground outside, every silent breath ... he heard it all.

Riddled with emotions and besieged with madness, Jerome quickly found himself sinking into the maelstrom; a raging torrent sweeping over him like a wisp being battered in the storm.

He had gravely disappointed the one person who had truly cared for him his whole life. He became enmeshed in thought, as Melfall became a blur and faded away only to be replaced by the unforgiving trees of Banneth Fell...

Garrick, Baylin and Mythos had been on the move almost from the moment the attack finished. They had only to tie up a single loose end, which had been done with cold precision, and their destination was set.

The shock of the attack coupled with the information Mythos had supplied was something that needed to be relayed back to The Reformation with urgency.

Garrick had worked under The Reformation for many years now and still, after all this time, felt uneasy about it. He questioned himself every time he had to go back and 'report'. It was as if they already knew everything; like they had ears everywhere; as if eyes peered through every shadow of every crease and crevasse of the world.

And still, after all this time, he *still* didn't even know their prime location. The whole sordid notion sent shivers down his spine, but he reflected, maybe that was why he loved it. Maybe that was the reason he felt his body tremble with excitement every time he had to go back and … 'report'.

***

Unaware and unconcerned of the time, Jerome found a place where he could sit, relax and think.

He pored over possible scenarios and outcomes of what he would say when he saw his mother again, but the cold of night was starting to settle into his calmed muscles.

His mind worked better when his body was moving and, now that he was stationary, his thoughts took an immediate change from resolving the issues he had at home to actually *getting* home.

Moreover, the clattering of his teeth and the shivering was making it impossible to think straight. The moon was barely halfway up and Jerome decided that heading home was the best plan.

However, the night had not finished playing, and as Jerome jumped to his feet he became very aware of where he was, or rather, very aware that he was a very small creature amidst a very big forest.

And then he became very aware of where he *wasn't* – somewhere he knew.

Like before, back at his house, his senses became highly astute.

The noises of the dark forest became that much more terrifying. Everything sounded as if it were right next to him prompting him to start walking ... and he did.

Every step he took rustled calamitously; every exhalation fogged his vision; every passing moment he tricked himself into believing he wasn't alone.

His walk turned to a jog, which was quickly followed by a run and then a sprint. The faster his feet moved the more he heard behind him, but nothing made him look back. He was completely out of control as he hurled himself through the trees until finally, unable to bear the fear anymore, he took a glimpse behind him ... nothing.

But the darkness alone made his speed dangerous and with his head facing the wrong direction, the inevitable became a reality.

He whipped his head back around and *thud!*

A thick branch caught him on his forehead.

His head stopped where his legs carried on, swinging him up before crashing him down. But even though the branch was firm enough to floor him, it was thin enough to allow a slight bit of movement and it sprang back and forth.

If Jerome had been conscious, he would have associated the rapid, slowing vibrations to a laugh – like the tree was chuckling at him, for being so silly as to not look where he was going, on a dark night ... at speed ... in a forest ... with lots of trees ... and lots of branches.

As it was, it was left to the entertainment of the forest's flora and fauna. This night had got the better of him, and he lay crumpled in a heap on the ground.

He awoke with the same shock, still lying in the woods, hoping hope beyond hope that last night was but a dream and today he would be back home.

It was not so – it was *never* so – and dwelling on it wasn't making the wet ground easier to endure.

A few moans and groans later and he had picked himself up, ironically, with the aid of the same tree that had knocked him down only hours earlier.

Upright and stable, Jerome tried frantically to find some familiarity with his surroundings, clinging on to anything that resembled … *anything*. But, it was all to no avail. There were no recognisable landmarks, nothing except the branch that rapidly reminded him of his forehead,

Which swiftly brought to mind the *thud!* as the pain trickled back into life. He gave the bruised area a rub, as he looked back and forth, wishing something could give him a clue as to where he was, but there was nothing.

The sun had peaked over the horizon when he started to walk again. The undisturbed ground beneath was shimmering with dew and, as he looked back to see the footprints he had made, he wondered where the future impressions might lead…

***

The morning had arrived faster than Driana would have liked. She had awoken from a nightmare and it had left her in a harrowing state of mind.

She took a moment to gather her thoughts, and the argument she had had with her son last night soon came to mind. She cursed herself that her fear and worry had taken such a hold of her, and her slumber had been one spent in unrest. She had wrongfully watched Jerome leave and made a vow – to not let that happen again.

But had he returned? Instantly worrying, she hastily rushed towards Jerome's bedroom and gasped when he was not there. She hoped her vow would not be too late.

She took another gasp and headed impulsively for the sitting room in the hope of seeing him there.

He was not.

She breathed and took another moment to sit down to think on last night's episode. Maybe he couldn't have got back in.

Maybe he was outside…

Springing out of the chair, she headed to the front door and flung it open, hoping, dreaming that she might find Jerome lying asleep outside.

To her dismay, he was not, but it did provoke an idea.

Peter may well know his whereabouts. Perhaps he was even with him. It wasn't uncommon for Peter to spend nights at her house, as it was vice versa.

She left in such hurry that she hadn't even presented herself; indeed, with the rush she was in, the world was lucky that she was even wearing clothes. The two houses were visible from each other and, with barely a minute passing, she was banging on Melissa's front door and very soon after, it opened.

"Driana," Melissa said, smiling, but quickly retracted it after noticing something to be the matter. "Won't you come in? What's the matter?"

"I won't," Driana replied. "You haven't seen Jerome, by any chance? He's not here with Peter, is he?"

Her questions were gabbled, and Melissa moved towards her friend. If she wasn't going to come in then she would go to her, and she did, taking her arm to give her support, to console her.

"I've not seen him, but I can get Peter. Maybe he knows."

Melissa rubbed her hand down her arm in a comforting motion, just before slipping it away and going inside.

"…Thank you," Driana softly and belatedly added. She was struggling with what to do if Peter couldn't help.

Driana and Melissa had always been close. It was made more so by their children's friendship, and with it, situations like this were not uncommon. Both had been roused early by each other's concerns, on more than just the occasional occasion.

However, *this* occasion *was* uncommon. The events of last night presented a tricky situation, as Driana knew: arguments can cloud the mind and make the irrational become strangely appealing. The more she thought about it, the worse the worry became.

Time dragged on as she waited, until eventually she saw Peter.

"Miss Davian," Peter said, approaching her.

"Hello, Peter. Have you seen Jerome? Do you know where he is?"

"I don't. I was with him yesterday, but we both went home, earlier than usual, too. I haven't seen him since."

"Could you help me find him, please? Could you take me to where you play?"

Both Peter and Jerome had always kept their *haven of tranquillity* a secret -- it was a special agreement -- and, more to the point, they didn't like to be disturbed while they were enjoying themselves, hence the reason why they had found a play area in the depths of The Fell.

"I wouldn't ask if it wasn't important, Peter," she added.

It was those words that changed his mind in an instant. He may have been a boy, but he realised the severity of the situation.

Peter disregarded the agreement. "Of course I will," he responded.

Quickly grabbing his coat from by the door, he followed Driana out.

During the course of the journey they walked mostly in silence. Periodically, Peter would point out which way to go and point to specific landmarks he and Jerome had used, but nothing else was really said.

They exchanged glances occasionally, but oddly there was really very little to say. Besides, Driana had enough on her mind.

So did Peter, who by no means was mindless of the situation.

They were approaching the clearing that Peter indicated was 'it'. Driana was impressed, to say the least, and could well understand why the boys both enjoyed being there.

She and Peter both furiously began searching for Jerome, shouting his name, combing the area, sifting through the surrounding foliage.

There was no sign of him.

Peter stopped, and then the conversation that he and Jerome had had began playing and replaying, over and over, spinning with vivid recollection. He had told him that maybe he should consider going to the city to be a fighter.

Would Jerome *really* have headed off to the city alone? The question kept buzzing through his mind and, as much as he wanted to tell Driana, he was worried.

It would all be his fault...

But how could he not tell her? If he *had* gone to the city then someone equally *needed* to know. He let a few more minutes slip by, for reasons of courage, to pluck up what he needed.

"Miss Davian," he began. "There is something I need to tell you."

Panged at her son's memory, and that 'need' was still a big word, she again held her hitched breath. "Yes, Peter?"

"Some days ago Jerome and I were playing. Well, we were *fighting* and he, well ... seemed very good at it. Anyway, I told him that he might..." – *this is it*, he dreaded – "... benefit from going to the city." The moment he said it, he regretted it, and he quickly carried on talking. "I don't know if that's where he is, but I just thought that you should know. I'm really sorry."

Driana took a moment to regard him and ruminate on what he'd said. He had his head down, but he looked up to see her looking at him.

It was clear that she was upset, but was Peter really the origin of it? Was he to blame?

The telling off Peter expected never came.

Driana was a graciously understanding person. Years of living alone, without the company of a lover or a fellow parent had made her this way. The sadness she felt was not the work of Peter, and nor could blame be placed upon him. He was just a boy, like Jerome, and likewise he had dreams. He should not receive punishment for encouraging a friend; he should receive acknowledgement for showing the gumption of honesty. And after all, it was *she* who had had the argument with Jerome.

"Thank you for telling me, Peter. It was … very brave of you."

"Miss Davian, I too am very worried about him. I can't tell you how sorry I am that I told him about going to the city."

"It's not your fault, Peter, but you should think about getting home. We don't want your mother to worry."

She didn't mean for it to be a double-edged statement, but it ended up like that, and it shredded her.

"I will keep my eyes open on the way home."

Attempting to hide her face from him, she said, "Thank you, Peter, for all your help. Get back safely now."

"Will you be able to find your way back?" Peter asked, as worried for her as she was for Jerome.

Words wouldn't come without tears, so she nodded. Reserved, but under instruction, he left.

She looked to the heath, where Jerome and Peter had spent much time sitting, and strolled over to it. There were two wear marks on the turf and, when she saw them, she sat. She moved her hand to the grass beside her and thought of her son also massaging the soft green tufts.

She observed the sun move overhead, as she whispered his name under her breath, in the hope of an answer, but all that returned was a whistle of the wind.

Wherever Jerome was, it certainly wasn't here and after wishing his safe return home, she began her own journey…

***

Very slowly her eyes opened.

She saw the stone ceiling above and then, turning her head left and right, she saw the cold, stone walls with a single arched window, admitting a tawny radiance. She had never been here before and she took a moment to think back.

She remembered reaching Toryn, but nothing else seemed to come back. Not even the preceding events came to her.

She withdrew herself from that train of thought and decided to attune her mind to more present matters.

Where was she?

At first glance it looked like a prison, but then why weren't there bars on the windows? And why *were* there flowers on the corner table?

Taking another moment, she wondered if the door would be locked – *that would be the real give away*. She acted on instinct, approached it and turned the handle – *unlocked.*

Bit by bit, she peered out of the door considering both directions. Neither way was more appealing – it was all a plain corridor. But staying in her room served no use, so she decided to have a stroll and see what was around.

She considered, her door had not been locked, so no secrets were being kept from her. She had just turned to start walking when a voice came blurting out from behind.

"Ah, so you're awake!"

She turned to face the man walking towards her. "Err – yes."

He was shorter than her, slender, well presented, a snood round his neck. "Good. I must say, we were all very worried. You've been out for more than two days now."

"Err – yes, thank you."

"However," he said, lowering his tone, "I'm surprised to see you up and about. You should be resting. You've obviously been through quite an ordeal."

"Err…" She had been taken completely off guard and found herself a little short on words. "I'd rather not. I have been asleep for … two days, you say?" Changing the subject, she said, "Excuse me, but where am I?"

"You are in Grey Keep, home of The Order," the man said proudly.

She had heard of The Order before, not in great detail, just heard of it. It was said to be the place where heroes reside, but she was sure there was more to it than that; and in all truth, she thought it was just a myth.

"I thought The Order was just a fairy tale."

"Oh dear no, we really exist. Come let me show you around. By the way, what is your name?"

"Galliana."

"It is an honour to meet you, Galliana. My name is Junus. Also, I apologise for the sparseness of the room. The knights here don't really care for decoration – they all look like prison cells, if you ask me – but I picked some flowers for you. Brighten it up a touch."

Galliana couldn't help but smile.

***

Meeting places with The Reformation were as mysterious as the organisation that held them. Garrick had been studying the randomness of them ever since he had begun his work for them, but no pattern had ever emerged.

Contacts were stationed in every city and major town, the nearest of these being Gatelock, a town twinned with Toryn about a two day journey south. That part of the journey was now over, as Garrick and his two companions found themselves amongst the city's bustle.

The question, now, was: *where do we find the contact?*

Gatelock was among the small handful of towns in which he had never met a contact before and so began the tricky bit of establishing where he, or indeed she, would be.

Specially designed clues lurked everywhere, in all the possible places to find the contacts. It was just a matter of knowing what to look for.

Most ordinary people wouldn't even notice them, for that was exactly why they were designed, but Garrick knew what he was looking for.

Something that could be altered on a daily routine, he thought. Anything that was too permanent was unchangeable and therefore not good when serving as a clue. But on saying that, things that are permanent can be indicated by something temporary, context changed to mean something else, and by which exposing a clue. It was all very complicated. He continued thinking – *something not as it should be…*

Gatelock was a market town, but it was also a mining town, rich with tin, he reminded himself, hoping to unlock some key piece of information.

Garrick scanned the square, looking for anything that seemed not to belong. Inns and taverns were often prime spots for meetings, so these would be the first places to check.

"Oh, why don't they just tell us where to meet?" Baylin exclaimed.

"Because then it would be heard." Garrick spoke through gritted teeth, trying to pacify Baylin. "And just because there are people around doesn't mean I won't *calm* you," he said again, threateningly, subtly tapping a crossbow shaped object hidden within his long coat.

Baylin knew all too well that Garrick's way of *calming* would be a killer, and so he grunted and turned away. Mythos and Garrick exchanged a look.

"Oh, boss, have a look at this," Baylin said, raising an eyebrow and looking at a few barrels.

"What?" Garrick replied.

"Look," Baylin said insistently. "Read what's written on this barrel."

"Let me see... 'Take to the Cider Cloak Inn'," Garrick read. "Baylin have you been drinking?"

"Not that. Look beneath it."

Garrick looked closer and, true to Baylin's word, there *was* something amiss. It was The Reformation's symbol – a sphere being orbited by another, smaller sphere. Admittedly, it had been hastily scribbled in chalk, with the centre ball looking more like an egg than a perfect circle, and the surrounding orbit resembling a skewwhiff halo than a perfect nimbus, but a symbol was a symbol, and this was a clue.

"Well done, Baylin. Now ... where is the inn?"

***

Jerome had been walking for hours and had still found no trace of any path. Every step he took without finding something recognisable was another blow to his hope. And then it wasn't just his hope that was seeking restoration; his grumbling stomach was starting to dictate.

And then he saw it, as if his prayers had actually been listened to and answered, and not just flung into the prayer pile of whatever god had half an ear open, and an ear-and-a-half uninterested, to the mumbling musings of the mortals beneath.

A rabbit.

A *real* rabbit!

A fluffy-eared, hopping *rabbit!*

Like a predator, he looked at it with an insatiable hunger. He even licked his lips at the thought of something to eat. Of course, there was just that one, single, *eternal* issue standing in the way.

He had to catch the damn thing. He shuffled forwards to a tree, took a little breath and then stepped out.

His feet felt lighter on the ground than they had before. Keeping his eyes on the prize, he considered that what was driving him was so much more important than just sport. Closer, he was so, *so* close … closer even than Peter had got.

Jerome was one step away and he prayed that the little rabbit spirit would keep its mouth shut.

With little adjustments, he poised himself.

He had his arms outstretched, legs bent, and was about to jump, but like every time before, the little rabbit hopped forward.

But only by a little bit…

It was still there.

Maybe three, four steps away.

He brought his arms back and straightened his legs, taking one, two steps towards it.

Be a deaf rabbit! Jerome prayed. *Ignore that annoying little rabbit spirit!*

Again, he lowered himself to a jumping pose, and then took off, a leap of faith.

But today, faith rested with the rabbit, and it hopped off, bouncing into the undergrowth and away.

"No!" he yelled, face full of leaves.

He lay there for a minute, prostrating himself against the soft rot of the dead foliage, before standing up and brushing himself down.

The frustration had at least subsided his appetite, and he carried on walking in whatever direction felt the best.

He was utterly shattered.

He had had nothing to eat or drink, but fortunately, in his exhausted state, he sighted a hollow in a large tree where he sat, slept and hoped...

The sound of darting water smashing onto the tree and reverberating around the hollow gave Jerome a startled awakening. With pitch darkness surrounding him, and the rain beating down relentless, there was little he could do but to tuck his chin into his soaking legs and pray.

For the most part, the rain had simmered down to spitting, and he was just at the point of sleep when, before he could barely make a noise, a hand came energetically into the hollow, grabbed him and threw him out onto the wet and cushy ground.

He landed face first and, just as he rolled himself over, a figure was visible.

He froze. Chills, sent in the dozens, crawled their way up his spine – like tiny demons on a hell march, each one pulling the hairs on the back of his neck up rigid.

"What would a person your age be doing in the forest unprotected at this time of night?"

Amidst the adrenaline, Jerome's voice was wavy at best. "I ... I g-got lost."

"Where were you going?"

"I was ... trying to get home."

"Where is home?"

"Melfall." Jerome gulped.

"This is an interesting direction then," the man remarked, plainly.

Jerome made no reply; there was nothing he could have said. There was a deep pause and the dark figure slowly backed away. Jerome heaved a sigh of relief and stumbled to his feet.

The stranger had so far evaded any light the moon offered, until now, and Jerome managed to get a description of him.

He had long, dark brown hair, black eyes – which, oddly enough, added a gentle slant to his over-bearing structure. He had a bed of thick stubble on his face and a slender physique that was concealed by a layer of dark clothing. It was too dark to see any closer details, if there were any. Hooked over one shoulder he had a bow and over the other, a quiver full of arrows. Over his right hip and attached to a belt was a scabbard, which sheathed his sword.

"What is your name?" the stranger said, after Jerome had brushed off most of the leaves and dirt from his clothes.

"Jerome."

"My name is Keldor. I am one of the Realm's Rangers. I have been following you for the past day now."

Jerome had heard stories of the Rangers of the Realm, as their group was called. In all honesty he couldn't be sure if they were true or just fantasy, but either way, this is what he had heard:

They were a highly skilled band of elite hunters. So the story goes, *on the dawn of their fifteenth birthday they are sent out of their home city or town with nothing more than a sword and the clothes on their back. If they return after half a year they are to become a Duke's Ranger. If they return after one year, they are to become a King's Ranger. If they return after three years they are to be a Realm's Ranger. As Jerome and Peter believed – the more time spent away, the more land covered and the more knowledgeable one would be of the realm; as a duke has dominion over a town, a king over a city and the realm, well, it's obvious.* Again, these could only ever be speculations, but Jerome and Peter enjoyed the idea.

"How old are you, Jerome?"

"I am fourteen."

"Then I think it best that I take you home."

"Is there anything to eat? I haven't eaten anything for ages. I'm *so* hungry."

Whether Keldor liked it or not, the choice was made at that very moment. He had to find some food for the boy or there would be complaints for the whole journey back, and then there wouldn't be a boy to take home. At least, not a living one.

"Very well, and then it's straight home." Looking around at the area, he continued, "Let's find a better place first."

Jerome followed as Keldor found a spot that he deemed worthy.

The rain had completely stopped, but drips and dribbles still came tumbling down from the sodden trees. However, Jerome was in safe hands and a fire was soon blazing from the skilled hands of the ranger.

"Jerome, I want you to remain here while I find us some food."

"But I want to come with you," Jerome replied, childishly.

"Now, Jerome," he said, taking a breath of fresh air and composing himself, trying not to let the petulance of the boy get to him … too much, anyway. "Let me get this straight with you right now. If you've heard anything of the Realm's Rangers, you will understand that I know a lot more about these parts than you probably ever will. I have lived here. Not just here but all around. And if I say 'stay here' then you will *stay here* … or I will sneak away and never return," Keldor whispered.

Jerome sat and sulked, as he lowered his head to his chest. However, it didn't take him long to realise that being by a nice warm fire was pleasantly comfortable, as he felt the heat emanate and thaw out the chill that had embedded itself in him over the past day. To be fair, he felt strangely glad that he wasn't able to go.

The sky had reached a noticeably lighter shade when Keldor returned with two rabbits. Jerome briefly wondered if he would ever get that good at catching a rabbit – let alone two – but the thought was replaced by more desirable things, as he watched, gluttonously, the ranger preparing both rabbits before placing them on the fire.

He had never looked at a meal so desperately his entire life and hopefully, never would again. Soon the rabbits were ready for eating and Jerome didn't pause. He sank his teeth into the succulent meat and within minutes had finished every last ounce. Keldor finished shortly after and as soon as he had quenched the fire and gathered up his belongings, the journey back to Melfall had begun.

***

The sun was just bursting its rays over the horizon, the light splashing over Peter's face, tickling him awake. Usually, Peter only awoke well after the sun was in full motion, but not this morning. Not only that, but the night had left him feeling out of kilter.

There was something that needed his attention. He slid out from under his warm blankets and perched on the edge of the bed. He sat pondering upon what this feeling was doing ... if anything.

When he first opened his eyes it felt plain, just like a simple craving for something – like a simple hunger for a particular type of food –, but now it seemed as if it was actually influencing him to *do* something. Something else. Something *more*.

Unable to bear it anymore, he picked up yesterday's clothes from the floor and threw them on. He then proceeded to amble down the stairs giving his mind every opportunity to think what this could be and what he could do to remedy it. Maybe a walk might take the edge off, he thought.

Although the sun was up, a misty layer of fog submerged the hamlet, but it was a mild freshness and his clothes kept him warm.

His walk took him along the street and into the woods. He savoured the wonder of the world in its early morning state, but as much as he enjoyed it, the feeling was just not going away.

On the contrary, it was getting stronger and more specific, implying a journey. It was madness, he thought; the feeling was actually telling him to leave. It all sounded far too absurd for Peter to handle, as it would anyone. What could make someone feel like this?

The walk, doing little to ease him, took him on a course back home, but he took every minute to delve further into the depths of his mind to try and find the root of this feeling.

A few minutes later he reached his front door and then it came to a conclusion; it *clicked* into place, just as the door *clicked* shut … *Nardil*.

He was supposed to go to Port Nardil?

He soon disregarded the question and spared himself the pain of arguing with the illogical feeling. His mind had already gone through enough for one morning, so rather than arguing with himself he decided to act upon his instinct. Which, it turned out, was a remarkably remedial action.

While it was still relatively early and his parents weren't awake, he packed up some clothes, got some water and a loaf of bread.

As for money, he knew where his parents kept some gold. They weren't a particularly rich family, but Peter knew that a single gold from the fifteen they kept spare would quite easily buy him passage to Nardil.

His little efforts so far had already gone a long way to relieving the pressure and it was here that he took a moment to glimpse around his home, as he let out a small smile. It was not, however, a smile of happiness. Rather, a smile to ridicule himself, as he faced the reality. This was madness and to everyone, even himself, this was a crazy thing to be doing. He still couldn't believe that little more than an urge was making him leave the people he loved, his parents, and his home. But he knew that if he didn't, the feeling would remain to haunt him further, and get worse, *maddeningly* worse…

His first port of call would be the inn. He thought it fortunate to live in such a heavily visited part of Aramyth, for he knew that there were bound to be adventurers all readying themselves for their next journey. That was what the hamlet was known for and that was what would get him to Nardil and maybe beyond.

There was only one more thing to take care of, for he couldn't just up and leave without saying something.

His decision was to write a note to his parents. He quickly grabbed a quill and some parchment and wrote a short letter explaining that he had left of his own accord. He would hate for them to think that he'd been kidnapped or even murdered. Either way, it proved difficult to construct a set of words that said he loved them but that he had to leave. It was so contrived and, no matter what he wrote, it all seemed wrong, but time was pressing on and The Feeling wasn't pulling any punches.

The Vale Inn was on the far edge of Melfall, on the southern side of the valley. However, it wasn't far, and he was outside the entrance within minutes. He entered and looked around.

Sitting at the bar were three people. Two of them looked like they had both seen better days and were either back from an adventure – and/or drunk – but the other looked almost pristine, as if ready *for* one.

And it was this man that Peter chose. He took a deep breath and headed over. He felt so out of place, as he leant against the surface of the bar, but he had no choice. It was either feeling like an idiot or feeling like he was going to explode. He opted for the former.

"Hello," Peter said.

The man turned and looked at the sixteen-year-old. His reply was without words and took the form of an odd look.

He was well built. His attire was composed of subtle and subdued colours, but Peter noticed an insignia on his clothing just next to his shoulder. He had no idea what it represented.

He had a deep beard which after a second glance was covering scars all around his jaw. His hair was dark brown and pulled back into a ponytail. To add to this Peter could see frayed and damaged hairs sticking out from all corners of his head. His eyes were blue and his nose was fat and crooked.

"May I ask … where are you headed?" Peter asked softly.

"Why?"

"I am looking to get to Nardil … and seeing as I have no way of getting there … yet, I was hoping that maybe you have a carriage … and room on it at your disposal?" *What was he saying?*

There was a pause.

"What are you doing? How old are you? Why do you want to go Nardil?" the man exclaimed.

Peter was lost for words, as he felt his cheeks beginning to redden.

"Well?" the man continued.

"I can't explain it. I've been trying to understand all morning," Peter blurted out.

"Understand *what*, exactly?"

"I just said that I couldn't explain. I just have to get to Nardil."

"You will have to try and explain. I'm not just taking *anyone* with me."

"I can't. It's madness."

"You're quite right it *is* madness," the man agreed. "Start from the beginning."

Peter obliged the man's request, explaining everything that had happened in great length being careful not to leave out any detail.

"Well," the man said. "And you say this feeling just started when you woke up? Was it a voice that was telling you what to do?"

"I don't know. I suppose it *was* sort of like a voice telling me."

"...Well," he said again, huffing. "I don't know *what* to believe." He stopped for a moment and considered what the boy was telling him. "Well, I don't see any problem you joining me."

"Oh, thank you," Peter said.

"Now, do you have a name? Or shall I just call you the mad one?"

"I think 'mad one' seems fitting, but my name is Peter."

"Very well, Peter ... the mad one." Peter grinned at that. "I am Pendrick. My carriage will be arriving shortly, and I hope you have some money, madness only goes part way to getting you what you want."

"Yes I have. Thank you, Pendrick."

A few minutes passed, furthering them in acquaintance, before a man walked in. He glanced over at Pendrick, who seemed to recognise him. Pendrick nodded to the man and then beckoned Peter to follow him.

Outside was a carriage with two horses. The animals let out their breathy sighs as they waited.

"I see, two of you this time, Pendrick? You know that'll be extra."

"Yes, old friend. How much will it be?"

"Six silver between the pair of you should cover it."

Both Peter and Pendrick paid their share of the fee, Peter handing over his gold coin and the driver returning him nine silver back. Pendrick was first to step on and Peter, still feeling quite strange to be leaving his home, climbed on after.

The driver had soon bagged and bound the money to his belt and once settled in place, started the horses and the carriage shuffled along behind, bound for Port Nardil.

In the carriage, Pendrick leant to Peter and said, "Well, Peter, the mad one, have you travelled much?"

"Not much," Peter said, nervousness at work.

"Then think about this: isn't it strange that this Feeling just so happened to lead you to the only person going Nardil...?"

***

The day came and went, as Keldor led Jerome safely back to Melfall. The journey was uneventful, but Jerome indulged himself, talking of adventures, hopes and ambitions. He noticed that Keldor seemed reticent to tell his tales. Of course, he was not used to talking. Company was not a luxury he had been exposed to, but that didn't bother Jerome for he was only too happy to be in the company of such a person, and what was more, a person to whom he could tell all his stories without interruption.

Night was in full grace when the two had reached Melfall. Jerome felt so happy to be home, but the worry he had become very familiar with crept back in.

What was he going to say to his mother?

She didn't even like him being out when it was dark; how was he going to explain his way around this one?

Jerome put his hand to the door ... and knocked three times, waiting patiently – as patiently as he could. The sudden rumble of activity that he was expecting to hear – that had come when he returned home late before – never came.

In fact, there was no answer at all, delayed or otherwise.

Perhaps she's asleep, he thought.

He knocked at the door three more times, this time harder. Yet, there was still no reply.

The curve of Jerome's smile – a smile that he had adopted simply from being home – turned down and a look of concern filled his face. A wave of fear flooded in, as he knocked again with real force, but still he heard no one.

Jerome turned to face his adult companion. Keldor could see the boy's eyes mad with desperation, and he tried knocking, but there was still not a shred of life coming from within the house. It would have been enough noise to wake even the dead, Jerome thought.

It was unlike his mother to have gone anywhere and not have told someone. So he decided to ask the neighbour, the local blacksmith, to see if his mother had mentioned anything to him prior to her leaving. He gave a knock at the door, which was answered soon after.

"Jerome, hello," he said, rubbing his eyes, recognising it to be the tailor's son. It was a surprise to see him this late – this *early* –, but that didn't stop his gracious attitude.

"Hello. I'm sorry it's so late, but my mother isn't home. Did she say anything to you about where she may have gone, or if she'll be back?"

"I am sorry, no. I have heard nothing. But I can't expect she's gone far."

The blacksmith shut the door, his strong arms and hands making it close louder than most, leaving Jerome alone with Keldor, and also a great deal of dread, for where could she have gone?

Slowly, he walked over to a nearby rock where he sat and felt the pressure from years of love and affection being stripped from within him.

His body pumped with emotion. He felt all the veins pound as he drifted uncontrollably to his knees.

He swayed his head back and – with the muteness of a breath but the rage of a squall – he threw his aching silence up, squeezed it out, filled it with so much *want,* so much zeal, that it would force the gods to listen, and afterwards, all he could do was bring himself back to the terrible reality.

He simply knelt there feeling twisted and broken, looking up at the starry sky. The excitement of seeing his mother again was rent from his soul, as weariness crawled all over him.

He closed his eyes to the world…

***

Valkyre slowly opened his eyes; a noise had interrupted his sleep.

Gently he turned and tilted his head accordingly; some-thing was drawing his attention.

It was blurry from his tiredness and, coupled with the abundance of darkness, very little could be gathered. The only key fact to become immediate was that he, maybe she – it was very dark – was definitely a person and not some animal or something falling over and breaking the dead silence.

After some adjustment and a little time, he concluded that the figure meant him no harm.

In contradiction, the figure began fumbling at the shackles that were holding him in place.

"They are held shut by magic," Valkyre said, exercising his right to speak.

"What kind is it?" the figure whispered, as if not really asking.

It was definitely a man.

"What kind?" Valkyre questioned, picking up on the quiet words. "Some sort of binding magic I would have assumed."

He heard the locking mechanism rattle and click, as the shackles loosened around his wrists.

The man seemed quite nervous and unsure, as he crafted the right magic to unlock his feet shackles. He did so in such a natural way, that of a master.

It was only shortly after balancing on his own two feet that he felt the vibrations of magic pulsing from this shadowed figure and realised this was a being of magnificence and awesome power. He felt massively humbled and for the first time in years, felt truly safe.

"What now?" Valkyre posed.

"To be honest, I'm not even sure what I'm doing here."

This man seemed very strange. It hadn't dawned on him, but everything about him was odd, anachronistic almost, something from a different time, *timeless* was the word he settled on.

He wore a long coat, which despite looking tattered and dirty – years of wear and tear – looked a good insulator. It hung open and hung free and was obviously comfortable.

On his legs he wore a textured material, while his top half saw home to a ripped smock of some sort, but he really couldn't make it out, and any desire to try paled in comparison to his desire to get out of here once and for all.

"How about we exit through that door over there?" said Valkyre, pointing.

"Yes. Good thinking—" Valkyre could see him begin to utter something, but quickly corrected himself, "Valkyre."

Valkyre overlooked his mistake and instead said, "How did you know my name?"

"Long story. Call it magic…"

Chapter III
Revelation

It was evening at The Cider Cloak Inn and Garrick had been keeping his eyes peeled for the contact the whole time. Mythos and Baylin had, meanwhile, been busily indulging in conversation and, although Garrick had had his few words, he still remained sufficiently disengaged to keep watch and shortly after, he caught the eye of a woman. She was stood at the bar and if it wasn't for the black attire with the recognised Reformation symbol, then he probably would have thought she was out for something else.

He returned focus back into the conversation, or argument, as it transpired.

"… No, Baylin, that is incorrect!"

"How can it be? If I—"

"Stay here you two," Garrick interjected. "I won't be long."

"Of course, we'll be here," Mythos confirmed.

"Yes, you had better be. I know you two and your arguments," Garrick said, as he lifted himself from the table and looked over to his contact.

There was something unreal about walking over to contacts. It wasn't nervousness; it was as though he were a lesser being. And his mind always carried to sinister places upon the notion that these people were the arms and legs of The Reformation. He himself was a nihilist with goals and ambitions, probably outside of the normal *happy, fulfilled* life; so what were they to be so close to an organisation hidden under the flames of ice, and the candles of dark?

Something more than just a deep-seated coldness, he wondered, taking the last step and collapsing his body against the bar…

"Come with me." The woman spoke without emotion and Garrick followed without question.

He understood the reason for her attire now – for no one would suspect anything *off* about a man following a woman, dressed in such revealing apparel, upstairs…

She led him to one of the rooms.

Everything like clockwork.

Always like clockwork.

The room was plain. There was a single bed with a bedside table and on it, a lit candle and a dagger, which she had just placed down. Apart from the bed, the bedside table, a table in the middle of the room with chairs tucked under, there was nothing else of note. The curtains had been closed and the only other source of light, aside from the bedside candle, was the candelabra on the centre table.

"Garrick, it is most fortunate that you're here," she said, sitting.

Garrick sat with her. "It is?"

"Yes … and important."

"Why?"

"If you spare the questions I may even get round to telling you."

"…Please continue," he said.

She took a moment to glare at him, her eyes serious.

"We have a new target for you."

"A new target? Forgive me for asking, but surely I am to receive new targets via a more … *silent* source?"

"You're questioning the way of The Reformation?"

"I am not. It is merely that I have never received a new mission in voice before."

"We have not time to go through such long protocol. Its severity must be answered with haste. Action must be taken now … and you will need some more serum," she added, handing him a small vial.

He brought his crossbow up from his side and began to lace the viscous serum not onto the tip of the arrow, but onto the groove so that *every* arrow would be laced as it left.

"The serum is meant for *you* not your opponents."

"It works better this way," Garrick remarked, ignoring her, and then turned sharply up, looking at her with dangerous eyes.

"What kind of target would require such attention? Not forgetting I'm a man down at the present."

"A boy."

"A boy?" Garrick laughed.

"Your hubris may be your death, Garrick. I warn you to not take this lightly. Your success is imperative to The Reformation and, possibly, will even lead you to a more handsome role within."

Crossbow laced, he returned it to his side. "…Very well. So, tell me about this boy." And he leant in and let the candlelight envelop them…

***

I'm on the battlefield again, running. My father is not with me. The fog is carrying the smell of blood and the sound of slaughter is ringing in my ears, but it is very faint, because the speed at which I'm running is making the wind rush past me.

The crest of the hill ahead approaches and I can see a figure dressed in full black plate-mail armour. As I approach, I draw my sword.

I stop just outside of sword range and I'm confused that he doesn't draw his weapon. Instead, he reaches up to his helmet and removes it. His head is slightly bowed forward so I can't see his face, but as he lowers the helm down he reveals … me. He's – I'm – all scarred. Pale skin is stretched over the bones and muscles and I can barely recognise it, but at the same time, I can completely *recognise it – me. It's the evil in me, the truth…*

This is me, and I sink to the wet ground. Now he draws his sword and I can hear the sparkling glisten of the sword. It wants me, calls for me with voice of chagrin and rage. But just before it reaches my neck, all the rudiments of evil flow from 'him', into the ground beneath and, like a black river, it courses into me, replacing me, eradicating me…

***

Jerome's eyes shot open, as he heard his name being said, and his body being rattled awake.

It was Keldor.

"What happened?" Jerome muttered.

"You were dreaming. What was it about?" Keldor asked softly.

His few moments of consciousness had brought with it remembrance of what had happened only hours before.

"It doesn't matter," Jerome said, as he rolled away from Keldor.

"I think it *does* matter."

Jerome drew a deep breath. "I have to find her."

"Jerome, I don't want to be the bringer of bad news but—"

"Then don't... Help me find her."

"Do you have any idea how hard that would be?"

"I *have* to find her," Jerome begged. "You have to help me. I have no one else; she is all I have. Please?"

"Oh for the love of—" He stopped himself and also took a deep breath. Jerome's accidental pathos tipped the decision for Keldor, and in his agreement he thought that even the trees would break their life-long silence to help this young figure lost in a world so much bigger than him.

Keldor had prayed he would never find himself in this position, but it seemed as though fate was stronger than prayer. "Fine. I will help you, Jerome."

Keldor released a sigh at the same time as wishing he had refused Jerome's request. He mused over the possible outcomes of such a quest. He'd never been one for faith, really, but maybe luck would bring the boy back his mother. But luck, he knew, had never been so kind to him. Maybe it would have been better to refuse the boy than let him live for years in the hope – there was that word again – that he would find his mother?

Maybe he would eventually forget.

"So where do we start, Keldor?"

"I have a feeling it already has."

Jerome nodded. It *had.*

"Jerome, how long will you spend searching?"

"Until I find her," Jerome resolved.

"What if you never do?"

"What do you mean?"

"…Nothing," Keldor said, recovered. "But, Jerome, if you resolve yourself to this, it'll never be over until it's over." That wasn't exactly how he wanted to say it, but he was trying to reason with someone who couldn't *see* reason.

"Of course, but that won't happen. Not with a *Realm's Ranger*."

Keldor looked up and took a moment for himself. He was simply unable to inject any modicum of reason into him.

Just as Jerome turned to follow Keldor his eyes glimpsed something standing beside a tree about twenty feet away. And as he took a double take, whatever lurked before had vanished. He brushed off the event and continued behind Keldor.

***

A few days had passed and beyond Galliana's original forth-coming attitude with Junus, her willingness to be consulted had receded.

However, she was frequently seen to be wondering around Grey Keep, to almost everyone's amusement, like she owned the place. But the humour was beginning to wane, wane from everyone except for one.

He was called Lord Percival Pembroke, although he never insisted on being called by his full title. He preferred Percy, just Percy, and he, above all, always found the time to try and talk to her. He thought that maybe some trauma had befallen and returned to her and that was why she remained so staid.

More often than not he found her in the hidden garden behind the Keep, looking out towards the trees and always deep in thought. In opposition, Percy was not an outdoorsman, but over the past few days he had developed a pretend interest, which, oddly, turned into an *authentic* interest.

He considered the surroundings quite beautiful, as he delicately approached the quiet and still girl.

"What's out there?" Percy asked.

Galliana spoke not a word.

"It's quite a remarkable view isn't it? You know, I must thank you."

Still no words from her, but she turned to look at him.

He gestured out towards the trees. "For showing me this marvellous view," he remarked, a reason he gave earnestly.

She frowned at him in a quizzical manner.

"But I must have seen this a hundred times, you're probably thinking? Very little, you'll be surprised. Maybe Junus has mentioned that no one here really cares for beauty. But you're never too old to change... And what better company?"

However kept she was, she had grown fond of Percy. She wasn't going to tell him this, but it surely was a fondness.

He was a large man, but he had a warm face and his grey beard and hair only added to this. Despite his age – she placed him in his late sixties – he carried himself as a man in his prime and the flowing white attire that he donned, as did most of the residents of Grey Keep, made him appear almost heavenly, maybe even god-like.

But something tickled her curiosity further; she knew there was more to him than just a grey beard and white attire. Firstly, she knew he was not a caretaker of the Keep. Was he a hero? Was he one of the myths that so many had spoken of?

Her silence, and, with it, her thought, was interrupted again.

"What happened to you before?' He looked deep into her eyes. He could see their pain. "Why so still?" Percy asked, pryingly. He knew the risk, but there was only one way to discover the truth...

***

The trip to Nardil was unadventurous, Peter thought, as the horses were reared to a halt.

Pendrick beckoned him out, and he did so; and to be firmly on the solid ground was a relief. Journey by carriage was neither comfortable nor relaxing.

The coachman was quick to find another fare and, without delay, the horses were pulling the carriage all the way back.

Peter and Pendrick signalled their farewells to the driver and then turned to each other.

"Now, Peter, the mad one," Pendrick said, "do our paths end here?"

Peter was a blank. "I don't know."

"Very strange," Pendrick said under his breath. He humoured himself, as he left; his last words to the boy, he thought, were truly representative of their entire time spent together, odd ... at the very least, *odd.*

Peter thought it lucky that he had been to Nardil before, as he waved farewell to Pendrick. His parents had taken him there a few times, so he wasn't entirely lost in its bustle. The streets were crowded and lively – as normal – which, along with its enormity, made Peter feel quite insignificant and perhaps, a little bit scared.

He recognised a couple of the larger buildings in the distance, as they stood sky-high above the rest of the city. One of them was the cathedral, haven to the guild of priests, known as the Western Keep. This was one of the oldest buildings in the land, along with the Aramyth Consortium in Arthak, and in it rested its founder, Gwyneth La'Crey, whom according to history was the first priestess. Although others before her were considered by that title, they never employed such a fullness of grace and sacrifice as High Priestess La'Crey.

The second building Peter recognised was, of course, the palace of King Finnigan I, which immediately struck the reality bell inside him.

Now that he'd arrived in accordance with the feeling, where was he to go now?

While he ambled along, he desperately tried to encourage The Feeling's next message.

Maybe an hour passed, while he tumbled through the streets, keeping himself to himself, wondering what he should be doing, when an image came to him.

A boat.

He had to catch a boat? That all seemed good and well, but this wasn't a quiet little village. It was a busy place with ample number of people who could keep watch of a mischievous youngster. He revised his thought pattern. Lots of people yes, but lots of places to hide. However, which one would he have to catch?

Instead of trying to answer this, he made his way to the harbour while thinking upon it. *It all seems to be fitting together rather well.* He cogitated onwards... *This feeling, like Pendrick had said, must have known that there would be a man willing to take me with him. It was saying to catch a boat in a port city. It can't be making all this up.* He felt slightly ridiculous going over everything like this, but surprisingly, it was the only way that any of it made sense.

It took him a little while to reach the harbour, and when he did he smelled the salt of the fresh sea air rise up his nose.

Moored up at the harbour that day, were three boats. The largest and farthest to his left was a cargo ship, called the Tynamere. He had heard of that boat.

The Tynamere and its younger and smaller sister, the Faramere were the two main cargo ships that transported everything from wine to weapons, metal to wool, between Nardil, the other port cities of Aramyth and the north-western island of Tirthewdin and beyond. The smallest vessel and the one in the centre was a passenger vessel, called the Bird Song. Finally, to his far right was the Sal-Nardil ferry, another passenger vessel.

From the looks of things Peter was clearly able to see, both from the ship's design and the passengers, that the Bird Song was for higher class people who like to travel in style, and the Sal-Nardil ferry was for the lower class people who, either couldn't afford the Bird Song, or simply weren't as stuck up to care.

Amidst thoughts, Peter looked right and saw the huge building, The Western Keep of Priestess La'Crey, perched upon the cliffs, a landmark and signal to all.

Besides this though, he had to find out which boat to get on, and then he would have to obtain admission on board that ship. For that, he would need a ticket.

That being the case, he would either need to fund one, or mug some unsuspecting holder. Shortly after some simple banter with surrounding people, he found out that a ticket for the Sal-Nardil ferry was ten silver – one more than he had –, not including the journey refreshments… a key element of a two and half day journey. So he was back to mugging someone.

Firstly, he needed to identify someone with a ticket and then lure them somewhere, then … then … who was he joking? He couldn't mug anyone. So he was back to square one, except without options one or two.

Of course he could always stowaway, and once on board, he could sneak around, scavenge food, hide. Yes, stowaway it was.

Then, it happened … *The Tynamere. Good.*

The Tynamere was the largest ship there, consequently, the easiest to hide on, and secondly it was a cargo ship. *Fewer passengers.* Because, cargo-ship travel was not recommended for any person *not* involved with the delivery. However, they always attracted some, and the shipping companies weren't about to turn down revenue. So a limited number of passengers were given board, *if only 'given' meant free…*

Enough wishing! He reprimanded himself.

So, the first issue of which boat had been dealt with accordingly; getting onto the ship was next on Peter's agenda. Taking an un-educated guess – the best that could be expected – the boat was still barely half full of its quota, giving him, hopefully, plenty of time to search for a crate with a loose top and preferably a soft cushion. Quite simply, his idea was to be carried onto the boat in one of the boxes.

It didn't seem that hard, as there were lots around, but it took him a good few minutes to find one.

It had the word *cabbages* chalked on the side, which he thought would be a good enough cushion. That was the first thing that deemed this box suitable, but also it was the fact that it was one of a good many other boxes.

He immediately set to work prying up a loosened edge and true to the indicated contents, inside was a large heap of cabbages.

As he settled down upon the green vegetable bed, he thought what a good-fortune gesture it was from the gods.

Although he wasn't a fan of cabbage, he thought, *better that than some sharp weapons crate.*

Soon he felt the box being lifted and carried, clumsily and with little care to its contents, onto the boat. A few minutes later, it was put down, though it didn't feel like that. Even though he had the full support of the cabbages, to Peter, it felt as though he'd been dropped on his head, and he had the ringing in his ears to prove it.

It was unwise to make any movements and possibly bring his position to note, until he was sure the boat was well under way and even then he would have to be careful.

Oblivious of the time, maybe an hour passed until he heard the deck hands shouting and signalling the boat to set sail.

He let more time slip by before he chose to move and, when he did, it was only to take a glimpse through the weakened lid of the box.

Turning over, being careful not to lift the lid obviously, he gently, with control, pushed it up with his head. It was a lot heavier than he remembered, as he glanced out of the slit.

The view was minimal, but he was able to guess that he was alone, only as far as the many crates that surrounded him, which hampered his vision somewhat. But aside from that, he was sure that no one else was around – another perk of a cargo ship. *It was far easier to watch non-moving items than living people, who were very capable of running-a-muck.*

He inwardly smirked.

With this in mind, he pushed the lid of the box well open and was about to bring a leg out when he heard footsteps from behind and a voice.

"What perfect timing."

It was a woman's voice. Peter froze. He hoped that maybe she was talking to someone else, and he waited for the second voice; but none came. Instead, the footsteps carried on towards him and stopped right in front of his line of vision.

"Look at you. Would you like a hand out of there?"

"Err … yes please," Peter said, slightly startled by what the woman had said – indeed, by the woman alone.

She pushed the lid up another foot with one hand and the other, she offered out to Peter for support. He landed clumsily – his legs had lost almost all use – crumpling to the floor. She helped him sit up against the crate and knelt down in front of him.

"Thank you for the help," he said, trying to calm his heartbeat.

She had shoulder-length blonde hair with the most phenomenal eyes, like a desert island – chestnut in the middle with blue waves lapping at the shore. Her nose was slightly pointed, but she exuded warmth and kindness. Her eyebrows were fair, but what made her face look particularly pleasant were the way her lips weren't overly red. If anything, they were a subtle shade lower than expected and even though they didn't stand out, Peter was unexpectedly drawn to them.

She wore a long green leather coat and, round her neck, was a hood also made of green leather. It was hanging down her back now, but Peter saw from its size that it would be used to completely obscure identity. Her boots stopped just below the knee and her trousers were black. Peter considered that they may have been silk, because of how the light interacted with them, but he didn't know for sure, and to stare any longer at her legs would have been rude.

"It's my pleasure," she said, pleased and almost expectant of him.

"But, how did you know I was here?" Peter questioned, thinking his plan to have been flawless.

"This isn't coincidence. I have been tracing you for over two days now, guiding you, sending you the relevant information to set you on the path here."

Peter was stunned. He had to ask, but he was quite sure what the answer would be. "So are you the reason behind this agonising feeling that I've been having?"

One side of her face grinned, a half-grin Peter thought it. "I am."

Peter was overburdened with all sorts of complex emotion. The guilt of leaving his parents was his initial standpoint. Why had she made him do such a thing? Once he considered that idea, the others paled in comparison.

"What appears to be the matter?" she asked, seemingly ignorant.

"Pardon me, madam, as nice as you are, and I mean no disrespect, I have left behind my family and life … for little reason, other than to deal with a silly feeling, which, I might add, has now gone. So thank you, but no thank you."

She saw his pain and gently rested a hand on his knee. "You poor thing, I didn't realise your human life was so important to you."

"Human life? What do you mean?" he retorted, startled.

"You are going to find this difficult and I apologise in advance, but there really is no easy way of saying it."

Peter was on tenterhooks. What was she going on about?

"You are a magus." It was so blunt it was almost impolite.

"Pardon me? A magus?" He disbelieved any possibility, even though he had no idea what she actually meant.

"You are a magician, a magus, a magic-user, thaumaturge, wizard, one of the magi of the realm."

…He didn't expect that… "A magus… Why can't I use magic then?"

"You can, or else you wouldn't have felt what I've been sending you."

"Why have I not been able to use it before then?"

"Have you ever thought you could use it before?"

"No but … you could be—"

"Lying? Then I redirect you to the feeling again."

"It could have been a headache and I just needed to get some fresh sea air." It was a long shot, even to his young and outlandish mind.

"You might, but how do you explain this?" She opened her hand to reveal a miniature tornado spiralling around, dancing over her palm. He kept watching as three, also tiny, trees sprang up and rooted themselves into her skin. They then proceeded to get battered about by the squall until all the leaves circled inside the maelstrom. He even heard the thunder and saw the lightening as the stormy chorus began, and then, amazingly, the tornado swept onto to the peak of his knee. It remained for a while and then *poof!* As her hand clasped shut, the image vanished.

"A magus is what you really are," she confirmed.

Peter remained silent.

"There is no point in questioning it," she continued. "There is no other way I could have sensed you. No other, logical," she eyed him purposefully, "way you could be here."

"I still don't understand how I could not have known before. How did I not," – he felt silly saying it – "cast any," – sillier still – "magic spells?"

"The answer lies in the basic, most fundamental, rule of magic. What you believe to be true … is. Even in games, you have still believed yourself to be non-magical. And magic is not easy to control, Peter."

"How did you know my name?"

"You know that."

"Then why didn't you mention it earlier?"

"I didn't want to alarm you."

"It's a little late for that."

They paused. He smiled. She half-grinned.

"So what is *your* name?" Peter asked.

Almost instantly after asking, a similar feeling to one before came over him, but it was actually pleasant. And then he heard her voice inside his head saying something. It was strange, he knew it was her voice and could hear words, but couldn't understand any of it. He tried listening harder, as he closed his eyes and then it appeared – *Garveya.* That was her name.

A moment later he spoke it. "Garveya."

"Yes. Now tell me how you feel."

Peter considered just that. Muddled was the best way to describe his emotional disposition. He missed his parents, but every second that passed, every moment, now that he existed knowing of his *new* life, he felt something sweet seeping into him. He wanted to discern this new reality, but he wanted to return home. He wanted both and the following question proceeded. "May I go back to my parents?"

Her face dropped, and his copied. "It's unfortunate and of course you can return, but magic attracts magic, and magical creatures attract magical creatures. That being said, there are a great many dark creatures out there who would feast on more than just your life. I'm sorry, Peter, returning home would not only be dangerous for you, but would put your parents at risk, also."

Peter fell even more silent than when he was wordless.

"Maybe in the future you could return, when you have gained some capacity to conceal your magic."

"Would it ever be untraceable?" Peter hoped.

"...I'm so sorry, Peter." She placed a hand back on his knee.

He stole a deep breath and held it. Feeling the frog in his throat, he began to exhale and close his eyes, taking all the time he required to allow every iota of air to leave. He repeated it once more, at which point he buried his head in his knees and then brought it up, sharply. His eyes were slightly red where the tears had begun to form against the bitter sea air. They subsided and he felt better, but he still had a long way to go before he would be free from grief.

"There will be plenty of time to lament, but keep in mind that there are benefits to being a magus, as you will see when I teach you."

"I understand," he accepted. "So where are we going?"

"Normally we would head straight to Alatacia. That's the home of the magi, in case you didn't know. And, while it's fortunate that I sensed you, it's unfortunate, as I have another more pressing task that needs attention." She took a breath. "And it's a dangerous one, too."

Before Peter could be allowed to speak, he was quickly put at ease.

"But stay with me and we'll both be fine."

He looked into her eyes and nodded; and as he became cognisant of his own magical impetus, he suddenly became strikingly aware of hers and the unconscious echoes of power that pulsed from her, and through him.

"So what is this task?"

"I have been sent out to track down some rogue dark magi. The first reported sightings of these individuals were in Tae'Lamere, but when I arrived there, information that they had travelled to Cearan was all that greeted me. However, again, upon my arrival at Cearan, there was news that they had moved on to Tryth. I would have headed there directly, but then I sensed you, so I arranged to meet you on this cargo ship from Nardil."

Peter nodded and then frowned. "So why not just summon me to Cearan?"

"Firstly, the journey to Cearan is more perilous – for *you* that is – and secondly, I've always preferred sea travel. So our destination is Sal, then on to Tryth and hope that they are there."

"Right ... good," Peter fluttered.

Garveya took a moment and then broke away from Peter to head to the side of the ship. Peter savoured the solitude. No actual words could describe what he thought, but in short, it had been a redefining few minutes. Just before, he was a boy hiding in a box of cabbages; now, he was one of the realm's magi. Although not fully in touch with what that meant, he was sure that it held a great responsibility.

Shortly after, Peter joined Garveya at the side of the vessel. Though they stood in silence, Peter could still sense the vibrations of an infinite power quake the air between him and his female acquaintance and he realised ... this was a familiar feeling, a feeling that he'd felt all the time before.

And as he gazed out beyond the horizon to a yearning future, a future which, as of yet, was unfathomable, the glare of the sun took him off guard, forcing his eyes down to the waves beneath.

The tranquillity of the sea became ever more desirable, but the uncertainty of his future continued to rumble beneath the surface. He shook his head and thought onward about their journey to Sal and then further on to Tryth.

And then he smiled.

***

Although Keldor was now laden with this young boy, he still had his agenda and needed to report back to the king of Cearan. Normally a journey this long would have only taken a little over a day, but the company was alarmingly slowing and after three days, the kingdom of Cearan was in sight.

Jerome had not been open with his companion as of yet and the original lurking shade beside the tree had eerily followed and plagued him all this way.

The city, which far away could have been appreciated in its wondrous entirety in a single view, became closer until the massive city walls shadowed every building. Keldor continued to take Jerome around the perimeter of the city walls until they stopped at a postern gate. This gate, Keldor informed Jerome, was a direct route into the city's centre avoiding the slums. He tapped at a closed peephole and it was swiftly snapped open.

"What business do you seek here in Cearan?" said a voice behind a pair of staring eyes. But not the only pair of eyes paying attention.

"I wish to speak with the king," Keldor replied, Jerome gazing at the eyes that were glowering straight back at him.

"Is the king aware of your arrival?"

"I am a Realm's Ranger: the king is *always* aware of my arrival, and I have important news." Keldor rolled up his sleeve to reveal a tight leather band secured around his wrist with the Realm's Rangers coat of arms.

"What of the boy?"

Keldor considered his young companion who, to him, was in a world of his own, but unbeknownst to any onlooker was still being fearfully scrutinised.

"The boy is with me. Now, open the gate."

The slit closed off and with that noise, Jerome disengaged himself from the forbidding skulker. The small, postern gate began to clink and rattle as gears and cogs inside engaged and disengaged until finally opening and revealing a quiet alley which led forth to a lively city street.

Keldor stepped through and Jerome's jaw dropped. He had never seen anything of so much magnificence in all his life. On raised land, at the far side of the city, the palace of King Josiah

II was on exhibition to everyone, Jerome being no exception with Keldor duly noticing his ogling.

"That is our next stop," Keldor said proudly.

"Are we really going to see the king?" Jerome's eyes were twinkling.

"…But first, I need to see an old friend."

Jerome trailed behind Keldor, finding it difficult not to get caught up in the ambience of city life. However, the surroundings lessened and the mood lowered as he was led into a seedy part of the city.

Jerome followed Keldor all the way until they were outside of a somewhat dank and gloomy looking shop, making it all the more gloomy as he was told to wait outside.

He leant back against the wall and was repelled back up to vertical, as he felt the grime beneath his fingernails. Turning round and looking, he saw the walls, either side of the filth-stained door, had streaks of grime and gunk running down them. Its location was more specifically near the end of a discreet alley called Mourning Street – the sign itself being as encrusted with glop as the rest of alley and reflecting it perfectly. Jerome supposed the whole alley to be a place that would normally have been missed if not looking for it.

Above the shop the sign read Borric's Grotto of Dark Creatures and Magic. It gave the occasional creak as it swayed aimlessly from the cold draught that soared its way down into the dark depths of the alley.

Another place was a tavern called The Firefly. Jerome could only assume that it might have been a nice place to go once, but now it had the random smears of lichen and the fungus growths to prove its age and care, or lack thereof. And to instil this further, most of the windows had been plated with planks. Yet, by the sight, sound and smell, the tavern was lively, if a bit disorderly.

Jerome glanced about more, in the hope of seeing maybe one patch of solace within the dark. Sadly, his illusion was as crippled as the backstreet itself, when his eyes fell upon a shop called Frogs.

Jerome spent as little time as possible looking at it. There were other shops, but by the time Jerome had finished looking at Frogs he was totally disinterested in the whole alleyway and had set himself upon a barrel, thinking only good thoughts about his future meeting with the king; but as the wind shot another cold burst onto him, the present found himself shivering, alone and ... bored.

Now having this as well as the unending wait for Keldor to finish talking to whomever he was talking to, Borric possibly, just added insult to injury. Additionally, that ominous pair of eyes were back and looking at him from within the shadows, and Jerome could tell they – and the It that was behind them – were getting angrier...

***

After three days of travel, Garrick and his two subordinates were well on their way to western Aramyth. Specifically, they had been charged to go to the small village of Morigan's Green, southeast of Arthak, and await further instruction.

Few words were ever exchanged on journeys like these. Each man kept himself to himself; all energy, effort and focus being channelled into completing the expedition, which was especially why, when Mythos blithely mentioned that today was the Feast of High King Terrowin, Garrick and Baylin stopped to look at him.

Of course, he was right, and they stopped to share a drink and five minutes on, they were back in full swing, jogging onwards to Morigan's Green.

***

It had taken time, but Galliana had finally taken the first step out of Grey Keep and into the city of Toryn. She had not ventured out alone, though, and it was Percy who had accompanied her.

Percy had spent almost his entire life under the roof of Grey Keep, never venturing out. So this was as much a baby step for him as it was for her. But they kept each other in touch. He, with his dry humour, kept her face equipped with a smile, while she confronted the flurry of celebration. After all, this day was Feast Day, the Feast of High King Terrowin, and people weren't going easy on the festivities.

Their journey began quite gently, as they carefully eased themselves into the crowd, but the deeper they went, the livelier people grew, putting Galliana especially off balance.

Her head became a bewilderment of chaos as more threw themselves towards her, into her, against her. Percy tried his best to keep her on two feet, but she collapsed and almost as soon as she did a hand was proffered down to her.

Ignorant of anything else, she accepted it and a man, silhouetted by the sun behind, drew her up onto her feet and slightly into him. She thanked him.

"It was my pleasure," he countered.

Percy was very much on the back foot. Something that he would never have allowed to happen had happened.

Thermion shifted his head shading Galliana from the glare of the sun, but more importantly enabling her to see his face...

His tanned skin and smooth face, for the briefest moment, made her heart flutter. Her life, up until this point, had seen her mostly removed from men, and consequently, she found it hard to contain herself, her cheeks blushing crimson again. And the delicate smirk that grew from the side of his lips suggested he knew.

"I haven't seen you around Toryn before. Have you recently arrived?" he asked.

She was highly nervous, but something about this man reassured her, and then it—

"Who are you to ask such a question?" she said.

"My name is Thermion. And it was a pleasure to meet you."

"...Maybe it's time we headed back to the Keep." It was more a statement than a question as Percy interjected and then turned to face Thermion. "It's been a pleasure to meet you, but it's late." Percy was a big man and even Thermion was slightly taken aback at his presence.

Percy began to cradle and guide Galliana away.

"...How do you fancy bumping into each other again tomorrow? Same time?" Thermion shouted.

She heard, and that was all that mattered. As he turned, he ignored the odd looks that people were giving him, and carried on enjoying his day and the Feast...

***

A few, very lengthy, minutes later Keldor emerged from the gloomy shop, located Jerome and then continued out of the elusive backstreet and into the wild crowd of Cearan.

Jerome turned to Keldor and asked, "Are the streets normally this lively?"

"Have you not realised what this day is?" Keldor said peering at Jerome through questioning eyes.

Of course, Jerome hadn't realised until now what everyone was celebrating. It was the Feast of High King Terrowin.

This feast was in celebration and, moreover, commemoration of the People's Revolution. He had played the story in his mind over and over again, just as his mother had told it.

Before the inauguration of the high king, over half a millennium ago, Aramyth was a land ruled by kings and queens, but kings and queens who respected their people. However, it came to be the rise of three monarchs: King Vian, Queen Casadriel and King Morrowyn. Such was the power-hungry nature of the three that they decided to steal the rule entirely for themselves.

Under cloak and shadow, they held clandestine meetings where they plotted and schemed, until the time came to put their plans into action.

Having amassed a secret, underground army – the black guard, as it would come to be known – they issued their orders and within a month they had overthrown the other monarchs, putting into power their own bribed and biased lords and ladies.

It happened so suddenly, with such force, that the people were left dazed.

With the iron rule of the empowered nobles – a name that belied an ignoble truth –, which was enforced by the black guard, the people of Aramyth were left with virtually nothing.

Settlements, ranging from the tiny riverine hamlets and villages, to the bulging towns and cities, were turned into slave communities, with every man, woman and child forced to work for little, often nothing.

The anguish suffered hung like a thick stench over all of Aramyth for everyone to bear.

However, it would be the three monarchs' individual, power-hungry thirst for supremacy that would be their undoing; each one's singular need for ultimate power driving a wedge straight into the heart of their evil rule; taking the focus away from controlling the miserable masses for enough time for a long-suffering, bitter group of peasants to band together and form a revolution, right under their noses, to overthrow and unpick the hands of the tyrannous triumvirate.

Jerome had heard this story many times before from his mother. A few minutes were always devoted to the memory of those that died for the freedom of Aramyth.

It was feted *on* the anniversary, *every* anniversary – all, it seemed, except this one. And Jerome quietly languished, considering how cruelly surreptitious change really was, and how fast it affecting all of his life.

Then he decided that he would not let himself forget the tradition, and he played the finale out, fixing together little collections of memories. He remembered how he always looked so forward to this bit. He relished the moment, and it was only when the feast was laid out and set to eat that Driana would unravel the close…

As far as the story goes, the slaves of the north formed an alliance with a man named Terrowin and consequently, he led them into the battle that was won on pure odium for the three leaders.

As much as Jerome, or anyone for that matter, liked to believe that Terrowin was a slave, he was not. It was a common misconception in the recitation of the tale, and a favoured one.

Terrowin had in fact been a nobleman before, and still had contacts – contacts that he was able to reach.

And so it was, that their fourteen year reign was ended after little more than a week of war, a demise that was finalised at the Battle of Northbury, in a final stand against Queen Casadriel.

Kings and queens were quickly re-established, but a new high king was appointed – High King Terrowin – and so it was decreed that the kings and queens would be united, united and powerful, but always under the watchful eye of the high king – a constant balance of power.

It truly was an exultant day, but it wasn't just that single day that was celebrated, but the whole year – a whole year to waste the wine, food and luxuries that the slave-driving despots had worked out of the people, hence the title of the celebrated day, the 'Feast of High King Terrowin'.

Jerome grew sad, as it just reminded him of his mother, but he brushed off the thoughts that were weighing him down and tried vigorously to put his mind to something else.

He thought about the slums that they had avoided by the secret postern gate – poor people begging for money from other poor people.

It was enough to temporarily draw his mind away from his bereavement, and then he didn't need his vivid imagination anymore to support him, for Keldor had led them far enough through the city that the royal castle was in beautiful, clear view.

The few shops and people on the path moved behind as they began to cross the royal bridge, with guards stationed left and right, each one in crisp uniform. At the far side, stood before the moat, Keldor gave a shout up to one of the lookouts.

"I am Keldor of the Realm's Rangers, and I have important news."

"What news is that?" the voice from the high wall returned.

Keldor rubbed his stubbly face in thought. Jerome was positive he saw a little smile. "News that your under garment is to be flown as the new flag of Cearan."

Jerome gawped. Keldor waited for the response. "Is that the same under garment sewn by your mother?"

Keldor tried, but couldn't quite find the words to meld a suitable retort.

"Not got one, Keldor? You know the forfeit."

Quick as a flash Keldor whipped his bow from his shoulder, snatched an arrow from his quiver and had it trained at a point high above the walls.

The speed, with which Keldor acted, followed by the tiny adjustments as he pulled back the bow against his cheek, stilled Jerome.

Then he released and the arrow went up...

Jerome was focused intently on the arrow, his gaze fully dictated by the flow of the ballistic, and he couldn't quite make out what had happened to it, until he strained to see a very thin container, perched on the wall, resting between the crenellations ... *with the arrow inside.*

It was an impossible shot, Jerome believed, from anyone's perspective, but as he saw the wind catch the arrow's four-fletch, blowing it around within, there seemed nothing to doubt the truth behind the impossible.

The lookout shouted down to one of the guards to drop the drawbridge and it sank slowly setting its place over the wide and deep moat. The two crossed over, Jerome still amazed at the fineness of Keldor's archery.

They walked side-by-side through the courtyard. Keldor threw a look back and up to the lookout, who, in turn, nodded back, and then they reached the doorway to the great castle.

The guards by which, unlike the lookout, did not hesitate as they drew up their spears in alignment with their vertical stances, permitting them entrance. Just beyond that, and before the cloister, a servant to the king was ready to escort them.

Such was the nature of the visit that no time was properly afforded to relishing the interior of this majestic palace. If Jerome could have stolen himself away from its beauty, and applied his mind for the briefest of periods, he may have concluded that the servant would have walked these halls on a daily basis and was now immune to its magnificence, and consequently wasn't about to give a grand tour.

Keldor wasn't immune; his benchmark for magnificence was just so much higher, for his eyes had glimpsed brilliances that no interior, whether regal castles of opulence, or mystic, woodland huts of the druidic sage, could ever outshine.

But to Jerome, and what little the simple village life had shown him, he had only seen the fancies of his mind's eye, of epic battles and the heroes born from within, of silent assassins leaping from roof to roof, of ships straying too far and falling off the edge of the world, of dragons making spears of the cities' steeples upon which they were perched, of the seraphim dancing to the tune of the wind…

Wondrous images, but nothing real… *This was real.*

Each part of the castle was a new fantasy world brought to life, starting from the very beginning, even before they had actually entered.

Just walking in and around the cloister, which treasured a luscious, lustrous garden at the centre, brought Jerome new waves of wonder. Then, upon entering at the far corner of the cloister, there was a corridor that bore right. The sunlight streaming through the arched, crisscrossed windowpanes was hued green, an affectation from the leafy vines that had been cultivated from the outside garden.

Each room told a new story, a separate tale to which Jerome attached so many ideas. His eyes bulged as they paced the regal carpets, passed floor to ceiling tapestries, which depicted mighty quests, artistry that only true power – not even pure wealth – could attain, as well as monuments and portraits of past monarchs.

So enamoured was he that he completely ignored the guards stood authoritatively by a big set of ornate wooden doors.

As they were admitted, his focus was demanded by the cupola roof, painted to mimic the heavens, and was more interested in the embedded white-stone columns, each one uniformly topped by intricately-carved, dwarf-like figurines.

So mesmerised was he by the way the dwarven finials had been shaped to look as though they held the domed roof aloft, that he completely missed the fact that Keldor and the servant were now kneeling. His head had been swimming in the clouds, listening to the sound of feet clapping on a shimmering floor; listening as the dwarven figures, holding up the heavens for eternity, passed the sound back and forth between each other.

Oh, is that the king? Jerome thought, as silence suddenly presided. *Oh, should I be kneeling? Kneel!* He knelt so quick, blink and you'd have missed it.

After a few moments, and a few thousand prickly heartbeats, the king motioned them to stand.

"You have brought me news, Keldor?"

"Your Majesty, over the past few months I have come to learn of an uprising."

"I don't like uprisings, Keldor. Be more specific."

"I can't be sure exactly, but within Banneth Fell, where I have never previously experienced any trouble, I found a collection of dark creatures."

"Do these things have a name and ... did you manage to deal with them?" the king asked.

"I did, and I took it upon myself to find out about them."

"Good, and what have you discovered?"

"Having spoken with a friend, and expert in the field, we believe they are called plague bearers ... or plague bringers. Apparently either term is acceptable."

Jerome wondered if the friend Keldor was talking about was Borric. It seemed likely.

"So what are these creatures then? What do they do?" King Josiah asked, leaning forward.

"They are a form of undead. The term plague bringer is appropriated to their stench and look, but as for a true purpose, no one can be sure. People say they're relics of The War of Unity, but that is only speculation."

The king paused and the room waited upon his word.

"You are not the only ranger to relay this back to me, Keldor," the king said. "And you have confirmed my beliefs. I have had this letter drawn up which I would like you to personally take to the high king."

"Of course, Your Majesty."

"One more thing, Keldor. Four Duke's Rangers have been reported missing. So be careful, yes."

"I will, Your Majesty."

Keldor bowed his head firmly and Jerome, seeing his action, imitated. They were both escorted out of the throne room, down the winding corridors and out into the cloister where the servant stood to farewell them.

Jerome was so excited that he turned back to wave for a second time, but instead of seeing the gentle looking retainer that had showed them through the castle, his eyes fell upon a beaten and bloodied version of the same man swinging, hanged, in the archway. The dead eyes looked at him. Immediately, Jerome flung himself around and yanked at Keldor's sleeve.

"Keldor, look!" With haste, Keldor exploded round, his expert senses surging to life, expecting to see something warranting that urgency, but on the contrary, found himself engaged in eye contact with a very confused servant.

"What am I supposed to be looking at, Jerome?"

As Jerome turned back with Keldor, he also only saw the gentle man and then he immediately felt the skin under his collar heat up. Desperate for answers that, whilst walking to leave the city and when passing the obscure Mourning Street, Jerome wondered if Borric might be able to shed some light on his visions.

"Keldor." Jerome gained his companion's attention, then wished he hadn't – he was having visions and wasn't ready to open up. *Too late* ... "I'm having visions." It slipped out.

Keldor's silence was agonising.

"I've been having them since we left Melfall."

"Visions? Voices as well?" his ranger friend inquired.

"No, just visions. They began with just a pair of eyes ... looking at me, but now ... back at the castle, I saw the servant hanging in the archway. I just wondered if your friend, Borric – I think his name is – might be able to ... help in some way."

"We can ask, but he deals more with Dark Creatures. The *magic* is more a sales pitch, that is, if that's what these visions actually are?"

Taking the right turn, they emerged into the shadows of Mourning Street and edged towards Borric's Grotto of Dark Creatures and Magic.

The shop was very eerie and was in the exact state Jerome expected, having seen it from the outside. Ornamented on the shelves other than the usual-*unusual* books were such things as: pots and jars, some labelled, some not, but all containing something peculiar and unspeakable, other trappings of magic dimension and all sorts of dead animals which included bats, rats, frogs and other ill-fated faunae.

Jerome speculated if it was all for show after what Keldor said. After all, it did seem somewhat cliché.

Keldor had gone to speak to his friend and the two of them approached Jerome, who at best was uneasy; at worst, quaking in his boots.

"So you're having visions," Borric said, an erudite quality to his voice.

"Yes. *And* they're getting worse," Jerome responded, keen to be helped.

"It's difficult to say," he admitted. "What form do these *visions* take?"

"Well, they began just with a pair of eyes, although, I was sure I could see something of Its figure. The last time was the worst, though. A man that was taking us to see the king, I saw him hanged in the archway, dead, swinging, and his eyes looking at me." Jerome's mind was transported back to that horrific moment as he recanted it.

"And you couldn't see the same figure with the eyes? It was just the man?" He paused. "Now think carefully. I have an idea on what this might be."

"I can't see It." Jerome thought back again, trying hard to look at all the details. It was awful. The man … he simply swung … left, gently right, gradually left… and then, he saw the gentle servant, *behind* the hanged version of himself. But there was no other figure, no pair of eyes. "No, it was like the figure had *become* the hanged man."

"Curious. Just allow me one minute."

He bustled his way to a bookshelf where he stroked his finger across the spines of a great many books, until stopping on one, which he whisked out.

It was a heavy book and dust exploded out from beneath it, as he collapsed it down onto a wooden table. The table rocked, disagreeably, and he unclasped the side of the epic tome before flinging it open. With a mad flurry he began turning pages, back and forth as he searched.

"Has someone close to you recently died?" Borric said, his head still in the pages.

Jerome glanced at Keldor for approval. Keldor's approving nod turned him back to Borric.

"No one has died ... I hope," – Jerome gulped – "but my mother has ... gone."

"Is your mother important to you?" Borric asked, quite mechanically, ignoring any empathy.

Jerome dropped his head and wiped his damp eyes. Borric was still glued to the pages as mumbles and the occasional word or two bounced out and, then, realising his question to remain unanswered, he looked up. A brief moment later and Borric understood Jerome's upset, as he let his mania subside and his control return.

With sincerity and care, Borric continued and gravely he said, "I believe you have a Dark Whisperer."

"A what?" Jerome babbled.

"Above Its name, which isn't factual I might add, there is not a huge amount about It that is documented. It appears that people who are victims of grief, or torture, or some kind of trauma, like yourself, begin to manifest these visions. It's not specific about 'what It does', but it sounds like a form of communication."

"What kind of communication?" Jerome demanded.

"It's not really clear, and I could still be wrong. Because, you see, in most cases where people have visions, it's – I'm sorry to say it, Jerome – because their mad. And those *visions* are generally just manic echoes of their minds slowly dying, and rarely do they take any continuous, logical stream. But *you* saw a pair of eyes, just eyes, and then the man hanging, *just* the man hanging. You're seeing only *one* thing, and it's trying to do only one thing: scare you. As for the communication, I imagine it's more of an instruction."

"How are people instructed?"

"From what I can make out, it sounds a bit like ... *hot or cold.*"

"What do you mean?"

He put the words together in his head and then said, "Well ... have you ever played *hot or cold?*"

Jerome knew, but appeared puzzled at the connection.

"You look for something and the other person says 'hot' or 'cold' depending—"

"Yes, I know," Jerome said, stopping him.

"Then that's how I imagine this thing will communicate with you. Except rather than it saying 'hot' or 'cold', the vision will get more horrific the longer you ignore It and more angelic the further you listen."

"And how do I get rid of It?"

"I wish I could tell you. But, there's nothing here. And, unfortunately, when there's nothing written down about things like that, then you can take it as a sign that it's ... never been done..." He paused, to give his words weight. "So, if ever you *do* find a way of ridding yourself of It, I would greatly appreciate knowing how. And if I were you, I would do as It wants. Some of the things people have said about the visions are best resigned to the dusty bo—" He stopped mid-sentence, and then muttered, "Wait, wait, wait, wait, wait..." as his eyes caught something on pages beneath.

And, as suddenly as his eyes caught whatever it was, he flitted over to a huge wall of books and flashed from shelf to shelf, running his fingers along the backs until stopping. The particular book, which he tapped, pulled out and then slammed down open on top of the tome, was tiny by comparison.

Everything paused, while his fingers shuffled through the pages, as though they were an intelligent appendage of the book. His head shifted left and right, eyes scanning sharply over the words, and his abrupt halt almost shook the room into motion, booming it like a war drum, the skin slowly rumbling to stillness. Jerome held on every breath. *What was he going to say?*

Borric inhaled, hard, and seized a moment to compose himself.

Referring to the tome beneath, he began, "These pages are a compilation of facts taken from real stories of *real* people and their experiences. They have been amassed, refined and mapped over years of labour. Rarely does it actually mention a name, but here," – he dabbed a pointed finger on a spot in the epic volume – "I missed it before, but when I saw it, I knew I recognised it. And here," – he grabbed the little, leather-bound pocket book he'd recently plucked from the shelves – "this is the journal of a forebear of mine, who attempted to help someone 'plagued by visions'.

"The journal itself stops a little beyond Marston, but the man showed no sign of ceasing, nor did the visions become any less engaging. I'm sorry, Jerome, that is the extent of my knowledge. I can help you no more."

Keldor thanked Borric for his assistance and then left, Jerome sauntering out behind his purposeful gait.

He was swept up within the ocean of his mind as the city around, people and shops, streets and all, paled away until they were both alone, on the quiet track to Arthak. The city's rumble behind was only just audible above the gentle rattle of the great wilderness.

Chapter IV
Dilemmas

Peter and Garveya arrived after a two-and-a-half day voyage. The ship had made good time as it moored up. The sky was clear and the moon brightly lit the quiescent streets of Sal. Once on hard land, Peter turned to Garveya.

"So, how does one go about finding these people?" he enquired.

"That is a good question. Do you remember I mentioned before about magic attracting magic?" Peter nodded. "Dark magi they may be, but I can still sense them and trace them, within a certain distance. They try and hide their magical aura, which is why I could sense you from so much further away."

"Can you sense them now?" Peter queried.

"Sadly not, though I think we should walk *while* we talk. We have still a way to go before we reach Tryth."

Step by step they began trekking down the moonlit streets. Quiet predominated, but Peter still had more on his mind.

"What are we going to do when we find these dark magi?"

"I have been ordered to do what is necessary."

"What do you mean?"

Without directly answering his question she said, "Peter, these dark magi are not something to sneer at. Though they look no different to you or me, they are not called dark magi for no reason. They are demons. They are evil, and they feel no remorse, or no remorse *I*'ve ever seen, and if you ever find yourself around one, then I suggest you find the quickest route out."

Peter turned his attention inwards. The ship journey had not left Peter well rested – it seemed there were no modes of transport that were comfortable, *perhaps in the future they'll find one that is*. His Feast Day was spent mostly feeling ill over the side of the vessel, and if he were being totally honest, he was looking forward to stopping for the night, but Garveya showed no sign of breaking. The journey continued, through and out of the streets of Sal, north to Tryth.

***

The travelling had got to Jerome. He was tired and weary and his legs felt like they were made of wood *and* jelly. Keldor, on the other hand, thrived. He was always alert and appeared to be ready at every corner.

They stopped for no more than a few hours a night, Keldor making certain to use up every drop of daylight, an experience Jerome thought he would never discover. In retrospect, would have been *happy* not to discover.

But on the plus side, Jerome was exposed to a great deal of new and exciting things. An eager student, he was quick to open his mind to the ways of the ranger, learning such things as setting up camp, making fire and catching all different kinds of game, *including* rabbits, though not by sneaking up on them.

Of course, Jerome was a beginner and mistakes were all part of the process, a process which required reward and punishment; it was just unfortunate for Keldor that some of these punishments affected him as much as Jerome. Every time he went without an evening meal he was painfully reminded of this eventuality, but he knew that it was only a passing thing and he was quite able to deal without food for a day – for a week, and sometimes more if needs be. He had before.

Over the course of the journey, Keldor had really begun to value Jerome as a companion and friend. It made it easier *because* of his desire to learn, but it was apparent that there was more than just a common interest.

It was unfortunate, but the solitude of Keldor's life and career had never allowed him to understand the worth of a friend, but with each passing day he felt more protective over Jerome, more worried about his ignorance to what the world really had to offer. But those were things that Jerome would discover.

He would have to learn to bear himself to the fear, square his shoulders to the task ahead and never look back.

As for his mother, Keldor had promised him that when his mission from the king was over, he would devote his time to finding her.

Jerome understood Keldor's commitment to the king, and the realm, and was thankful.

And while they had all this time together, he was quick to pick up everything Keldor was teaching him, and was soon able to find his own food, *most of the time,* light a fire and cook his catch.

Unfortunately, due to his youth and lacking strength, he was unable to build an all-weather shelter and was limited to the preformed shelters nature had to offer.

"The best ones sometimes," Keldor had always added.

Jerome didn't mention it, but his Dark Whisperer still plagued him. It was something he was getting as used to as the early mornings and long days.

It was an evil that seemed to be irrevocably stitching Itself into his life.

When Jerome slept and Keldor had a moment apart, he reflected on the limitless quantities of information that could be absorbed; for even he, a person considered to be a distinguished ranger and survivalist, still learnt things.

And he hadn't realised it, until now, but he was even learning things from a fourteen-year-old boy.

***

After having returned to Grey Keep, and after chiding herself for her behaviour with Thermion – namely her blushing, feverish state – Galliana had sunk back within herself. The voice that she had found with Percy had diminished and died away, and even he was now unable to console her.

A few days on and she was still voiceless, nothing able to shake the words from her. The only communication were her eyes, emoting lonely anguish and Percy quickly grew anxious. He wondered what might open her up and then the idea came to him. It was a moment of madness he thought, surely it was, but it might just work.

He was going to arrange a meeting with Thermion. Maybe his presence could jolt her free from her internal prison.

He immediately set to work making preparations to leave. Unlike others, he was still very much in the baby-step phase and leaving wasn't just something he could simply up and do.

It took time.

He needed to make sure he was presentable, both on the outside as well as the chain-mail armour beneath, checking for any snagged circlets.

He needed confirmation that his hair and beard were well groomed and respectable, but it was the mental grounding that required the most time.

He thought about the plan and remembered Thermion talking about 'bumping into each other again tomorrow'. He was aware that it had been a couple of days, but he hoped that Galliana had made enough of an impact on him that Thermion might still be there, wanting to 'bump into her' again.

He had just finished finalising *the plan,* each step plotted meticulously, when there was a knock at his door.

He soundlessly cursed under his breath for the disturbance and then – in that evanescent moment between being sat, ignorant to everything beyond his room, and the time it took to answer the door – he realised how much this girl had shaken his world. He could think of nothing that would have worked him up this much before.

It was, of course, Junus, the faithful caretaker of Grey Keep. *Probably to tell me that council have decided a new rule about ale strength or some such nonsense!*

The council that Percy so disrespected often created humdrum rules about the whats, whys, this and thats of the world, so much so that he had lost all interest in them.

If they had nothing better to do, than to spend their hours dwelling within their own bureaucracy, then he would give them no time at all … and he used to be so much more.

He quickly put a cork on that train of thought and invited Junus to speak.

"Lord Pembroke, I have—"

"Percy, please," Percy implored.

Junus did not respond to Percy's interjection, and Percy wondered if ever he had called him 'Percy'. "There is a man waiting for you in the main hall. He asked for you."

"By name?" asked Percy, allowing his curiosity to flourish.

"He did not, but he did indicate you by mentioning Galliana, when you two went out on Feast Day."

Percy could hardly believe it. He knew who it was and then, like a blanket of wisdom wrapping around his mind, he became highly understanding. He was not the only man to have been stricken by this girl.

Thermion was busy looking at the surrounding exuberance of the main hall when Percy walked in.

"I wondered if I'd find you here," Thermion said, applauding himself.

"Is it me you've been looking for?" Percy wondered, although he assumed it highly unlikely.

"Not exactly, although I have a feeling I need to speak to you first."

Percy disregarded Thermion's comment and continued, saying, "What made you think I'd be here?"

"Where else might you find a well-dressed old man looking exceptionally uncomfortable outside?"

Thermion's parrying question had a good slant, but his next comment, "That and The Order's coat of arms was an absolute give away," confirmed to Percy that he was a very observant young man.

"Walk with me," Percy invited.

And he led him around the beautiful, water-based architectural features and walkways of Grey Keep.

"Galliana is a very delicate girl," Percy said.

"So *that*'s her name," Thermion said, with a relishing tone.

"She has," Percy continued, "not said a word since we last met. You are the last person to whom she has spoken and," he took a breath, "I think she may 'open up' to you."

"Well, there's only one way to find out," Thermion concluded to Percy, and in agreement, they went back inside Grey Keep.

* * *

The triple functioning, well-oiled machine that was Garrick, Baylin and Mythos had stormed eastern Aramyth and arrived at Morigan's Green in quick time. From there, they had located their contact in the only local tavern, and then no time was wasted, as they left immediately after new information of their target's next destination.

* * *

Very little had happened on Jerome and Keldor's journey and even less had happened before the decision had been made to set up camp for the night. Keldor was moments away from dropping his impenetrable guard before his eagle sense honed in on a solitary figure making its way through the surrounding trees. Keldor immediately began his investigation.

He bounded from tree to tree, hiding behind each one so as to keep hidden, but as he reduced the gap between him and his unsuspecting target, he noticed him to be badly injured.

It was indiscernible from a distance, but he was stumbling, using almost every tree as a crutch.

It was his left leg that had sustained the injury – his limp clearly indicated – and shortly after, he collapsed, sinking into the undergrowth.

Keldor didn't dawdle as he picked him up and carried him, over his shoulder, to where Jerome had already begun getting a fire started.

Jerome, eager to lend a hand, cleared and arranged a spot on the floor where the man could sit and lean.

Keldor set him down, and between the pair of them, they prepared food and tended to the man's wounds, some with herbal remedies – not that they were druids, by any means – and others simply with clean water and bandages made from spare clothing.

"Thank you, thank you both," the injured man mustered.

He was a messenger, an Arthak messenger to be precise. Keldor understood this, even from before he had picked him up, but then, very little escaped Keldor. Jerome, on the other hand, required telling, his capacity to observe and reason was still in its infancy.

"What attacked you before?"

"Green-skins ... dozens of them. It was as though they were waiting for us."

"How many of you?" Keldor interposed.

"Ten of us," the messenger continued. "I only just made it out; they slaughtered everyone else. I don't know if I should have stayed and died, rather than running."

"You made the right choice," Keldor confirmed. "Your duty is to your king and to the message that must be delivered. You're no good to anyone dead."

Full with sorrow and close to despair, Keldor's words rang true, as the man calmed and realised the sense.

"Yes, you're right and I must be on my way," he said, staggering to his feet.

"You should rest a little before you continue on," Keldor beckoned.

"If it were for anything other than the utmost importance then, believe me, I would, but this can't wait."

"What must the message contain to need such urgency?" Jerome said, dying to ask.

Keldor felt slightly embarrassed at his young companion's impetuousness, and Jerome felt it, his face reddening, but the messenger recognised a similar impetuousness in his younger self, and showed understanding to Jerome's dilemma.

He leant towards him, like he was about to tell a secret story, a soft curve in his lips. "I can't be sure," he began. "I am not privy to such information, and I would never betray the secrecy of our sovereignty, but," – and he invited Keldor to listen, as well, – "the word is that there's an increase of dark creatures. Armies of them, people are saying... It may be about that, but all I can tell you is that I need to get this to Cearan, on the highest authority."

"I would implore you to stay, at least rest tonight, but I appreciate the duty we have of being in service to our king."

Keldor helped the man to his feet and they shook hands, before setting off.

His damaged leg still forced a limp, but he was steady and, even ignoring the limp, had the direction of a man keen to fulfil his obligation.

After waving the man off, Keldor returned to the warm atmosphere of the fire.

He was a man who lived purely by instinct and rarely did he dwell upon anything, but the information haunted him, especially since he had arrived at a similar conclusion, *and* it was based upon reality, not speculation.

Concern filled his mind as he pondered upon the severity of the situation.

How far had this plague spread?

***

"You! Goblin!" shouted the hulking ogre, who towered feet above the small green goblin. "One human not dead!"

The ogre picked the small goblin up by the neck and shook him furiously. He finished by hurling him into a structural tree, around which the tent had been erected.

His head struck first, but his spindly, bony body barrelled up over, slamming his back against the hard wood. The goblin landed in a heap on the floor, arms and legs twisted together. However, he managed to pick himself up and, moreover, dust himself down.

"You was meant to kill all! Why one not?"

"Misto not know one was alive. There was others supposed to kill them as well."

"I not care! One not dead! You should have killed!" the ogre continued to bellow, as he again picked up the goblin by its neck.

"Misto is sorry, but I not knows one was alive."

"Goblin, you be hurts!" the ogre roared, heatedly.

The giant shifted his grip from around the little goblin's neck down to his flaying legs. Once he had them firmly clamped between his massive hands, he proceeded to belt his head back and forth across the same tree with which he had earlier been acquainted.

"You, Goblin, will learn that humans be all dead or me will kill you!" he ordered, while punishing the small creature...

***

"Keldor, are there many green-skins in these woods?"

"Hundreds; this is green-skin territory," Keldor said, unwavering.

Dread began to overcome Jerome, as Keldor let spill that they were in the middle of a giant green-skin melting pot.

"Aren't we going to ... do something?" Jerome pleaded.

"What do you propose?

"Did you not know that there were green-skins in these woods?" It was a rude question, but Jerome felt he had no other choice.

"Of course I did."

"Then—"

"Why did I lead us in here?" Keldor completed Jerome's obvious question.

"Since the War of Unity, almost fifty years ago, a peace treaty has existed between humans, green-skins and magi, so there has never been any need to worry before. I'm just assuming that the truce seems to be a little more tenuous than it used to be." Keldor answered his question.

"I see."

"Are you able to carry on moving tonight?" Keldor asked.

Jerome checked himself. He felt tired, but he gave the nod anyway, and they were up and on their way.

But just as they began the hard slog into the night Jerome caught those horrid eyes glaring at him...

With the tiredness at an abundant level, Jerome found himself able to put the visions out of mind, even if not out of sight, as he fell into a meditative state where everything became a blur.

Keldor probably wouldn't have approved of it, but he'd walked for longer than he cared to imagine and, to be honest, right now, he didn't care what the ranger thought.

Keldor had quickly, and then patiently, followed the tracks, tracing where the injured man had come from and considering what manner of incident had led to his injuries.

It was the natural route to follow, as the dispatch unit had come direct from Arthak, and Keldor was impressed with how far he had travelled bearing in mind his injuries.

The minutes ticked by and light began to flood over the eastern horizon, Jerome following glumly behind, kicking the loose, dead foliage on the floor ahead as they walked.

Although not outright following the tracks, Keldor still stayed on target, wondering how much farther it could have been. And then shortly after wondering, he stopped.

"There!" Keldor whispered sharply, as he pointed directly to a small clearing in the near distance. "If I'm not mistaken, that is where the attack must have taken place."

Jerome looked towards it and noticed nothing of why the attack 'must have taken place', he mimicked childishly, as Keldor flitted his way over.

Jerome followed scruffily behind, thinking *ahead* to be no different to the massive amounts of *behind* that they'd spent ages covering.

However, to be within its confines was a far different story. Gazing around, he saw the scarred trees, the pitted and stained floor. More and more smatters of blood became present with every glance; the bells of war had rung here and stayed to haunt the vicinity, making its daunting presence ever more unwelcome.

Keldor was wrapped up sleuthing the event piece by piece. Jerome watched as he studied one area at a time and then marking out certain movements.

The jigsaw puzzle had been completed as he slotted together the final moments of the nine men's demise.

"That's that then," Keldor remarked, plaintively.

"That's what, Keldor?"

He inhaled … and exhaled. "…A massacre, Jerome. The bodies have all been dragged away, too. Very un-green-skin like."

"What do we do?"

"We do as planned," Keldor stated. "Head to the high king and report our findings. And we do it quick. Something's spooked the inhabitants."

***

There was no way of describing the feelings that whirled inside Jerome, as they walked into the morning, through the day and into the evening.

He had experienced so much since the seclusion of Melfall, his home.

Responsibility was the biggest thing and although it was only simple responsibility – taking charge of lighting a fire, catching food – it was responsibility nonetheless.

It was as though the blanket, that had kept him so blind, had been removed.

And it was ironic. Looking at it subjectively, all of those things he had to do – the fire, the food – he would before have thought robbed him of his freedom.

But on the contrary, it had given him a new and more *satisfying* freedom – the freedom to know that he was able to take care of himself, to be independent.

…It was then that he was yanked back to his mother and his life *before* she had gone. Internally, he reddened as he played over moments from before he met Keldor, as he looked at how he would have behaved. It left him feeling confused and numb, if not slightly embarrassed.

Keldor looked at Jerome. He was not one for silence. Since knowing him, he had been anything but. So seeing him like this worked thoughts of their own into Keldor's head.

"Jerome?" Keldor said, capturing the boy's attention.

And it was like someone had struck the candle to life behind his eyes, and his blue gaze met Keldor's.

Who continued, "You're very quiet. Is there ... something you want to talk about?"

"Oh, no. I was just thinking."

"About what?" Keldor pried.

"Oh, nothing much. Just thinking about what's happened ... what might happen ... my mother ... and father ... general things," Jerome let dribble out.

"I know this might be hard for you to comprehend and especially at such a young age, but I can assure you that this is not your fault. Whatever you may have said to your mother... What is her name by the way?"

"Driana."

"...Whatever you may have said to her, she will have forgiven you long ago. You are a kind boy, you are—"

"Am I?" he asked. "I threw it back in—"

"You feel bad?" Keldor pointedly questioned, cutting him off, just as he had done to him.

Jerome stopped. Paused. And then nodded.

"What *good* person wouldn't? Remember, it is your remorse that makes you human, not your regret."

These words stuck inside him, lodged in deep. Jerome looked down to the ground as a tear seeped out from his eyes. He understood it. He could not change the past. He could only hope that the future would see him do the right thing.

His thoughts flowed as the moon rose, phasing the air into deep calm. Keldor stopped walking and Jerome assisted as together they prepared the area, but just as Keldor was about to rest, he suddenly – *again,* Jerome thought – jumped into a state of awareness. Jerome sat up.

It was different this time. Something felt different. *Bad* different.

"Wait here," Keldor ordered.

But before Jerome had time to ask what was going on Keldor had leapt into the night and Jerome was alone.

A few minutes passed and Jerome had already prepped the area and got a small fire going, when a figure came into the dim light.

Jerome's first thought upon hearing the movement was Keldor, but it didn't sit right with him.

It sounded clumsy, and Keldor was anything but clumsy, and then, before he could take any evasive action, he was hooked up by the back of his neck and, staring into his eyes, was a vulgar, green-looking creature of exceptional build.

Jerome had never seen a green-skin before. But it didn't take a genius to work it out.

And then the fear hit him.

He had no comprehension of how scary it would be, as he hung petrified beyond belief.

In self-defence he began shouting and kicking, trying to find a way to get it to release its grip, but seeing the futility, he stopped just as quickly as he began.

The green-skin stood, wall-like, immune to his feeble strikes, immune and then outwardly confused.

To him – at least Jerome assumed it to be male – he was as light as a feather, and the green-skin was quite able to endure almost any blunt force that Jerome could assemble. And as he ceased, it remained immune … and then immune *and* angry.

The green-skin was raising its gnarled club up, but before he had a chance to start bludgeoning Jerome, there was a grunt, a loud grunt coming from behind him.

To Jerome, it just sounded like a noise, but when the club was lowered, it became clear that it was a language and the grunt a most fortunate command.

Jerome's sigh of relief made him feel quite light-headed and, as the blood returned, he looked around to see Keldor, who was also detained.

It put an immediate halt on any hopes of escape, as there were also about five more creatures of similar kind present, and then, as his eyes inured, lurking in the background, he saw many more green-skins who were busily scurrying around.

In the grip of the green-skin, Jerome remained still, his hope relinquished, but he remembered and valued the grunt that saved his life.

They were soon trudging through the woods making their way to an encampment, which was littered with smaller camps, where there were green-skins of all sizes sat together, talking – *grunting,* Jerome thought – laughing, but as they passed every crowd, all talking – *grunting* – stopped and they were greeted with sneers in the language of silence. The exuding hatred was as torrid as the heat from their fires.

They were led to a central camp, where they were pushed to the ground.

A massive central figure bellowed an earth-shattering roar, silencing everything within hearing distance. All stopped. Even the green-skins that were beginning their taunt backed off.

Once properly registered, the silence was broken by a shorter figure standing next the central hulk.

Neither Keldor nor Jerome could understand what was being said, but they were sure that whatever it was, they were the subject, and when it was over, a few of the smaller creatures scampered out from the audience with rope and bound them.

The congregation ended with the behemoth striding through the crowd and everything in its path shifting to one side. The littler one, initially to his side, followed behind, head down and hushed, into the chief's den.

"What's going to happen to us, Keldor?" Jerome said, shivering from the cold.

"…I can't be sure…" Keldor said.

But he did.

They were going to kill them.

Jerome tried to block out the cold atmosphere and get some sleep. He thought it wouldn't be difficult, but whenever he closed his eyes a gust of cold air shot past him, leaving an unpleasant tingle that wound its way up his spine.

Not only that, but the thought of impending death – Keldor hadn't said it, though it seemed obvious and ominous – wasn't helping his attempted sleep, and the wicked eyes weren't easing their adamant scowl either.

Fortunately, after an age of trying, he did manage to doze off, where he came to be running down the battlefield, sword in hand, with the one intent: killing his archenemy.

Vanquishing men to his left and right, he approached the figure in black.

As before, he removed his helm, and standing before him was his reciprocal, evil image.

Their swords clashed, the fight came to life. Each attack Jerome made was countered and, in turn, each attack made against him was blocked and parried.

It was equal both sides, but then, a sudden shock broke his fight, as he felt an arrow penetrate his back. He dropped. His hand weakened. The sword fell from his limp and lifeless grip. He let out a yelp, leaving his neck clean open for the finishing blow.

He saw the sword come flying down in perfect alignment, but just before it made contact he awoke to find himself sweating, breathing hard in the cool night air.

He took a few minutes to place himself before trying to fall back to sleep, but even granting that he was still tired and suffering with massive sleep deprivation, he could not return to his slumber and wished, in that short instant, for a little piece of calm in an otherwise turbulent journey.

This pervaded his main stream of thoughts, but death – the idea of it – soon became the overriding issue.

He did not shut his eyes again.

Instead, he tried to take in the cool and pleasant welcoming of the moonlit night, and he savoured it, for – he thought – it might be his last. It was for the first time in his life that he truly saw how beautiful the effect of the moon was, as it vivified the trees with a cerulean tinge.

Sounds in the distance broke his focus as he peered round the tree, which was obscuring much of his vision, to grasp a glimpse of what was happening.

It seemed to be coming from within the main tent. Two figures were silhouetted against the material. One of them was huge and bulky – Jerome deduced it to be the earlier hulk – but the other one was very short and scraggly.

And it was here, in what Jerome took to be his final few minutes, that he spun a thought for his mother and his friend Peter, hoping that wherever they may be, they would be faring better.

"Peter, welcome to Tryth."

It was night upon their arrival, but it was nonetheless entrancing. The moonlight was something Peter always loved. He would even go as far to say that he preferred a bright night to a sunny day. A *dark* night, on the other hand, was a different thing altogether...

"It's amazing," Peter exclaimed.

"Yes," Garveya said, jocularly at the youthful excitement of her companion, "and there will be plenty of time to appreciate it, after we find a place to rest our heads for the remainder of the night. After all, we're not even in the city."

"Agreed," Peter confirmed.

They approached the gates and Garveya knocked.

"What business do you have here in Tryth?" A deep grunting voice spoke from the city-side.

"My son and I wish to spend the night; we have been travelling for quite some time."

"Very well."

The gates creaked open, stopping well short from a fully open state; just enough to let Garveya and Peter slide in. After the gates had been closed tight and the tired guard – working the graveyard shift – had finished the motions of locking and securing this entrance to the city, Garveya further beckoned his attention.

"How may I help you, madam?"

"Just quickly, where can we find an inn to keep us for the night?"

"Depends on the quality, and as I wouldn't dare guess on what you would like, I shall open the options for you." He cleared his throat and hid a gentle yawn. "There is the Barrel Roll, a little way up the hill from here. Or you may choose the Tailors Mail? Or, on the upper end of the scale, you have the Red Cap. A fine establishment, but it all depends on how far you wish to walk, and how much money you have to spare."

"Thank you. Where can we find the Red Cap?"

"Wise choice," the guard said. "Follow Cobble Street until the end. Turn left down Fenwick Street. At the end of that, you will find yourself in Golden Square. The Red Cap is directly opposite. You can't miss it. Is there anything else I can help you with?"

"No, thank you. Good night."

"Good night, madam. Enjoy your stay in Tryth."

"I am sure we shall," Garveya said, adding a feminine touch.

Garveya led Peter away as they started up Cobble Street and, while they walked, a harmless question began to form within his mind; a simple word, but a simple word with a big consequence.

"Son?" Peter humoured, plainly wondering the need for the pretence.

Then quicker than Peter could fathom she replied, "Would you prefer partner?"

He instantly turned red. Even the cold draughts shooting between the streets could not numb the heat building within, and without helping it, he remembered her legs, and then all too soon was drawn to her other womanly aspects.

His mind raced, trying to find something to say, but nothing could be said to neutralise the blush that was blithely grinning from both cheeks.

He looked down, trying to hide it, but it did not stop Garveya from enjoying watching him squirm, and the journey, which should have taken but a few minutes, made him feel an old man, as they eventually stood overlooking the entrance to the Red Cap.

It looked quite dormant, but they took the guard's word and entered.

The plush foyer was lit by a few unobtrusive candles, and waiting on the other side of a counter stood a man, smartly dressed and awake, ready to tend to the needs of any guest, would be, or current.

"Good evening. How can I help?" the man invited.

"Good evening, we would like a room please," Garveya replied.

"Of course. That will be one gold for you and your…?"

"Husband," Garveya completed.

"Husband, of course."

He handed over a big, well-polished key and with it, directions to their room, which they followed, to the letter, to the door.

Peter wondered what the man had really thought of their relationship.

He would be a man without assumption, or rather a man who would completely conceal *any* assumption and make no comment regarding them.

Either way, the single difficulty of a double bed was presented, a situation neither had considered.

But as he lay on the chaise longue and thought – vividly so – he wouldn't have minded sharing a bed with Garveya, *if only she felt the same.*

He couldn't let go of those thoughts of her and with each dwelling urge it became very troublesome to think on anything else.

The big calm that was his life in Melfall had ruptured and brought forth a plethora of convolutions, effectively rocking each part of his rapidly developing world.

He tried his best to eradicate the thoughts, but nothing could diminish them, so instead, he refocused his mind to other things, namely his parents, who surely, by now at least, would have found his note and had the time to wonder…

This consideration of home also spurred on other thoughts and he remembered his friend, Jerome, and gave prayers for his safety, hoping that he wouldn't need any.

These final bursts of freedom allowed him to sleep.

***

The small goblin that had earlier received the severe beating was stood in the same ogre's presence. The ogre did not seem at all changed from his earlier mood and the anger from before still resided in each crack and pore of his evil animation.

He bellowed at the minute, trembling figure, coming up no higher than his knee.

"Humans outside, tied to tree because you did not kill!"

"Misto did not know humans was alive, so did not kill."

"I's does not care! We now has humans here. Others will come! You are stupid goblin! You are stupid … very stupid goblin!" the ogre affirmed, his own stupidity not allowing him any other insult.

The colossus then moved a step closer towards Misto, closing the gap until he was within arm's reach. He then picked him up by the neck, and with his other hand, seized a huge rock from a counter behind him. He held it tight, the rock adding to the thump of his fist.

Misto then began to take smash after smash as the ogre repeatedly thumped him round the head several times with his stone-fist.

After a dozen or so strikes, the brutally mauled goblin was hurled out of the tent, catching the loose flapping doors on the way…

***

…All Jerome heard were the roars of the hulk and the thumps received by the little green-skin, and amazingly, there were no whimpers. Not a single cry was voiced, even when he was chucked out. The small thing just lay there, breathing heavily and deeply.

Eventually, the goblin found the strength to get up and Jerome marked its endurance.

The goblin then promptly twisted and stretched all the discomfit out. He then looked around and surveyed the surroundings before meeting Jerome's eye and then slowly and cautiously started approaching.

Upon connection, Jerome immediately shut his eyes hoping not to draw attention to himself, but was convinced that the green-skin had seen him.

When he was sure that it was coming over, he began to panic, breathing thick clouds of condensation, worsening his panic.

He soon heard the light tapping of feet on the ground getting nearer, but inside, he was very aware of the heavy thumping of his heart.

It was so loud; surely the green-skin could hear it. Maybe, they could hear things humans couldn't.

Stop being paranoid! he told himself, *it's your heart!*

The footsteps were close now, but still he kept his eyes forced shut, so tight that they began to water and then almost freeze beneath his eyes.

He was so scared that he almost missed the high-pitched squeaks jumping out of the little figure and then, to his disbelief, he felt the ropes that bound him being cut.

What was he doing? Stupid question, Jerome. Why *was he doing it?*

When his restraints were completely loosened though, the questions subsided and reality took over. He slightly opened one eye to see what the little green-skin would do next, and to his surprise it was also freeing Keldor.

However, when Keldor was liberated his hand viciously snatched the green-skin's thin neck. Instantly, the creature began to struggle helplessly and with the same alacrity, Jerome reached for Keldor's hand, urging him to release the tiny green-skin.

Keldor glared at him, rebuffing his want, but Jerome stared back with even more fervour. He loosened his grip from around the goblin's neck, but did not put him down.

"Why?" Keldor said, quietly but heatedly.

"He cut us loose. We owe him," Jerome reasoned.

"We owe him nothing. He is just another green-skin."

"Think about it, Keldor. He has risked himself, at the least, let him explain…"

Keldor appreciated and respected Jerome's reason and calm at this hour. Slowly, he released the goblin. As soon as he was free though, he rapidly scurried behind Jerome who turned to face the goblin.

His fear had completely evaporated and he took a deep breath, a breath, he had thought only minutes earlier, he would never take again.

"Thank you," Jerome said.

"Me only wanted help you and friend," he hastily replied in a shaky tone – the language barrier an instant give-away by his basic errors – glancing over Jerome's shoulder at Keldor.

"But, why?"

"Me not like this place, they be nasty to Misto."

"You're called Misto?"

"Oh yes, Misto Cuts." The little goblin stood firmly to attention, dignifying himself with his introduction.

Jerome looked round to Keldor beckoningly.

"Oh no," he denied, finally getting the gist of Jerome's beckoning eyes. "No, no, no! I refuse to walk around with a…" – his tone filled with disgust as he glanced over Jerome's shoulder to Misto – "…goblin."

"You haven't got a huge amount of choice really. Any moment now this goblin could shout the alarm." Jerome signalled to the goblin behind his back by waving his hand in an upward motion.

"Yes, Misto could!" Misto confirmed.

"No, Jerome, he couldn't," Keldor riposted. "He is the one who cut the ropes that bound us. He would not only get the blame, but he would probably be executed with us as well. This leaves *us* … with the choice of his fate."

Keldor's tone put Jerome on the back foot, but strangely, drove Misto to step out from behind the protection of his back.

"You be wrong," Misto began. "Me is set for death anyway. Maybe death is better for me than life. So … mees wants you to be nice or mees *will* yell for help."

Misto began to lean back, filling his lungs with a fresh gasp of air, but just before he released, Keldor's machismo was beaten, as he snatched at reason, clamping his hand over the goblin's mouth.

"Very well, goblin."

"Misto is my name, Misto Cuts," the little goblin said, again to Keldor, standing crisply and dignifying himself during his second introduction.

"Don't push me, goblin."

Misto was quite capable of looking after himself, and did not succumb to the bullish outlook of Keldor, instead, he responded equally. "Now, *human,* you may needs your weapons?"

Keldor was shocked, but oddly, his estimation of Misto went up. Yet, he was still a goblin and he had strong views about them, but his preliminary anger and disgust had departed and he could now think straight.

Keldor pulled the attention back to the re-acquisition of his weapons, and Misto was not hesitant. He trotted silently into the darkness and both Jerome and Keldor couldn't help but think that they wouldn't see him again.

With time running rapidly away and the cold night air nipping at every part of exposed skin, their unease worsened.

"Should we make a run for it? While we're free?" Jerome queried.

Keldor's eyes were flipping from left to right, trying hard to contain both sides of a vicious mental argument.

"I don't know," Keldor answered, a few seconds after Jerome's question.

After many thoughts on when seemed best to leave, the little goblin returned. Relief was felt between both and was expressed with a silence in Jerome, a rest for Keldor's eyes and a smile between them both.

Misto placed the weapons on the damp, tufted grass at which point they both noted the strength of the little creature.

Keldor acted with haste, equipping himself as if for the thousandth time, but as he was about to equip his dirk, which would belong in his hidden back scabbard, he looked at it and wondered about Jerome, who up until now had remained weapon-less.

"Jerome, do you know how to use one of these?" he said, resting the blade in his hands, hilt first. It was quite a lengthy weapon, almost as long as his swords, but it looked more refined and almost more lethal, with a gentle curve at the head of the beautifully ornate hilt. *Yes!* He wanted to say *yes!* but the boring truth, Jerome thought, was more appropriate at this time.

"I ... don't..."

"Take it anyway," Keldor said, gently pushing the handle towards him, "you may need it." He marked his youthful companion's reserve, but thought it the best decision. Jerome took it, and the sheath in which Keldor kept it. "And," Keldor said. Jerome looked up. "Take care of her."

"I will," he said, honoured to have it at his side.

Contrary to Jerome's earlier dreams about swords, they were a lot heavier in real life – and this was only a dirk.

"Now, we move," Keldor concluded and, fully armed and prepared, the three crept out of the camp and into the deep shade of the trees...

Chapter V
Curse of the City

Keldor and Jerome, along with their newfound companion continued the last leg of their journey to Arthak. The road ahead was quiet and still, but they had to make speed, for a second capture probably wouldn't be twinned with a second escape.

They had made their way out of the tall trees and the sun had begun to crescent up over the horizon when suddenly Keldor stopped, along with all conversation.

"Something's not right," Keldor said, trying vigorously to discern what it may be.

Jerome and Misto remained completely silent, allowing Keldor time to work it out.

Eventually, after many minutes of failed deciphering, he allowed the continuation of the journey, but he was not content and the pace had quickened. The fear of something terrible was bothering him.

It was during the very last stretch of the journey that Keldor was granted enlightenment and, for a second time, stopped the walk *and,* again, the conversation.

"Something's wrong," Keldor stated. "Something is really wrong. I didn't realise before, but we should have been able to see the Arthak Concordium," he further asserted, "the Aramyth Consortium."

"The Aramyth Consortium? Keldor, what's that?" Jerome asked.

Keldor rolled his eyes. "First of all, do you know that every city has a concordium?" he asked, to which Jerome responded with a shake of his head. "So," and he breathed, preparing his explanation, "every city in Aramyth has a concordium that seats all the members of power within. These are collectively known as the concordia and, individually, they discuss citywide issues and form settlements and accords between the municipal guilds and factions.

"Knowing that, the Aramyth Consortium exists in the capital city, Arthak. The confusion is in its name; it is called both the Arthak Concordium, when referred to by the city, or more popularly as the Aramyth Consortium and it is the central, realm-wide concordium – if you will – where all the meetings are held between all the cities and towns. Though, as well as deciding and homing all this, other topics, that span beyond the Aramyth coast, are also discussed, such as issues regarding our northern sister lands… Can you name them?"

Taken a little off guard, Jerome said, "Err, Gorthahn aaand … Tomei?"

"Good. The warring Gorthahn and Tomei, but let's not forget Tirthewdin."

"Tirthewdin? You mean the tiny isle in the middle?"

"None other. It *all* gets discussed. And decades, *centuries,* of those discussions and history remain stored within its walls. This building is the heart of Aramyth, so let us pray that nothing severe has befallen it." Keldor reflected upon his words and a short breath later spurred them on.

Keldor, Jerome and Misto completed the final section to Arthak and to Keldor's worst thought, the city they expected to see brimming with life, lay in ruins, crushed, dead.

***

Over the dead city, Garrick's eyes scanned. Within its crippled walls was where their target, this boy, was meant to be; and this occurrence, the demolished metropolis, as one of many, was no odder than any other mission on which he had been sent.

He had learnt to forgo his human instinct to question the surreal and plainly clairvoyant twists that often went hand-in-hand with The Reformation's bidding.

However, this didn't stop Baylin from calling on those human instincts.

"Well *this* isn't what I expected at all. What about you, Mythos?" Baylin forthrightly blurted out.

"Be quiet, Baylin," Garrick said.

"It was just a question."

Garrick put his finger to his lips and shushed him.

"We move as a three, working street by street. Do you both understand?"

Once in agreement they crossed the threshold into the ruins of Arthak.

***

The day was still very much in early morning bloom when Keldor, Jerome and Misto began their *search and rescue* expedition.

The decision had been made to split up, but before beginning, they had agreed a specific rendezvous point as a precaution. They started together and, as the streets branched at a crossroads, they too each branched off, Misto first, trailed by Jerome.

Being alone in the wilds of Aramyth was a loneliness Jerome had come to accept. At times it was even something he valued, especially with the situation in which he found himself. It gave him time to think over where his mother could be, or how Peter was, or, if he felt alone enough, where his Dark Whisperer might be leading him.

However, there was something inherently wrong with a lifeless city, and with each dead street that he passed, he simply couldn't adjust to the growing solitude.

The longer he walked, the longer his wishes to see another living being were crushed, the more he became positive of something ominous; and to add, with the silence overbearing, his eyesight developed an acuteness that allowed him to be more aware of certain haunting details that he had previously missed: such as the absence of bodies, or the enormous claw-like scars on the walls of some of the great structures.

He wondered how he could have missed such sights, as now, they appeared to jump out at him, tempting him to contemplate what ghastly gargantuan might have caused this devastation. And worst of all, once he'd seen that, he noticed that *every* building, in some way, had been marked.

The morning's chirping of birds and clanging of cathedral bells was more than enough to rouse Peter out of his slumber.

It had been a restless night with little but agonisingly, yet desirable, graphic thoughts. He still felt as tired as when he went to sleep, maybe more, but he took a deep breath, told himself he wasn't at home anymore and that lie-ins were out of the question.

He looked around thinking himself to be alone, but all too soon *she* came into sight – *she,* who had made his night's sleep more of a fidgety rumble with the bed linen.

Garveya looked at him and smiled – *half-grinned* – which he took with a childish pessimism.

He wondered if she had any idea.

And then his face went as white as snow as he recalled her reading his mind earlier on board the ship.

It made his stomach rapidly flutter with butterflies to think that she was probably *well* aware of the situation, of how he felt.

He wasn't sure what was worse, having these thoughts about her, or thinking that she may even know about it. He writhed internally for a moment and then again breathed, accepted that nothing could be done and got out of bed.

He hadn't paid attention before, but she was already good and dressed, making his enervated slope out from under the covers that much more degrading.

Peter hoped the rest of day wouldn't continue in this doomed state, but he couldn't imagine his mind changing at any particular time.

"So, where are we headed?" Peter said, trying to think positively.

"The concordium will be our first stop."

***

Like Jerome, Keldor and Misto had also noticed the disturbances on display throughout the city and neither could find anything to which to attribute the lack of bodies or the scars that lived on every structure.

With every street that was searched and cleared, Keldor became convinced that no one could have survived a catastrophe as big as the one that had left such an aftermath, but there was something else triggering alarm bells; he just couldn't put his finger on it...

***

The morning's fog had lifted and the patent devastation rattled the chimes of fear within Jerome. He was finding it hard to bear and he almost gave up completely, but before he acceded to turning round and heading back, he noticed a square surrounding a church up ahead.

He began to make for it and, even though it had sustained damage, like every other structure, it granted him some solace.

Seeing the house of peace relaxed his frenzied soul, but then something he was dreading came back to trouble him further ... the vision.

He was almost fully under the canopy of the great stone church by the time the It had made Its presence known. The sun only just touched beneath his forehead, stunning him slightly before he shifted out of its blinding brilliance and into the gloom.

Moments later, details that were impossible to see from the over exposure came forth and with it, the most horrifying vision...

***

Keldor's tingling senses were not something he ignored, at least not anymore. He would always explore and pursue them until they either made sense, or could be rationalised and right now, they were neither.

So, he immediately moved into the shadows and kept to buildings where the walls weren't plain. He utilised the natural noises surrounding him along with every stir of movement and gliding between the pair, he made himself virtually invisible, undetectable.

He drifted from street to street, keeping as hidden as possible until he spotted a figure up ahead. Instantly he began analysing: male, carrying weapons, his head movements and body language suggested that he had training, and then, something he didn't expect occurred.

The distant figure made a hand gesture.

The sort of gesture one would make to another person.

He fixed his gaze upon him until out of sight and then he thought. The probability of someone else, obviously not from the city, walking around, maybe searching, seemed low.

What might he – *they,* Keldor amended – be doing? *Maybe they were seeking survivors?* He returned his concentration to the figure and played it back slowly. *He didn't look as though he was interested in finding any survivors,* but more than that, he evoked something sinister. *He didn't care about the city, or its inhabitants. He was looking for someone ... or something* and this was an event that required attention.

He needed to get back to the rendezvous point.

***

Garveya led the way through the streets until finally stopping outside the concordium.

"So why are we going to the concordium again?"

"Do you know what the concordium is?"

"I think so. It's the place where the city is run, yes?"

"Indeed. And, between you and me, we have a number of magi set up all across Aramyth, in all the concordia and even the Aramyth Consortium. Although I care not to think of them as spies, they do very similar and necessary work. We have no quarrel with non-magic folk, but there is a history between us and, as such, we need to be aware of their movements and motives. There's the treaty, made at the end of the War of Unity, which hangs in the balance, but in truth, neither side is really open to communication. So we have no other choice but to keep people on the inside, ears open and mouths shut. And also, they are not just here to procure information on the movement of humans. It is thanks to our connections in Tae'Lamere that we heard of these dark magi."

"I see."

"You seem worried," she said.

"No. Not worried." It was a small lie, but he didn't want to feel any less manly than he did right now, especially not around *her*.

"You know, there really is no need to worry."

"I understand."

Garveya did not wholly believe his answer, but she appreciated that he was new to this, and didn't want to make him feel any worse than he already did.

Together they walked into the concordium of Tryth through the grand doors. The outside belied its true size, as the foyer, and all of its internal designs, towered, monolithic, beyond anything he had seen.

This really was the central hub of Tryth, and he wondered if any of the other concordia were as spectacular.

"Welcome!" a man said from behind a desk, eager to catch their attention.

He was one of many sat behind overly furnished desks and his voice cut through the gentle mumbles of duologue and the activity of daily life within.

Upon approach, they both noticed his desk to be by far the messiest. The more Peter looked, the more objects he found: from quills, to parchment, to flowers, to books and just for good measure, two lit candles. He saw them to be time candles, a very accurate and simple method of timekeeping, as well as providing good light. *Clever,* Peter pondered.

"Now, how can I be of service?"

"I would like to speak to Councillor Talley please."

"Of course, madam, I just need to take a few details first."

The man rummaged through his desk, opening and closing draws, lifting up books, peeping behind his beloved flowers, until he found the relevant parchment.

He inked his quill and poised himself in position, with a little circle of his hand, to take down the required details.

"What are your names?" he asked.

"Emberlin and Peter."

"Son?"

Oh, here we go again! Peter thought.

"Husband," Garveya promptly answered.

Not even a flinch! How can he think we're married? Why does she keep saying that? Peter continued on his train of thought.

"Are you residents of Tryth?" he asked.

"We are not. We live in Cearan."

"And finally, what is the purpose of your stay?"

"We have friends who live here."

He jotted down the final piece, checked it over once again, referred to his time candle and added the little extra formalities until filing it neatly within a draw of his desk.

"If I could ask you both to take seat," he indicated a row of chairs against the wall behind. "I shall alert Councillor Talley of your arrival. If she unavailable, is there anyone you would like me to fetch?"

"No, thank you, just Councillor Talley."

"I shall be just a minute. Thank you for your patience."

"Thank you," Garveya said as they walked over to the chairs and sat down.

The man scurried off and, as the minutes ticked by, they both came to the conclusion that these chairs were designed for appearance and, most assuredly, at the expense of comfort.

Peter asked about the name Emberlyn, and Garveya said it was her mother's name.

Beyond that small exchange very little else was said, and a short while after, the man returned looking calm and collected, but alone.

"I am afraid to tell you both that Councillor Talley is no longer working here. I didn't get the memorandum until now. I am sorry for the inconvenience. Is there anything else I can assist you with?"

"Thank you for your help, but no." Garveya was about to turn her head when another question sprang to the forefront of her mind. "Just quickly, can you tell me how long she has not worked here?"

"I can't tell you for definite, but I am sure that I saw her yesterday, if not yesterday then the day before."

Garveya thanked him and exited. Peter followed behind and something about her disposition made him uneasy.

"What just happened?" Peter said.

"I don't know what is going on, but something is amiss. An informant would never just leave their position without prior warning and a *lot* of prior warning at that ... unless for an emergency. Peter, this is bad."

"What do you think has happened?"

"I don't know. She's either been found out and gone into hiding, or been taken. Outside of that, I can see no other reason why she would not be at work. And *if* she found something out then she would have sent word to Alatacia. It just doesn't make sense... Come."

"Where are we going?"

"To her house... If she has indeed discovered something, she may have left a clue."

***

Dangling upside-down, hanging by a broken leg, was the remnants of a mutilated figure.

This was the worst image Jerome had seen. Worse even than the hanging servant to the king.

Protruding out was the other leg; its angle from out of the torso was such that it appeared snapped out of the pelvic joint.

The rags that were draped over the body were shredded and ripped and beneath some, infested gouges crawled with life.

One arm hung inert, gently brushing against the head, whereas the other had been brutally severed just below the elbow. The rough tear of sinew, muscle and flesh revealed massive trauma.

As much as Jerome tried to pry his eyes away, he couldn't resist, and they fell onto the head.

Up until then, it was just a random body, but the face made it personal. The neck had been slit and the body exsanguinated, but as the jaw rested open and the tongue drooped, the pain-stricken eyes seemed to look through him.

Riddled with fear, he captured every detail knowing that, worst of all, turning away would not be the end. The 'eyes' would find some other way of shocking him.

His best course of action would be to stay, to bear it. *It was not real*, he began to repeat to himself. It became worse. He knew it was getting the better of him.

It was winning.

"You are not real!" Jerome thundered.

And then, in an instant, it was gone. He briefly wondered if he had got the better of it, but before he had a chance to detail and categorise the event, something else snatched his interest.

The body had been masking an entrance. Not the designated church entrance, but something beneath, something, Jerome wondered, no one was supposed to see…

***

Together, Garrick, Mythos and Baylin behaved with total interdependence. Their behaviours and movements were completely reciprocated. As one stopped, they all stopped; and with the echo of a young voice hurtling towards them, they all paused and then, in a flash, they all adjusted course and ran…

***

"Misto, there you are!" Keldor exclaimed, catching sight of Misto walking towards him from another dead street. "Did you have any luck finding survivors?"

"No luck."

"Come on, we have to get back and wait for Jerome to arrive."

"Why? Is it not better that we's look for him?"

"No, Misto, that is the point of having a rendezvous point."

"But we's must find him. Others are in the city and—"

"Exactly, and we stand more chance of running into them than we do Jerome. No, we're best off waiting where we agreed."

Keldor's words finalised the conversation and they headed back.

**

The trip to 4 Wavers Lane, Councillor Talley's house, was completed mostly in silence. Peter looked to his female friend from time to time and, above his desires for her, could see her mental focus.

Wavers Lane was a very small street and, to Peter, seeing the busy flow of people on the roads either side, it looked as though its main purpose was as a through road and not a very prevalent one at that.

From outside, the house looked in normal condition with no immediate signs of a scuffle, but after entering Garveya knew differently.

"She was taken from here. Of that, I am certain."

"How do you know?" Peter asked.

"There are magical traces dotted all over. Help me look around."

"What are we looking for?"

"If she discovered something untoward then she would have made a note of it. We're looking for a small journal, bound in red leather with a brown leaf emblazoned on the cover. Each one of our city informants is given one."

"Where do we start?"

The house was quite small, being comprised of only two downstairs rooms and a hall, and two upstairs. They carefully searched every surface and bookshelf until it became clear that the book was not there.

With the book's added disappearance, Garveya became certain that these events were not just coincidental or simple bad luck and timing.

"It's not here."

"I agree."

"So what do we do now?"

"Did you notice the carriage marks on the road outside?"

She led Peter outside the house and straightaway he picked up on a track of faint depressions in the dusty road.

"Do you think that a horse and carriage took her?" Peter asked.

"Do you not?" Garveya wondered, confused at Peter's reticence to believe.

"It's just that this lane looks to be the subject of many carriages a day. What makes *these* any different?"

"I'm impressed with your deduction, but two things confirm my suspicions. Look at how close these marks are to the house. If someone were using it as a thoroughfare then they would be more central, and finally, how else would you get someone out of here without drawing too much attention?"

Peter took these points on board and accepted his error.

"It's not a certainty, but there is little chance that whoever took her did so without a horse and carriage, so we shall visit the livery stable next. There will be records that we will need to gain access to."

"But won't the records be a lie?" Peter pointed out.

"I expect on the surface, but they can't hide the addresses to where the coach was driven. And that's all we care about."

Continuing to think about it, Peter asked, "...Is this really going to work?"

Garveya considered him. "...What do you mean, Peter?"

"I mean ... wouldn't somebody have *seen* if they were kidnapping someone?"

"You'd be surprised how few people pay attention."

Peter thought for a second more. "...No, I mean, would they *really* have hired a coach?"

"How else would they get a coach, if not by hiring one?" Garveya was hinting at a smile – her half-grin beginning to peer at him – at Peter's attempts to find the wording.

"No, I mean, *if* they hired a coach, would the driver not have seen?"

Garveya's half-grin was gone. "The driver would *probably* have seen, Peter," she said, a slightly belittling slant in her tone.

Peter finished what he was trying to say. "…And then reported it to the law?"

"Ah, I see."

Took you long enough, he mentally said.

A second later, she smiled, with an unnerving amount of knowing, and said, "You see, Peter, silence is a commodity like anything else, and can be purchased and sold as such. Yes, the driver would have seen, in fact the whole company may even know about it, but they would have been paid to keep their mouths shut. Either paid, or threatened. Or both. As far as *commodities* go, both work well."

He nodded and then said, "So how are we going to get to the records?"

"Let's worry about that once we get there."

"Are we going to use magic?"

"No. If there are dark magi plaguing this city, as I'm even more convinced about now, then using magic would be like shouting out in the middle of the city. And we don't want to draw attention to ourselves…"

***

With curiosity and caution as his ally, Jerome forwarded towards the exposed entrance and with each step he became overwhelmed with compulsion. His ears were picking up faint traces of sound. He listened, still approaching the ingress, and the sounds became voices, voices that called to him. It was clear the connection between the voices and his advance, but he was hesitant to listen to the temptation.

With his senses peaking and his emotions in overdrive, he took a long stare forward. Upon closer inspection, the entrance was more a descent. The voices grew louder and, just before taking a foot down, he stood still.

Trying to recapture his sanity, he cleared his mind and strained to push the voices out.

However, his reticence was not received well by his tempters and with rapidity they began to butt against his repressive attempts.

Jerome was struggling to keep the voices at bay, which were now bombarding his ears, and so he decided to employ his body as well as just his mind.

With time against him, he turned and what he hadn't bargained for was that the voices had more than just sound to plague him.

The calm city he was expecting to see had been blotted out by a horde of demons, violently twisting back and forth in his way. Their pitch screeched between the high and low, intermixed with groans and wails. In natural reflex, he pursed his ears, but he lost his footing as the fright spun him back round. He whipped his hands away from his head and began to frantically calculate his imminent descent.

His tumble down the uneven slope left him relatively unscathed, although he was aware of a couple places that were going to bruise up.

Slowly he opened his eyes and adjusted to the low light.

With his eyes attuning to the gloominess he began to wonder into where, exactly, he'd fallen.

None of the objects reflected holiness or peace, quite the reverse. Four beds, all, in some way, discoloured to a red maroon. Jerome suspected blood, but he didn't care to elaborate. What caught his eye, more so than the beds, were the gruesome looking instruments hanging above each.

He feared the worse, but his nightmare took full form when he noticed the straps on both sides of the beds, and the human shaped compressions upon each.

He wrenched back with a small vocal intake. He was really struggling to keep from crying and he probably would have broken down, but he suddenly realised that he wasn't alone.

The tears subsided. Fear took root again.

He quickly gathered together any courage left inside and spun round, expecting to see something horrendous and fitting of the grim environment; but what he saw was nothing of the kind.

She was … an angel. Jerome felt a deep desire to speak, but she raised a finger to her lips, compelling him to silence.

Once sure of his quietness, she indicated to the entrance behind him. Three figures came into view all outwardly looking as though they were searching.

***

"I could have sworn the voice came from around here," Baylin said.

"As did we all… Mythos, can you sense him?"

"I can't sense anything in here. This whole city is in magical mayhem. I couldn't sense an army of magi, even right around the corner. Indeed, if you want my honest opinion, I think we should leave this city. There is something deeply disturbing about it."

Garrick nodded, confirming his understanding, although they didn't need his word to see that the boy wasn't in the area. They hastily began their journey to the outskirts.

***

With some simple directions from the city guards Peter and Garveya found their way to the livery stable. It was located in a quiet, picturesque district of the city where the only people around seemed quiet and outwardly friendly.

Growing up the wall, around the door and windows, was a beautiful white flowering creeper. It gave the building a very honest and welcoming grace. On the other hand, the inside told quite the reverse.

It was stuffy, insalubrious and extremely unwelcoming.

Garveya gave the room the quick once over then examined it closer to try and find any sign of where the records might be.

She counted three doors, including the one from which she and Peter had entered. Their loneliness was only fleeting though as a man emerged from the far door. He was a studious looking individual clothed almost entirely in black with a monocle hanging from a top pocket.

"I thought I heard the door. Can I help at all? I run the finest ship in all of Aramyth."

The man certainly knew how to sell his wares, Peter thought, doubting his confidence when, abruptly, his name *'Peter'* being called inside his head, interrupted his thought process.

It gave him such a fright that he jumped and couldn't help blurting out a 'what'. Initially he thought that Garveya had actually said his name, but when he realised the contrary, he quickly tried to fumble a response to cover his embarrassment.

"I mean … how can you boast that? I mean … Aramyth is a big place."

Peter's ill-thought-out response stunned the man blind and he simply could not tie a comeback together. It took Garveya to break the silence and she didn't hesitate.

"Why don't you show me where you keep the horses?"

"Yes, of course. Will your son be—"

"Husband," Garveya interjected.

Peter secretly clenched a mental fist.

"Will he be joining us?"

"He will not. He gets terrible sneezes around them. You should see him when we travel long distance."

Peter didn't like being spoken about in the third person, especially when it was so blatant, but she surely had a reason and the man escorted her out through the side door.

"Peter," Garveya telepathically whispered.

Peter was still unsure of how to form a reply but he relaxed himself and just tried to think the words.

"Hello?" he strained.

"I can keep him distracted for a few minutes while you go and search for the records."

"Where are they? What am I looking for?" Peter thought, employing the same technique as before.

"You'll just have to look. Try and find something that mentions 4 Wavers Lane. We're looking for a destination. You can do this, Peter, I have faith in you."

"I'll try."

Peter was not confident in his ability at all. And as the adrenaline began coursing through him, pumping his heart at an inordinately high rate, he realised the enormity of what he was going to do, but he dug deep and remembered whom he was doing this for.

With haste, yet careful not to make too much noise, he set foot towards the far door.

Taking as much care as possible, he turned the handle and opened it, while trying his hardest to govern his own unstable emotions. But peculiarly, when he got the other side of the door and heard it *click* shut his nerves calmed and he was able to think straight.

With a fresh breath and a slightly soothed soul, he began assessing the room and its contents.

It was much smaller than the main reception area and quite cosy, if Peter were being honest. However, its size seemed made no impact on how many different chests and cabinets were present.

Just looking at them, and considering the overwhelming amount of luck he would need to find just a single document, threw him straight back into turmoil. But he surprised himself as he, again, staved-off those doubting and useless thoughts of failure.

He kept reminding himself of the reasons behind his actions. And also, it wouldn't have been right for it to feel comfortable.

He was now a magus, not a boy from Melfall, and he had to step into those shoes … big as they were. And the first step was to find these records.

He quickly shuffled to the first potential, document-containing, subject – a cabinet with two shelves, both piled high with paper documents, each pile bound with twine.

He didn't want to be under-cautious and not check something just to realise he'd missed something, but he was painfully aware that there was a huge amount through which he had to sift, and not much time. Again, he took a deep breath – *they seemed to be working well today* – and remembered that what he was looking for was only a matter of feet away.

After a superficial rummage through each pile, it seemed clear that they were not what he was looking for.

An attempt at logic told him that what he was looking for was going to be a recent event, so probably not tucked away at the back or beneath.

His next target, which upon closer inspection was locked, was a small chest next to the over-stacked cabinet. He decided that he would return to that later, if he was unsuccessful, and so he moved over to the desk, where he hurriedly started throwing open the draws either side.

"Peter, have you found it?" Garveya interrupted.

"I need more time." Peter tensed the words out. He was still not used to the concept of telepathy and was sure that he was pulling a silly face every time he tried to think-speak.

Right now though, that was the least of his worries. He still had to uncover these elusive *records* and this side of the desk was not bearing any fruit.

"Peter, I can't keep him busy for much longer. You're going to need to get out of there ... quickly. We'll find some other way to get the information."

The adrenaline started its second wave over him, but worse this time and, as he launched himself to his feet, he took a brief moment to think about anything he may have moved.

And then ... he found it! Quite ridiculously it was lying in plain sight on the desk. *Very recent,* he thought.

"Peter, do you hear me? Where are you?"

It was difficult, but he couldn't concentrate when he had her speaking in his mind. He recognized that he only had a brief window of opportunity and those *shoes* weren't going to fill themselves.

To accompany the good fortune of locating the records, they were easy to understand, and with lightning speed he scanned down the margin containing locations, notably the *travelling from* section, until his finger fell upon *4 Wavers Lane.* The date and time also coincided. *So far so good,* he celebrated as he marked his finger along to the *destination – Fallon House, the Crescent.*

He had done it! And he felt the biggest smile grow unashamedly upon his face.

But, his split second elation was promptly replaced by fear, when the door handle began to rattle. Subsequently, he was frozen stiff, unable to move.

The door just began to creak, Peter contemplating the punishment of his crime, when, unexpectedly, it stopped taking Peter's breath with it.

He wondered if the man had already noticed something amiss, giving him reason to stop, but then it closed.

"Get out of there, Peter!" The hurry in her voice was unmistakable, and he realised that now was going to be his only feasible opportunity for escape.

The door was no longer an option. He considered hiding under the desk, but almost straight away put it in the stupidity container.

He looked around and saw the window. It was marginally open and it seemed a far better option than to spend his day sat under a desk and probably end up getting caught.

With caution *and* celerity nipping at his heels, he made for it and flung it wide open. The door handle rattled again and that was his cue. It was time to leave and pray that it wasn't a bramble patch beneath, into which he was going to dive…

***

Jerome watched, as they remained hovering around the entrance, ostensibly unaware of where he was, until moving off. He waited until absolutely sure that they had gone, before turning back to the angel, but there was nothing there, nothing to watch him except the grim haunts.

***

Keldor's mind was racing. Even now, he was still going over and over, repeating the gesturing man's movements, gleaning any and all information he could.

Soon, they were crossing onto the last street leading to the rendezvous point, and Keldor's eagle eyes suddenly focused on a small green-skin, exactly where they were supposed to be meeting.

He followed his first instinct and looked to where Misto was, at his side, but there was nothing there. He had vanished.

Being a rational man, Keldor wondered if there was any possible way Misto could have evaded him. The answer was yes – unlikely, but nevertheless possible –, but as he came closer, it didn't explain why Misto was now stood all that way a away and *also* looking as perplexed.

"Human, why yous be there? Yous were here."

"Misto, it was *you* who was next to me, here. Don't you remember?"

"Of course mees does. It's yous that's forgot."

Keldor stopped arguing. "This may be above your tiny green mind, but do you think it's possible that we've both been affected by the same…" – Keldor was reserved about using the word 'ghost' – "…thing?"

Misto thoughtfully hummed, then said, "But what would bes affecting us? And whys we just see each other?"

"I don't know, but we'd best wait for Jerome. There are no survivors in the city."

"Where's we going when the boy comes?"

"The cities will hear of this soon enough. What is more important is informing the magi. I think *they* may be able to shed some light on what has happened."

Misto wasn't over the moon with the suggestion, but was less happy to argue about it.

***

Under the navigation of Garrick, they swiftly reached the outskirts of the city and waited patiently. Garrick was on edge and concerned about the boy's whereabouts, courtesy of the forsaken metropolis.

He had never been given faulty information before and, although he didn't doubt it was possible – maybe even inevitable – he was going to make sure that this wasn't going to be the start of a new fad.

"Do you sense anything yet?" he demanded.

Mythos was deep in concentration, but the only thing he could sense, outside of the city's demise, was Garrick's tension. And *Baylin* could have sensed that...

***

It was not a bramble patch, but a hedge and because it had been pruned to a shallow depth it was very hard, almost as painful as cobblestone, and then some.

The rough, uneven surface poked through Peter's clothes pricking him everywhere that it touched and he was still not out of the woods completely.

Trying to ignore the discomfort, he rolled off the low-cut topiary and onto the hard, cold stone road and from there, he bounded round to the front side of building where he sat, relaxed and reflected, while rubbing his scratched skin.

Soon after, Garveya strolled out. Peter wasn't sure, but she looked as though she even *winked* goodbye to the man.

"What took *you* so long?" he asked, standing and smiling.

"Oh very funny, did you find what we need?"

"I did. Fallon House, the Crescent."

"I knew you could do it," she said, hugging him.

His face reddened, but he couldn't help but enjoy it. "I think you had a great deal to play in my escape, though."

"That's not important, you did it. Anyway, we have as little time now as we did before. But first, Peter, I don't know what is going to happen here and I'm concerned. Can you find your way back to Councillor Talley's house?"

"I'm not going with you?" Peter inferred. Why else would she ask that of him?

"Not now. It's too dangerous."

"But I can help."

"You already have. And you will be helping me by doing this, but you must promise me, that if I don't return, you will not come and search for me. If I am unsuccessful, then others will come from Alatacia and they will find you."

Peter wasn't going to lie; it hurt and her face emoted understanding, but it also expressed conviction and that drove Peter to a gloomy acceptance.

***

Keldor's career as a Realm's Ranger had put him in many situations. He had been from tip to toe of Aramyth and never had he imagined looking into a dead city with a goblin. Periodically, he would peer over to Misto, who was as silent and, to the ignorance of each other, also thinking the exact same. Drearily time ticked along, and eventually they saw Jerome running back.

"You're here?"

Misto and Keldor shared another glance.

"I ran here with you two beside me," Jerome continued. "We have to get out of here… There is really something wrong with this city," he said, out of breath.

"Why do you think we's been waiting?"

"Did you have any luck finding any survivors?" Keldor asked in duty, as he was confident of the answer.

Jerome shook his head, still puffing.

"Right, we could – probably *should* – go back to Cearan and tell the king, but – like I said to the goblin here – I think it best we let the magi know about this, if they don't already. So, when you've got your breath back, we'll be going."

***

A few minutes on and Mythos' senses tingled. He mentioned it to Garrick, who clearly had much pent up frustration, but as soon as the news hit his ears he switched into hunter-mode and the chase was on…

***

On her own, with only a few directions supplied by locals, Garveya navigated the streets of Tryth, passing the concordium and the city cathedral, until standing at the top of some steps. As she began to make her way, she realised she was winding down what seemed like an alley with an assortment of buildings either side, the walls of every one indicative of degradation and squalor. From the way things appeared, she expected The Crescent to be an exceptionally rundown quarter.

With every sharp corner she turned, she began to slow with the building presence of other magical beings.

She couldn't be sure how many there were, but she knew that if she could sense them ... then they could sense her.

Up until now, Garveya hadn't thought much of Peter. His company had been something that she had just accepted, but being without him in this time of concern and doubt allowed her insight into what was going on beneath the surface – and she missed him.

He had grown immeasurably from when they first met and he had most certainly started to fill the proverbial *shoes,* as she had seen when having a prying gaze inside his mind.

The alley soon came to an end and she emerged onto The Crescent, aptly named due to its shape. However, what the name didn't indicate was its grandeur.

It was Tryth's best-kept secret; it was incredible.

Everything about it was epic, from the ineffable designs to the delicate and untouchable statues.

With uninterrupted clearness on the whereabouts of her targets, she started along the gently contoured street until her magical faculties peaked – right outside Fallon House, just as she expected.

Well done, Peter!

It, like all the other edifices, was stunning, the main attraction being four white stone pillars facing out frontward. The middle two supported the central and cardinal stone canopy, while the two either side seemed more for visual symmetry rather than actual structural integrity.

Keeping with the aesthetics, there were also five white steps, composed of white marble. It didn't look the usual haven of dark magi, but nothing on this street looked as though it *should,* and with the utmost care Garveya took her first step over the threshold.

The white-mirrored floor of the atrium, along with the reflected loftiness put her on edge. It also didn't help that the room was almost completely bare apart from a couple of tables either side.

Upon further inspection, she noticed tiny scuffmarks on the beautifully polished floor.

Clearly, they were not here to stay – the marks denoting signs of packing up and moving out. Just beyond each side table was a pristinely varnished wooden door, but the dark magi weren't in there.

They were upstairs; she could feel them, three, maybe four, of them.

She was also aware of a kin magus – she assumed Councillor Talley – and something else. It was minimal, whatever it was, but that meant nothing.

Through all her training, the one thing that stuck with her the most was never to turn a blind eye to the minimal.

Her focus became the staircase at the far end of the room. Like the rest of the atrium, it was excessively adorned and embellished, from the ornamentally carved volutes to the individually crafted balusters. It led to a small mezzanine floor maybe ten feet wide and half that back.

The *tap* of each footstep resonated with distorting clarity, the closer she came to reaching the grand staircase the more caution.

She climbed the stairs and, now she was on the mezzanine, was faced with a choice. Would she take the left staircase or the right? Then she considered that this could be used as a tactical advantage. Then she considered that it could easily backfire and she could fall victim to a skirmish.

So, whatever she did, it would need to be executed to perfection.

Vigilantly, Garveya made her way up the left stairwell and soon she found herself to be only a subtle slide away from having a clear view of the room. A gentle inhale later and she whipped her head round, but before she could ascertain how many she was facing, a flurry of fire burst her way and drove her head back round the solid balustrade.

Luckily, she had been prepared for such a *warm* welcome.

The difficulty she was having now, besides being outnumbered, was that she couldn't start firing bolts of deadly magic for the fear of hitting Talley. And she still didn't know what that *hint-of-something-else* was.

This getting her nowhere, she called for a change of tactic. Her two options were: using the opposite set of stairs to divert attention, or use some sort of stun spell. She favoured the latter option as the stairs may well come in handy at a later stage.

She began conjuring, rotating and twisting her hands in a strict series of motions, unique to her, until she was ready to explode the finale.

It needed to be powerful, though. Powerful enough to shine through the thin eyelids, so she took her time to net all the right ingredients and then it was ready.

She turned to face the dividing wall, tucked her head down and shut her eyes tight. She hoped, that even through all these safeguards, she would know if it worked.

Ready as ever, and without wasting another second, she flung her hands up and released the dazzling conjuration. As hoped for, the light did pierce her own preparation, but it wasn't blinding and when it died down she still retained the vision to get a look at the playing field.

Craning her head round, she counted: *one, two, Councillor Talley, three* … and then two more, *a fourth dark magus and* … she gasped, *Peter.*

With her advantage quickly diminishing she fired a pot shot at the nearest, blinded dark magus. It looked promising, but without the risk of seeing if it was a hit, she sharply retreated behind cover, and then heard the distinct hiss and crackle of black magic pouring her way.

***

Peter and Garveya had only been divided for a few minutes before he had been ambushed. Beyond that, he could recall nothing. First he was there – innocently walking to Talley's house – and now he was being woken up by something unutterably bright.

With his senses slowly returning to him, he felt a dull throbbing coming from the back of his skull, and it was only when he tried to soothe it, that he realised his hands were bound behind his back and his feet bound in front.

He was sat up, back against the wall, neck-aching from where his head had been allowed to rest to one side.

He snapped open his eyes to discover where he was and what was going on. He saw three people, each in dark, light-cloth garments, throwing a deluge of fury towards the left side of the room. Also present, was one similarly dark-attired female, lying on the floor, maybe unconscious or ... *dead* – Peter didn't like that idea.

Looking round to his left, he saw a woman who, like himself, had been bound at the hands and feet but her restraints didn't stop at that.

She was also gagged, blindfolded and upon closer inspection had something fastened around her ears. She had been totally sensorially deprived and, through wondering why, he concluded that she might be a magus; and then maybe even thought about the possibility of it being Councillor Talley.

Being only a few feet away and with their captor's attention drawn elsewhere, Peter began to manoeuvre himself towards her, pivoting between his shoulders and feet. He realised the consequences of what he was doing and that there would be severe repercussions, if he were to get caught, but he had to find a way of helping; and after the slow and grinding effort of rolling his shoulder blades and heaving himself, he could have sworn he felt some give in his hand restraints...

There was another loud crack associated with the release of magic, stopping him mid-heave, and then a further retorted salvo, but the room settled back to a dull hush and he continued grinding his way along.

Since beginning his minor traverse across the back wall, he had lost focus on where he was going and overshot on the last heave, brushing past the lady, as he lowered himself down.

There was something about her that made him feel comfortable. Whether it was her utter helplessness or whether she had some magical effervescence that he was invisibly detecting, he couldn't put his finger on it, but he was going to do something and that began with freeing himself.

As Peter wrestled with the frayed and splintered rope, it bit back, burning and grazing his wrists raw, but he tried to avoid thinking about the pain and rather on freeing the helpless magus – he was *sure* she was a magus.

***

Garveya was still stuck and only able to hurl the occasional strike over the top or around the side, but she was conscious of Talley and, *poor Peter. He would have been fine had she not involved him in this.* She berated herself and then made a deal that her every action from this moment on would be devoted to getting him out of this.

Still unable to properly form an offensive, she decided that now would be the best time to use her advantage. She needed to draw attention to both sides; it was imperative to make her enemies blind to where the next attack was coming from.

She looked across to the far side and saw the other staircase go up in exact reflection to where she was now. If she could create some decoy then it may serve as an adequate distraction and ultimately confuse the dark magi.

***

Peter had struggled until his hands were a swollen memory of their former selves, but he had been successful and he could now dedicate his energies to freeing the lady.

So far, no one had turned around to them and he reasoned that, if he were quick, he would stand a good chance of loosening her binds before the encounter was over, giving her the chance to upend the outcome.

He set to work and immediately, upon touch, he felt the lady's aura change. She could tell that he was a kindred spirit, and he could tell that *she* could tell by her subtle lean forward, supplying him that slightly bit better angle to reach the knot.

***

Garveya had shot a similar, but lessened, version of her initial light display to the other side and it collided with a deliberate thud.

Without hesitancy, she propelled herself to beyond the safety zone and began incanting the words for a lightning-imbued strike. This was only intended to stun, she knew that, but she didn't have the time to incant for a fatal discharge.

Upon releasing the thunderous bolt, she saw that her first strike had been a clean hit and this one was going to be the same.

However, an attack she hadn't expected was heading her and it looked accurate.

Although she managed to hideaway without taking any critical damage, it did strike her shoulder and she felt it blister and bubble beneath a black vapour.

The smell of burnt skin hovering around her nostrils quickly tested her premature thoughts of victory and thrust her back into a place of uncertainty. But just before she ducked back around she was positive she saw Peter freeing Councillor Talley.

***

And just as he broke the back of the knot, Peter looked round and noticed that it was Garveya on the other side. As soon as her hands were free, the lady instantly pulled down her blindfold, gag and ear coverings.

However, one of the remaining dark magi, who had turned and seen this, had fixed his concentration towards the woman and had already begun to manipulate magic to his malign biddings.

The death hex wound its way towards them, twisting and reappearing at the front and fading and crumbling at the back.

With swift reflex, the lady blocked it by flicking her hands up and knocking it off course to the window above their heads.

The spell feathered into smoke as it hit the glass, but the defence did not faze the dark magus, who already had another invocation developing.

Peter had never seen such strange clarity, as he perceived tiny particles grow, stretch and wrap into shade enticed towards the man's hands.

This, as opposed to the woman's colourless altering, gave Peter true insight into the difference between the two groups of magi.

The magical creations clashed and nullified each other in the middle and they both returned back to generate something else that would outdo their rival.

Peter was encapsulated in the magical challenge, but he thought about Garveya and turned his head to where she was hidden.

He couldn't make out much, as the reverberations of power distorted the air between him and the rest of the room, but he couldn't locate the other dark magus. He darted his eyes around until he caught sight of something ducking down low against his side of the hard wall, mirroring Garveya's position.

**

From behind the confines of the staircase, Garveya found it hard to take her mind away from the searing pain in her shoulder, but she worked hard to overcome it and thought about Peter, *still helping,* saving Councillor Talley. It gave her hope and she let that settle, just for a moment, before strategising her next assault.

However, she was just in the junior stages of the next design when her magical senses were triggered by a presence. It was close, whatever it was and it was building up. She couldn't identify what was causing the swelling, as magic didn't work that way.

Once they were released, they would only ever diminish, but this was still growing and then she realised that it wasn't a single spell, it was one of the dark magi on the other side, directly behind her.

She felt the gentle shockwave, just before the release of a spell, instigating her to dive away, just before a massive hole was blown open.

Rubble and wood-chip from the wall exploded out and rebounded off the far wall. The majority of the dust settled down, but the powder from the stone and brickwork still infused the air, leaving a memorable mark of the eruption.

Garveya felt on the cusp of consciousness when she decided her next move.

Covered in dust and debris, she lifted and shook her hands, sifting the dirt away and then began shooting non-lethal strikes towards the newly made hole, hand after hand in swift succession.

***

Talley was locked in a sustained strike with her aggressor and Peter could see her energy waning. He could feel it. And he thought that, although *he* could do nothing with his power, maybe she could put it to good use and that may give her the edge in her current locked combat.

In his mind, and in principle, the idea seemed simple enough, but when it came to it, he wondered how he was going to transfer his power over. After all, it wasn't like a bag of food that you could easily give away.

He referred back to when he first met Garveya and his experience of using magic. He didn't think of it at the time, but she had simply touched him and that had awoken his dormant magical soul.

He hoped that it would be the same now, as he rested his hands upon Talley and tried to open himself to her.

Suddenly, he felt a pair of ethereal hands reach inside, attaching to every modicum of power within.

A perfect conduit had been formed between the pair, as she channelled his power – *pulled* his power – direct into her and then pressed it out.

Her declining fight against the dark magus burst back into life, as she pushed with an even greater command than before.

The face of the powerful evil that opposed them felt the increase and quickly responded by drawing deeper inside, mustering every degree of force that could be harnessed.

But it couldn't be sustained, however, and then neither, Peter considered, could his.

Suddenly, Talley yanked even harder at his power. For a moment it was painful, and then it was weirdly euphoric, and then strangely soporific. But he couldn't sleep; he had to fight; and he strained against the taxing drain. All he had to do was keep his hands on her and his eyes open, while she wrangled his power out of him.

He regulated his breathing and focused his eyes taking his attention away from the combat and into supplying as much energy as he could without passing out.

Then it stopped and the strain upon his being shut him down momentarily. Every muscle throbbed, as his hands slipped off her and onto the rough wooden floor, but he needed closure on the situation of the combat.

With his head resting on the ground, he opened his eyes and saw the room from a slanted perspective, but it was enough to see Garveya and Talley deal the final blow to the last dark thaumaturge.

Soon though, he lacked even the energy to hold his eyes open and everything became a blur ... and eventually black.

***

Peter slowly regained consciousness with a smooth feeling of energy trickling into him. But it wasn't the usual waking up sensation he was used to. Whereas normally he would feel exhausted for quite some time upon opening his eyes, he felt truly alert and awake and then he realised that this wasn't a natural wake up. Garveya and Talley were both replacing his power with their very concentrated verve.

"Are you all right?" Garveya said.

The energy felt good and soothing and he nodded his wellness to her. Gently, they helped him sit up against the wall, relishing the feeling of life returning to his overworked body – relishing *her* touch.

"Peter, this is Councillor Talley. She and I have to have a little talk. Will you be all right here while we do?"

Again, Peter nodded and Garveya took Talley off to one side.

"I didn't think that the cities were so rife with dark magi," said Talley.

"I'm not sure they are, we've been aware of these since they arrived in Tae'Lamere. We can talk more about it, but I want to question one to find out how many more there are."

"Of course, but first, what is the story about Peter?"

"I'd love to tell you, but there isn't one. Until a few days ago, he didn't even know he was a magus. He had been living a human life in Melfall."

"Are you taking him to Alatacia?"

"Eventually, yes, but I need to find out more about what's happening."

Garveya and Talley distinguished a single conscious dark magus and walked over to her. It was the first one Garveya had dispensed with and she looked up at them both with a heavy defiance.

"What is your name?" Garveya said, opening her line of questioning.

She looked away, uninterested.

"What is your name?" Garveya repeated.

"What does it matter to you?"

"Tell me your name or not, I don't really care, I was just ascertaining out how stubborn you're going to be … and I can work with this…" And the dark magus smiled.

Garveya knelt down beside her, putting her hands on her head as she began probing her mind.

"What are you doing in the city?"

Garveya felt the stubborn walls come up, but she was ready and knew how to get around such basic mental defence.

"We are looking for The Destroyer of Magic," Garveya heard.

"Have you ever heard of The Destroyer of Magic before?" Garveya repeated out loud.

"I haven't, but whatever it is, it sounds…" Councillor Talley said – or *didn't,* because it was clear what she meant.

"What is The Destroyer of Magic?" Garveya said to the dark magus.

She remained disinclined and Garveya crossed back inside her mind.

"What is The Destroyer of Magic?" Again the walls shot up, but like before, Garveya was easily able to navigate beyond the rudimentary defences. She could find no further knowledge of it and she even went as far as to understand that the name was nothing official.

She changed the subject.

"Are there any more of you?" The trick, Garveya knew, was to push her mind to close off certain parts and moreover, draw the focus away from guarding information that would also hold the answer. Here, she outwardly implied that she was looking for how many there were, while she could be looking for how many were left.

"Renith. He has left for Blaile." Garveya picked up on it and the strain that held the mental walls up collapsed, indicating that she now held the final piece of the puzzle.

Garveya released her hands from the dark magus's head and stood up.

"Renith is the last one. I will be heading to Blaile."

"Are you not taking Peter?"

"I think it is best that he stays here with you. Will you be able to deal with this?"

"Yes. I should have it cleared up by tomorrow, and then I shall return to the concordium and explain my absence."

"Very we—" Garveya stopped. "Wait. What did you just say?"

Talley was taken off guard at Garveya's question, but she tried to think back. "…I shall continue work at the concordium?" Her question was over-inflected towards the end, because the question she was *actually* asking was, *'Was that what I'd just said?'*

Garveya was onto something, but didn't let on to what it was just yet. "Did you just say that you *hadn't* informed the concordium of your absence?"

"No, I hadn't the chance. Why? What is it?"

"The man ... Peter and I saw at the concordium, he told us that you had handed in your notice."

"Then he was lying."

"More to the point, I think that *that* is Renith. That would explain why he seemed so disorganised, so ready to help us. He'd only been sat down for a matter of minutes. That is the final dark magus, I'm convinced of it, and he *tricked* me ... and now Peter is in danger. Councillor Talley, we'll need horses, Peter doesn't understand void travel yet and I haven't the time to teach him."

"Of course, just outside the eastern edge of the city lives a man whose allegiance is to me. Mention my name, Moriah Talley, and he will help you any way he can."

"Thank you."

They shared a smile and then Garveya, with Peter, headed out of the city where they met up with the contact. He supplied them with two horses and soon they were riding out on the path to Blaile.

***

With Arthak behind them, Keldor, Jerome and Misto made good headway, and as the hours moved on, Keldor mentioned the man, to which Jerome added the three men he had seen. Keldor said very little as he kept his conclusions to himself, but insisted they pressed on.

Not far behind, Garrick and his entourage trailed and, as always, they remained quiet, exchanging nothing just in case of unwanted ears.

No one would have known they were following, except what they hadn't banked on was that they were shadowing a

Realm's Ranger, a master of such activities, and Keldor always knew when he was being tracked.

He knew why, but he *didn't* know why – *what it was that told him* – whether the wind carried what the trees said, or whether the ground sent vibrations through him, revealing to him the secrets of what was around.

Either way, with the knowledge of being pursued, Keldor's next task was to become familiar with who, or what, was so interested.

His technique went essentially unnoticed by Jerome and Misto; with only a curious question from Jerome, as to why a particular tree shared a very similar resemblance with an earlier tree, and a silent happiness from Misto, happy to be rid of his fellow green-skin kinsmen.

However, a very big turning circle and an amazing sense of navigation allowed Keldor to effectively retrace his steps and ultimately get a look at those showing an interest.

Conversely, what Keldor wasn't allowing for was that, while most people wouldn't have suspected such a stunt, Garrick wasn't *most people* and the second Keldor started, Garrick knew what was happening and furthermore knew that it was Keldor, someone with whom he shared a previous life.

Garrick, Keldor knew.

Keldor, Garrick knew.

Realisation dawned at the same time, but neither was willing to divulge any information about their pursuers to their companions.

Keldor picked up the pace.

As did Garrick.

Keldor forced the group to run.

As did Garrick.

They became so close that the tracks in the ground were still springing back, and eventually Garrick caught his first glimpse of Keldor in a long time.

"Keldor, I can't go much further," Jerome begged, still running.

It was a foretelling that Keldor would not have been able to avoid. Maybe if he were on his own, then he probably could have eluded Garrick, and the light-footed scout, and the robed man, information garnered from the earlier inspection of the tracks.

But as it stood, Jerome lacked the endurance to keep up and the savvy of blending in with the surrounds.

He was still a boy with so much to learn.

Slowly Keldor began to cease running. Jerome eagerly followed with Misto easing himself still. Keldor had no doubt that Misto shared his ranger abilities and also considered the possibility of escaping if it were just him and Misto, but how far would they have got?

These games of cat and mouse were rarely concluded in favour of the *rodent.*

Keldor breathed, mastering his emotions, as he turned about to look into the stark woods, knowing that, somewhere close, three pairs of eyes were staring back. Maybe, if he examined hard enough he could see them, but he didn't need to; he knew where they were and that was all he needed to rebuff their evil resolve.

"Who *is* this man?" Baylin whispered.

Garrick had never previously witnessed anything like it, but before he decided to do anything, he savoured the feeling of supremacy. However, the originality soon wore off and he began to raise and aim his crossbow at Keldor. Carefully he judged the distance, the height, and took account of any wind factor, of which there was none.

"Boss, what are you waiting for?" Baylin questioned. "Take the shot."

With swift resolve and even swifter execution Garrick left-hooked Baylin square in the jaw.

After recoiling and recovering, Baylin rapidly expressed a desire to speak, to question, but Garrick assuredly nullified it with the threat of another punch. Mythos remained deep in silence. He had no need to speak.

"You have no idea who that is, do you?" Garrick posed.

"Does it matter?" Baylin spat.

Garrick understood Baylin's background. He was Lyrian, a Warrior of Lyre, to be precise, and to Lyrians, death was as much an accepted part of everyday life as sleeping and breathing. They were the land's mercenaries, mercenary by name and just so by nature. Nevertheless, Baylin was out of place saying that, but it threw Garrick's mind into clarity and he became still.

"So are we going to kill him?" Baylin pushed.

Garrick's nihilistic demeanour flourished, as he thought over his place in life. It wasn't right to dispatch of such an opponent in this way. Keldor was a man of huge talent and he considered, and reconsidered, the idea of killing him.

He had him in the palm of his hand and all he had to do was pull the trigger, send an arrow flying his way, puncture his lungs or rupture his neck; he wouldn't last long, but it wasn't the *killing him* that filled him with fire; it was touching death. If death were the only adventure, then Keldor was Death's scythe – and a scrap like that was an opportunity he could *never* pass up.

"Not yet," Garrick said, settling, "but when I do kill him, and, believe me, I *will* kill him, there shall be honour, and he shall know that it was me." Garrick smiled and Baylin shared his enjoyment, but Mythos remained silent and thoughtful.

However, as much he wasn't going to kill Keldor, he did have his assignment, and it needed to be completed, regardless.

He carefully re-aimed at the boy, who was stood only feet away from Keldor, his specific instruction being *not* to kill the boy, but to capture him.

Garrick processed the information through his logic stream and the only coherent solution was to wound the boy, *in the leg should suffice*, he deliberated. At that point, the only options open to Keldor and his green-skin companion would be: leave him, stay and defend him or run and attack. All three satisfied the assignment, but the latter two would provide Garrick with his much desired taste for death.

He peered down the sights and the invisible crosshair appeared to shift naturally to account for the distance and other varying factors.

With his eyes following the boy's exhausted movements, and his fastidiously calibrated aim working to seamless precision, it was just a squeeze away – just a very gentle squeeze. And as he slowly began to press the trigger, he felt the slight jolt of the finely sprung instrument coming to life … just as he felt the beautiful high of controlling life and death.

Keldor stood poised, waiting for the inevitable and, slithers of time before, he grew very aware of the arrow. He slightly tensed, from the knowledge that Garrick would never miss, but he did.

Then Jerome yelped and fell to the ground gripping his leg. Keldor turned to him sharply, analysing the severity of his injury. It was not a fatal wound, but it did assure Keldor of one thing – Garrick never missed, so what did they want with Jerome?

"Good shot, boss!" Baylin praised.

Garrick was silent, inwardly counting the seconds for what was next to happen. He wondered which course of action Keldor would take. Maybe stay and defend … he hoped so. As for the boy, he could only guess the sound of his cry, but even that echoed around his ears, stirring his hateful tides.

He witnessed Keldor turn to the boy and put his head down to his. Then surprisingly he saw Keldor jolt back. His mind raced, wondering what could have caused his unsuspecting action, and then he didn't need to wonder. Keldor would have seen it first, but the boy was beginning to glow.

Very soon the light was spilling out all the way to Garrick and beyond. Desperate to keep watching, but struggling to bear the brilliance, he threw his hand in front of his eyes and shut them.

But it was still penetrating. He moved his hand further round until he was hugging the top half of his head. Even so, beneath his arm and his tightly clamped eyelids, he was still very aware of the light's depth.

Still increasing, all muscles tensed, the light began to furiously brighten more until exploding and then quickly vanishing.

Garrick released his head and threw his arm down in an eager attempt not to miss anything, but yet, even against all of his guards, the light had left markings on his eyes and it took a few seconds to adjust.

As everything began to settle, something curious caught his gaze, as well as Keldor's. A trail, etched in smoke and dimming radiance, began forming up from where the boy had lain, and just as it reached the treetops above, it rapidly grew in speed and then shot back towards Arthak – a shooting star.

It hadn't occurred to Keldor or Misto that Jerome was as much a ghost – or whatever was haunting the city – as they had appeared to each other earlier. And just as Keldor realised this, something even more pressing came to realisation, something from which escape seemed impossible, a wish at best, and Keldor didn't like wishing.

"We need to move," Garrick initiated.

Not another word required articulating to get Baylin and Mythos in travelling mode, destination Arthak. This time they wouldn't get it wrong and they crept into the brush and away.

"Mees thinks this could be bad."

Keldor agreed with the goblin.

"Is it worth wes running?"

"If it were," Keldor said, placing an unwanted wish, "I wouldn't be standing here."

They each stood in their unique weapon-ready stances as the surrounding stillness began to crawl with life, slowly releasing a mass of intent green-skins.

Chapter VI
Conclusions, Part I

Jerome woke up feeling more alone than before; he felt somewhat abandoned. And to add, his time spent unconscious had done nothing to remedy the sleep deprivation that had been affecting him for well over a day now.

As he stirred and stretched, he felt every filament of his being ache, but eventually though, he got to his feet and then he remembered, after having placed his hand on a hard and crusted bloodstain, where he was.

Also, now that his eyes were more sensitive, he caught a glimpse of an alcove.

Countless possibilities of where it may have led came to the forefront of his imagination, but either way, after thinking it over, he was in no frame of mind to dredge up any more surprises that this place may have lurking. The darkness had concealed it well before, and so he left the darkness to continue its good work while he focused on getting out and finding his companions.

The pungent, fusty air of the desolate city hit him hard and he became very aware of how tired he really was. He could barely remember anything of his earlier route. Instead, he was drawn to how much it felt as though the weight of the world was attached to his eyelids and, oddly, the only thing keeping him from falling asleep was the lingering presence of his Dark Whisperer, which he sensed with every intricate movement.

He scarcely had the energy to begin walking let alone resist the temptations, and he succumbed. He put his faith in the Dark Whisperer, which happily took the reins of his soul and began leading.

It would take on different forms, varying from the grotesque to the angelic, each one designed to force the correct path, and street after street he began weaving his way out of the city.

"Do you have him yet, Mythos?"

Mythos could still sense the devastation of Arthak even this distance away, but he had yet to have a trace on the boy. He answered Garrick with a shake of his head, but was suddenly forced to immobility as something else captured his magical mind's attention.

He was immediately familiar to what it was and recognised it at once as a magus.

Taking a moment, he wondered why there would be a magus travelling this way with such urgency – under void travel, no less – but the alarm bells came to a cease. The question had an obvious answer.

"What is it, Mythos?" Garrick said, picking up clearly on Mythos's brief disturbance.

"I assume the magi of Alatacia have finally sent someone to find out what's going on with the city. No doubt they would have sensed it."

"Do we need to be concerned?"

"I don't think we will be troubled."

"That better be the case," Garrick warned, "or *they* won't be the only casualties."

***

Weary and unaware of all but his fatigue, Jerome made his way out of the city, pulled by images of deceptive beauty and pushed by an evil, squirming horde that would materialize should he veer off course.

Once he was outside of Arthak, the images ceased to be so brusque, but he knew they were there. He could sense the wriggling wickedness creeping next to him, waiting for him to turn his head and marvel at its evil vicissitudes.

Every tree started to look the same as the next, just as every bush, fern and shrub had its twin. Jerome's walk resembled more the mindless perseverance of a zombie than the youthful gusto of a boy, but still, he continued.

He daren't stop; he daren't stop and be forced to witness some atrocity. His eyes and mind were too weak to bear any more. His only choice was to carry on, and little by little he continued.

**

Peter and Garveya had ridden for a good few hours and needed rest. They were over halfway through their journey to Blaile and she hoped that they would be there in time to thwart Renith's plan, whatever that may transpire to be – *The Destroyer of Magic*. Until then, Peter needed to learn a few things, starting with the basics – shielding.

"Peter, Fate, in all her infinite wonder, has brought us together, but also, in her grand and somewhat confusing plan, slotted us into a tricky situation. We're going to have to face this enemy together."

Peter was humoured by the way she talked of fate as a person. "But you took on four of them and succeeded. Surely one won't be an issue?"

"That was different. I had Talley and you helping me. *And* a good position. You can *never* underestimate the value of a good wall," she said, as though reciting something *she*'d been told from a teacher. "We will not, or *may* not, have those advantages here. If anything, Renith will be the one with the advantage. And let's not forget that he was able to deceive me. To completely obscure power you need to *be* powerful. The idea is ironic, but … sadly, the truth doesn't deal in irony. This is not going to be easy, and you need to know a thing or two about shields."

With a flick, Garveya shifted her hair back and was about to speak when Peter said, "…I heard you and Councillor Talley mention something called *void travel*. What is that?"

Wanting to teach him, but understanding his need to know, she tried to craft a passage that would give him an insight, as well as a good basis, into how magic worked, at the same time as answering his question. "…Magic is a wonderful thing. It can be used to create an infinite number of outcomes, but some things are easier to achieve than others. There is a common misconception about *spells,* which, to the uneducated, are a particular set of words or movements that result in an event. But the idea of *spells* is limiting – I mean, how many different outcomes for a spell can you think of? Hundreds, thousands, millions of things, all differing in some way. Is it *really* possible to categorise every single one, wrap them up, give them each a name and call them a *spell?* Not really, but fortunately, that is not what magic is. Not how magic *works.*

"To fully understand, you need to think of magic as an ever-present thing; an energy that can be harnessed and used to do the magus's bidding ... and that could be almost anything. But like I said earlier, some things are not so simple to achieve. The concept of going back in time, for example, has yet to be accomplished. It can be slowed down, marginally – which is just a perspective thing, anyway – but as of yet, no one has succeeded in reversing it. Neither, properly, has invisibility been achieved. Can you imagine trying to stop light from reaching *every* pair of eyes?

"But the other main concept, of teleportation, while it has not been fully accomplished, *has* been exploited, and it is from it that we get this idea of *void travel.*"

"I think I understand," Peter said, as she took a little break.

"Because teleportation involves every part of your body and spirit being moved a considerable distance, only the very strongest of thaumaturgists can attempt – and I mean *attempt* – such a feat. For the rest of us we rely on void travel.

"Teleportation, in essence, is just a form of moving. This principle does not change; what changes is the rate at which you move, relative to the distance you travel.

"It all starts with walking, and once you're doing that, you can then concentrate and perform a *void hop* and jump a very tiny amount. For a beginner, you may only succeed in performing a few of these *void hops* in a minute and *only* while you're walking, but consider being at a full sprint and performing somewhere between a hundred and a thousand void hops a minute, each one spanning a foot at a time. Huge distances can be eaten up very quickly... But I can teach you

more about that when we get to Alatacia. For now though," –
she gave him a *be-quiet-and-let-me-teach-you* look – "you need
to learn about shields."

And he didn't ask any more red herrings…

***

As well as heavy eyes, Jerome's legs were now numb, but he
had delved into the pit of soul and discovered a little well of
energy, which he was now furiously dipping into. He didn't
know how long it would last, but he hoped that his Dark
Whisperer might allow him a minor reprieve.

He followed, or rather adjusted his course according to the
visions he was subjected to and they usually adhered to a
pattern. However, on this occasion, the pattern was disrupted.

He had just finished passing another very similar looking
tree when, from out the corner of his eye, he noticed two odd
figures.

His first assumption was that he had veered off course, so
his response, as always, was to turn away from it. But, what he
hadn't expected was to find three more alike figures striding his
way.

He stopped, confused by the inconsistency and wondered
what was happening. He turned his head to where he had come
from, half expecting to see nothing. But when he actually
became aware that these things were real, it was too late to
contemplate an escape and now they were spilling out from
every direction.

Jerome pulled the dirk from his side and stood ready. He
had turned full circle time and time again, but not been able to
assess a safe fleeing point as the area seemed over-encumbered
with these things.

They moved so hauntingly, like zombies, directly focused
and yet, strangely unaware. Their eyes, of brushed metal lenses,
were emotionless and perfectly reflected the very real fear he
felt. Their skin was like ancient, weathered vellum, where
darkened cracks had formed around various places on the blue-
ashen canvas, a canvas that hugged the cheekbones and skull

beneath, so tightly that it accentuated hollows and prominences, which until now were new to Jerome. A sallow-green, turquoise tint appeared stained over the surface, while yellow discolorations bloomed, feathered in cysts and excrescences.

These features were the uniform that bound them together, but different genders could be attributed: in particular, females, mainly from their bodily features and generally longer hair, and males from the patchy spots where beards had once grown.

He saw them; saw as more came, breaking free from the arboreal confines. He matched these phantasmagorias to the things Keldor had talked about to the king. Yet still more came, and with each revealing, Jerome was powerless to their relentless march. He was completely surrounded.

Completely.

***

She came out of nowhere at a horizontal spin, sword out in front and, just before passing one of the creatures she angled the weapon out, letting the blade, assisted by the power of her movement, slice its way through, decapitating it. She moved with such graceful athleticism that Jerome could only compare himself to an oaf. Her landing was perfect, with all but a leaf being brushed up. And as she stood to face Jerome, she flicked her hair round to the side, revealing her face. Jerome stood gobsmacked, stunned by the last few seconds.

"Do you know how to use that?" she said briskly, looking down at the dirk Jerome held.

He stuttered and muttered somewhat, then uttered, "Err … not really."

"These don't appear to have much in the way of dexterity, so you should be able to strike a couple." When he didn't say anything, she continued, "If you aren't confident, just keep an eye out for them… Do you understand?"

"Uh-huh," Jerome mumbled, baffled.

It was impossible to count how many there were and either way, he failed to see the point, as the more he looked around to try and glean a number, the more he saw.

She turned her back to him, pressing herself against him, allowing them full circle coverage. Then he heard her make the first strike. He stood, holding the dirk, not sure what to do, but trying all the same to look dangerous.

"You have no idea do you?" she asked.

Jerome didn't even know what she was referring to, let alone find a yes or no answer, but he rolled over the possibilities, over the events of the past few days, to anything that she might *possibly* be talking about. Not a single thing came to mind; he didn't have a single clue, and his answer was simple:

"No."

She was silent; he was intrigued.

"What do you mean?" Jerome continued.

He heard another slash and slice and then she said, "Do you have any idea who you are?"

One of the creatures was getting uncomfortably close to him, and he was disinclined to answer her question with anything other than a plea for help. But before he vocalised it, she slipped in front of him. It was as though she could sense his fear, and adeptly, she sliced through the creature. It groaned while crumbling to the floor. But what he found the most unsettling was watching as the creature brushed past the foliage, and seeing it wither under its touch. He didn't care for the foliage, but it wasn't about that. What would it do if it touched *him?*

"You do know that you're magical, yes?" she remarked, just before returning round, planting her back against his.

"I'm not." And that response was about the only thing he *didn't* end up mumbling.

"Maybe not a *full* magus, but magic does exist in you."

"I … How? How … can you be sure?"

"How did I happen to find you in the middle of one of the biggest woodlands in Aramyth?"

He heard the words, but failed to put meaning behind them, as the approach of two more creatures overwhelmed him, taking first priority.

"I-I need help," he urged.

They were getting closer and she wasn't turning around. The amount of adrenaline that coursed through him before paled in comparison to now. He felt his body tremor as he looked down to see the dirk shaking in his hands. Everything, from the tip of his head down grew icicles. His eyes watered, as every pore tried to find some way of releasing the dread.

The building anxiety pushed a fainting feeling his way and his senses devolved into a haze. His hands were numbed and his ears felt blocked as muffled versions of familiar sounds thudded around the concaves of his ear. His rapidly diminishing gaze was fixed avidly in front, but the monsters weren't stopping.

He tried pushing back, to move away from the danger, but he only felt her body, pushing back just as hard as he was against her.

However, he then felt something other than the fear. He felt the warmth, and it began to transfer across, jolting his mind away for a brief moment, allowing a granule of reasoning to take root.

She is fighting. She is not able *to turn around and help. I am going to die unless I do something...*

It was enough and, although still frightened beyond anything he had previously experienced, his senses returned and he found adequate strength to stand his ground.

The dirk in his hands stabilised and, as he traced the atrocious details of its face, he lunged forward, piercing the rags and then its skin, feeling the little extra frictions of organs inside rupturing and bursting. He had turned away just before the lunge, but its groans made it manifestly clear what he had done.

Jerome took a breath and looked down towards his hands, which were turning white from the rigour, and then he caught another sharp breath when he saw the black blood rolling in globules down and round the weapon, until building in a pocket between his hands and the hilt.

His stiffened fingers had cramped up and, as the blood had nowhere else to go, it began dripping off either side. It was thick and sticky and he felt his body lock tight.

When she initially rested her hand over his, he wasn't even aware. It took a thrusting kick to the impaled creature to get him to loosen his grip and, even then, he was still, for the most part, unresponsive.

"You're fine. It's over," she said, holding his shoulders, softy rocking him back to focus.

"I-I … what have I done…?"

"…You saved your life." It was matter-of-fact.

He heard the words. He even understood them, but something inside insisted that what he'd done was inherently wrong. But she had a very calming quality and the tension that had him wrapped up tight loosened and he released the blade. When she had full control of the weapon she put an arm around him and escorted him out of the killing zone, to a place canopied by thick-leafed, low-hanging branches.

Under the viridian ambience he sat, back against a tree, knees up, arms draped loosely by his side. His breathing was stuttered and irregular, not dissimilar to the aftermath of teary exhaustion.

She let him breath and reclaim some calm, and then said, "So, you are a magus," introducing something new, something *different*.

It captured his attention instantly, but he was disinclined to believe her. "…But, I don't … *feel* any different to how I've *always* felt."

"And there's no reason why you should," she offered straight back – like it was obvious.

"So let me get this right; what you're saying is … I can cast … *spells?*" Jerome asked, not able to help the excitement of it, but also, not able to help but be a little pessimistic of such a statement.

"If there were spells to cast, then yes. But, that's not how it works."

"I'm confused. Wouldn't I need to have magical parents to be a magus?"

"I've never heard of it otherwise, and … I'm assuming that because you don't know…" she said, stopping to reword her question. "Do you know who your parents are?"

Driana immediately came to the fore. And it stung. "I never knew my father, but my mother, I don't think she's … magical, but … she is … missing. I'm looking for her."

She was aware that he was on the verge of further upset and played to his sympathy. "I'm sorry to hear that." She paused, to allow time for her honest words to suffuse. "So, you don't think she's a magus?" she asked carefully.

He shook his head, struggling not to fall back to tears.

"So it's likely that your father was a magus. Unless they were both non-magical, but as I said, I've never heard of anything like that before. And it would explain why you're not emanating as much magic as I would usually expect."

"What do you mean?"

"…I think you're a demi-magus. But I don't want to confuse you anymore than you already appear to be."

There was something comfortable about the silence that proceeded. It gave them both the time to become used to the other. Granted, he was still bewildered by the news, as was she that he didn't know, but the peacefulness saturated into his belaboured soul.

"So, is that how you found me?" he asked, restoring the conversation.

"Yes. Although, I was already heading in this direction to investigate the magical disturbance north of here."

He wondered. "Do you mean Arthak?"

"Do you know something?" she said, pouncing upon his knowledge.

"Well … err … the city is … destroyed."

"…Destroyed?"

"Completely," he confirmed.

"People?"

"I don't know what's happened to everyone. There were … no bodies."

"We knew something bad had happened, but I didn't expect that."

Pause. "…I don't think anyone did," he said.

Elisa fell silent again and Jerome watched her think.

"We should head to Alatacia. I need to report back and you ... well, you *belong* there."

Curious at her words, he enquired further. "Alatacia?"

"Home of the magi. It's where I've come from. It's a two-day journey south of here. Will you be happy travelling with me?"

Jerome liked that she asked. It seemed such a simple thing to do, but it accorded him importance. "I will, but I need some rest. I've barely stopped."

"Of course. We can leave when you're ready."

"Thank you."

She smiled, and he couldn't help but return it, but amidst everything ... he still thought of his mother.

"You'll like it there, you know," she said, seeing his smile fade.

"Alatacia?"

"It's a very special place, unlike anything you would ever have seen. The trees reach the skies and beyond, the rocks and stones form and shape to will ... the world plays and changes as it needs. The two different magi have their separate guilds: the Pure Magi and Battle Magi... There is one other, the Blade Magi ... magus."

"Magus? Is there only one?"

"There used to be a lot more, but something happened," she said and took a breath. "If you meet him, he may tell you."

She was sincere and her words spoke honestly to Jerome's heart, compelling him to adopt her deepest emotion. And with the silence surrounding them, she looked deep into his eyes only, then, to turn away.

Jerome's initial compulsion, to reciprocate her passion, turned to confusion.

"What is it?" he asked, leaning forward to her.

There was a complete role reversal, with Jerome becoming the comforter and her, the comforted, but as soon as his hand touched her she snapped back, snatching away the emotion that was so evident.

"It's nothing. You just ... reminded me of someone long ago. Anyway, never mind me. How are you feeling now?"

"Better, thank you."

"Are you able to travel?"

"I think so."

"Good, but if we are to travel together then I'd like to know your name."

"Jerome."

"My name is Elisa and it's a pleasure to meet you... How old are you, by the way?"

Jerome hadn't realised; he hadn't had the time to think, but it was his birthday.

"I'm ... fifteen, today. It's four days after Feast Day."

She flashed a smile at him. "Happy birthday, Jerome. Now, we should best get away from here. We'll rest soon, I promise, and tonight we will begin our journey."

***

Keldor chided himself for getting captured ... *again.* He would never have allowed himself to be that unaware, but he was focused on Jerome and his welfare. He cursed himself again. It was his fault and his fault alone that he was tied to a tree and worse, tied to a tree with a goblin. He dropped his head – this was the second capture of which, he was sure, there would be no escape.

"Misto be sorry," a little voice squeaked in apology from behind the other side of the tree.

It wasn't the goblin's fault, he knew, but saying, "...You don't need to be sorry," was hard anyway.

"Mees thinks we both be sorry." It was aptly put, Keldor considered.

Oddly, despite his prejudice, he felt an affinity with the goblin, for Misto was now as much an outsider as him. He reflected his place as a Ranger of the Realm and the solitude that it brought.

Although respected, he wondered if he was *feared* and the thought brought him discomfort. Were the people that he so protected afraid of him? It left a bitter after-taste, but then his mechanical and straightforward thought process was cut short by an earth-shattering roar.

It was loud and incomprehensible … and as it finished rattling it drove the hairs on the back of his neck shooting up to attention. As for Misto, he knew exactly what it meant, and he recognised the savage ogre behind the voice … as well as the revenge that must be paid.

"Misto! You not be hurts! You be dead."

"No, Misto be alive."

"ARGH!"

***

That was the only distinct sound Keldor could make out as he clenched himself tighter to the tree, aware of the altercation behind and little able to do anything other than avoid the fray. A rough minute later, a few soft squeaks from Misto and a barrage of loud grunts, and the violent clash rippled to a close.

Keldor heard the thud of something huge hitting the floor, vibrating the ground beneath. Following on from that, he heard the pushing and scuffing of leaves and then in quick succession, footsteps running away, ruffling the crisp foliage with every step.

He waited, wondered, to think what would happen next until he heard the pitter-patter of feet trotting back and then the clash of weapons being dumped. Keldor, as always, had been theorising and positing what had actually happened, but as he felt the ropes being sliced and then fall limp to the ground, he stopped; he was free and little else mattered.

"Quick. Not good. Must go!" Misto hurriedly said, peeping round.

"What—"

"Not now. Must go!" repeated the goblin, this time with more urgency.

"Misto?" Keldor attempted.

"MUST GO!" rebuffed Misto.

"M—" he retried.

"GO!" the goblin finished.

Keldor ended all hope of trying to converse with Misto and instead, placed his efforts in making an escape, where he would make sure there would be no third time – as he didn't believe in luck and, even if he did, he wasn't prepared to test the waters of superstition.

Keldor threw a final look back to see what may have happened and sighted a particular ogre-shaped pile beneath a blanket of leaves.

He looked down to the little green-skin before beginning their sneak into the woods and on to Alatacia.

He wondered if Misto would ever speak of what happened, but as they disappeared within the thicket it seemed neither important nor relevant. He had a hunch that Misto would be a lifelong companion – and that was good…

***

During the brief time when they had rested, Garveya's attempts to teach her young companion had only ended in failure. Although just a simple defensive shield, Peter was only ever capable of developing it into a broken and unstable configuration, easily penetrable by Garveya's simple, yet harmless, attacks.

That evening they arrived at the small indistinct village of Blaile, where they dismounted their tired horses and hitched them to one of the bordering trees. The sun had dipped beneath the treetops and dusk presided.

The settlement itself was comprised of two small rows. The structures on these rows consisted of several houses, several trading posts, namely: a blacksmith, a mailing house, a tailor and the village hall. Through the centre of the village lay the dusty, worn and well-walked road and just short of the woods on the far end of the village was the focal point, a church.

Slightly separated from the other buildings was the local inn, the Shadowed Glen. Peter queried its name, as he understood that tavern and inn names always heralded a relevance to the local customs, clientele or surroundings.

Looking around for anything noticeable, he spotted a stump, now being used as a table. Obviously the stump was the remnant of a tree and this precipitated looking further afield; he saw similarities between the stump and a few weeping willows growing nearby. The name's meaning was now clear to him and he returned his attention to Garveya.

She knew that Renith had passed here as the atmosphere still held inklings of magical vibration, but she couldn't get a clear sense of where he was. However, she expected this, as it wasn't the first time he'd concealed his power.

"Where is he?" Peter asked.

"I'm not sure yet."

"Can you trace him?"

"Slightly, but he is … exceptionally good at hiding it."

Peter was silent as he watched the dusk get darker and the darkling sky blacken.

"Follow me," she said.

Garveya slowly followed the dusty path to where the village buildings ran either side. She had switched off almost every sense, including her hearing and sight, in order to boost her capacity to sense any magical interruptions.

The idea of *seeing* without seeing was a principle that she was still mastering.

From her teachings, the mind's eye provided a much more detailed view of the world, but far more complex and harder to understand. Where the eyes simply view the surroundings as three-dimensional shapes and facets – and, more often than not, erroneously – the mind can see the world as an encryption, removing beauty and colour and replacing it with pure and continuous detail – detail created by magic's interaction with everything else, and not being limited by the straight lines of light.

Peter tailed slowly behind, very aware of Garveya's concentration. They were just about to pass the village hall when she stopped and turned.

"Stay behind me."

Peter nodded and moved to the side, letting her take the lead. They closed in on the village hall and, as they neared it, a strange sensation washed over Peter making him feel light-headed. However, Garveya was not watching him at this point. Her attention was fixed on the door and as soon as she put her hand to the handle the door burst open, blowing her backwards and flinging her painfully to the floor.

Before Peter could process the event, she was back on her feet and ready with a shield, a quick response to the impending attacks.

The deadly energy that disrupted its way through the open door drew light in as it headed towards Garveya.

Almost powerless, Peter unhooked his backpack, peered round the door and flung it towards the antagonist in the hope of hitting him. In retrospect it was a bad idea as the attention that was so directly focused upon Garveya vehemently turned towards him. Then it was he who was the subject of a new bolt of anathema, singeing its way onwards.

He barely managed to evade its path by clutching the side of the door and swinging his weight around. With Peter out of the immediate way, another bolt charged its unholy power towards Garveya, but she drove her own specially crafted hex into his, countering it, causing sparks to jump and explode from the centre.

The power play continued with both Renith and Garveya crafting their separate and unique invocations with each one meeting in the centre and dispersing out.

Peter, now totally useless, stood beside the door watching the calamity when he was hit by a shocking reality. Renith was casting faster than Garveya and that was pushing the meeting point for their magic towards her.

Soon she would no longer have the protection of her spells and worse, Peter could do nothing.

Garveya also began to notice the inevitable and her bolts became sloppier as she started backing off towards one of the nearby willow trees Peter had previously sighted.

She was close to the tree when Peter observed that, with Garveya's capitulation, Renith's attacks also became sloppier and quicker as he desperately tried to penetrate her ballistic shield ... and then one of them did.

It struck her leg and she yelped, collapsing to the floor from the sheer exhaustion.

Without thinking, Peter sprinted out, eager to come to the aid of his female friend. He forgot all about the circumstances as he held her head and looked at her closed eyes.

But the combat had not finished and Peter felt the near proximity of a fire-bolt scorch the hairs on the back of his neck. His natural reaction forced his head down nearer to hers, and then he looked around and saw Renith. He was standing just outside of the village hall with pomposity written all over his face.

The humour that he relished stung Peter to his core as little spots of fear and anger slowly erupted inside, willing him to act. But he wondered what he could to do.

With Garveya incapacitated and a powerful dark magus rapidly bearing down, he began to shake Garveya in an attempt to wake her, but she remained still.

Close to giving up, Peter turned and saw Renith orbiting his hands around a central space summoning malevolence into a growing mass between. The phrase 'do or die' sprang to mind; a phrase that he and Jerome had said so often with little effect. He hadn't appreciated its full meaning. His did now.

Time insufferably short, he tried to prepare his mind for what Garveya had taught him. That was the first step; now he needed energy, and he reminded himself of his little internal emotional eruptions. These he pulled to the forefront of his mind along with the goal, and third step – protecting Garveya. The light-sapping mass, wriggling with deformity, was released and now it was only Peter standing in the way.

He pushed the energy that lingered on the tip of his mind out, willing the shield to go up, praying that it wasn't broken and more importantly, that it could withstand the attack – whatever tangible bane it was that had been summoned.

Peter didn't have time to consider if the shield worked, as the collision between the two ended in an explosion knocking him back. It was a momentary blackout and his recovery showed that his shield had worked … for the most part.

He was alive, but as he floated back to consciousness something had come with him, something had remained from Renith's attack. And it was ... eating him, eating away at his soul.

He felt somewhat proud that he had protected Garveya even if was just for a moment, but now there was little else he could do. The black particles were embedded in him now, and their appetite was not sated yet...

However, this last acceptance was slightly premature, as the blast had not only knocked *him* in and out of consciousness, but also Garveya.

Acting fast, she laid her hands on Peter, pinched some of his power and began succouring the nefarious parasites and curing him.

It was an instant rejuvenation for him, while, from her deceptively unconscious state, Garveya fired a shot at Renith – who also appeared visibly stunned from the contact between his attack and Peter's shield – giving them both time to retreat behind the willow, which Garveya had originally made for.

Dazed but half-ready Renith, regained control, destroying Garveya's simple magic and then pummelling the willow tree with an array of attacks.

The weeping willow had a sizable trunk and offered ample protection, but Renith's assault kept them very aware of all their body parts.

"You managed to make a shield. Peter, well done."

"Only just though, and it couldn't have been *that* good."

"Trust me, it was good enough. Now, keep well in."

Her words put his soul at ease. Garveya shifted her weight to her tiptoes, keeping her knees bent and body down, ready.

The varied bombardment was erratic and to have any chance of success, Garveya needed to make the unpredictable predictable.

"When I say, put your hand out and take it straight back in. We need to draw his attention. Be quick, though."

From then on, as she studied the timings, she became very aware of Renith's aptitude for magic, but she focused on his attacks.

One to the left, another left, one to the right ... left or right?
"Peter, now."

Renith saw the hand poke out and wasn't to be confused. He knew it to be trick and he stopped firing and instead waited, keeping his attention directed at the *other* side.

Garveya prepared the most part of her spell behind the cover and then she quickly leant out, choosing the same side from which Peter had put his hand out. She knew a dark magus would know of trickery and, of course, it was always a risk, but she hoped *he* wouldn't expect it from her.

Then she opened up her magic, her planned attacks. The power of the dark magus quickly formed into a shield.

However, the hastiness of it caused it to be flimsy and ill-prepared to match up. As such, it was rapidly falling against her very prepared offensive. And soon, his shield was ruptured all over – a buckler full of holes – as he began retreating back to the security of the village hall.

Desperate to land a strike, Garveya upped the volume and dropped the effectiveness until one bolt penetrated his dying shield, hitting him on the waist and driving him firmly into the room's shadows.

***

From within the confines, Renith gathered himself and sidled out of the back. Clutching his injury, he crept along the rear shadows of the village, between the buildings and the treeline, leading to the church, where the evening sermon was under way.

Abruptly, he barged through the large and elaborate wooden doors, hushing the cleric at the end and putting a pause on the mass.

Renith was unfazed by the silent stares of the village populous, as he thrashed his way up the central passageway, pushing the priest aside.

The initial silence was now a rumble of voices with Renith standing unceremoniously in the high position.

"Everyone out!" he shouted.

The crowd ignored his order and rather than quieting, the sea of voices erupted into severe unrest. But, avid for getting his way, he began blasting shots above his defiant audience. Incited by the noise, the unrest matured to uproar, with everyone hastily leaving their pews, desperate to reach the exits. Mothers grabbed their children and men assisted their wives as all hurried one another out.

The emptiness presided and the building returned to true resonance with every sound amplified to brilliance. And under the heavenly acoustics, Renith heard the cleric's prayers.

And he turned to him. "Pious priest, your devout loyalty to your god impresses me... It's just a shame that I'm only one listening."

The cleric lifted his head from prayer, looked to Renith and said clearly, "He is always listening."

Renith exuded something along the same vein as an eye roll, or a *tsk-tsk;* but it was an inaudible, invisible mark of derision. "He may have an ear open to your whining mumbles, but why would He answer your selfish prayers, oh righteous priest?"

The cleric's face bore into him, a mark of clarity enduring. "I am not praying to be saved," he said, as if it were obvious. "To ask for such would be irreverent. Whatever His plans, I shall always follow."

Renith couldn't help but be intrigued. "Enlighten me then, priest. Tell me ... what would demand your last words?"

"Safe passage to Heaven."

Renith laughed, and the church seemed to laugh with him.

The cleric returned his head to his folded hands, and returned to his whispered prayers.

"Holy priest, I cannot deny your safe passage," Renith subtly said. "...But first you need to get to the afterlife."

***

The threat of violence had momentarily passed and Garveya and Peter reorganised themselves before beginning the hunt for Renith.

They were just before the threshold of the village hall when they both heard the low hum of a ruckus.

They were about to enter, when a horde of people burst from the church, desperately running for their houses.

With the mass moving in one direction, Garveya and Peter headed the other, running for the church, eager to lay the menace to rest.

The twilight hour was nearly over and the only light was the gentle trickle that spilled out from the stained glass windows of the church.

The alarming silence added an extra layer of caution to their encroachment upon the holy vicinity. Renith had no need to hide his magical prowess anymore, just as Garveya had no need to sense it, but their power resounded back and forth signifying the final showdown to be just a spell away.

Garveya took the first step through the agape doors and into the echoic building. The benches either side made evident the quick evacuation, no doubt instigated by Renith, and the damage marks dotted above the embellished archway gave Garveya a clear understanding of what happened here.

Fortunately, there were no bodies anywhere ... except one. Her eyes fell upon the corpse of a man in holy vestments with his hands to his head, bowed down in worship ... lifeless. She knew the dark magi to be so iniquitous, but understanding a malicious act like that was something she could *not* know of.

Both she and Peter adopted cover between the pews as they listened ardently to anything that would give up Renith's location.

The stillness was palpable, as Peter glanced across. His distress was unmistakable and Garveya could do very little to comfort her young acquaintance.

At the far end of the church, just below the rafters, was a strange white luminescence. Quite rapidly, it expanded and Peter quickly analysed that it was not benign.

With deviations in colour, it began to whirl and spin, and then whirl and spin faster until reaching a climax that led to devastation. A massive tempest began spiralling above, tearing up the pews, behind which they had both assumed cover.

The joists that mapped the ceiling snapped and descended into the spinning cyclone, taking with them all-size fragments of heavy stone blocks. The vortex continued to spin for a little longer until all of its energy had been consumed, at which point the revolving mass of debris began to fall.

Peter and Garveya were both prepared for the incoming plummet and their shields held, as debris fell down and bounced off.

Once everything was grounded, Garveya quickly sought out Peter, just to find him doing the same. He smiled; she half-grinned.

But their connection was cut short, with bolt after bolt of darkness scourging its way down between the piles of detritus, causing random contusions to the already ruined church.

Garveya could sense the hatred inside Renith. It seethed out of every pore and he was riddled with it; every ounce of his self was held together by it. This destructive anger was the fuel for his desire to bring death upon them, as another dread-bolt weaved through the destroyed chapel.

Garveya had deliberately kept quiet, bringing her patience to aid.

With every curse that Renith expelled, she became surer of his location and when she had built a complete mental map, with his position pin-pointed, she released a mass of lightening-imbued magic. She liked lightning; it was good, she had discovered, as it had useful properties, because, although she had a good idea of where Renith was, she couldn't be totally sure and the lightning would encompass a wider area.

Her invocation carved its way through the delineations and deviations of the building out of her sight.

A thick pained wail reverberated its way around the stone structure.

The cry told Garveya that she had been lucky and that it had struck him and, hopefully, more than just tangentially. Still drawing on her patience, she waited to make sure that no surprise attacks would come and, when she was confident, she stood and made her way across the ruin.

Renith was lying, breathing heavily, with a fatal laceration across the left side of his chest. He was bleeding out and was almost certain not to last much longer.

Peter watched from the far side of the room, as he saw Garveya finish what needed finishing.

He saw her bend down in a similar way to the dark magus back in Tryth. He assumed her to be collecting any last information that may be pertinent.

Her return to standing meant a great deal to Peter; it marked the end of a huge turning point in his life, a point that, upon looking at it retrospectively, he risked not seeing the other side of.

And now that Garveya had given him the capacity to learn and the freedom to flourish, he looked forward to the long journey ahead to Alatacia.

But *really,* he just looked forward to being with *her.*

***

Jerome had slept well over the last few hours, his Dark Whisperer leaving him be. It was much needed rest and, although not enough to fill his energy well, it was a good start and was enough to get him on his feet and ready to get the long trip to Alatacia underway.

Evening bloomed and Elisa waited for Jerome to get himself together. Everything had been done: the fire staunched and covered, any signs that people had settled concealed, and they were ready to go.

However, some old visitors had returned…

***

"He's very close," Mythos whispered.

Garrick didn't reply; he needn't to.

He'd heard his academic acquaintance and had hunkered down into hunter-mode to try and get a visual on where the boy was.

"And he's not alone."

"What do you mean…? Keldor and that ridiculous goblin were captured. Who could possibly be with him now?" Garrick questioned.

"If my senses are correct, he is with a magus."

"I thought you said they weren't anything to worry about."

Mythos was a savvy individual, with an intellect to match most, but he knew that *being smart* with Garrick was, ironically, a highly idiotic course of action, and his desire to be sententious or pedantic was put to a close and he chose silence as the favoured course of action.

"Can you still trace them?" Garrick asked.

"Maybe even better than before." It was a half-truth, but Garrick wouldn't know.

Garrick held his gaze, wary of his studious accomplice. He wasn't a thaumaturge and, as always, he took what he said with the utmost caution.

He returned to his hunter directive, scanning every tree, bush and fern.

***

Elisa had encouraged Jerome close to the ground the moment she caught a hint of someone else, someone magical, but after this immediate alert she recognised the same individual from before while she had been under void travel. She thought very little of it at the time, however, something wasn't right and she hastened to think that Jerome had something to do with it.

She regarded him and something about him seemed different to anything she had, up until now, experienced.

She knew that he was a demi-magus and so his aura would, of course, be unfamiliar, but that wasn't it. And it frustrated her that, no matter how hard she tried, she couldn't put a finger on it.

"What is it?" Jerome asked.

"We have company."

"Is it bad?"

Elisa ached over a way of trying to answer his question, but couldn't, while Jerome took her silence as exactly what she had been hoping to achieve with words.

Yes. Very.

***

Both Garrick and his two companions, and Elisa and Jerome were in a standoff, with neither party willing to make the first move. But this was familiar territory for everyone except Jerome, whose impatient spirit was beginning to lose control. However, underneath the layers – below the anxiety of Jerome, under the gratification of Baylin and even beneath the taciturnity of the hunter Garrick – was an ethereal battle between Elisa and Mythos. She was building the walls of distraction while he worked to tear them down. He was most certainly adept, but she was prepared and the battle between them was relatively balanced, with the favour tipping back and forth, each waiting for the advantage.

But the supervening advantage that came affected both in a way that, unknown to the other, was helpful.

To Elisa, Mythos's attempts to overcome her walls came to a close, while Mythos, on the other hand, seemed convinced that he had successfully broken them down and now had a fixed location for her and the boy.

Elisa was highly suspicious of the strange ending, but she made the most of the auspicious circumstance and beckoned the restless Jerome on the beginnings of the journey…

Part II
The Journey

Jerome and Elisa had travelled for two days. After day one, they had entered a particularly dense woodland, which Elisa informed him to be the Tenebrae. The overbearing pitch and gloominess left Jerome feeling quite claustrophobic, which initially he struggled to deal with. But Elisa's calming persona, and his own boyish zest to explore the future, allowed him to overcome it and, against preliminary concern, find peace.

They also talked, and during the periods of rest they learnt a lot from each other, about each other. Admittedly, most of Jerome's stories centred on Melfall, his mother, Peter, his brief stint with Keldor and Misto... He missed the bit out about his Dark Whisperer.

But her stories were so much more interesting: Alatacia, magic, adventures. What wasn't to enjoy? And every time she mentioned magic, in particular the *art of magic,* he felt his heart race.

By the end of the second day, Elisa told Jerome of their impending arrival, and the excitement that had dominated his mind changed into a nervous tension. But he took it as a good thing, because change was something he was slowly coming to accept; and this was going to be a *big* change...

Of that, he had no doubt.

Chapter VII
Tiny Spells

The Tenebrae was a place of constant caliginosity. Even when the sun was up, and Jerome could see the bright heights above, down below was a dim wash of gloom, but there was something so remarkably stunning about it. Jerome likened it to a distant world, untouched by human hands and, within the depths, it had been allowed to bloom.

It had been like that for the whole time inside, but now there was a change. The air had thickened and a mist was building, and with each untouched and moss-ridden tree that they passed the mist became denser and heavier.

The mist was now thick fog.

"Is this really the way to Alatacia?" Jerome asked, a glint of worry in his voice.

Elisa just smiled – something he couldn't see – and said, "Wait and see."

The fog was so thick that it was like wearing second layer of clothes. Visibility had been completely removed, so much so he even considered closing his eyes.

Resisting that though, he continued pressing forward until the thick fog subtly began to subside.

As there had been darkness, there was now light, and it enticed him forward, the fog fluttering back to a light mist; his every step onward was like an anodyne, curing his blindness, at the same time thinning the darkness.

Now it was only pockets, occasional puffs of mugginess, and then…

…he was somewhere he'd never been before.

"*This* … is Alatacia," Elisa announced.

Speechless, his mouth agape, Jerome surveyed. Just as the king's palace in Cearan had done, this place was also showing him more new wonders, more awe, more bewilderment.

He hadn't believed her before, but he would never have believed that something quite so beautiful could exist. And Elisa had not been wrong about anything: the trees, both distant and far, were endless; the rocks and the cliffs appeared so perfectly formed, like the might of The Creator was on exhibit.

Jerome and Elisa were standing on one such cliff, while to their right, a massive waterfall, coming from the nothingness of this world's ceiling, was gushing down gallons of water – so clear, as though molten crystals.

Beyond the lake and spanning the distance between it and the treeline, Jerome saw what appeared to be a communal area. Carpeted mostly in grass, it was filled with people doing all manner of things. Some were sparring, some, Jerome assumed – his heart fluttered again –, were practising magic, while others meandered, spectating.

He turned around, not sure what to expect, and saw the deep nebula through which he and Elisa had arrived.

"Think of it as a portal, Jerome," Elisa said, enlightening him. "Although we are still very much in Aramyth, even *still* within the Tenebrae, this whole place exists in a different dimension."

Jerome thought about it and then looked at her. "How?"

"Alatacia flourishes because, in the minds of everyone here, we understand and believe it, and therefore it is."

"Alatacia is just a dream?" Jerome concluded.

Elisa bobbed her head from side to side, going over whether or not to let his half-right impression be *right enough,* or whether she should battle it out against his youthful and limited understanding.

At last, she said, "It is as *infinite* as a dream, where the rules differ hugely from what you're used to, but it *is* real."

"And if someone were to walk through the Tenebrae, would they end up here?"

Her head again bobbed left and right until she said, "There is an element of permission to it as well as just understanding. A person not looking for it would simply walk through and be none the wiser."

"But it seems so real," Jerome questioned.

"…And that is what makes it so." And she secretly crossed her fingers, hoping that she'd said enough to solidify a *right enough* impression in his mind.

He was quiet while he thought. Finally he said, "I suppose. So where are we going now?"

Uncrossing her fingers, she said, "I'm taking you to see the queen's council, so we can discuss what will become of you."

"That soundsss…" He held the word and Elisa could see his concern.

"This is a *good* thing, Jerome. We will decide what guild of magi you will join. Do you remember the different kinds?"

"I think so…"

***

Peter had been in Alatacia for a day so far. His journey, though longer, had taken less time than Jerome's, as Garveya had taught him the basics of void travel.

Shortly after arriving, Garveya had accompanied him up and through the heights of Alatacia to the queen and her council, where he was given the choice of two guilds of magi: Battle or Pure. His choice to train as the former was made by two deciding factors. The primary was that, because he had spent so long with*out* thaumaturgy, he would benefit from extra support, such as using a weapon, something that the Pures didn't use. But the second more germane factor, if not necessarily the most important one, was that Garveya was a battle magus, and she was his inspiration.

So with his decision made and granted by the council, Garveya was chosen to be his mentor.

Because, even though he thought he concealed it well, *everyone* knew he liked her. The queen's council might well have declined the idea, but the truth was: she liked Peter, too. And they would prove to be a good match for each other.

***

Jerome and Elisa had made their way down the precipice, along an extraordinary path that, as Elisa had mentioned, had been naturally formed, but was so ... faultless it was hard to believe.

Now that they were at the bottom and the huge lake – with its gentle flowing and ebbing wash – was so close, Jerome was able to fully take in the sheer scale of everything.

Being perched at such a height had been quite deceiving, but now that he had his feet kissing the ground, Jerome could, and yet absolutely *couldn't,* fathom the place.

The trees – ever growing, never ending – in the nearing distance were the principle point that his eyes were drawn to and, up each, Jerome could see structures dotted intermittently.

She spoke to him while they walked across the busy plain.

"I told you it's unlike any place you've ever seen before."

He nodded, starry-eyed. "What are all those formations growing up the trees?"

She looked to where he motioned. "Where we live. All those buildings that grow up the tree will continue to grow, and with every new magus that is born, a new structure begins forming at the base. And so the eldest, most powerful magi live at the top."

"Where do *you* live?" he asked.

"You'll see," she responded, another grin.

They continued walking.

Before, when he he'd said 'I think so', regarding the different guilds of magi, he'd not been entirely accurate, so he asked, "What kind of magus are you?" in the hope that she'd give up the knowledge.

Her knowing grin suggested she knew that he *didn't* know, but she was kind and said, "I am a pure magus, but I have been dabbling."

Once she'd said it, the other one, *Battle Magi,* came to mind, and he said, "Dabbling?"

"Dabbling," she confirmed.

"...What do you think *I* will be?"

"I couldn't possibly say. It is not for me to suggest or incline you towards any decision. It is for *you* to make."

Pure. Battle. Pure. Battle. It was a tricky choice.

The trees towered over them both and when they had reached the base of the biggest tree, Jerome gazed up to see the myriad of life within the beautiful architecture of nature's design.

***

It was as Jerome had entered Alatacia that something started stirring within Peter. Even in this short time, his magical awareness had developed with tremendous speed, to the point of having a constant connection with magic and its eternal flux. And it was something within that flux that sparked a familiar feeling. Garveya had encouraged openness and so he was without reserve to question it and discover the cause…

***

The beginning of the upward trek started, like any ascending voyage, from the base, and in this case, from the trunk of the great tree. Watching, like a baby opening its eyes for the first time, Jerome saw the bark begin splitting in several places, like a pattern, and then bend out to form and winding staircase.

Having looked up and seen the endlessness, Jerome was shocked that it only took a minute to reach to the summit.

He puzzled over the idea that maybe this tree knew where they were going and so adjusted the steps accordingly, but that still didn't actually *explain* anything. *Troublesome* was how he left it. But he expected it; after all, he still didn't have a firm grasp of Alatacia, let alone its mechanics. For now though, he let acceptance take over, but made a point of getting his head around it later.

And the acceptance was a much-needed commodity, as when he looked over the edge to see just a light template of the lower world beneath, he was dumbfounded and dumbstruck – utterly silenced.

Elisa tenderly coaxed him away from the side, encouraging him to follow her along the sturdy bridges and pathways that intertwined every tree, and soon they were outside an extremely grand formation, the grandest of all.

Its age was apparent by the colour and definition of the wood that created it – from which it was made. It was also much bigger than the structures beneath.

Elisa knocked upon the majestic door and a moment later it opened, but not in the way Jerome expected – *never* the way he expected. Rather than opening as if by a hinge, like a normal door, the wood manipulated and contorted into an open state and, when it had finished, Elisa led him in. Once they were both inside, Jerome heard the door creak and crack shut.

However, the moment that sound had stopped his ears detected the same natural wooden grind, as he clocked three other doors all starting the same process.

This he only registered before again, his eyes was drawn elsewhere, this time to the centre of the floor, to where something soft and unusual lay. Upon closer inspection, Jerome could see it was an intricately detailed flowerbed, with all manner of infinitesimal plants, blended together, living and swaying to the same imperceptible breeze of its own tiny ecosystem.

The pure perplexity of the teeny garden beguiled him and Jerome was keen to discern as much about it as he could. Then, while enraptured, he started to witness little amorphous and pallid shoots spearheading out from the floral patch, this setting into motion a whole life cycle. The little shoots were now budding, leaves sprouting, until maturing into saplings.

The development was so rapid, as they began to criss-cross in and out of each other, joining to become a single system. The saplings then shot up farther, until reaching an invisible point a few feet about the ground. Like water that had been thrown at an invisible surface, the entity then began to separate and spread out, while becoming thicker and denser, but still keeping to the same height. In similar fashion to their vertical growth, other shoots heading in similar directions also merged together forming an incredibly tight mesh.

It was only in the final slowing stages that Jerome could see that it was growing into a table, and when all the shoots had stopped, the uneven surface began to weather, affecting an aged metamorphosis.

The leaves that were so young and vibrant only seconds before were now nothing more than etchings within the profound wooden grain, like skeletal fossils.

It finally clicked inside him: the truth behind Elisa's words, that everything here was alive.

Now that the room was ready after its transformation, people began to enter from the two side doors, taking place around the circular table. It was all hush as they looked to the central and grandiose entrance.

Shortly after, a man walked in, followed by a pristinely-dressed – clothing that seemed as alive as the room (bedizened by nature) – female.

Jerome's logic told him that she was probably the queen, but his logic had so far been of little help and he was all too open to correction. Very little was as it seemed; but perhaps this would be different.

The majestic female took position around the table with her male entourage and looked around to her kin.

The door behind her closed, and all eyes fell upon Elisa and Jerome.

"Hello, Jerome," the regal lady spoke.

He resisted the desire to ask how she knew his name. Compared to the events of today, that was probably the most explainable thing.

"Hello," he said. Unsure of any specific etiquette, he just tried to be as polite as he could.

"I have to say, it's not very often that we find familiar magi outside of Alatacia, but don't you find that some things happen all at once?"

Didn't she mean magus? It was, after all, only him. But despite not knowing what she meant, he didn't want to appear rude and so nodded.

"Your Majesty, he is a demi-magus," Elisa said.

"Quite," the queen said, clearly aware of it. "I haven't seen a demi-magus for a very long time. Do you know why you're here, Jerome?"

He'd got to thinking while he'd been here. In fact, he'd done a *lot* of heavy thinking over the past week, and her question, although innocent enough, sparked Jerome to say, "Not for the same reason you think, Your Majesty."

No doubt, it was not the answer she, or anyone, was expecting. Everyone was confused, including Elisa, and the queen responded, "What do you mean?"

"You think I'm here because I'm ... magical." It still didn't feel right, but he considered all the things he, perhaps *everyone*, always wished about – dreamed of – doing with magic: flying, teleporting, time travel... "The truth is ... I wouldn't be here if my mother hadn't disappeared."

Saying it made the little tear glands start working.

"I see. So you don't think that being here is ... a calling?" she said, inflecting her question.

"I'm not sure what you mean." And then maybe she was referring to— "Do you mean that my mother's disappearance was ... *meant* to happen?" he said, half-affronted half-pained, the little tear glands holding back a touch.

"Not at all," the queen immediately retracted. "That is not what I meant at all, and I would never suggest that," she said, apologetically. "But ... here you are and you *do* belong here... However, I'll leave that for you to think about."

Each word she spoke gave Jerome an uneasy sense that she knew exactly what was going on.

"And," the queen continued, "this is not to discuss *why* you're here, but to be glad that you are and indeed, now that it is so, what will become of you. Has Elisa told you of the different guilds?"

Jerome's nod motivated her to continue.

"And what would you like to be, Jerome?" she continued.

"...I don't really know the difference."

"If I may interject?" said one of the so far quiet members of council.

"Of course you may, Slayne," the queen said, invitingly.

"If this boy is a demi-magus, he may do very well as a Blade."

That *was the other guild of magi Elisa had mentioned,* Jerome suddenly remembered.

The gentle susurration in the room completely hushed, and the queen carefully considered Slayne.

Suggesting that someone follow one of the particular foci was, not so much prohibited, just not done. But *this* was different, and she said, "And you would be his mentor?"

He waited, to give his, 'I would,' answer more weight – more sincerity.

The queen looked to Jerome. "Jerome, do you have anything to say?"

It was only after he was asked this that he considered the man who had offered to mentor him.

He was larger than the other magi around the table. And looking closer, despite his size, he stood out more than any of the others – and, he felt uncomfortable and somewhat ashamed at thinking it – but not in a good way.

His clothes were a little darker, but mostly, he just looked scruffier.

Where everyone else was preened and dressed in opulence, he looked unkempt, worn out… He looked tired, like he'd given up long ago.

Jerome didn't want to say anything, for fear of saying something rude, but the pause was only getting bigger and an answer was only wanted more.

The queen broke the silence and she said, "Whatever decision you make does not have to be final or eternal. The paths we take can be altered and changed. Take Elisa," – she briefly looked at her then back to Jerome – "a pure magus, who has chosen to learn some of the Battle's way." *Dabbling,* Jerome remembered her saying. "Take yourself, until recently you didn't even know you were a magus." The queen looked to Elisa, who looked to Jerome. "I think that under Slayne's guidance you can become great. But you have to believe it. You have to want it."

It made sense to him. His earlier reservations hadn't gone yet, but something about what she said gave him a little confidence and then he decided.

And he nodded, saying, "I accept."

"I think that's a wise choice, Jerome. Does anyone have anything to add?" she said, opening it up to the table.

"Your Majesty," Elisa said, gathering everyone's attention. "There is something else I need to talk about."

"Go on," said the queen.

"I have news of Arthak."

"Thank you, Elisa, but we have already heard." And there was a glint of pain swimming in the room. Everything felt sad, felt as if in mourning.

"You have?" Elisa puzzled.

"Indeed, by a non-magus, named Keldor. He arrived with a green-skin a day or so ago." The queen was talking while Jerome was faintly smiling. "Now, are there any other points that anyone else wishes to raise?"

When there was nothing else to offer, the queen adjourned the meeting by stepping back from the table. The other magi copied her backward step and, as they did, the table began a new process.

Jerome watched the ancient wood begin to crumble and break up. It was slow and gentle at first, but before long the whole table had been dissolved to dust and Jerome watched as the table fragments reached the floor and then travelled towards the little garden.

"It's natural, Jerome," Elisa said, aware of his curiosity. "Like everything that comes from the ground, eventually it all returns."

She soothingly moved an arm around him taking his mind off nature's course and giving him peace to leave.

***

"Jerome!" shouted someone from behind, as he took a single step out.

He knew that voice, but he said it anyway. "Peter." He said it, because he wanted to – because he couldn't help it. He turned and, although he knew who it was, seeing him face to face gave even greater elation. They were little bits of home – *real* bits of

175

home, not just memories. Jerome hadn't quite registered it, but Peter was already running towards him and they hugged, carefree of whatever the world may think. Swells of emotion, built from the sheer relief, dampened anything beyond their embrace. It was a break from the madness they had both suffered and endured, and they gripped at each other's backs, making absolutely sure that the real bits of home were as real as they were visible.

The two female magi, Elisa and Garveya, allowed their young companions time.

And slowly they broke apart. Neither had realised it, but they had both become teary-eyed and as they backed away from each other, inviting the world back in, they wiped their tears with their sleeves, and they chuckled – it was funny – but they were still buzzing from the high of seeing each other.

"Elisa," Jerome said, absorbing the last tear in the material of his sleeve, "this is Peter. He and I grew up together in Melfall."

Peter extended an arm to Elisa. "Hello, Elisa," he said, something akin to formality in his voice.

Garveya and Elisa shared a look and a smile and, without either one knowing, the same thought – *after the embrace they just had, they were already pushing away and hiding their emotions.* But they were just boys, eager to be men, and she took Peter's hand.

"Garveya," Peter continued, stepping back from Elisa, "this is Jerome." Briefly he considered whether to repeat what Jerome had said about growing up together, but he thought it unnecessary.

Just as Peter had, Jerome stepped to her and extended his hand to Garveya, which she took.

Elisa and Garveya were not previous acquaintances, mainly because they were of different guilds, but it seemed clear to them both that they would be spending a lot more time together.

"I find it hard to believe that two magi were living together in the same hamlet, and yet had no knowledge of who they really are," Elisa said curiously; Garveya was just as intrigued.

"You're a magus *too,* Jerome?"

"*Demi*-magus, but I'm still not sure what that means yet." Jerome remembered the queen mention *magi,* not magus. And the reason was now clear.

"...Do you have a guild?" Peter asked.

"Blade magus."

"Blade?" Peter questioned. "What's that?"

"To be honest, Peter ... I don't really know," he chuckled. "Anyway, what guild are you?"

"Oh, it had to be the Battle Magi, didn't it?" he said, unable to stop a grin – a grin that Jerome emulated.

"It's so good to see you again, Jerome. We have to have a proper catch up, perhaps train together, if you'd like?" Peter meekly asked, as if clutching to the thought that this may still be just a dream.

Jerome didn't wait. "I would like that."

There was a brief silence while, for the first time, the future looked brighter than it ever had before.

Elisa and Garveya exchanged friendly glances, and it was Garveya who interrupted the two boys. "I hate to break up your reunion, but Peter, there'll be time to catch up later. For now we really should continue."

Peter was not upset at her statement. Just *seeing* Jerome again was something – in itself – *magical,* especially since the last he knew he'd gone missing. Then he thought about Driana, and remembered what he'd said. What would *she* be thinking now?

Saying goodbye was like all the times before and they left each other's company in good spirits, but the thought of Jerome's mother had strummed an uneasy chord inside Peter.

***

Elisa took Jerome to her dwelling. It was a fair way down from the top, but looking over the edge, it was still a fair way up, and *still* took next to no time to reach. In similar fashion to the council's domicile, her door also opened without the use of hinges, not taking into account that every piece of wood is different – different knots, growth rings, grain, basic structure – and would therefore move and shift in a way unique to itself.

Jerome stepped in and *wow!* 'Amazing' seemed an understatement. Growing all around the walls and ceilings were hundreds of vines, some leafy, others willowy. It had a very serene quality and left Jerome feeling open and unrestricted, as though the room could, and would, respond to him. The central table, Jerome was sure, was conceptually the same as the one in the queen's residence, except smaller; the main differences were the lack of a special flowerbed beneath, and there were also seats – permanent seats – around the queen's.

"Do you like it?" she asked.

"…" was Jerome's speechlessness.

"You're very welcome to stay here until you have a place of your own."

He finally found his voice and said, "…That is very kind. Thank you, Elisa."

Jerome spent the rest of the day with Elisa. After showing him around the rest of her living quarters, she took him down to the communal green where all kinds of events were taking place. The most interesting, Jerome thought, was the Battle Magi sparring against the Pure Magi.

It was taking place in an arena that Jerome could have sworn wasn't there when he first arrived, as it took up a large portion of the green, and when he posed this to Elisa she told him that it was not a permanent landmark, but was formed to fulfil the needs, like everything in Alatacia.

The arena itself was down-set into the ground with a steep and unscalable surface all around. The ground at the base was mainly grass but towards the centre, was churned up muck.

After watching and talking for some time, it appeared that these events were not uncommon and were often decided upon by internal guild factions all vying for more control, to tip the balance of power. It was all Jerome needed to understand that powermongery was something to transcend all race, class and society.

He and Elisa spent the rest of the day watching, but Jerome was tired and as soon as the blue sky above was speckled with starlit serenity, he made his return back to her residence for some much required, uninterrupted sleep. The only clear sound, as he drifted into nothingness, was the tranquil drone of the waterfall.

***

The next morning arrived, and for the first time in a long time, Jerome was glad to be awake. Today, he thought, was going to be the start of a whole new way of life.

The blankets of leaf-blossomed vines, acting as a curtain, mellifluously drifted to the sides to let the sunlight through, and as the room illuminated, he looked round and saw all sorts of floral organisms stirring, waking and moving.

Feet planted on the floor, he stretched and the room seemingly stretched with him, the stems of plants erecting from their drooped state, the flowers blooming with the dawn of the day.

Like the residents of Alatacia, it wasn't just them that slept, it was everything: the houses, the trees, the water and the sky. *Everything was alive...*

Fully dressed and ready, Jerome contemplated when his training would start. He didn't, however, expect it to be the moment he walked into the main room.

At the table, sat at one place, was Elisa and at another, he recognised immediately, was Slayne. They both turned to him and all of a sudden he felt very *observed.*

"Good morning, Jerome, this is Slayne. As you know, he is going to be your mentor."

Heavily encumbered by surprise he looked at Slayne. He was much bigger up close and that only aided his discomfort. But there was something different about him today, Jerome wondered. His worn-out tiredness, that bedraggled look that initially promoted reticence within Jerome, looked replaced by a new spirit, like he'd decided to give *whatever he'd given up on* another go.

"Good morning, Jerome," Slayne said, his erudite eyes scanning him.

Jerome returned the greeting and, after Elisa's request, took a seat at the table.

"Slayne has been telling me about your future training. It seems that you're one of a kind."

"One of a kind?" Jerome repeated.

"As a demi-magus," Slayne said, "you have a huge amount of potential. It's just a matter of preparing it."

"It sounds complicated," Jerome ventured.

"It's a lot easier to think of it like this… You are a demi-magus, all human, half magical and half not, and, for the purpose of this explanation, to make it simpler, imagine you have two different souls. But, it's *not* as simple as just *halving the power*. Your non-magic soul is currently the dominant one and because of that, your magical capacity is severely restricted. And as frustrating as that will be for you, it is what is going to put you way up in the thaumaturgical food chain."

It was clear to Elisa that Jerome was very engaged in the whole idea.

"Elisa, if you're not opposed," Slayne said, breaking topic, "I would like to take Jerome and show him more."

"Of course, he is your protégé," Elisa mentioned.

"It has been a pleasure meeting you," Slayne said, bowing his head to Elisa. "Now, Jerome, do you have a weapon?"

Jerome remembered the dirk that Keldor had given him. He could still remember the thick black blood oozing onto his hands, the fear still gripping him, the taste of death still building in the back of his throat, but through trying to conquer those painful memories he couldn't remember what had happened to the weapon.

He handed Elisa a despairing look, in hope that she may know, and before he said anything, she straightaway left the room and came back … with the dirk, clean and ready for him.

The quick nervous tension that had developed rapidly drained without leaving any trace, as she held it out, hilt first.

He fastened the sheathed dirk hastily to his belt for fear that it might *run off* again and almost completely blanked Slayne's complimentary words about it.

Jerome briefly mumbled some thanks, but he was so glad to have it back that he didn't give much notice to anything else. Slayne wasn't bothered though and they headed out.

He led him down to the communal green, and then beyond, heading into a crag and then out the other side, into another green expanse, quiet and unused, a tad dishevelled.

Jerome stood gawping, as he watched Slayne begin to move and control the land in front.

The layers of grass and mud shifted and folded back on themselves baring a hard surface beneath. Jerome wasn't sure *what* Slayne was creating, but by the hands of invisible artisans various structures began assembling. And then stopped.

Which confused Jerome, because the finished piece wasn't nearly as *finished* as he would have expected, with most of the walls ending in a jagged and toothed edge and the main edifice appearing as if left to ruin, like a forgotten temple of an ancient tribe.

But Slayne seemed pleased enough with it though, and that would do for Jerome. He followed Slayne into the enclosure and when they were both inside Slayne stopped, turned and looked directly at Jerome.

"I didn't want to say any more in front of Elisa, which is why I have brought you here."

"What do you mean?" Jerome asked.

"It's for your sake… You must be excited about all this? And I didn't want you to feel *embarrassed,* but the only way for you to fully understand what you are might make you feel … not *quite* as excited." He paused to inhale.

And continued, with his fresh breath, "Most importantly," – and exhaled – "a blade magus, despite the name, is not defined by the sword alone, as most may have you believe. Certainly the magus is great in the art of combat, but you see, a blade," said Slayne, drawing and demonstrating his own sword, "has *two* sides, just as the blade magus has both the weapon *and* the magic.

"However, and this is the part that may upset you. Now, listen to me carefully. You *are* magical; it's just that, right now, you have a very *limited* magical capacity. However, that is what will eventually be your strength. Because of your dominant non-magic soul, your magical side is massively subdued and therefore you will find using it remarkably difficult. Your friend, whom I've heard so much about, will develop very quickly and way beyond you. But I must remind you that it is not permanent, and one day it will flow through you with the same ease.

"For now, though, we just need to work on something I call … 'Tiny Spells'."

"Tiny spells?" Jerome said, curious. What he'd said had stung a little, but Slayne was so enthusiastic that Jerome was filled with hope.

"Yes," he said. "As hard as you will find it to craft magic, you still can, but what you create will all be much smaller versions. Where a magus will be able to hurl a boulder, you will be able to throw a pebble. Sounds silly, but a pebble in the eye can be a very useful trick. It works like this, when a new magus is born they will either become a battle magus or a pure mag—"

"So what's the difference between a blade and battle magus? They both fight and they both use magic," Jerome asked, cutting him off.

Slayne forwent punishing him and answered, "I see your confusion, but there is a *big* difference. Granted, both use a weapon, but the battle magus cannot fight and cast at the same time, whereas we can."

His clandestine tone added to Jerome's confidence and he almost felt good about his magic inability.

"To continue, though," Slayne said, picking up on where he was interrupted, "in order to fully master magic, a magus needs to train from a very young age, in which case, they forfeit the weapon. Or they spend years, either during or after, trying to master that, too, with one, almost certainly, being sacrificed.

"However, like I said, because your magical knowledge is still very much in its infancy, we have plenty of time to get you mastering the blade. Then we can intertwine the magic and then one day you will be superior to almost every other magi."

Jerome smiled and looked around. "So this is where it all begins."

"I know it's nothing impressive right now," he admitted, regarding the dereliction, "but I'm sure we can return it to its former glory."

"We? Former glory?" Jerome questioned.

"I don't know if you know, but up until yesterday I was the only blade magus."

"…Elisa mentioned something about it to me. But she didn't explain why or what happened."

"But I wasn't *always* the only one," he said, ignoring Jerome's obvious desire to find out. "There were many of us and we had a guildhall just like the Battles and the Pures, but after it happened, it didn't just spell destruction for the Blades but also the guildhall in which we assembled."

"You mean…?" Jerome said, cottoning on to his meaning.

"*This* used to be the guildhall of the Blade Magi. And, as you can see, it hasn't been used in a very long time."

Strangely, Jerome found a sense of purpose being within its walls, knowing that it was steeped in such history. And in complete contrast to his initial feelings he now felt honoured to be stood within.

"But why have there been no more?" Jerome asked.

"…To be trained as a Blade you first need to be a demi-magus."

"And what – makes? – a demi-magus?" Jerome quizzed, struggling to find a better way of wording it.

And Slayne began, "…Back when the magi were still young, they walked among the non-magical societies. They were, in reality, no different. Just humans … with a gift."

And? Jerome eagerly waited for him to continue and said, "So what happened?"

"They stopped being accepted."

He hadn't answered the question. "…Why?"

"Fear, I suppose."

Slayne could see that Jerome remained unsatisfied and would probably end up asking another 'why?', so he saved him the trouble, and continued, "The thing is, Jerome, it only takes one person."

"…To do what?"

"To poison the mind of another."

"Poison with what?"

Does he ever stop? Slayne thought. "…With the thought that, because magi are powerful, they will use their power for badness."

"I understand."

Finally. "…So, one person becomes two, two people becomes a group. And, once a group forms, *everyone* wants in."

"So they were made to leave, the magi? What if they didn't?" Jerome quickly asked.

"They weren't killed, if that's what you mean." That *was* what Jerome had meant. "But they were met with derision and hostility. They didn't *have* to leave, but they were given no other choice *but* to leave.

"And those who were espoused, pairs of mixed magical capacity – shall we say? –, were either made to split up, or leave together. Some had children, and, eventually, those children became known as demi-magi. And since magi no longer lived among the communities of the non-magical, no more demi-magi, or very few more, were ever born. In truth, Jerome, you are the first demi-magus I have seen in years, *hundreds* of years."

Jerome's initial thought was *how old is he?* But he chose a different line of questions.

"So, humans and magi, they don't get on?"

"Even though magi *are* human."

"But—"

"I understand," Slayne said, stopping him, not without wanting to confuse the eager teenager any more than he already was. "You might say that they don't get on, but there exists a treaty, more a curtain of acceptance than outright peace. It was decreed after the War of Unity, and was also formed with green-skins. But nothing's *really* changed…"

Jerome felt overloaded by this massive intake. It really brought to light how little he'd known, how little he knew, how much *more* there was still to know. And he took to thinking, to wondering.

"…Do you think they ever would have?" Jerome asked.

Slayne briefly wondered how much of the *conversation* Jerome had had with himself, before conceding to the fact that he wouldn't be able to unravel the mind of a fifteen-year-old. He had to ask, "Who and what?"

"...Do you think that the magi would ever have ... abused their power?" Jerome asked, finding the notion uncomfortable.

And Slayne thought. He thought about how to answer such a delicate question. "...I've seen and met a lot of people over the years, and the truth is, *most* people want little more than a happy, prosperous life. But you always get the exception."

"...You mean they *would*."

"I mean that if *one* of them *did,* there would have been lots more to stop whoever it was. But, it's hard to say, as no one can ever know what will happen or what *would* have happened then. We can guess. Make informed decisions. And *hope* that what we do is the right thing. But if your *heart's* in the right place, the *right thing* probably won't be that far away."

Jerome nodded. It was a lot to take in. It was a new world.

And Slayne watched Jerome digest the information, a glimmer of a smile creeping onto his face. No doubt, he asked a lot of questions. But Slayne considered his young protégé, his burn and thirst for knowledge – a healthy trait to have. You can't learn to *want* to learn. You either have it or you don't. And Jerome *was* interested. And those who were interested were always easier to teach.

Yes, it would be fair to say that Slayne liked Jerome from the start.

"So, where do we begin?" asked Jerome.

***

Slayne and Jerome stood inside the remains of the guildhall, weapons out, edges gently touching.

"Before we begin, the first and most important thing to know is: a blade is *not* a toy. It is designed to kill. Never use a sword ... or a *dirk,*" – he looked at Jerome's weapon – "without knowing that. Do you understand me?"

Jerome nodded and said, "I understand."

"Good. Now, the weapon is an extension of your body," Slayne instructed. "You need to feel it as you do your arms and legs, as you do the heat within. Now, pay attention. Watch my shoulders. That is from where the next attack will come," Slayne said, bringing his sword round and to Jerome's left.

In all fairness, he couldn't tell anything about the attack from Slayne's shoulders, but he did raise the dirk in time.

"Good," Slayne remarked, "but try and think about moving your weapon in the opposite direction to the attack. Logically, a static block will work if you're stopping an attack, like the one I just showed you, but the real thing will be far different. You need power. Power from motion. Move the blade across your body and force the attack away."

Again Slayne came in for another attack, this time on the other side. Jerome had to think and though he saw it, he couldn't get the dirk to do what he wanted, and he ended up ducking, awkwardly.

"Look at my shoulders," Slayne said.

"I did, but I don't understand what I'm looking for."

Slayne could see that the idea was frustrating him, so he showed him what he meant.

"I understand. Right, Jerome, look at your hand."

Jerome did.

"What is it attached to?"

"…My wrist?"

"Which is attached to…?"

"My arm."

"And what connects your arm to your body?"

Ahaa…

Slayne enjoyed watching understanding take root. It had a signature like no other. "It's a subtle movement, but it's there. And I promise that you will eventually see it. *And,* if you think about it, the *real* movement comes from the collarbone."

Moving his hand beneath his neck, Slayne rubbed across the line of his collarbone to his shoulder.

"Break *that* and you'll completely disable the arm."

Head bobbing up and down continuously, Jerome said, "I understand."

And he *did* understand.

Slayne and Jerome reformed, blades touching. Slowly, Slayne moved to attack and, although it wasn't a natural movement – and the shoulder thing *still* wasn't telling him anything – Jerome *did* succeed, with a slight motional hesitation, in blocking the incoming offensive.

"Better! But you'll need to be quicker than that. Follow…"

Slayne began a slow and continuous flow of strikes, varying from side to side and up and down. At the start, Jerome really struggled to keep up and sometimes had to duck to avoid being hit.

Sometimes he had to step back, embarrassingly losing his footing, but Slayne pressed on, forcing Jerome to think and, more importantly, to act. And the longer Slayne pushed, the easier it came. The more he *drove* Jerome to move, the more *able* he was to move, until, strike-by-strike, block-by-muscle-pounding-block, the minutes dropped away, pulling the hours along with them.

Several hours and many hundreds of blocked attacks later, Jerome was shattered. Every sinew and fibre, from the surface to the core – including the spaces in between – throbbed and ached.

But it was the evening's feeble limp back to Elisa's, behind Slayne's brisk stride – just like Keldor's purposeful gait – that was the hardest part of the day, and as he lay on the bed, his body burning, the waterfall's gentle drone did make it a little easier; so much so that he almost completely overlooked the evil eyes of his Dark Whisperer, still glowering malevolently upon him. But that was it; that was all…

And he overcame the fear, as his eyes fell shut, allowing sleep to set in.

***

The next morning, Slayne was ready for him again, something Jerome soon discovered, sauntering out of his room, muscles bleeding and energy low. But his new mentor was unswerving in his resolve to train, and down the great tree they travelled, across the green, through the cliffs, towards the site of the Blade's guildhall, which he promptly engineered to assemble.

Looking at it, Jerome could see little differences. It was by no means complete, but something – just a little *something* – about it seemed just a *little* more pristine, a little *less* forgotten.

"Same again today, Jerome," said Slayne, unsheathing his sword and encouraging his tired protégé to copy.

His dirk felt heavy, much heavier than yesterday, but as the blades tinged upon collision, and Slayne initiated the first attack, he felt his body slip into a natural state. He felt his body pick up on something ingrained.

Agreed, his burning muscles didn't burn any less, nor did his heavy eyes feel any less heavy, but the repetitive co-ordinated hits were much easier to defend and also predict. He found his eyes not focusing on the sword, but – like Slayne had said – at his shoulders. He actually was able to pick up on the acute alterations and associate them with a defensive movement of his own.

"Good," Slayne said, stopping. "Now, change hands."

Flabbergasted, Jerome replied, "What?"

"Change hands," Slayne repeated.

Jerome had so far favoured his left hand, but when Slayne had finished his command, he felt it fly behind his back and stay firmly in place. The dirk fell from his uncontrolled hand and it clanged unpleasantly against the stone floor, piercing his ears.

Ignoring it, Jerome desperately tried pulling his clamped hand back round, but Slayne's magical decree was not to be fought against – at any rate, not *won* against. To say the least, it put Jerome firmly on the back foot. That, and he now had to use the wrong hand.

"You are a blade magus, and need to have full command of your body. You must have the perfect symmetry and excellent balance of a blade. Now ... up!"

Jerome despairingly picked up the dirk and held it out in contact with Slayne's sword. It was such a wrong feeling. He couldn't judge anything; even gripping it with the right degree of strength took concentration. Nonetheless, he consoled himself somewhat. He at least had his minor ability to predict the attacks – keeping a firm watch of Slayne's shoulders.

Slayne began and whether Jerome liked it or not, so did he.

Like yesterday, the sun rose to its peak, dipped beneath the horizon, and they didn't stop until it was dark.

Exhaustion had a new meaning, Jerome thought, as Slayne broke for the last time.

Unable to find the entrance to his sheath, he rested his dirk upon the ground and sat next to it.

"I hope you don't think we're done for the night," said Slayne – Jerome did, rather he prayed –, "because I've got more lined up for us."

Internally pulling the biggest sad face he'd ever pulled, Jerome rose to his feet. Suddenly a whole string of beacons, dotting along the perimeter of the walls, roared to life, hurling out so much light that Jerome instinctively lifted his hands to shade his face. The initial eruption of light was over and the fires settled. He dropped his hands.

With the slight crackle of each flame humming all around, Slayne continued, "I know you're tired, Jerome. I know how you must feel, trust me. I was once a boy like you, but I want to pass on now what my mentor taught me then."

It was nice for Jerome to hear him talk like that; to feel empathy and Jerome was captivated by what he would teach him ... unless it was more blocking.

"Right now you are tired because you have no energy." *Did he really say that?* "It is the same principle for magic; without energy, magic will not work; it will be tired. So, we need to learn how to *get* energy."

Jerome sat forward and made sure to listen.

Slayne continued, "There are four fundamental elements which contain the world's power: earth, air, fire and water. Have you heard of them before?" Jerome nodded. "Just before we go any further, you need to understand one more absolute and universal fundamental – energy *cannot* be created; only changed. Now, where were we? Yes, each elemental energy will offer a different kind of force and, consequently, will generate a difference in spells; each one better for different kinds of magi.

Some, more often than not, link themselves to one of these elements, so they can become more efficient at drawing from it. This has its downsides though, because, although it will be an effective means to obtain power, if you take away that element from them, what are they to draw upon? Some may choose to be linked with two. It's better, but like I've said many times before, we are not like the other magi, and we shall be using all four; learning to be a perfect conduit."

"Are *you* a perfect conduit?"

"Not as perfect as I'd like to be," he said, smiling, "but I'm working on it. Anyway, I'm not important. For you to survive as a magus, you need to be as cunning and ruthless as you are valorous and honourable … *especially* you. Where you lack in magical prowess, you will need to gain in wiliness, deception if needs be… Now, onto the basics. There is no such thing as a set spell with one single outcome. However, that doesn't mean that there are an infinite number of possibilities. There are limitations and, just before you get too excited," – *don't worry about* that, *Slayne,* Jerome thought – "time travel, invisibility, teleportation are all unattainable as of yet."

A little subdued at the mention of all that, Jerome still held out for *flying.*

Slayne carried on, "But I can assure you that there are still plenty of things you can do, things that are *still* being learnt. And the sooner you realise that, the more likely you will be of victory.

"Take that stone," he said, pointing at one of the many small pieces of rubble littering the floor. "I want you to move it."

"Move it where?"

"Let's not get ahead of ourselves. Just try and move it first of all."

Jerome stood and then said, "How?"

"Three steps – prepare your mind, draw energy, think of the goal."

The thrill of *learning magic* had staved off most of the tiredness, but after hearing what Slayne had said, none of it really made any sense and he felt his eyes grow heavier again.

He knew what he had to do, rather what Slayne had said to do, and so started... Through his mind, he imagined thoughts of moving the stone, *step one*, as well as attempting to feel an energy that wasn't there, *step two*, until the absolute assurance that it hadn't worked, because as Jerome thrust his hands out towards the ground, stone in sight, *step three*, not only did it not move – not even vibrate a little – it looked even more immovable than the walls between which he was stood.

It was embarrassing, as Slayne and he shared eye contact.

"...This isn't a song and dance routine, Jerome. The physical side isn't for show, it's how the magus summons and manipulates magic. Try arming yourself while doing it, it may offer you some strength."

Like clockwork, Jerome moved his hand to his scabbard, and when he felt it empty, he looked, only to remember that he'd left his dirk on the floor – too tired at the time to fumble it back into its sheath.

He took it as a lesson – to *always* sheath his weapon – as bending down to pick it up now was so much harder than if he just had to grab it from his waist.

Small a movement as it may have been – to simply bend down and pick it up – to Jerome, right now, the floor looked to be a hundred feet away and the dirk looked as if it weighed a similar amount to a giant's two-hander.

Nonetheless, he picked it up, took a long, slow inhale – and an even longer, slower exhale – and then shook his head.

"Stop," Slayne said, seeing Jerome's premature admission of defeat. "Jerome, what I'm about to say is fact. This *magical essence* that you're trying to reach will *not* be something new. You are a magus and you always have been. It's not something hidden deep within you; it's something that you would have felt for as long as you can remember. You don't need to go to a new place to find it. Try looking for the familiar."

Now *that* made sense! He retried the inhale-exhale fad, save the headshake at the end, and closed his eyes to have a look inside for *it* – this *magical essence*. *Step one*, the stone is going to move. *Step two*, he wondered if his first breath in and out counted as the air elemental. *Step three*, suddenly the back of his eyelids came to life and he could ... see. Not everything, but he could see ... the stone and he could see ... his hands, oddly though, not in their usual colour frame. Looking at them moving in front, one was clasping his dirk, which he also couldn't see, they weren't any colour at all, but they were ... *there*.

He focused back to the stone and then he grew aware of a build-up in his fingertips. He wasn't sure what it was, but the growing charge began to elongate down and towards the floor, more directly, towards the stone. And it was that stretch that pushed his hands out, this time with meaning and purpose – not a 'song and dance routine'.

It was almost there. Almost touching; and then gradually the little, *giant, massive, I-can't-move-this-stone-with-my-mind* stone began to scuffle, *rattle-rattle,* upon the solid ground beneath and then stop, as the last drop of power dissipated away.

Jerome slowly opened his eyes, feeling more tired than he had after the whole day's training. His gaze fell upon Slayne who was looking ... *proud?*

"Good work," Slayne congratulated, with honesty.

"But I didn't really know what I was doing," he admitted.

"But you did *something*. And *you* did it, too. Jerome, for the most of us there is an element of guesswork, but you have done something truly amazing tonight and you should be proud. Now you just need to learn concise magic so you can squeeze out every ounce of the magic... Tiny spells," Slayne recited and Jerome understood it as he nodded, and then he stilled. His lethargy was more than visible and Slayne said, "Get some rest. Tomorrow will be another busy day."

Jerome checked his waist for the dirk that Keldor had so kindly given him. The feeling of almost having lost it the day before still triggered the adrenaline and it made his nerves jump through hoops. But he had it, it was safe and now he was looking forward to some richly deserved sleep.

"Oh, and Jerome," Slayne added, "you might consider shaving."

That was the last thing he expected, as he stopped to listen. He hadn't thought about it before, but his words drew his attention to his face that he stroked, trying to feel for any hair.

His cheeks felt smooth and his chin felt no different. The only part that got Jerome's mind going was a delicate mass of fluff beneath his nose, *but surely that couldn't be it?*

Still stroking his face, he moved beyond the walls of the Blade's broken guildhall, when he stopped to turn and admire it.

He only looked for a few moments, but it was enough to see Slayne, still training. There was something about seeing it that struck a truth inside Jerome.

It was because Slayne worked so hard that he was so tough, that made him a blade magus. He couldn't believe it, but the passion Slayne presented reached completely beyond his tiredness and he felt a strong compulsion to return and demonstrate his own passion for greatness.

It was a great sensation fighting for something this hard, and when Slayne saw the return of his protégé, he welcomed him proudly back inside the walls and the training continued, taking all the time they needed...

Chapter VIII
Everything Changes Now, Part I

The minutes ticked over into hours which spilled into days; and as the days rolled into weeks, the weeks pulled the months along with it, until three years had come and gone, and the two innocent young boys from the secluded hamlet of Melfall were now men. Jerome had just celebrated his eighteenth birthday and Peter was well into his nineteenth.

Only weeks after arriving, Peter and Garveya had become *official*. But there was something special about them. The ease with which they communicated telepathically made them kindred spirits and a match made in Heaven, with a stamped seal of approval from Mother Nature herself.

Jerome, on the other hand, had not as yet found *the right person* and, instead, spent the majority of his hours training. However, Peter was keen to spend time, indeed train, with his old friend and their friendship had grown ever stronger.

But in the hours of solitude, when it was just Jerome and the Great Beyond of Alatacia, he yearned in secret silence for someone with whom to share his burdens, even though, right now, it was the burden that was holding him together.

His quest to find his mother had become more of a pastime, with his early petitions to the queen's council having been met with disapproval.

This didn't change his desire though, and instead fed the yearning monster within. And the longer it had sat with him, the longer it had begun to dawn on him. He wondered the connection between the quest for his mother and his Dark Whisperer. He couldn't be sure what it was and he tried not to dwell, but it stuck with him until he couldn't shake the idea away.

As for the visions themselves, they had lessened and become more an unremitting pestilence, which he suffered alone.

Only Keldor had any idea of his visions, but even so, Jerome was sure that he'd forgotten by now.

On his occasional return visits to Alatacia, with his small green-skin companion, Misto, he was as he always was, functional and, in a perfunctory way, kind, honest and gentle, and Jerome felt a real affection for him, as well a great venerability; after all, Keldor had allowed him permanent tenancy of his dirk.

The fluffy moustache which Slayne had mentioned, had now become a fluffy memory in comparison to the rough stubble that now lined his face; his shaving routine, unlike Peter's, was far from quotidian and more an unorganised spur-of-the-moment thing. But also, unlike Peter, he had no need to gussy up; there was no *special somebody* there for him, except Slayne, Keldor, Misto and Elisa and *they* didn't count.

The years of relentless schooling had brought on the completion of the Blade's guildhall, with their combined attention and energy holding firm the walls, which now stood as they always had, and the rest of the thaumaturgical com-munity revelled in this benchmark of time.

With little else to do, Jerome's swordplay was now excellent, and although he wouldn't yet match up to Alatacia's finest, his appearance and youth belied a fine melee artist.

However, his magical effeteness still put him bottom of the 'thaumaturgical food chain', as Slayne had so masterfully put, but he remained in high-hopes as he clung to another of Slayne's famous phrases … 'Tiny Spells'.

However, something else he mentioned also stuck with him – the idea of a *second life*. If he understood correctly, because he was a demi-magus, he was currently in his *first life,* a life almost entirely devoid of magic and unable to sustain immortality, but eventually, he would lose his mortal coil and enter his *second life,* where he would be able to fully enter the ocean of magic.

But it was the journey there that stuck with him the most… Like any *life,* it always had to end with *death.*

***

Up until now, all had remained relatively calm, but something was about to erupt from deep within the confines of Jerome's soul. It was an ordinary day, like any other; Jerome was amidst the usual daily grind of training, specifically with Peter and in particular using the other hand – although he had long since lost the feeling of a dominant side – and as always they were well matched. When they had been younger, Slayne had made them spar with sticks, but now that they were men, and in all fairness – Slayne confessed – quite handy with a blade, he had no qualms. And it was during this session that Jerome's Dark Whisperer suddenly let loose and raged unholy vengeance. The normal, quiet pair of eyes, which just watched and stared, suddenly developed a mouth; a voice … and It used it.

The initial sonic blast ripped through him like a fire ravaging a dead field, but it was the howling shriek that followed which collapsed him to his knees, hands on his ears and screaming. As he managed to peer across, the mouth continued, but he saw the thing growing in size, expanding way beyond anything before. Three years of silence and this 'Thing' had finally reared Its ugly head up, not to be ignored again.

Peter acted immediately, crouching down to him, holding his arms and trying to get through. Jerome could see him, he could even see his mouth going, panic looming in his eyes, but no words could rise above the perpetual deafening howl.

The ringing was starting now, his ears' natural defences kicking in, trying to block out the invading noise. He tried shaking his head; he tried smashing his fists; he tried using his hands and arms like a vice, anything to quash the mind-splintering screech.

Just an ephemeral moment before losing it, and passing out, and the noise suddenly stopped.

Yes, the ringing still remained but now, at least, he could recover and also hear Peter's voice slowly beginning to cut through.

"Jerome, are you all right? …Jerome? Can you hear me?"

Still knelt and clearly shaken, Jerome tried to placate his concerned friend by gently shaking his arms off his own and nodding to him.

"Jerome, what happened?" Peter said.

Vague was best, Jerome decided. He didn't want his friend to think him mad, after all the years he'd spent hiding It, after all his hard work at concealing It, at bearing It.

"Nothing, let's carry on," he said, confident of his brush-off.

"I've known you for a long time, Jerome, and nothing like that has ever happened. What are you not telling me?"

"Peter, I'm just a bit stressed right now." Inspiration came to him. "It's my difficulty with magic. It's getting to me."

"Fine, if that's it, Jerome," – *if that's what suddenly makes you starting hitting the ground and clenching your head then,* Peter disbelieved his friend – "fine," Peter said, standing, but added, "I would like to think that you can count on me whenever you need."

"I can count on you, Peter," Jerome said, assuring him, and also stood. "Anyway, help me take my mind off It. Let me win, eh?" he said, falsifying a chuckle.

Peter didn't buy it, but he raised his sword to Jerome. They each had their unique stances and every journey to the finish was as unique as the last, and just as fun.

But Peter still didn't buy it, nor did he let Jerome win. He was quite able to do that on his own. But he didn't today. This day was Peter's day.

***

Long day, Jerome thought, as he returned to Elisa's. No other accommodation had yet been allocated to him, but he was fine with that and Elisa had never complained; never complained or had anything to say, until now. She was sat, obviously waiting for him, at the table with concern plastered across her face.

Her tone, though, was as calm as ever and she spoke. "Jerome, have you had a good day?"

That couldn't be what she wanted to ask, but he answered, nonetheless, "Yes, it was good. How was yours?"

"Is there anything you want to talk to me about?" she asked, skipping his return question.

The truth, Jerome inwardly smiled, and then sighed. *Long day … looks like it's going to be a long night, too.*

"No, there's nothing, why do you ask?" Jerome lied.

"The queen has been to see me. She is concerned. Maybe it's worth paying her a visit." Jerome hadn't recognised it, until that last bit, but she was petrified.

"Elisa, you seem bothered. Is everything—"

"Of course I am. You're in danger!" Not loud, just firm. Elisa didn't shout.

"Did the *queen* say that?" Jerome asked, feeling a mild fear creeping his way at the thought of danger.

"The queen doesn't do house visits on a whim, Jerome. Something is very wrong and I'm … I'm concerned for you."

She meant it and she didn't very often 'mean it'. For her sake, and maybe a little bit for his, he decided to take her up on the idea. Maybe the queen could help, and that would be better, he thought, as he left and headed up the great tree to the majestic quarters.

Every time he was up there he just had to look over the edge. It was his own little routine and it still fascinated him, but the normal spot, reserved for the old smile, was instead a pattern of sadness. And he meandered to the queen's residence.

He wasn't paying attention as the door creaked to its open juncture. His head was down and he was too engrossed in his melancholy to notice the preassembled council, waiting for him – Slayne included.

"Jerome," the queen addressed him and he looked up, *oh,* "I think we need to talk…"

***

The assembled council said nothing and their presence immediately rendered him speechless. But as he scanned the faces, his eyes falling on every one of them – principally Slayne's – they each observed him speculatively. This unwanted pressure and then the sudden cognisance of being subject to the finest and strongest magi in all of Aramyth, all at the same time, was too much and he could do nothing except let it all out, and the tears welled up and fell out.

It may have been three years for his Dark Whisperer, but it had also been three years for him.

An agonising and painful solitude was now releasing in a flood of embarrassing tears. It became worse though, as he desperately clambered his hands to his face, trying to hide his emotional peak, but all that did was make him feel hot and sticky beneath – and *still crying.*

The queen was quick to put Jerome at ease and excused everyone out – including Slayne.

And what would he now think?

Alone, she quickly glided over to him, resting a hand gently on his shoulder.

"We're alone now, Jerome. Everyone has gone."

For the most part, the tears had run their course and the hand caressing his shoulder gave him internal permission to lower his hands and reveal his wet, red and sticky face.

He felt deeply uncomfortable, but with the embarrassment he had already encountered and endured, he found nothing wrong in wiping his sleeve over his face, clearing away most of the emotional leftovers.

"Come," she said, gesturing him to follow and leading him out into the night air.

It was rejuvenating having the coolness nipping at his swollen eyes. She looked at him intensely, regarding him.

And then she broke the silence, saying, "You're a quiet soul, Jerome."

"Your Majesty?" he questioned.

"You don't talk very much and … it's good to talk."

"It's hard to talk sometimes," he said.

"What do you mean?"

"…There's not always someone to talk to."

"What about Peter?" she suggested. "Can you not talk to him?"

"I can't talk to him as much anymore. He's with Garveya."

"Slayne?"

"He is my teacher," confronted Jerome.

"And friend?" she countered.

"Of course," he confirmed.

"…Me?"

"What would you like to talk about, Your Majesty?" His response was both terse and facetious, and she saw right through it.

"I like you, Jerome. How long have you been here now?"

"Three years," he answered, "almost to the day."

"I know something is bothering you. The others may not, but I can see deep inside." She waited, listening for a response … nothing. "It must be hard having limited magical capacity."

"That's not what's bothering me," he snapped.

"So, there is *something*," – he'd fallen straight into her trap – "bothering you."

"…It's complicated."

"Is it your mother's disappearance? I would have let you go, but it would have been certain death in your state. Even now it's dangerous."

"You mean I *can* go and find her?"

"This isn't a prison, Jerome. But you know that leaving when you asked would have been the wrong decision. But that is not what is troubling you." She paused and changed tone. "I don't know what It is, but I know It's there, and It's getting worse isn't it, Jerome?"

He stuttered in disbelief. "H-how did you know?" She was the first person to mention It. And it was an oddly relieving thing, having someone know and, even better, not shying away from something he considered madness. He had coped – and mastered – the fear presented by his Dark Whisperer, but now someone was here to help.

"…I can't help you, Jerome," she bluntly said.

He gulped then reproached himself for his premature thoughts – that someone *could* actually help. He wasn't sure how he felt now; maybe frustrated that he'd been tricked into opening up when he had been coping just fine on his own.

"It's better that I know. No, I can't help you, but keeping it to yourself is not the solution. Trust me," she said, peacefully gliding into his personal space and winking, "seeing things is not the worst affliction, especially in this world."

Her garments – of nature's design – mirrored the night and appeared sleepy, as if he could lay his worry into them.

"But what do I do?" he said, grasping for any sign of hope.

"This isn't going to be what you want to hear. You need to leave and hunt out whatever this thing wants of you."

"So," he said, about to refer to his petitions to search for his mother, "I need to leave *anyway?*" It was another terse and facetious comment, and like before, she was ready.

"Jerome, I don't *want* you to leave. If there were a way for you to stay then, believe me, I would find it."

She was sincere. Her sad eyes pierced straight into him, supplying full understanding and he accepted the truth.

"I understand," he said, not needing to say it, but voicing it gave it far more credence.

***

He took the rest of night to himself.

After his conversation with the queen, he was no longer tired – not that he really was before – and he was going to make the most of his last night and morning within the beautiful, surreal paradigm of Alatacia.

The point he'd made of understanding how it *worked* three years ago had fallen swiftly by the wayside, but he didn't care. It was left as something contemplated, and *only* contemplated.

He spent the last few hours before dawn in the guildhall, under the invisible – but ever so present – scrutiny of the ancient members of before.

He relished the energy of their souls; it fed him.

Morning was fast approaching and the moment he became aware of first light, he left the soul-filled walls to appreciate the sunrise.

And it gave him a stunning farewell present: an exquisite, harlequin sky undulating from beyond the amaranthine vastness, with a red sun to boot. It lasted only moments before the colours faded and normality reclaimed its hold over the distant scape.

Even so, a moment it may have lasted, a lifetime it would be remembered.

By now, he was enraptured and totally unaware of the footfall behind him.

"Jerome," a voice said.

It took him by surprise, but it was welcome and he didn't need to turn – the voice was…

"Peter," he said. "How did I know you'd find me?"

"Because, no matter where you've gone, I've always been able to find you, and nothing's changed. We found each other here and, just to let you know, you're not going anywhere without me."

"What made you think I was going?"

"I don't need magic to know what's going on inside you. Oh, and for the record, I *knew* something was bothering you."

Peter had moved beside his friend and they were both reminded of being boys again, sat on the turfed heath in their hideout under the canopy of The Fell.

"It's complicated, Peter. I don't want to leave, but I have to."

"You've always been complicated, Jerome," he said humorously, pulling him in with a strong boyish hug.

Jerome smiled and wriggled free.

"I don't want you to leave either," Peter continued.

"Oh, I can imagine," Jerome said, sarcastically. "No one to train with?"

Peter's silence caught his attention more than his words, and he looked across. His eyes were sad and sincere. "No … because I'm going with you."

"…You don't have to, but that's thoughtful though."

"Don't give me any of that. You're like a brother to me, Jerome."

Jerome took a breath. That meant so much to him, but he broke the silence and presented a new scenario.

"What about Garveya?"

"She will understand."

Jerome's heart was in his throat and they sat quietly, taking in the glorious beyond. The nostalgic silence captured them both until neither registered the footsteps behind.

"Boys," another voice said.

Snapped back to childhood for that harmless moment, their heads whipped round and Elisa was stood over them both.

"I see what you mean," she said, also mesmerised by the ending sunrise. "I still have not tired of the view... Jerome," she spoke, quite mercurially, "you didn't return last night. I was afraid for you."

Her tone and words emulated a vocabulary direct from his mother. But rather than feeling reassured, something about it was remarkably uncomfortable. However, he hadn't the time to contemplate the ill feeling before the reminder of his mother and his childhood memories took him over.

"What's the matter?" she continued.

"I have to get my things packed," he said, perfunctorily.

"You're leaving?" Another mercurial mood shift put her in concern. "Where are you going?"

"I wish I could tell you, but I have a feeling that it might be a one way voyage."

Her reaction was quick and beautifully unexpected. "I'm going with you."

He had come down here to gain a moment of serenity, not amass an entourage, but their kind, offering words were not something he was going to oppose.

"I don't know how this will end..." Jerome let the words hang, but Elisa and Peter stood firm in their resolve. "This is my fight."

"And we will help you fight it," Peter muttered, getting the nod from Elisa.

Jerome was honoured to have such friends and fleetingly everything was fine, but like the sunset, it lasted only moments and was replaced, with unfair rapidity, by the inevitable future. But like the sunrise, the memory, he was sure, would stay with him for a lot longer...

***

The council gathered; everyone eager to discover what had been discerned from the young magus. The queen entered following her personal retainer. The assembly held on her every movement, the hush deafening as she formed the words and thought.

Pause. "My fellow, magi, sad news." She broke the silence. "He is troubled. Something lies within him."

"Is It evil?" a voice asked.

"It may be, but we have to remember that *he* certainly isn't," she appeased.

"What is going to become of him?" Slayne was the keenest to discover what was to become of his young pupil – and friend.

"He and I talked last night. He has decided to leave."

"Decided? Or was it agreed?" Slayne was overrun by emotion and his connoted undermining of her was understood, even accepted.

"I am well aware of your concern for him, Slayne. I am sorry that I cannot bring better news."

"You realise I will leave with him."

"And I will not stop you. Undeniably, I would expect it."

The atmosphere was still. Each was in quiet contemplation. It dawned on them all that Slayne was the only remaining blade magus, and now he was leaving.

It was a morning of firsts as the queen adjourned the meeting. The strict order of events for the hundreds of years before was as always, queen first, followed by her second and lastly the council, but not this time.

The queen stood firm, as everyone else left, all but Slayne, who remained behind with the queen. The partitions of rank and stature were entirely removed, as the royal woman took position next to the last and complete relic of the, once fabled, Blade Magi.

"Majesty," Slayne said.

She was looking for more than formality from her long-time friend. But she could see his inner struggle and his deco-rum was all that was keeping him together. Their goodbye was stilted, as she left him standing alone with only his thoughts.

The sunrise was over, but as Slayne left for Elisa's, he realised that a great journey had only just begun…

***

Over the years since Percy and Thermion attempted 'to find out' if his presence would break her silence, Galliana *had* rediscovered her voice.

On the outside, she could look tranquil and carefree, but no one could really tell what was going on beneath, what secrets were lurking under the skin.

Every word she pronounced, her eyes spoke different. Yet they hoped that whatever was plaguing her would eventually diminish without leaving a mark. It was high hopes, but they had no other way of knowing. All they could do was try to be there for her at every turn.

The concept that was *the three of them* was a moot point. Even though, in reality, there *were* three of them, it was really, at any given time, only ever *two of one* and *one of another,* and the *two* always included Galliana.

The trouble arose from Percy and Thermion's relationship, which was similar to two poles, both of the same orientation, never able to connect, but ardently drawn to Galliana, with one always pushed away.

They were both of such different stock, Percy's cautious wisdom butted hard against Thermion's brash impatience. But for Galliana's sake, they both dealt with it.

All this said though, they did do *fighting* very well – practising as Percy would call it; scrapping as Thermion would – and, by token of the rest of their relationship, their fighting-practising-scrapping styles couldn't have been more diverse.

It was accepted that, between the pair, Percy was the finer swordsman, but his age had slowed him down and, by continuing the theme of every other angle of their association, where Percy was inhibited in one way, Thermion thrived. And as much as these were physical battles, truthfully, every one was a battle of wills.

Galliana, the then seventeen-year-old girl, was now a fully blossomed lady and she had a life – though minimal– within the city of Toryn.

Although she was deeply intrigued by Thermion, he had a dangerous quality. She could never quite put her finger on it, though. It was as if something were warning her away from him. But slowly, she managed to see past most of that and with careful words and small steps from Thermion, they forged a calm and civil relationship. However, she still remained chaste.

This relationship – though unsupported by Percy – did not bother him. She always made time for him, to be with him, to talk with him, to even sit in silence with him. To him, she could confide in totally, without any fear of admonishment or judgement. To her, he was a man she needed, but like her, she could see that something cryptic – maybe dark, even *evil* – was going on under the skin. Whether that ghosts of the past or something *else,* they both knew it about each other and both reserved the right to remain silent, and not challenge the other.

***

Three years on.

Three years of uni*mag*inably boring baby work, and Garrick found himself skulking in the darkness of the only reputable inn in Gatelock – not the original contact point of the Cider Cloak, but a much finer establishment – namely, the Last Point, its name bred from the age long habit of it being referred to as the *last point* of call, before the Marchlands.

His failure to retrieve the boy had resulted in his disgrace and conclusive reproach … and was the reason why he could now be found drunk, in the corner of a pub, surrounded by the upper crust.

He was at the lowest of the low and to make matters worse, Baylin and Mythos still had to accompany him. It would have been difficult to tell who had it worse, but tonight they were looking for nothing more than a good time; this day was a day of merriment – no reason – well, at least, it was meant to be.

Garrick was on his seventh drink and the alcohol was really taking its toll as he tilted, quite unaware, over the side of the table.

He had just downed the last portion of ale and now he was free, he thought. But then he felt someone brush past him and, in his inebriated state, was convinced in a malicious manner.

Senses considerably dulled and mind dowsed heavily in booze, he tried to focus on who had dared to assault him, but when he caught a glimpse of The Reformation's symbol, he quickly pushed aside the alcohol's take on him.

He was good at that.

He was a master of his body, of his abilities and capacities and, although he was sure to have a raging headache on the morrow, he would be able to function for now, and then detoxify later.

Standing up, his body sinking slightly with the straightening of his legs, he stumbled over to her – maybe he *had* had too much to just ignore all of it.

"Come with me," she said, looking disparagingly at him.

He followed, a slight sway subtly weaved into his gait, while he watched her behind, thinking – and this, he was sure was the alcohol – that she was quite attractive...

The upstairs room he was led to was medium-sized and of much higher class than any room the Cider Cloak had to offer.

Plush, red furniture was dotted around with a deep crimson drape hung in front of the two ceiling-to-floor windows.

Like always, a table had been set up in the centre of the room with a lit candle, a quill and ink, a pile of documents and two chairs facing each other at opposite ends.

They sat.

"Garrick, it seems fate is smiling upon you," she said.

He was quiet, listening intensely.

"You have a chance to correct the mistakes of the past," she continued.

Garrick, who had been calm and sat back in his chair, was now leaning forward, eyes twinkling at what she was saying. He theorised as to whether she was talking about the *boy* – he adjusted for the time difference and considered that he would now be a man. He tried to veer away from wishing, but he couldn't help but wish, and then she confirmed it.

"We don't like mistakes, Garrick. People who make mistakes either end up dead, or they may as *well* be dead, as I'm sure you've experienced. I don't know why, but The Reformation has deemed you ready to right your mistakes. So, what do you have to say?"

"I'll need some more serum."

"You walk a fine line, Garrick," she said, taking a small vial and handing it to him.

He unhitched his crossbow from his side and, like before, laced the groove with the viscous liquid. She was as critical as she'd always been by his use of the formula, but she accepted it. If he got the job done then that was all that mattered, and, to be fair, he rarely failed … but this boy wasn't the ordinary catch.

She knew this and she just hoped that Garrick's machismo attitude wouldn't stand in the way, like it had last time…

Downstairs, back at the table, Mythos and Baylin looking bewildered, secretly praying for something better than they had had for the past years, Garrick gave them a nod. But this was a good nod and they both saw that.

"How fast can you gather together some Warriors of Lyre and meet back here?" Garrick said to Baylin, utilising his time as a Warrior of Lyre.

Lyre was Aramyth's southern-most town, and the only town to be almost unchanged since the inauguration of the high king.

As a town that was already rife with depravity, it quickly became a haven for the worst of the land, its name becoming synonymous with crime and brutality. In Lyre, you either learn to fight, or get used to dying – if that's something you *can* get used to. Garrick hoped that Baylin still had the respect of his, once, fellow kind and the response followed shortly:

"Three days," said Baylin, quick to respond. This was exciting and he wasn't going to miss *any* opportunity.

"Good. Three days. Mythos you stay with me while we plan the next step."

Mythos's taciturnity produced a nod. He wasn't like the Garricks and Baylins of this world. The pure desire for malevolence didn't course through his veins, but this was what he did, and his motto in life: *either to do it properly or don't do it at all.*

He also didn't *have* anything else.

***

Everything packed and ready, weapon at his side, hanging limply from the old and worn leather sheath, and Jerome had a group of three not including himself: Peter, Elisa and, surprisingly, Slayne, whom he couldn't be happier to have on side.

Considering that, at the outset, he thought he was leaving alone, to have his life-long friend, his initial rescuer *and* his mentor with him, gave him a massive surge of hope. However, he still had no idea where he was going or what he was getting himself – and them – into, but it became patently clear that, when he turned to see his supporters, everything was going to change now.

Goodbyes said and affairs in order, they made the way up the cliff side to the foggy portal, beneath the forever waterfall, and passed through.

Quickly the fog thickened, the darkness restoring itself, until eventually thinning and leaving them to the unsettling pitch of the Tenebrae.

Jerome saw the eyes and they mordantly smiled at him, he was ready for his orders…

…and the Dark Whisperer was ready to give them.

***

A week on from Feast Day and Percy and Thermion were repelling each other in true poles-apart style; fighting, scrapping, sparring, arguing – whatever they referred to it as – they were doing it. It was always within the confines of Grey Keep and always within a designated ring, depending on the room's size and shape or, if they were outside, the premises' size and features.

On this occasion Percy had the upper hand and Thermion's anger was building at a rate of knots. This was good for Percy; anger was the hardest emotion to control and Thermion did not possess the required mental athletics for such a deed.

His strikes became quick and manic, and all Percy needed was to block until the wrong attack created the right opening. He was in his element, and it was just a matter of time.

One, two, he counted, *three, four – upward block – staying calm, nothing to rush,* Percy remembered. Impetuousness was the character of losers. *Five, six,* he continued his counting, turning it into a meditative precept, and then a mistake… Thermion's shoulder backed a touch, a clear sign of a lunge. With the opening in sight, his whole body followed through, arm outstretched and then suddenly, paused.

The anger, which danced so wildly in his eyes, departed. His breathing was rapid, his body heaving with every sharp and muscled intake – big movements and noises compared to the abrupt stillness. Then, as his eyes adjusted, stopped in perfect status millimetres from his head, he saw Percy's sword. No shakes, no quivering and no question as to who had won. The sword hovered so close by that Thermion could hear the lustrous singing of the blade's metal.

"You should wear a helmet," commented Percy, detracting from his victory and snapping into *normal* Percy.

"I don't wear helmets," Thermion replied, defiantly.

"…If you don't wear it, it can't protect you."

"It won't need to. It won't happen again."

"Care to put that to the test?" asked Percy, offering a rematch.

"Anytime, old man," Thermion accepted.

"This 'old man'," – smiled Percy – "just handed it to you."

They had reset their positions and were just about to clink their swords together when Galliana disrupted their practise, a new event in any case. There was no colour in her face at all, and abandoning their pugnacious attitudes, they went straight to support her.

"Galliana, what's the matter?" Percy asked, his concern evident. "You look like you've seen a ghost."

It took her a moment to respond, seemingly because she just hadn't gauged who had spoken, or even if anyone had.

The two men flicked each other a furtive glance until she finally said, "No, I'm … I'm fine." Her voice was wobbly. It was not *fine*.

"What do you need?" Thermion said, his turn to speak.

"Nothing… I just need … some rest." She glanced up, suddenly horror-stricken, and then shot her head back down.

"Come," Percy said, retrieving the speaking permit. "I'll take you to your room."

***

The next day and Galliana's ailment had not lessened. It was odd because, although she was still ashen and distracted, she was suffering no physical defects. But the worrying thing was that her tolerance of it was shrinking, made clear by the almost continuous stream of tears.

Percy and Thermion had, on the whole, sat at her side the entire time and they took shifts in keeping a watch over her, but this time, when Thermion was alone with her, he decided on a course of action, something he had not talked over with Percy … and for good reason.

"If there's something not right, then staying here won't solve it," he broached, rubbing his hand over her clammy forehead and gently parting the strands of damp mousy-brown hair.

"But I-I can't leave. I don't … know where t-to go. I-I…" she mumbled.

"I will go with you. I will keep you out of harm's way," he assured.

That planted seed of leaving generated a sudden catharsis. Her dull breathing deepened, her sullen eyes began dancing with life and her cheeks started to swell with colour.

"I should tell—" *Too late*, she thought, as Percy strolled back in, sharply aware of some discreet interchange.

"What's going on here, then?" he pried, as he pulled his empty stool closer to the bed. "You, all of a sudden, look a lot better."

"I think that," she began, "whatever it is that is wrong with me, it will not get fixed here."

Astute Percy fixed his eyes on Thermion, but said to her, "What are you saying?"

Thermion was looking back, his eyes saying, *"What?"* in his same underlying and aggressive mood.

"…I think … I need to … leave," she said.

And then Percy looked back to Galliana. "Leave here? Grey Keep? Toryn?"

"Yes," she asserted, answering all three mini-questions.

"What has he said to you, Galliana?" Percy began. "Do you think that leaving here will really help you? It will only drive you onto a path of temptation."

For a moment, Galliana's expression filled with bewilderment and then flicked back to angst.

"I'm sorry, Percy. I have to go."

The room became embraced by silence. All of a sudden, she came over quite light-headed, wondering if it *was* the right decision. It was hard for her to distinguish between the feelings of leaving and her feelings regarding Percy, and which one it was that was unsettling her.

"You will come though, won't you, Percy?" she pleaded, her eyes piercing through him.

He breathed, deep in contemplation.

She threw him another pleading gaze.

"I don't know. I haven't left these walls for … a very long time. I don't know if I can."

"Can you do it for me?" she implored.

He paused, carefully choosing his words. He fanned over the many possible things he could say, but he landed firmly on the truth. "I don't know if I can." He let his weakness escape him. "I just don't know."

He stood up, a writhing knot of emotion, and left the room.

To Galliana, the closing of the door was an affirmation of Percy's decision, and she could not hold back the tears.

However, Thermion was quick to wipe them away with his thumb, his palm rested softly on her cheek. She felt extremely delicate at that moment and his touch – coming from that same unsettling thing *about him* – made her cringe slightly. Her tears backed down – the disquiet backed them down – and he decided that maybe she needed some alone time. He left her.

***

Here was the place where Baylin had spent his whole child-hood, and much of his adult life. It was Lyre and it was just how he left it – with perfect lawlessness and sin running wildfire through the streets.

Night was in session and the streets were laced with blood, with echoes of long-departed street brawls still punching the air. If luck shone brightly enough, then perhaps one was still discovering its outcome, with gore being shed into the midnight ambience, and maybe, if luck's eyes were burning black, if there were enough people and enough eyes to capture the moment, he could play his own hand, dispensing with a life by the shadow of the moonlight, clutching tight the body of a dying man and feeling his life add to the mausoleum in the sky. He was home.

He wound his way through dim avenues, familiar sights and sounds pervading until reaching the hub of the Warriors of Lyre. It was the perfect masquerade, Baylin relished, gazing at an unnoticeable building, one of many in this quiet lane. Anonymity was seconded only by the degree of ruthlessness of the souls inside. The faded words above the door read, 'Evil Hath No Place Here'. *How wrong it was...*

The ramshackle insides were covered in cobwebs. It looked like it hadn't been entered in decades. But that was how it always was. He remembered the route, stepping forward to the far end, passing all manner of detritus to his left and right until coming face to face with a picture. It hung at a crooked angle to the wall, again, just like it was *supposed* to be. He wondered if it was all too predictable as he tilted the picture, something clicking on the far side. Then some cracks, previously hidden –

rather, made unnoticeable – by the dilapidation, appeared and slowly the wall opened.

On the other side, everything was different. The rundown affectation of the main room had changed totally into a beautifully baroque and slightly circular anteroom.

A chandelier above cast just enough light to bring out the rich ruby reds of the shaped wooden room.

He crossed to the door on the far side and pushed, forcing it open. It was only held closed by its snug fit into the frame. Walking through, he closed it behind and headed down the stairs, which were illuminated by several burning wall torches. He was now well beneath the rumble of Lyre and as he reached the bottom of the stairs he opened the last door, entering the true centre of the Lyrian Warriors.

It opened up onto a platform overlooking a large room and upon his entrance, every figure beneath suddenly glared up to him. The steps zigzagged down, left, then right and finally out, at a ninety-degree angle from the original ledge. Everyone watched as he coolly wound his way down, staring back just as hard.

Stopping just after the last step, he remembered the ground beneath, soil, sand and rubble. It was just as always, he kept thinking, and then it was too much to contain as he let a smile turn his mouth up at the sides.

He glanced around, exhibiting it and slowly every face changed its tune, reflecting Baylin's humour. And then uproar, as the whole room filled with cheers and greetings.

He truly was home, but he reminded himself, not permanently. The people, some familiar, others not, returned to their business as a gentle drone filled the atmosphere. He could see the man he was looking for and he held his gaze, a subtle grin still remaining.

Winding in and out of the people and tables, he neared the seated figure until reaching his table. It was bigger than the rest and he had a little posse around him, not for protection, but for the status – for the fact that he could.

"Baylin," he welcomed.

"Minister Cutler," Baylin acknowledged.

"It's good to see you again. But," he dipped his head, "I'm curious, what brings you back?"

"The Reformation has a favour to ask."

"The Reformation should know that we don't do favours. Agreed, we have done work for them before, it does not make them an exception."

"Of course not, and you should know, having worked for them before, that they always reward well."

Cutler looked at Baylin, eyes thinning.

"Sit down, Baylin!" He laughed, invitingly.

Baylin pulled the nearest chair out and sat.

"How many do you need?" he continued.

"The usual."

"Oh, so it's like that? Tell me, what target would warrant such attention?" His eyes twinkled like a child's.

"A boy," Baylin answered.

The response he thought he would get of 'A *Boy?*' never came. Instead, he looked highly cogitative. He took his time to answer.

"I hope this boy shows his appreciation, having Aramyth's finest after him," said the minister, grinning sardonically.

"Still as arrogant as before, I see."

"Nothing's changed. Why should *I?*"

Baylin smiled and allowed him his conceit.

"So," the minister said, finalising the details, "is it just the normal slay'n'pay job?"

"No death, at least not for the boy."

"Maiming?" asked Cutler, a slightly pleading look.

"...Maiming will be fine."

"Maiming's good – I like maiming; I can *do* maiming." Another evil smirk lined his face.

It was Baylin's turn to return the grin and, with wickedness polluting the atmosphere, the deal was closed by a shake of hands.

***

Galliana and Thermion had very little packed. A backpack for each, stuffed to the brim with food and water. She was leaving in much the same way she had arrived. The halls of Grey Keep had never felt so empty, as they made their last checks, but Galliana secretly hoped that Percy would come and see them off. No, that was wrong. She ragingly prayed that he would come along. But with the completion of Thermion's final inspection, she cried hidden tears and they left; left Grey Keep, left the grounds, left Toryn. South was the direction. That was where she needed to go.

The hours rumbled on as she fearfully recalled the journey she had made to Toryn, and the landmarks of Dewdrop Wood that had been painted onto her eyelids came to life, reminding her of that awful night.

Exhausted from having travelled like this after so long, Galliana and Thermion settled down for the night. She knew that tomorrow would be the real test and that, along with an aching desire for Percy to be here, was her last thought before drifting away into oblivion.

***

Why did mornings always have to come so quickly? She inwardly muttered, as she folded her blanket back into her bag and took a swig of water from the bottle Thermion had proffered.

"Thank you," she said, handing it back to him. He took it and placed it back in his own bag.

She sighed and the walk continued. She simply didn't understand him and nothing allowed her to put a finger on it. He seemed dangerous, but she tried to remove that thought; for being in the middle of nowhere with a dangerous man was not a situation she wanted to find herself in.

No sooner had that thought vanished than she laid eyes on the run down shack in the near distance. *This is a mistake*, her mind was telling her, but as she tried to turn back, she was only met with a force that turned her straight back round, driving her, spurring her onwards.

She cursed every heavy step. She wished that the ground would just swallow her up, rather than remain firm for her to have to make this painful journey, confront the past. But soon the shack was near – *so* near – near enough to see a dead body resting on its side against the wall. Maybe whoever it was had been sitting upon death and maybe animals would have pulled it over, desperate to clutch at the meat. The skull was detached, ripped from the neck vertebrae, the open jaw making it appear to be eating the earth beneath.

Unable to recoil, her steps became slower as she neared the body, the tension bubbling away in the pit of her stomach.

The decomposition was complete, with only the rags of aged clothes flapping in the unwelcome breeze. However, the vile aroma that she was expecting never came.

Thermion had bent down to inspect the dead man. "That's a Ranger of the Realm!" he exclaimed. "Look at the emblem."

"A what?" asked Galliana, unaware of the title.

"It's a long story, and he's only a Duke's Ranger—"

"Only?" she gasped. "He's dead!"

"Indeed, which is what I find all the more intere-*curious,*" he said, quickly changing his words to suit Galliana.

"Why would that be interesting?"

"Well, *trained* isn't a word I use lightly, but this lot really know their stuff. Whoever-*what*ever," – he quickly exchanged, again – "killed them … you can use your imagination."

"I'd rather not, thank you."

His smile was only because of her response, but neither she, nor he, was humoured.

Conversation stopped as Thermion led the way in, but before she had a chance to even peek through the door, he'd put his hand behind him to stop her.

"Oh no," she uttered uncontrollably.

"Oh yes," he confirmed.

She had to know. It had been playing on her heartstrings for three years now and she wasn't going to let a little decomposition get in the way. Pushing past Thermion, she turned in, only to be confronted by two more bodies. She could not have been prepared to stand against the overwhelming horror, and she felt her body wretch.

There was no smell, but something was creating it. She could fabricate it, the rich, rancid and slightly sweet malodour. It wasn't there, but it *was* there, penetrating her nostrils.

Thermion laid his hand upon her back, rubbing her gently.

The bile burned the back of her throat – the fear now in full control of her – as she heaved, but she managed to hold everything back except a minor acrid morsel, which she swallowed back down, leaving a burning, lingering aftertaste. Then again, she raised her head up, was presented with the images of two dead bodies, but this time she could control her gag reflex and she took a moment to scan over the room, trying hard to ignore the patent death.

An overturned table, four knocked-over stools, a window on the far side and a closed door were all the features, but the only thing capturing her gaze was the closed door.

Thermion was busy assessing the room while she gingerly made her way closer to that which held her focus. Each creak over the rickety, wooden floor shot prickles through her, until she had her hand clasped firmly on the handle.

Again, she cursed this as being a bad idea, but with the desire to discover the truth pushing the door open, she could barely keep on her feet, before the raw, grim horror met her running-wild emotions, driving her into unconsciousness.

***

Oh that's bright! Too bright to bear as Galliana, even with her eyes closed, moved her hands up to block the source. And when she was comfortable that the shade would sufficiently protect her sensitive eyes, she opened them.

She took a deep *awake* breath and stirred a little, regaining control of her arms and legs, control that was unduly stripped from her. And then she remembered what she had seen, but not before her ears started working and she heard talking.

"…You think *you* could have stopped her going in there?" Thermion's voice was overrun with anger.

"Shh, she's waking up."

Slowly she dropped her hands and let the dazzling sun stun her before her eyes adjusted, and then one of the figures stepped in the way and a big grin appeared from ear to ear.

"Percy!" she exclaimed trying to jump to her feet, but failing – her legs still were still weak. Instead, Percy leant down to her and she flung her arms around his neck. "You changed your mind…" she whispered, mid-embrace, into his ear, his white beard grating on her skin.

But it was more than just the discomfort of his beard, because beneath his aged, softened cowl, she saw a chain-mail coif hugging his face. As well as that, another new addition was the hulking shield he had hitched to his back. She felt its sharp, metallic edge with her hands that were hugging him. She had never seen him wear such an outfit, but her elation at seeing him by far outweighed the discomfort.

"Is this a new dress code, Percy?"

"I haven't worn this for a *very* long time." His eyes portrayed an inward struggle and Galliana could see the depth.

"I'm so glad you came," she said, assuring him that she really was.

"I didn't think I would get out of Grey Keep, let alone Toryn. But," he said, glancing around, "this isn't so bad." His bravado was a very see through guise and Galliana could see the little white lie.

He was such a good man and he meant more to her than he would ever know.

"What has happened here, Galliana?"

The floodgates began to open. All the memories of before came gushing back into her mind.

Tentatively she began, "This is where we were hiding, my mother and I." Her eyes began to glisten, glisten more than usual, upon the mention of her. "My father had gone missing and no one helped. We waited for him to come back, but he never came." The glistening build-up had now begun to fall in rivulets down her cheek. Percy placed a hand on her knee to comfort her, but she seemed unaware. "He never came, so we left to head north towards Jericho, where we have family.

"We were looking for somewhere to rest, when we saw this place and—" Her whole body was heaving now and the words were becoming lost, but she breathed in hard, held the frog in her throat, forcing it to sit and wait until the end.

"And we were about to sleep, when we saw – people coming, bad people and she sent me away. I tried to say no, but she ... she..." She couldn't stay the frog any longer as she threw herself against Percy, draining her sadness, tears that had been waiting for three years.

Together, after giving Galliana some deserved attention and sympathy, Percy and Thermion created resting places for the dead and Percy finished these with suitable eulogies.

Her anguish was palpable and both men respected her desire for a quick and speedy departure.

***

Under the unnerving command of his Dark Whisperer, Jerome and his three fellow adventurers had made their way south-east. Very little had been said regarding his directions, but all had wondered. As for the torturous visions, Jerome had learnt to mask them well, but it saddened him: Peter, his closest friend, a friend that just before they left, had said he didn't need magic to see inside, *but he couldn't see this*. It was remarkably lonely and the days rolled on until they had reached the borderland city of Gatelock.

"Is this it, Jerome?" Slayne asked.

"I wish I knew," Jerome answered, earnestly.

"You mean you don't know where we're going?" berated Slayne.

"Not exactly," he said, defences coming up. "And right now I'd rather keep my sources secure."

Slayne wasn't used to being spoken to like that as Jerome continued on, taking little notice of any place within the city walls. Peter accompanied his friend up ahead, while Elisa slowed her pace until in line with the, still, bewildered Slayne.

"He's having a hard time," Elisa broached.

"I can see that," Slayne growled.

"What were you like when you were eighteen?"

"It was a long time ago."

"Don't hide from the question."

He was silent.

"He's *lonely,* Slayne," Elisa continued. "His mother has disappeared. He's only just become comfortable in a new home, which he's now had to leave, and I don't know about you, but haven't you sensed it yet?"

"Sensed what?" responded Slayne, eager to take the question away from his reprimand.

"I hadn't noticed in Alatacia, but I can feel the presence of … something, something I've never felt before, inside of him."

Slayne took a moment and then he said, "The queen mentioned something about this."

"Is that why he had to leave?"

"She wasn't clear, but I do know what you mean," Slayne admitted.

"Then shame on you!" she said, not loud, just firmly. "He could be having a horrendous time right now, who knows? We, who have been practising magic for years, must protect those less able than us. He will tell us when he is ready. And we need to be there for him when he is."

Her words scolded him, but that's what they were meant to do. He deserved it and then, being that bit wiser, caught up, with his head slightly drooped from the telling off.

And just as they had entered, the city, the streets and all the people within, faded as they passed on by, leaving it behind as just another landmark. Jerome noted the Last Point inn, on the obscure boundary of the city, and it served as a morbid reminder that this journey was sure to take him to the very edge.

Chapter IX
Meeting on the Edge

The eastward journey from Gatelock was desperately dull. Conversation had all but dried up a day or so after leaving Alatacia, and here they were, five days on and Jerome was quite sure that his three cohorts were feeling the same. The only one who didn't appear bored out of their wits was Peter. No doubt, he was in constant telepathy with Garveya, which made Jerome doubly jealous, as it wasn't just company Peter had, but excellent company. All *he* had, he considered, was his Dark Whisperer and the other two, simply their reveries.

But it wasn't just the dearth of words being exchanged that deadened everything. It was the austere scenery, too. Just a few plain trees – not dense or sparse – and a few minimal accents in the land were all there were to be admired.

Then *thud!*

An arrow impacted into a tree inches from Jerome's head, forcing him to the ground, his hands keeping him balanced. His heart rate shot up, twenty-fold, and the blood circulation came close to bursting out of his tingling skin.

Thud!

Another arrow, sticking out from the same tree, just to his right, again only inches from his head. *Staying down is not an option,* he thought, looking worriedly at the arrow – *is it familiar?* He glanced ahead and nothing, and then to his left and *mercy!* Perhaps the only interesting feature so far and it was only a few metres away. A ledge, about ten feet high, overhung a rocky hollow. Either side, it levelled out, forming a steep, grassy slope up to the top. As well as the shelter of the lip, there was also a shallow wall of rocks, like a parapet, comprised of seven rocks, three of which came up to waist height. Although not exceptionally tall, Slayne and Elisa considered them vital defensive support.

Timing was out of the window, as Jerome plucked up the courage to make his move across. And it couldn't have been better judged, because as soon as he'd taken his first step towards the cavern, another

thud!

drew his attention to exactly where he'd been resting, the flattened grass now strikingly punctured by an arrow. Another step, another

thud!

It was like someone was taking deliberate pot shots at him. Elisa, Slayne and Peter were almost at the hollow and it was a revelatory insight to think that Slayne and Elisa were probably already aware of that feature – and every other feature before – just in case of such an incident arising. He assumed that Peter, who was at the back of the pack, acted not upon instinct but as a follower.

He was nearly there and the barrage stopped just as he dived in. Elisa was quick to assist him to his feet, dust him down and check his wellbeing.

"That was close," Jerome mumbled, allowing a little satisfactory *I'm-still-alive* grin.

"Maybe a little too close," Peter added, his face not that far off sheer terror.

They all waited, giving themselves a little time to catch their breath and work out a plan of action.

Slayne and Peter were behind one of the three rocks each and Elisa, who had been on her own, now had Jerome with her.

Nevertheless, whether Jerome liked it or not, she had adopted a very maternal attitude towards him and she was happy having him there, as she rested an arm around his shoulders.

And that was important to her, to offer him some time of comfort because, as she peered over to Slayne, the truth became evident, *what were they going to do now?*

***

They had been waiting for no more than an hour before setting first sight upon the boy. However, that was first thing Cutler was curious about was that he certainly wasn't a boy, not anymore. But what piqued his attention most was that, against Baylin's word of him being untrained in the art of weaponry, he knew *exactly* how to handle himself. Cutler knew how to identify a warrior, slightly from his gait – the way certain muscles carried the body – but mainly his attitude to the weapon that he carried. An untrained individual would avoid making contact with it, every touch being followed by an uncomfortable glance down, whereas a proficient person may rest their hand upon it, allowing it to be as comfortable and as much a part of them as the hairs on their head.

He counted four, the 'boy' – *young man,* he modified – at the front, a woman, a more mature man behind her and another younger man at the back.

Arming his bow with an arrow from his quiver rested against the tree, he brought it up close to his face and pulled the string back.

He remembered, *just maim*. He enjoyed maiming just as much as killing. It was a far more effective way of winning in combat, he mused as he aimed down the arrow towards the *boy*.

He never got a chance to release though, as he saw him suddenly duck.

Another arrow?

He wondered what the intention was. He was sure that it wasn't one of his Lyrian companions. He was the only one with a bow. *Who was this mysterious attacker?*

Maybe it was Garrick, someone whom he had never worked with before, thinking he might get a lucky hit in. But he scratched that idea; they wanted him alive and *that* arrow was never going to be the *maiming* kind. Of course, the whole thing now required a change of plan, because they ceased to have the element of surprise.

***

Garrick, Baylin and Mythos watched from a distance. This location had been carefully picked because it offered good cover to an assailant, but very little to a defender, as well as offering a hugely diverse series of plans that could be branched off. For example, the unique feature that was an apparent place of cover, may well have offered just that, but it would leave the habitants of such at a complete disadvantage.

Garrick relished these moments – the art of combat. He lived for the thrill of it and he enjoyed racking his mind, searching for ways to overcome issues such as this, such as the one presented to him three years ago by The Reformation, such as the one he was going to eviscerate once and for all. He had to restore his name.

He spectated with pleasure, as the arrow shot by Jerome's head, protruding out from the tree. Seeing his fear and sudden action made his blood fire up. He obviously wasn't going to give up quickly. *Good.*

He wondered if it was a deliberate way of pushing the boy and his three fellow travellers into the trap, but then he felt an idea pinch him – a bad pinch – *those arrows look familiar.*

***

Jerome appreciated Elisa's warm touch, but it was enough now and he lightly finessed her arm away. He needed time to think, and that was difficult when he felt like a child. It was a horrid, sobering thought to think that whoever it was out there wanted him dead. It sent chills down his spine and just as he was recovering from the myriad of emotions, his Dark Whisperer jostled Its foul presence into sight.

At that point, he had been looking to his right towards Slayne, who was at the opposite side, when his eyes stopped upon a demon writhing in a ghostly haze. Instinctively, he did what he was now programmed to do and turned his eyes away so that he was looking at the left exit, just beyond Elisa. However, this time the vision wasn't what he expected; it was the angel.

Snapping back to Arthak, he suddenly remembered the angel, who helped him evade capture, and she was the same now. He flicked back to consider the other side again and the demon that inhabited not only remained, but also roared back at him. The message was well and truly understood, as he turned back to the angel, who was even more beautiful than before.

It was clear, and he didn't know exactly how he knew, but somehow someone – some*thing* – was going to attack from the angel's side.

Shifting past Elisa, and moving her away from the side, he withdrew his dirk and stood at the ready. He heard Slayne say, "Jerome, what are you doing?" but he was so focused that it sank into background noise.

Almost instantly, the angel moved to the side and as she did, a figure bounded round the side with his weapon ready for a lunge. With this joyous forewarning, he relished in his capacity to parry, which he executed with so much force that his attacker stumbled off balance. The look of surprise on his face tipped Jerome's confidence and he drove his weapon into the man's side and then kicked him off, driving him away until falling clumsily onto the ground. He thought that was it, but then suddenly an arrow shot into the collapsed body – *another familiar arrow.*

It came so natural to him and not one part of him writhed like he had during his *first kill.* He briefly wondered how much his mind had been desensitised and warped by the images presented by his Dark Whisperer. That, in itself, was a haunting idea; the prospect that he was losing his humanity one day at a time was not a thought he wished to dwell on, and not one that he was able to, before his cogitation was blunted by the beautiful angel dissolving into horror. All of her dreamlike aspects began peeling away, the light of her pacific aura blackening into the writhing demon, previously on the other side.

Again, instinctively he was forced to gaze the other side where the angel had now reappeared. He witnessed Elisa's perplexity, but ignored it.

"Slayne, your side!" he shouted.

Without hesitation, Slayne was on guard and a transitory second later he was in mid-block with a raging attacker. He fought with such beautiful elegance, such mastery.

"Jerome, what's going on?" Elisa snapped his attention.

Looking at her earnestly, he couldn't articulate a response as he fumbled his words.

She was about to try and get another answer out of him when he saw the angel revisit his side. He didn't fumble the words anymore. They came easy to him.

"Out of the way!"

Whether it was the force behind his voice or the fear in his eyes – or both – she let go as he soared towards the angel, dirk at the ready. However, this one was more ready than the last. His smooth shift around the edge almost caught Jerome off guard and now he wasn't ready.

A noticeable shift in his shoulder indicated an attack to Jerome's head, which he promptly blocked, shifting his blade horizontally and driving it upward. It was a disadvantage that he was in, and not one for which he hadn't prepared. Rather than just slipping his weapon away, he angled it vertically, forcing his opponent's blade down and into the trap of his hilt.

Locked in combat, the Lyrian pulled Jerome up close and raised his knee, driving it into his stomach.

Jerome spluttered – he wasn't ready for that – as he tumbled back, cracking his spine on the rock, which, ironically, had given him so much protection.

Sword freed, the Lyrian acted fast, drawing back and working up to plunge into Jerome when a magic bolt came flying over his head, striking him square between the eyes. His body went limp and his legs crumbled beneath his tense body.

Clutching his stomach, which was bubbling with cramp from muscles in spasm, Jerome shot a look behind and saw Elisa, breathing hard and still in the pose of attack. He tried to lever himself up, but along with a battered stomach, his back was alight with agony. Peter nipped past Elisa to aid his friend, who stood limply, buckled forward to ease his stomach, but grasping his back as well.

"Jerome," – Slayne sought his attention – "don't lose confidence." He felt better, but he was more concerned for Elisa.

They exchanged a look and a silent conversation followed.

"I'm sorry for shouting, Elisa. Thank you. You saved me."

"Anytime, Jerome."

Her soft, barely perceptible, smile in return eased his conscience, but his stomach was still in a tangle of pain and it took him by surprise, making him groan and cough.

***

Cutler had ordered three of his men to advance and flank the enemy. To his surprise and dismay they had all failed, although he couldn't see the individual battles, because of his placement above and behind the alcove.

When he had concluded that none of the three were going to return, he started to debate if where he was, in fact, was a good vantage point. *Nothing to be done now though!* He let the anger go and signalled three more men to approach. He prayed that they would have more luck.

***

"Boss!" initiated Baylin.

Garrick's gaze was firmly affixed on the skirmish, but the urgency in Baylin's voice caught his attention.

"We have company. King's Rangers, I believe. Three of them about fifty feet away." He pointed to a denser collection of trees behind.

"Damn! Damned Rangers of the Realm!" The vitriol spoke louder than his words, as he swiftly re-engaged his hunter-mode. "They couldn't have picked a worse time." But now it was a gruesome sarcasm that lined his throat, each word becoming drenched in it, as it travelled out past his lips. "Stay here." And the order was adhered to.

He was going to kill them. He was going to kill them all. And it would be bloody and desecrating and unbearable.

He had to find some way of alleviating his mood. And then it occurred to him … he felt thankful for their mistimed interruption … but *they* wouldn't.

***

All too soon the angel was back in vision and Jerome had barely recovered from the vicious blow to his stomach. No, the pain wasn't bursting his insides like it had before, but he was still bent double. He couldn't fight like this, but he needed to warn Slayne, Peter and Elisa of an unwelcome guest.

"There!" he muttered, his stomach tensing, bringing with it a flock of searing pain.

He was indicating Slayne's side and he was quick to step into position, but he hadn't realised that the angel was now on the other side, too. Elisa and Peter had moved him to the centre and now it was just Peter, defending alone.

"Peter, your side." Another tidal wave of pain ripped through his stomach as the words tensed his insides.

Cleverly, Peter had decided to back off. Rather than stepping into an unknown space in front, he pulled the enemy into his comfort zone. Jerome had never seen his friend fight, not from such a spectator's perspective. He fought well and Jerome wondered if he fought that well against him – or if he pulled back. A gentle smile lined his face as he remembered their early attempts at fighting. It seemed so long ago – and the smile was gone.

Peter's early take of the upper hand led to victory and the Dark Whisperer went back to quiet. Jerome's stomach had now settled and he returned to standing keeping a very sharp eye either side, but nothing, nothing but an aching silence.

***

A change of tack was required, Cutler thought, as he saw his three men go in and, ultimately, not return. *They must have help,* his arrogance peeping into visibility. With six men remaining, including himself, he needed to exercise control of this situation before it was just him.

He signalled the last lot to follow his lead as he made his way forward. Once in his new position, and confident that his men were also stationary, he made his presence known.

"We only want the boy!" he bellowed.

***

Jerome's blood ran ice-cold. They meant him, no doubt; he was the only one young enough to be called 'boy'. But what did they want from him? The cold blood, icing up his veins, then began to boil from the strain of being the centre of attention. He'd really only just recovered from the strike to his abdomen before this new level of discomfort was introduced. His first glance was to Peter, who eyed him back with the same puzzled look.

"Give us the boy, and everyone else will live!"

It was hard to hear any emotion over the loudness in his voice. Another hot and cold spell fluttered over him, but it wasn't because of the demand for him, it was because he was going to give himself up.

The panic in his eyes turned to resolve and immediately captured Elisa's attention. He was about to drift past her when she, for the second time, grasped his shoulders and made him face her.

"You're not thinking of going are you, Jerome?"

"It seems as though we don't have any more choice. We can't hold out here forever can we?"

"That's not the point. We hold out for as long as we can. I didn't come all this way with you just to watch you give yourself up."

"And I appreciate that. I appreciate *everything* that you … and Peter and Slayne, have done for me," – his eyes filled with sincerity and resolution – "but *I* didn't come all this way to watch my friends get killed. And if I have a chance to save you all then I will."

The honesty in his voice silenced her as he freed himself, but she found a response.

"You don't have to be a hero, Jerome."

Peter was about to stop Jerome when the voice called again, catching them both off guard.

"This is the last chance before we kill everyone!" The voice echoed unbidden through the winding barrens.

Peter had missed his window of opportunity as Jerome had already sauntered, unbeknownst, to the side and out.

***

Jerome's head was down as he turned the corner to the left, when his eyes caught hold of a pair of feet and then another pair just behind that. Instantly he flicked his head up and couldn't believe his eyes. Only a couple of feet in front, restrained by a sword at the neck, stood another similarly attired attacker. The man doing the restraining looked old, but it clearly wasn't a *decrepit* old – even though he had a white beard – it was an *experienced* old. At a complete loss on what to do, he just stood.

The old man moved his lips and mouthed a 'shh', of which Jerome took complete heed, but now he was still, and unable to speak. With a speed belying an old man, he whisked his sword down and battered the man on the back of the head, knocking him out. He then carefully lowered him to the floor, resting him against the steep angle of the slope.

Looking up, he indicated to move back under the shelter. Jerome promptly followed the command as he captured the sight of his friends once more. Their presence was an elixir and he drenched himself in it. And the sad faces that he had left behind turned to confusion. The old man behind, who was busy keeping his eyes all around, followed close behind until almost scooting Jerome in.

"Jerome?" a perplexed Peter said.

Jerome shrugged – a very relieved shrug. He hadn't been keen on going out there. But then he remembered *why* he was and, then, so did everyone else.

"Fair enough!" the bellowing voice boomed and that was it. Jerome fleetingly entertained the idea of going back out, just in case there was a chance of saviour for his friends, but he was stilled by the arm of the old man.

"They wouldn't spare anyone's life. These are Warriors of Lyre," the old man informed.

"Warriors of what?" questioned Jerome.

"A nasty bunch; I was only able to recognise them from a past experience."

Everyone looked confused and stared, speechless.

"My name is Percy and, although I'd like to get to know everyone's names, we should save the pleasantries for when people *don't* want us dead. Besides, more will be here, and tomorrow is a day I would very much like to see."

"What else do you know about these Warriors of Lyre?" Slayne asked, brought back to reality.

"From experience, they operate in groups of twelve."

"That leaves us with seven then—"

"Six," corrected Percy.

"Well done," Slayne said, an obvious remark towards Percy's age.

Percy dismissed Slayne's words – he didn't consider himself old; what man did? – and continued, "They will only improve in tactics. We need to have our wits about us."

Considering that Percy had only just met the group, he fulfilled the role of *leader* remarkably well.

He had arranged the defence as follows: Slayne and Jerome on the right hand side, Peter and he on the other and Elisa in the middle ready to supply magical back-up.

***

All five men had been signalled to continue the assault and Cutler removed himself from behind his vantage point, out into the openness of the barely-trod barrens. He was farthest back and he had his gaze solidly planted upon the alcove. He walked with care, gentle each time he had to rest a foot upon the uneven ground, and even gentler in lifting it up. Slowly he approached, but something caught the corner of his eye and he whisked his head round. He saw something, of that, he was sure, and it was niggling in his mind. *This is not good, whatever it is.*

Flitting from tree to tree, Cutler made his way to where he was convinced he had seen something. He glanced to the alcove to see the state of the attack and was surprised to see only three men approaching, two going for one side with the other on his own.

He returned his concentration back to discovering where the other two were, and also to locating the unknown figure. He wondered if there was some connection.

Using the mental map, which he had compiled while arranging this skirmish, he traced his way to where each man had been positioned.

There was nothing where the first man had been, at least nothing out of the ordinary. It was the same for the second location, but the third was different. There was the trampled ground, but a smattering of blood caught his eye and it told him with clarity, *this is* not *good*.

But before he could get a better look at the situation, he suddenly felt someone – someone small – jump on his back and move an arm – a little green arm – round his neck, holding still a very sharp knife.

"How many's more?" the goblin questioned, the soft, basic linguistic errors shining through.

Cutler's reticence to talk was met with a tightening of the green arm and a sheerer angle of the knife, which was now carving a little red notch into the skin over his neck.

"How many's?" continued the voice.

He was at a loss. The knife was sharp and the wielder clearly sharper.

"Three going in," he relinquished.

"Any more's waiting?"

He had never succumbed before, but the cutting blade of the knife forced more out. "No!"

"Why's you want the boy?"

"We have no interest in the boy," Cutler said, his tone rife with disdain.

"Then who's does?"

"Why?"

"Tells me!" forced the little green-skin, drawing another drop of blood from Cutler's neck.

"The Reformation!"

As quickly as the words were out, the arm, along with the knife, retracted. The weight of the figure was gone from his shoulders and he was left to look over the mayhem caused by the little individual.

He took a furtive glance behind, but as expected, there was no trace, no sign, of any living activity. It was a hard decision to make, but the only one that wasn't suicide was to abandon and revise a better plan.

He left making one promise, that payback would be sought and, more importantly, accomplished. He would find the *boy,* find his family, find his loved ones, and seek him out through any means necessary.

***

"Your side!" called Jerome back to Percy and Peter, pre-empted by the vision of the angel.

He stayed his eyes on them as they instantly became engaged with the emergence of an attacker. However, he was forced to turn about by a searing screech coming from behind. It stopped the second Jerome had turned and the demon, from which the screech originated, precipitously changed into the angel.

Oddly, it was something he'd grown used to, seeing these horrid delusions blending in with the natural surroundings, but seeing it in perspective behind Percy made him wonder how maddening it was. He brushed away the madness and armed himself next to Slayne. The attack was coming.

Indeed, shortly on from his premonition, a figure came round. Percy was right when his words 'they will only improve in tactics', rang in his ears. This person had skirted a good couple of feet away, and then, to Jerome's biggest fear, another crept round.

Facing them, were two of these Warriors of Lyre and they each looked as though they sought something more than just a mercenary mission, but savagery. Jerome quickly scanned them and their stances were perfect. They responded and moved with each other, their personal miens accounting for, and supporting, their fellow counterpart.

Jerome admired the symbiotic relationship, but then became fearfully aware of the flaws in his own stance. He was letting the fear get to him.

"Now remember what I've taught you, Jerome." Slayne's voice was a whisper, but it was a gloriously welcome whisper and he felt comfortable in the shadow of his mentor.

He forgot about whom he was fighting and concentrated on himself – turning his feet that minimal amount, to gain that little bit of extra balance or twisting the blade a touch more to instil a better, stronger arm locus. All these little instructions Slayne had supplied him with over the years of tutelage replaced *Jerome, the child* and welcomed back *Jerome, the adult,* the adept, the fighter – and hopefully, the survivor.

Slayne waited, forcing their first move, which they took in flawless unison, one step, one march. *So close,* Jerome thought, his nerves going through the roof. His palms were sweating and the dirk was slipping in his grip.

One more step closer was taken in complete silence and again without a single break in their defensive stance. Their weapons were touching now, as they stood poised, on the brink.

Jerome became convinced that he saw a gentle smirk rising from his aggressor and then it erupted, abrupt and manic, but at the same time, controlled and precise.

He was amidst three fine melee artists, and right now all he could do was to try and keep the attacks defended, and forgo any attempt to strike.

He wondered if Slayne would do better without him, but he averted that thought and took some solace that his logic was holding out, insofar that no attacks were getting through, even with sweaty palms and an over-worked adrenal gland. And he could see it frustrating his attacker. *Focus, Jerome. Focus.* It was only a matter of time though, before he made a mistake and his sword arm dropped a touch leaving a slight window of opportunity, which was taken unrelentingly.

His only choice, to avoid getting sliced, was a big shift to the side and *damn it!* His eyes closed, automatically. "One thing you absolutely mustn't do is close your eyes", Slayne had said, and the words rang in his ears as he berated himself and snapped them open again.

His focus was realigned to his aggressor, whose grin had returned and fortunately bringing with it an interim of calm. *He's playing with me. Fine!* Jerome made a mental stamp; abandoning all fear, *let's see who's playing, now*. He needed to make a few attacks, but he knew what to do…

Jerome raised his dirk against the Lyrian's sword. It looked small in comparison, but it offered much more play with much sharper handling properties – speed as opposed to strength, just like him; it offered a better fighting style for his relatively slight build.

He took after his mother in that respect. This time Jerome needed to initiate the combat and with a swish, he targeted the Lyrian's upper body. Even with a feigned shoulder movement, it was blocked and then riposted. This was as good a time as any as, rather than forcing a block against the strike, he moved his body down and thrust his blade behind the Lyrian's, pushing it in the same direction making it slam against the stony edge of the alcove, shooting off little bits of rock and dust.

"These are immune!" he heard Elisa shout from behind. *Immune to what?*

He hadn't time to think… Now he needed to regain posture. It was a surprise manoeuvre from Jerome, but this Lyrian was an expert and wouldn't let surprise detract from quick reflexes and good fighting.

In fact, the Lyrian was so quick – much quicker that Jerome expected – that he was already ready for another attack. *Oh damn, move!* Jerome was quick to act as the attack plummeted down and again his eyes closed. He sprung his eyes open; he needed concentration for this next bit. And then he was back on his feet, dirk at the ready and concentration at its optimum. The fear was no longer in his eyes and his palms were sweat-free.

Jerome waited; he needed to wait, to have patience, this next bit was so important.

Holding the Lyrian's gaze, he made a deliberate high thrust to encourage an upward block; he needed his sword out of the way.

He needed his sword out of the way, not only to avoid striking him, but also to allow the little stone a direct path to the Lyrian's eye.

This series of events he had planned. He needed something to shatter free some debris from the rocky edge – *the Lyrian's heavy sword;* he needed to duck and gain sight of a single piece – *a timed duck disguised as a reflex dodge from an attack;* and finally he needed the concentration to move the stone – not *have his eyes closed.*

The chunk went straight into the Lyrian's eye and his free hand followed. Jerome didn't delay as he drove his dirk into the exposed warrior. The principle was straightforward, but he forgot about his partner who was ready with a defence, which knocked his dirk down and out of his hands, just before he could lance the Lyrian.

All the confidence and pride, in which he had bestowed unto himself, was unduly reft from him and replaced with panic. The stone was only – and could only *ever* have been – a temporary window of opportunity and now he had failed. After all he had done what else could he do? His opponent was better than him.

The Lyrian had regained his composure and found no reason to hold off the execution. Nothing in his way, he made a decisive and punishingly clear retraction of his sword. Jerome watched as this man held his life totally in his hands, his power over him on display for the world to see. He closed his eyes, wincing from the imaginary pain and waited…

…And then he opened them, stunned that he was even able to. An awful lot had happened in that short time, too. For one thing, the Lyrian who was about to take his life away was now lying face down at his feet, an arrow sticking out of his back, directly beneath his head. And then it all made sense. He thought that the arrows were familiar – *Keldor.*

To his left, Slayne had just impaled his enemy. Jerome watched as he pulled his sword out, letting him slip lifelessly to the floor. The fatal wound to his chest was in such a place that allowed blood to spill out rigorously and pool out, expanding and filling all the imperceptible depressions of the grassy floor, staining each verdant blade several shades of vermillion.

"That leaves three," Slayne said, wiping the blood from his blade.

***

"Two," a hidden voice said, but Jerome knew who it was.

However before he caught sight of him another voice was audible. "None."

From behind a tree, about a dozen feet away, Keldor emerged, a subtle grin lining his face. A myriad of emotions whirled inside Jerome, a barely containable amount and then, just as his eyes began building for a downpour, Misto tiptoed around.

Jerome was not used to crying and he felt embarrassed, but he was quick to receive reassurance. And as he slowly started to recover the hold on his emotions, wiping the tears from his eyes with the back of his hand, he let loose a giggle. Keldor, Misto, Slayne, they all shared in that tranquil flash of humour and then they all calmed.

"You almost shot me," Jerome amusingly berated Keldor.

He laughed. "I needed to get you to safety… And I think we both know that I was nowhere near shooting you."

Keldor was right. If he wanted to hit him then he wouldn't have any trouble. "Well, you succeeded."

Keldor and Misto had not visited Alatacia much over the three years. It wasn't the life for a Ranger of the Realm to take *time off,* or for an exiled green-skin to *sit about.* They spent their time as the moderators of Aramyth, as wardens of the wild, as the secret unspoken, who worked without reward to keep everything *just-as-it-should-be,* and do it all without anyone knowing.

Peter, Elisa and Slayne who had both been introduced to Keldor and Misto, greeted each other and then all attention turned to Percy.

"A member of The Order?" Keldor extended his arm out to him.

Percy took it. "A Realm's Ranger. I never thought I'd see the day."

The invisible respect between the pair fluttered inside Jerome and he turned to Peter, who also had an equally ogling stare.

"Nor did I ever expect to see any magi of Alatacia," continued Percy as he hailed Slayne and Elisa.

Jerome and Peter had moved together, like the friends they were, and both shook Percy's hand. Although neither looked as veteran or as old as their cohorts, Percy showed no disrespect. Quite the reverse, he beamed with admiration.

"So what brings a member of The Order so far out?" Slayne asked.

"I am not travelling alone, but in answer to your question, I'm not sure what's out here. I could ask you the same thing. This isn't the usual activity I would expect in such remote climates."

Naturally, all eyes fell to Jerome, and then he realised that he'd yet to give any reason as to why they were walking, and he suddenly flushed, all the blood roiling his insides. He couldn't let them know the truth.

They would think he was mad. Perhaps he *was* mad.

"The queen said I should go, but I'm still not sure why…" It was a feeble lie and he was convinced that it wouldn't hold. But what he didn't know, and could never sense from over his own self-consciousness, was that everyone knew something was wrong, and he had their full support.

He was in the company of friends.

***

Wiping the blood from his weapon, Garrick returned to the side of Baylin and Mythos. He felt better, his nihilistic attitude throbbing from the kills, but the frustrating failure brought him straight back to anger.

"Aramyth's finest, Baylin?"

Baylin was speechless and Garrick left him to churn.

"They had unforeseen help," Mythos interrupted.

"So it seems, even with all that serum I gave them. But our old friend is back." Garrick smiled.

***

Percy led them away from the alcove, about hundred or so feet, to where Galliana and Thermion had been waiting.

"I bring friends," Percy announced, on the approach.

"Glad to see you made it, old man," Thermion said, poking his head up, jocularity infused in his tone. Although, he hadn't realised quite how many friends he was bringing as he composed himself.

"How is she?" Percy whispered quietly to Thermion.

"Nervous, but staying strong. Can we trust them?"

"With my life," avowed Percy.

With his confirmation, Thermion immediately relaxed and motioned to behind the tree, encouraging Galliana out.

***

It was very uncomfortable suddenly being confronted by so many strangers, but she held her nerve and the truth was that everyone was on edge, everyone except Slayne, who was, if anything eager.

However nervous, they all remained impassive, everyone except one: Jerome.

She was – Jerome couldn't find words to describe her, but as his mind saw it – somewhere between Heaven and beyond.

As she glanced – furtive, penetrating glances – from face to face, she caught his, and it was as though she could see inside him, touching his soul and all that was contained within.

He saw her brown hair, wavy, draped back behind her left side, spilling over her right, following the contours of her—

He couldn't look any longer. He *couldn't!*

Her every curve, every feminine feature and texture was arresting him.

240

He felt his heart like he had never felt it before, pounding, pounding so hard it could bash its way out of his chest – as though it had never properly worked until this moment.

Then he realised his breathing had increased, undoubtedly to account for his *pounding, pounding* heart.

And then he was powerless against her redolent design, but *something* in him turned his gaze down – his shame, his shame that his eyes were still slightly red from his earlier tears, but most of all, the shame of his Dark Whisperer.

The shame that he was plagued … cursed.

It made him feel untouchable … unlovable.

Unloved.

And even though he was looking at the ground, trying hard to eradicate his nerves and generally regain some composure, he couldn't escape her scrutiny. He *couldn't!*

Her face was etched forever on his mind, and projected out everywhere, brazenly onto the canvas of the world.

"Something bothering you?" Peter said, a little nudge.

His voice was steady and undeterred and Jerome wished, *wished* he could tell Peter the truth, but with every descending degree of the sun, everything became so much harder, so much more excruciating. And inescapable.

"I'm fine. Just – just still recovering from … back there." He insincerely flashed his hand behind, indicating where they had been, but he remained focused at the ground.

Peter knew there was more, and he hoped his friend would open up to him, sometime, but it would be when he was ready.

"Whenever you need me, Jerome, I'll be here for you." That was all that needed to be said.

Nerves under control and breathing calm, Jerome looked up and assessed the new party. It still hadn't been addressed or fully understood why they were all out here, but it seemed everyone had a taciturn grasp and for reasons, outside of anyone's control, they were all here to support, and to be supported. This day would see the last part of Aramyth before the Eastern Wastes – the Marchlands – the edge of the world, as they knew it.

He caught Galliana's eyes once more, but this time it was her who took a stealthy look away. Why? He couldn't be sure, but this young, quiet, tormented man would never be the same again...

Chapter X
Land's End, Hell Begins

Marston was the very last remnant of human civilisation before being in the folds of the Marchlands. In its heyday, Marston would have served a very similar purpose to Melfall, both on the borders, both with few inhabitants and both inundated with travellers all seeking fame, and most seeking its elusive counterpart, fortune.

Now, it was just a myth expressed through bedtime stories or campfire tales, told by descendants – told to keep the history alive. But, with evening upon them, as they moved through the final fragments of humankind, they could see that very little, outside of the anamnesis, existed.

Of note, the only significant structures were the old inn, which was the only complete building, a few crumbling walls and a solemn altar, but no church. The party headed inside the nameless old inn to make use of the shelter.

Inside, it became clear that over the years since its demise this old inn had received relatively recent, structural repair, a token of the fact that travellers and adventurers would take care of the last standing structure between Aramyth and the miles of nothingness.

It was far from perfect, but it was nice to know and see such commendable attitude existed among kindred spirits.

His rumination was abruptly disturbed by Keldor picking up a knocked over table and assorted chairs and stools.

"This should do 'til morning," Keldor said, addressing the crowd, examining the dusty, cobwebbed room. "I think we should each find a room upstairs and get some rest; this may be our last chance. I'll take first watch."

Jerome listened and it made sense to him and from the actions of the rest, it seemed everyone else thought the same.

It was a big building and as they each made their way to separate rooms, 'goodnight's were met with smiles. It was as though the edge of the world brought this diligent tribe of strangers together.

But as Jerome lay lonely on the rickety bed in his room, he couldn't sleep. It made him smile, for it simply couldn't get any worse. He tossed and turned, thought of that girl – somewhere between Heaven and beyond – and once she was in his head, she was immovable. He wondered if Peter had the same yearning for Garveya. Then he thought about *her* again.

And with a head full of thoughts, he crept out of bed, out the room, down the corridor and down the stairs to the main room. With no sign of Keldor, he opened the door and was straight away apprehended.

"Jerome." Keldor's voice was very loud. Jerome let out a sigh of relief. "What are you doing up? It's only been an hour, you must be exhausted."

Keldor had made himself a little post outside. Although, as Jerome saw, it looked a lot more than it was at first glance, because he had all of his weapons out – some resting against the wall, some laid flat on the floor – when, actually, all it really was, was a low stool, surrounded by an arsenal. Jerome still wondered how he carried it all around. And did all that extra weight bother him?

Closing the door behind him, Jerome said, "I can't sleep."

"I worry about you," Keldor said.

He ignored that. "I haven't thanked you yet, but … thank you for saving me."

"You know I would never have let anything happen to you. I think you fought well."

Compliments from Keldor were few and far between. "You mean you saw the whole thing?"

"I did. I had to get better position from the beginning, but yes."

"Why didn't you kill him earlier?" There was a trace of frustration in Jerome's voice.

Taking a breath, Keldor answered. "Is that really what you would have wanted?"

"… Yes." His shoulders slumped and his head dropped.

"Are you ashamed?"

Jerome was unresponsive to the question.

"Listen, *listen!*"

Jerome snapped his head up at the command. "You won that battle today. Your brains and your skill won it. It was bad luck, that's all.

"I don't know how, but you've found yourself caught up in the middle of something very strange. And, although I can't begin to imagine what this Reformation wants with you, I *can* tell you that they'll have to get through me first. And I'm sure most people in there," – Keldor indicated the inn – "would do the same. Look around, how many people do you know who would follow someone here?"

Pause. "I can think of quite a few." And Jerome smiled.

Then so did Keldor.

"Where's Misto? You two have become quite the couple."

"I would prefer duo," Keldor drolly rebuffed. "He's out there somewhere, doing his thing. Anyway, he'll stay around while you keep watch; he doesn't sleep very much at all." Keldor grabbed his weapons and sauntered inside, maybe even a little disgruntled at his green-skin's ability to sleep less than him.

***

Jerome had no idea how long he'd been outside, minutes, hours. He was too caught up in his own thoughts to care, but the only real relief he had been permitted was a temporary reprieve from the visions of his Dark Whisperer. It allowed him the freedom to glance up at the moon and watch as groups of clouds passed over and then continued their sky voyage on to reveal an even brighter moon, its light blooming and blossoming into the coruscant night.

"It's Jerome, yes?" A female voice took him by surprise.

He whipped his head round. *Oh no,* his regular, relaxed breathing shot up twenty-fold and his head hit the metaphorical clouds that he was only just watching, *it's her.*

"Y-yes," he stuttered.

"I can't sleep," she said.

Offer her your chair. Where did that come from? He wondered, rather, he implored. He already had enough on his plate: a Dark Whisperer, half of Aramyth's most deadly after him, The Reformation, a missing mother, being a magus who can barely use magic… The last thing he needed was a *conscience.*

He stood up and said, "Would you like to sit down?" indicating the stool.

"I can't stay still. I think I'd like to go for a walk."

"Nice night for it," he said, and she looked at him… "Oh, you mean with me?" he spluttered, giving his new conscience a quick bash round the head.

She chuckled and he helped his battered conscience back onto its feet. But beneath her chuckle he noticed that it masked some sadness. He could tell, because he felt the exact same; every laugh and smile covered a truth that Jerome thought too horrific to unveil.

They began walking.

"I'm at a loss," he said. "You know my name, but I don't know yours."

"I asked – I think his name is Slayne – your mentor."

"Oh, what has he told you?" *Maybe slightly blunt,* Jerome's conscience working over-time.

"This and that. So what brings you out this way? It seems you know where you're going."

"It's complicated." His concise response cut short the conversation, but keen to carry on talking, he tried a different tack. "Tell me about yourself, where do you live?"

His naive conscience may have produced a direct question, but she was happy to answer, *fortunately,* he thought, threatening his new inner being with a clenched, losing-my-patience fist.

"I used to live in Gatelock. My father," she snatched a quick breath – a *painful* breath – "used to work in the concordium, but he went missing…" She recited the curtailed story to Jerome, who listened intently. The tears that she had spilled before did not come to the surface, but she still found herself trying to remain in control of her breath.

"That's awful. I-I don't … I'm sorry. So that's why you're here?"

"I don't know why I'm here. I'm scared, I can't tell anyone anything. No one ever seems the right person to tell."

"And I am?" His conscience's scrupulous hands were held avidly in the prayer position, but were suddenly dropped by a thunderous roar coming from the side, coming from his Dark Whisperer. Promptly he spun his head, but what surprised him more was that Galliana copied him, as if privy to the same abhorrent noise. And then their heads turned back, becoming a *double take,* looking deep into either one's eyes, with the realisation of each other's Dark Whisperer. But to finish, the comedic *double take* became a fearsome *triple take,* as they whipped back round to the side.

"Err … Jerome." She was first to speak, but he was thinking the very same.

Plague bringers, dozens of them, heading their way.

In lackadaisical comfort, they had walked to where the lonely church altar stood, held firm by the solid, and very much intact, foundations, a fair distance away from the inn. Jerome turned back to her and then, effectively, manned up.

"I need you to do as I say." His tone was sincere, but calm and collected. In contrast she was very much out of her comfort zone and all her movements were snappy and hysterical. It was odd, but he hadn't been aware of how fast his heart had been beating. It was only now, with combat lingering on the horizon, that he realised himself to be more comfortable preparing for battle than talking to a woman – not just any woman though, a very special woman.

From another direction out of the pitch marched another load of plague bringers. At least, that's what he thought they were; he couldn't be sure, and then he didn't care. They were surrounded, any chance of escape wholly extinguished.

Frantically, Jerome dredged over scenarios and strategies, working through endgames and, it was hard to admit, but they all had less than satisfactory outcomes. However, the best plan was use the altar and hope that the plague bringers would filter round the sides, giving them more chance to fend off and, fingers crossed, hope they're stupid enough not to crawl over the top.

"Stay with me." Jerome encouraged her towards the altar. "I need you to keep eyes around. We just need to hold them off until everyone else arrives."

"How will they know?"

Misto, maybe, he hoped. *Best not say anything to provoke false hope.*

The gap was closing fast and Jerome was ever more fearful. He started to remind himself of his first encounter with these things, and how much the black blood stuck to his hands. Confidence waning and his mind conceding against troubling memories, he lowered his dirk, but something made Galliana reach out – for hope, for *something* – and touch him on the shoulder.

And it was as though the stars had fallen into alignment, as though he'd been sprinkled with light fantastic. He reversed the feeble clasp of his dirk, as well as his attitude of the situation.

It wasn't pleasant as he ran the blade through the soft, fleshy middle of the first plague bringer; it wasn't meant to be, but as he completed the execution he became very aware of Galliana behind him. What would she think of him doing that? He passed the thought on as something to worry about *if* he would get a chance to think about it – if they made it out alive.

It stumbled back, pushing against the mindless mob behind and then crumbling to the, quite intricate and ornate, foundations of the ex-church.

"Jerome, they're getting close." Galliana's words may have brought bad news, but it was his panacea – *she* was his panacea – and his weapon came to life. He was able to hold them off for now, but his stamina wouldn't last forever, and it didn't look like the plague bringers' numbers were dwindling.

***

"Quick, must go, Jerome in trouble." Misto was stood in the open door of Keldor's room, rather the room that Keldor had deemed his. It didn't take much to rouse him from his sleep. He didn't even think he actually slept anymore, able to get what he needed, but always teetering on the edge of sleep, just in case of moments like these, when he could snap out of it.

"Jerome? Where?" Grabbing a sword, bow and quiver. Nothing else was important.

"And a girl, by the church," Misto added.

"Jerome and a girl? Good on him. Go and wake everyone else."

"You goes and wake everyone else, I found him."

"Oh, really? *Are you going to do this now?*"

"Absolutely." Misto's eyes said it all.

With supreme vigour, Keldor opened his mouth and pulled in a massive lungful of air. Channelling all the frustration acquired from Misto, he opened his mouth and pounded out the words, "Attack out front!"

***

Surrounded by innumerable corpses and a tiring arm, he remembered his training and thanked Slayne as he slipped the dirk into his other hand, giving him a new lease of energy. He had been keeping an eye on the inn since the start, hoping that backup would arrive.

The battle-rage, like a bubbling torrent, was coursing through him as he tore limb from limb, but he was continually drawn to focus upon what these things were. He watched and was reminded of their nocuous touch, as they passed flourishing, living greenery, to see each leaf wither and die. To bear witness as *life* was ripped from every green pore. It made him wither inside just to think of it. But maybe that was what attracted these things? Maybe it was them; them and their beautiful, fresh, effervescent *life* acting like a homing beacon, summoning up all the creatures from the abhorrent stomach of Hell.

He became even more convinced when, from over the sea of the mindless mob, he saw them begin to curb away and head towards the inn, which was thankfully spilling out his friends: Peter, Slayne, Keldor, Misto, Elisa, Percy and ... the man with whom Galliana was obviously involved.

No! Now was not the time to have a crisis of character, he ordered himself. This was good, *surely,* and to add, he was finally beginning to make a dent in the endless waves of these hellions.

It was like a postponed, yet ever-building, eruption, watching his companions burst through the enemy lines allowing him time to rest after – Heaven only knows – how many he'd killed.

As the last fell and the dust settled, all that remained, outside of the thrumming drone still hazing the air, was an encircled mass of gruesome dead.

Jerome had an instinctive feeling to comfort Galliana, but when he turned to see her, her ... man, was holding her hands and ... doing all the comforting.

He turned away, pushed away by the feelings of being superseded, discarded, forgotten. Maybe he was being over-dramatic, but this horrid feeling dancing in the pit of his stomach was so real, so much stronger than the acid already inside; it was trying to burst its way out, rattling through every index of him, growing more frantic with every failed attempt to escape.

"Hey, how are you?" Peter's refreshing voice broke his nightmare. He undervalued it massively, *and* him. He felt like he hadn't seen him enough in Alatacia.

"Alive, but that's about all any of us can hope for."

"Well, that's *one* way of looking at it," Peter said, taken a little aback at Jerome's pessimism. "I hope you're not like this after every fight."

The injected humour deepened his young smile lines, but as he turned back to Galliana, he realised that it was just another fake smile, one of the many thousands, no doubt, that he had pasted on his face to pacify the loved ones around him. And then he realised he *still* didn't know her name...

***

With only a few more hours until daylight, they all headed back inside the inn and slept, except for Slayne, who kept watch – *inside.*

Although sleeping was the last thing any of them actually did. Elisa, Keldor, Misto and Percy, knew stories of what was beyond Marston and it wasn't sleep worthy material.

Galliana and Thermion talked, Peter was busy in telepathic conversation with Garveya and Jerome wasn't even tired. Now to add to his new found conscience, his Dark Whisperer, the bounty on his head that half of Aramyth's most deadly were looking to claim, The Reformation, his missing mother, his ineptitude at magic, his *conscience* and ... *Oh!* the heavens had released their evil grip and let rain a universe of suffering upon him, as now, on top of everything else, he was smitten. And the aching that tried so hard to escape him before trickled down his face, and into the old, used pillows below.

***

Between the nine of them they had enough food supplied for a hearty breakfast – hearty may have been the wrong word, as it was mostly bread, salted meat and water, but there was lots of it. Galliana caught Jerome's eye early on. She looked eager to talk to him, but he tried to block her out of his morning thoughts – failing miserably, of course – as she had dominated his whole night. Come to think of it, he hadn't spent much time, after meeting her, thinking of anything else. Occasionally he would think about his mother, seldom did he spare a thought for his 'one day' magical prowess – it gave him a soft internal flutter, but little more – infrequently did he pore over where his Dark Whisperer might actually be taking him – maybe he would give It a name –, but he couldn't take his mind off her. She was just there, in every bit of everything.

Outside, the morning breeze was strong and crisp, but refreshing. The bodies that had been stacked morbidly on top of each other had all but disintegrated. The tattered excuse for clothes was all that remained and even *they* had almost all gone, picked up by the strong current of the mighty wind and fluttered away.

It was deathly quiet as they waited, stood like children on the desecrated remnants of a moribund world. And it was as

though his Dark Whisperer knew that he was ready – receptive –
for new instructions as It appeared, beckoning him forth.

***

Eastward bound from Marston, and it wasn't long before the last
relic of humanity was no longer visible. In the distance were the
sheer peaks of the Burning Bluffs, jutting out ominously,
bleaching the land with a leaden saturninity.

Also, the land that was so fertile and green, which, in its
barely-touched state, rolled with a blanket of wild grassland,
suddenly stopped and became dry and arid, ruinous.

Jerome stood on the boundary, behind him the lush,
flourishing display of life, ahead of him the barren, expired
Marchlands. Looking along the edge, the anathema didn't stop
and although the line was scruffy and uneven, it was perceptibly
straight as it continued into the horizon, defining the clear break
between what was seemingly good and pure and what was evil
and tainted; the quietus slowly creeping forth, consuming, an
insatiable hunger, an unquenchable thirst.

Looking up, the sky reflected the land beneath. They saw all
the rippling, billowing features of the sky cease in perfect
alignment with the eating death beneath. But it wasn't hot. Even
though the sun's rays were uninterrupted, it was like it had no
essence, no power left in its empyrean home, deep in the sky.

As they walked, the party reorganised itself over and over,
forming little pockets – duos, trios – which conversed, taking
shelter in each other's *life*.

***

"Do you know what's ahead, Percy?" Slayne had found him-self
quite familiar with Percy.

"I know little beyond Marston. I believe that mountainous
region," – he indicated ahead – "to be known as the Burning
Bluffs, so called by apparitions – people coated in fire –
running, escaping … something. I don't know how much truth

there is in that. I don't like to think of it, but I look around and feel … pain."

"You and me both."

And they walked.

**

Both women, Galliana and Elisa walked together.

"How long have you known Jerome?" asked Galliana, eager to break the monotony.

"A little over three years now."

"How did you two meet?" she said, continuing the inquisition.

Elisa was going to comment on why she was so interested, but chose instead to answer her question. "I found him alone, lost, looking for his mother… He's always been quiet. He hides himself, keeps himself wrapped up in his thoughts. I know, because occasionally he drops the mask and I know I see good, but I couldn't begin to tell you what keeps him occupied though."

"I think I may have an idea." Galliana's response – which implied a deeper, more knowing, knowledge about Jerome than Elisa (someone who'd known him for three years now) – roused no reply and they continued in comfortable quiet.

Elisa didn't question how Galliana might know.

Elisa didn't care that her own knowledge was surpassed.

Elisa cared only that *someone* might be able to release Jerome from his solitude.

**

Keldor and Misto always walked together. Keldor still felt ashamed about his original behaviour towards Misto, but no grudge was held. They had formed an unwritten bond that, with every quiet step took, and taken, only strengthened.

**

Peter walked mostly on his own and in silence, at least an auditory silence. Inside, he was busy enjoying his telepathic link with Garveya, and was mid-conversation when he was interrupted.

"I see you always looking so calm," Thermion said, catching up.

It was impossible to place blame for an interruption when you're having a non-verbal exchange. "I have someone very special to keep me calm," Peter answered him.

"God?"

Peter chuckled. "Goddess, maybe."

"I'm not sure I understand," Thermion retreated.

"Sometimes, neither do I."

And Peter continued with Garveya.

***

Jerome's solitude was anything but dull. The constant correction offered to him by his Dark Whisperer – which he had still to name – had become more subtle, the bleeding of a wound or the twisting of a knife, and he followed, keen to finally unravel this mystery. But there was something else. For some reason, after the morning's unrelenting obsession with Galliana, he thought about his mother. He wondered how much he had changed – if at all – and what she would say. These were scary thoughts, but it was wondering if she would actually be waiting at the end, which occupied his headspace.

They headed forth, eating up the distance between them and the Burning Bluffs.

***

Within the monolithic juts of the Burning Bluffs, the most terrifying thing became its sheer scope. Each of the intrepid nine had all geared themselves up, but it wasn't until they were inside, under its canopy, completely in the play of its hands, that the fear could be really understood. The minutes and hours ticked over, every second not allowing a single, solitary flash of release. This was its game. And no matter how much they didn't want to play, little did they know, that was exactly what they were doing.

Unhindered by the clear sky, the man in the moon beamed down malevolent mischief and however tired they were, not one was inclined to stop and rest.

With every twist and turn through the blustery, whistling cliffs and fissures they were wrought by evil, but they made it out of the mountains of madness and so began the Marchlands.

Then, the echoing sounds of crying captured their attention, making them turn and, littered all over the Bluffs, in stark contrast to the night, were thousands of people, dowsed in fire, burning, falling, dying. The flickering conflagration of bittersweet oranges and dazzling yellows danced, twining around the immolated, masking a pain most horrible. Among the shrieks, indistinguishable words clawed their way through the fire, ricocheting around their ears, playing mental images and then—

...

Just the bleak graveyard of an untold number of people remained. The moon's mischievous grin had returned to a tender ember in the sky, and they rested.

**

The sun's deadened rays were enough to pierce Jerome's thin eyelids and he opened his eyes. Everyone had their own separate routines to wake themselves, whether that shaking off the tiredness or taking a more placid approach and just stretching it away. Whatever methodology they employed, they all indulged in some food and water.

"Jerome," Keldor said, summoning him over.

Jerome shuffled over, a piece of salted meat in his hand, a piece of bread being chewed up in his mouth.

"I don't know if you know anything about what's on from here?"

He shook his head, as he continued to chew on the piece of bread, while stuffing in a morsel of salted meat.

"I didn't feel it necessary to mention anything before, and although I'm not overly familiar, my predecessors have passed down information to me, and other Rangers of the Realm, should I ever find myself here, and … well, as you can see, I'm here."

Jerome was busy eating, but listening intently.

"Those mountains," he waved his hands forward, "just beyond them is the old city of Verilis. People call it The Dark Realm. Not sure why. It's dead now, destroyed … 'by a blast from the heavens'," he said, as if reciting, "or so they say. It's plagued now – that could mean anything – but I just thought you should know. At the rate we're travelling we should be there just after noon. Anyway, finish eating."

Jerome swiftly said, "Hang-goo," – *his mouth's full,* Keldor humoured – not wanting him to go unthanked, and then swallowed, "…for telling me."

***

True to Keldor's word, they were stood at the base of the huge cliff face at almost the exact time he said they would. Splitting it down the middle was an enormous fissure, which, at the top, looked like a small crack, but at the base, was a monstrous opening. If Jerome thought hard enough, he could compare it to the great maw of Hell, open-wide and gaping, tempting any stray souls in. He didn't need tempting though. He had all the encouragement he needed, courtesy of his Dark Whisperer that created angelic visions just before the hell-mouth.

It was cold between the sheer stone crags and, in surreal truth, the walls appeared to ache, reaching out with icy hands and sapping all happiness away, but they pressed on, spurred on by each other, not prepared to give in or give up. Time became nothing and each step began to blend in with the last, but soon they saw the light at the end of the tunnel, piercing the gloom.

***

It was like a huge basin, the cliff edge surrounding them like a prison. It was desolate and, not only was there no sign of a city, there was not even a glimpse that anything had existed here for a very, very long time, except one thing, a lone spire poking out of the ground. Jerome wouldn't have noticed it, had his Dark Whisperer not brought it to attention. Nevertheless it had, and the party, as always, followed behind.

Despite the fact that any degree of humanity existing here would be considered rare, this looked especially odd. The spire was at a very slight tilt and as they neared everything became clear. This was the very top part of a steeple. The rest – who knows? – was somewhere beneath.

Now that they were close enough, they saw it to be the upper aspect of an arsenal tower, but with a centre point which had a circular, sharp and pointed roof. There was a strong, riveted wooden door that was very slightly below ground level, but looked as though it had been opened.

"This is where we're going?" asked Slayne, who seemed very dubious. The emotion was mirrored by everyone, except Galliana, who looked sure that this was the right path.

Jerome nodded and Slayne began to prise open the door. Once he had shifted the door past the ground level and, indeed, past its initial stiffness, it opened with relative ease, with the final push slamming it against the stony architecture of the tower.

The sound carried throughout the gigantic basin, resonating and reverberating off each aching, *aching* cliff. But there was nothing alive to scare, except them, and it made them realise just how small they were in contrast to the stark barrenness.

Jerome gave his fellow travellers a *sorry* look, before entering. The darkness made everything all the more worse, drawing perfect attention to each breath and every movement.

It was a spiral staircase, which carried on going down, down, ever more down.

Behind, they heard the door slam shut. With a brief pause to analyse and conclude – who knows? – they continued.

Down…

Chapter XI
Welcome to The Dark Realm

Then they were at the base. The steps stopped and then, somehow, light bubbled into reality. Jerome pushed open the bottom door and stepped out into Verilis, The Dark Realm.

The shocking clarity stunned him. It was a city. It was a city, with buildings and roads and signs. He looked at the building from where he'd emerged and saw it to be a garrison. The steeple carried on up into the extremely high ceiling, but he was enticed back to marvel the scale of this lost city.

It was the abundance of light that really piqued Jerome's mind. There was no direct – or even discernible *indirect* – light source, but the place was lit up like day, just without the vibrancy. It was as though a very thin, blue film had been painted over everything, stripping away all the real depth and textures, leaving it cold and haunted.

The ceiling looked composed of stone and resembled what a mountainous region might look like if viewed from above … in reverse. The surrealism came when noticing that some of the higher buildings seamlessly melded in with the upside-down stone mountains, creating new and strange caves and grottos. Jerome imagined these to be dotted throughout this weird and fantastic realm, buried forever beneath the annals of history.

But they weren't going to be alone down here. He felt the subtle nuances of life creeping into the well of understanding. It was abounding, scuttling below the surface, rumbling within the walls and, then, the earth began to tremor: once, then twice.

Something – something *big* – was bashing its way to them, nearing with every calamitous quake.

Jerome turned to see Keldor, Elisa, Misto, Slayne, Percy and Peter – Galliana and Thermion he assumed were still to break out of the barren garrison – when he heard something blast out behind him.

It was more the sound of collapsing buildings, yet there were those clouds of dust – agitatedly awoken from a long slumber – and they floated, expanding, into his periphery.

But it was the faces of those in his party, watching them all slowly look up, seeing the terror seep into every inch of skin, that brought the demon into reality and he turned.

Everything felt slow.

Twisting his body, he saw it.

Jerome saw what he thought to be feet – it was using them as feet. Its body was black, a shiny shell with two prong-like claws curling and stabbing through the cobbled street ahead. Then he saw, on the other side, another set of claws, also piercing the cobbled road as though it were butter. Sweeping behind were a number of tentacles – their gruesome sound as they slapped and lapped over each other turned his stomach.

He was just about to look at its head – if it was going to be that simple – when a thick, many-jointed – *dis*jointed – *thing,* which he took to be an arm, swung for him.

With fleetness of foot, Jerome lunged sideways and hit the ground before *it* hit him, but he still felt it, the hard-steel muscle of the monster – beast, demon, *thing* –, the whump as it drove through the empty space, distorting the air as it moved.

Face down, Jerome's head firmly pressed against the cold floor, the beast let loose a gigantic shriek. It was clearly angry that it had missed, but Jerome got the impression that it wasn't going to surrender itself just yet. He rolled over, realising that he was at a great disadvantage, and just in time as plummeting towards him was another one of its – *eight?* – arms.

Although clear that they were arms, there were massive differences. Outside of the fact that it was a colossus and every part of it was gargantuan, the arms seemingly had two functioning elbow joints and from the second protruded another smaller – still giant – limb.

From the way the finger-like appendages were long, he thought them to be primarily used for grabbing and restraining, but the other one, which was clearly used for its *bashing power* – death a most likely outcome – was fast coming down towards him and he rolled over again. It shyly missed him.

But it did hit the ground.

And the ground was shattered beneath its thunderous blow, churning up the stone street, bouncing Jerome up and then landing him, hard, back down.

He barely noticed his shoulder popping out, and back in, above the dread, but as he lurched onto his haunches, pain tore through him.

***

Galliana was the last to emerge into the cerulean, underground city and the last to clap eyes on the huge beast.

She saw Jerome as he turned away, and the party, who were all static, yet it wasn't until she saw the nearest of the beast's huge, colourless arms almost crash into Jerome that everyone began starting to form up and act.

Her heart hit the roof of her mouth, as she saw him hit the ground and then roll over, making a near miss of the downward smash from the monstrous giant.

Keldor unhooked his bow and was ducked behind a near boulder, a creation from the catastrophe this thing had brought.

He fired arrow after arrow, forcing its attention and when a strike came towards him, Keldor jumped and rolled away from the boulder. It crushed into a million pieces beneath its heinous strength. Misto was ready and as the arm hammered through the slab, he latched on, driving his dagger firmly through a natural break in the armoured shell.

It howled and flung its arm up, taking Misto with it.

***

Slayne and Peter moved round to support Jerome and help him to his feet and hold his footing. Slayne held him up one side, while Peter, unbeknownst, gripped his bad shoulder.

And Jerome spluttered, "Badshoulderbadshoulder!"

Moving his grip down behind Jerome's back, Peter quickly and apologetically muttered, "Oh, sorry,"

"Are you able to fight?" Slayne interjected, to the point, no time for 'are you all right's?

Jerome nodded. "Just need my weapon. Peter?"

Peter, eager to make up for landing on his friend's bad shoulder, held Jerome's scabbard, while he outdrew his dirk. It was always going to be difficult with either arm disabled, but because he had his scabbard affixed to his right side – still favouring his left arm – his right hand would stop the sheath from moving, allowing the dirk to come out freely. And as it was his right shoulder that was now defunct, it was down to Peter to help him.

Green-skin-included, the monster lurched back, releasing another pain-stricken howl, giving them another few moments to get ready and assemble some form of offensive.

* * *

Galliana had remained, for the most part, totally stationary. Without any fighting experience, she could do little more than watch as the demon writhed and attacked.

She felt so tiny in comparison that nothing else began to matter. She daren't turn back for her evil visions would forever plague her. Although for whatever reason, they had lessened somewhat since meeting Jerome.

She could only guess that both his and her visions were in some way connected, both searching and leading them to a common goal.

Silhouetted by the colossus, she wondered if that was why she felt an affinity for Jerome. Was it that? Or was it just *him?* Either way, she couldn't take her eyes off him. She felt like she was betraying Thermion, after everything he had done for her, being there at every turn, supporting her, encouraging her, but something just wasn't *right* about him.

Elisa saw her, motionless and exposed. Grabbing her arm, which felt cold – *freezing* – even through her coat, she pulled her behind one of the newer piles of rubble and kept her there.

And from there, she began conjuring, mounting a magical offensive.

Percy and Thermion, although still repelling poles, knew each other's styles. They knew how the other fought, how they worked … and that was a strong advantage in combat. They carefully surveyed the battlefield: Slayne, Peter and Jerome were to the left, Keldor and Misto the right. They decided to hold the centre, with Elisa behind, magic ballistics piercing overhead.

***

In mid-swing, Misto kept his purchase on the dagger with both hands, as he was swung back and forth and side to side. The beast continued lashing, but eventually stopped as it became clear that the little goblin wasn't going to budge. The beast accepted its new addition, but the moment it stopped, Misto took the opportunity to stab his secondary knife into another break in its hard crust. Another wail and Misto was quickly travelling again, but this time he had double the support.

Keldor had, meanwhile, regained his posture and had already started firing arrows furiously at the wailing beast. Even for him, trying to accurately puncture the tough outer shell was proving difficult. Every arrow kept bouncing off and landing ineffectively on the floor.

Maybe he should try the Misto way of doing things?

But quickly disregarded the idea.

***

Another strike in Jerome's direction caused all three to duck, but Slayne took the opportunity to get a better position and he bent forward and sprinted under and past the prong-footed legs of the beast – as though it were a huge arch – to the flaying tentacles at the back. Just as its feet were, the slippery feelers were also offering stability.

With Slayne gone, Peter and Jerome were back upright and ready, his shoulder now feeling like a block of lead, useless and pulling down hard. He had bent his limp right arm up and was holding it across his body, his hand clutching some of the loose material just below his left armpit. On the whole it was stopping the pain, but his arm remained unusable.

In an emotion akin to that of frustration, the monster started flailing its eight arms about in a flurry.

Percy and Thermion were both knocked back by the same arm, powerless against the pure ineluctable force that turned them into little more than little model soldiers being carelessly knocked over by an angry child with a calamitous arm, wiping out his whole army in one fell swoop.

They landed together in the bed of rubble that Galliana and Elisa were positioned behind.

***

Another of the beast's arms collapsing down between Jerome and Peter split them apart. Jerome had to make a painful dive, and he yelped when he hit the floor. Peter quickly scrambled over to tend to his friend.

"Did you see that?" he said, offering his support.

"See *what?*" Jerome accented, getting to his feet jolted his shoulder.

"A potential weak spot, between the arms."

Tucking his right hand back under his left armpit, Jerome squinted to see and said, "How are you planning on getting to them?"

Peter looked sincerely at his friend. "We annoy it…"

***

Even with its arms flaying, Keldor had evaded any attempt to knock him back and instead ran with his bow and arrows, attracting attention to him, having seen Slayne move to the back and hoping to give him the best chance.

He was preparing to do something. Keldor was sure he could see the faint glimmers of *something* of an idea.

The attention that Keldor was so keen on acquiring quickly arrived, and the beast bowed its head down, stopping in front of him, merely feet from the ground.

Its eyes were black and lifeless, but beneath, Keldor could see flickers of movement, judging and scanning him.

It was ferociously huge, and the acrid breath puffing from out of its nostrils made Keldor's eyes sting and subsequently leak, like the gaseous ordure lathered his lenses with acid.

Two huge stalagmitic teeth were exposed from both sides of the beast's mouth. The viridian colouration at the base of each saw home to beds of mollusc-like creatures, clumped in formations, a chiaroscuro effect drawing living pictures of the entities into shadows.

But that brief moment spent regarding each other ended. Keldor saw its huge glands, just beneath the huge hard jawline, swell and contract, like it was producing something.

Keldor hoped that, whatever the substance, it wouldn't be flammable: *maybe that was just the stuff of children's stories.*

The monster then began manipulating its huge hard jaw muscles, pumping the venom into its abysmal mouth, where the liquid was then swilled and blended.

Until it was released – a spray of thick, mucilaginous ooze.

Keldor was already moving, and his leap took him out of the spray, most of which he avoided, but a light amount nipped the side of his smock – which was fine.

What wasn't *quite* so fine was the natural ignition switch that sparked the dregs alight, turning the liquid into a molten stream, while chucking off roaring sparks that quickly detonated the rest … including the dab on Keldor's smock.

Two things, in the following order, *also* sparked up in his mind: *not the stuff of children's stories! Damn!* And he didn't have time to dwell on his next thought. The fire was spreading and it was getting remarkably hot, remarkably quickly.

He started patting at it uncontrollably, trying to dowse the fire, but the flames licked higher, happily gnawing through his clothing.

Misto, who was still attached to the flaying arm, finally got another break and noticed the same weak spot that Peter had spotted. While it was spewing out the deadly goo at Keldor, he began puncturing the unarmoured area. The creature barely flinched.

There were a few minor convulsions, but that was the only response to the blood and gore now spurting from the several incisions. Misto was sure that it was oblivious, even as the limbs slackened and hung limp.

**

Slayne's idea, to run behind it and gain a new vantage point, had initially been to simply to slice away at the tentacles, but he reconsidered and, looking at them, and seeing the very serious, reflective scales that were burnished from the top to the tip, he decided on a new ploy.

Craning his neck, Slayne looked up to where the flaying tentacles joined the main torso. It was a smooth transformation between its spinal column and the net of snaking appendages, each one widening and webbing together at further points from the floor.

Higher up its back at selected intervals particular vertebrae were raised into sharp spikes, each one spearing up from a prominent column. This column grew taller and more pronounced the closer to the head, until it was virtually at waist-height: a wall built from toughened cartilage.

Protruding out, both left and right, over its shoulders – where the *shoulders* would have been – were two thick plates. These plates skimmed close the armour-plated surface of its back, but then he located another potential weakness.

Just beyond those shoulder bones, at the base of its neck.

All he had to do was get there...

**

Just as Peter had, Percy and Thermion had also discovered the potential weak spot between its arms, which was corroborated when Misto disabled one of them.

After they had returned to their feet, they readied their swords, because, now, it was bowing down, looking at Keldor, its whole body arched over.

Jerome and Peter abandoned their idea of annoying it and, instead, ploughed into its arms.

And then it spewed fire…

***

The fire was spreading over his smock and Keldor was running out of options. His panicked tap-tapping was doing nothing but fanning the conflagration, and the temperature was literally extricating the beads of sweat from his face and beneath his smock.

Panicking, in trouble, his only choice was try and struggle free from the flame-ridden top, and a struggle it would be.

Frantically he threw his hands down and started fumbling with his belt buckle, trying to undo it. A few moments later, after realising that that was *all* he was doing – fumbling – he started tugging at his smock, praying for a rip, a slit, a frayed edge, *anything* that would allow him to tear it open…

The flames were licking at his neck, scorching his well-cultivated stubble, when he felt a pair of hands suddenly push him to the ground and begin rolling him over. It made it slightly worse, only because it was pushing the intense fire into him and then, even more randomly, he became immersed in water. *Glorious water!* But where did it all come from? And who was rolling him on the floor?

Looking up to his surprise, he saw … *Galliana?* Surprised not because he doubted her moral integrity, or doubted that she had the character to save someone, but she barely knew him. However, she surely wasn't the reason for his soaking.

Scanning a little farther afield, he saw Elisa, hands out, held in post-incantation. He caught her gaze and nodded his thanks. Then he quickly returned back to the present, and more importantly to Galliana, who, even more astoundingly, didn't have any weapon to speak of.

With the beast still close, beckoning his death, he wouldn't force Galliana back to go back to Elisa, but before he had a chance to decide anything, he heard the beast's glands, which were again swelling and, for a second time, filling.

"With me," he said, grabbing Galliana's hand and taking her to a place where they had at least some cover.

The largish pile of rubble wasn't perfect, but it was something and, there, he looked at her face, all blackened and charred from the fire she had negotiated. This fell into a rare category for him to remember: people didn't often save him, and *she* had risked life and limb for him.

From previous experience, he didn't like to put things to the test more than once, and waiting for the beast to spill its flammable contents was something he wasn't prepared to just let happen.

Glancing around, developing quick-fire ideas he caught Misto's eyes and then suddenly, the plan came together...

***

Misto caught Keldor's eyes, just as he had caught his, and the plan fell into place as easily as dropping onto the floor, off the limp, dead arm. Carefully, with sly and deft footsteps, Misto sneaked towards the beast's head via its underbelly, and assessed the underside of its jaw.

Like the rest, it was covered almost entirely in scales, but he wondered if, at this close range, he could pierce between them, prying them apart. Well, he had to be able to or the plan wouldn't work.

Goodbyes Keldor, goodbyes Misto.

Glands almost full, the sodden Keldor said, "Stay here," to Galliana, and then dived and rolled beneath the head of the beast.

Immediately, with Misto, he started stabbing at the breaks between the scales surrounding the venomous sacks.

However, Misto's first suspicions, although not *entirely* accurate, were truer than he would have liked. Their weapons were hardly piercing the toughened crust and only a few trickles were dribbling out.

And now the beast was angry.

***

Slayne, however, was halfway up the spine. He'd made his run for it while the beast had been hunched over, attending to the *annoying human*. It was an inappropriate time for humour, but living beyond this was only a probability, so he reserved his right.

Back to the issue at hand, this wasn't like any old obstacle course, conjured by mentors to account for real-life scenarios; this was a long distance run, up the spine of a beast – may as well be a dragon – with the addition of razor-sharp backbones, which needed avoiding.

He was getting close and he thought he was going to make it, but then the monster started to rear up.

It was all or nothing, he thought, as he put the speed on, risking losing not only the chance for a strike, but also his footing – and no doubt more… Close as he was, he was still a way away from being able land the blow.

No other choice afforded to him, he had to make a jump for it and he cast himself up.

And with a single arm, he managed to grip the shoulder plate.

One arm holding him from an unwelcome greeting with the floor, he thrust the blade deep in and with the grace of God, it sank.

Blood jetted out from the gash. The beast began raging.

And with the beast reeling, cries that shook the blue world, Slayne slipped. Tumbling uncontrollably towards the ground, he unsheathed a dagger from his back and just managed to stab it into one of the flailing arms, halting him, holding him.

He held tight, for that was all he could do now, hoping that he had done enough.

Trying to reach behind its head while letting loose bellows that resonated through every ounce of its giant body, the creature tried to pull out the sword that was slowly killing it. Its whole right side had been disabled, its arms hanging loosely, and the three active arms on the other side were all busy clinging and clutching.

From their various positions, the party watched as it fumbled and groaned. Each second it failed to reach the blade, was a second that it wasn't trying to kill them, was a second longer they had to live. And then mercifully it began to slow, easing its arms down to the side. But that wasn't the end, and Keldor saw, from the way its venom glands began to empty and pump into its mouth, what its final plan was.

It wasn't going to be a lonely demise.

The beast was just about to release the last mouthful when Elisa dived out and shot up a surge of flame-infused magic. The gentlest, tangential touch would have set the ignition, but *this* magic wasn't going anywhere other than straight into the mouth of the beast...

And the inferno burst and erupted from out of its cheeks, raining down fire ... on everyone.

Keldor ran over to Galliana and used himself as a body shield. Peter dropped his sword – a disadvantage of being a battle magus – and formed a guard, deflecting the liquid fire over and away from himself, Jerome, Percy and Thermion.

Elisa created a small arched defence above herself while siphoning a stream of water towards Keldor and Galliana, cooling and quenching any fire that got too close.

Against what Slayne would have considered his better judgement, he dropped from the limp arm and neared himself to Misto, at which point, he also conjured a shield and the fire ran in rivulets down the domed shelter, smoking and cooling as it touched the chilled cobbled street.

Then all movement stopped from the beast; the flailing, the grumbling, groaning and wailing all ceased, including the last dying flaps of the slithering tentacles.

Almost imperceptibly at first, it began to topple over and it was Slayne and Misto who needed to do the final dive away as it dropped, knocking through and destroying the whole row of old residential buildings, from which it originally emerged.

The dust settled and the party slowly reformed by the old garrison, each one taking a mental register of everyone else, checking for casualties.

The silence was refreshing, but as everyone looked at each other, they were all far from refreshed.

"Welcome to The Dark Realm. At least we made an entrance." Keldor's words brought little humour, but Jerome winced as he was briskly reminded of his shoulder. Elisa's smile was also wiped away as she headed straight to him.

"I don't suppose there's a magic that will fix me, is there?"

Elisa paused and looked at him. It was a harmless enough comment, its genesis from innocence, but she couldn't bear to see Jerome – one of her boys – hurting. "If there were a way I could make it better…" she said, but it dribbled away.

Jerome could see that she wasn't to be humoured, and her reaction – the way his mother would surely have behaved – repelled him, and he couldn't help easing away from her.

He didn't *want* to be pampered or mothered. It was all too nostalgic and he wasn't in the mood to go through the memory banks of his past.

The party – barring Slayne, who was retrieving his sword – looked at him as he released his strong grip across his body, shifting his arm down and letting it sit by his side.

He was crying inside, the pain was terrific, spiking through him, but he gritted his teeth and got on with it, and then it was still by his side, and the pain eased. He closed his eyes, opened them, looked at the party, looked to Elisa, silently apologised – she silently forgave him – and then looked back round.

Waiting in the blue shadows, stood with prominence and expectation, was his Dark Whisperer. The ghastly change to the angel showed the way and, as he looked to see the headless body of the dead gargantuan, Keldor's words ran circles through his mind.

The sound of smashing wood, as that of a door closing, turned him back momentarily, but he returned his ever sought-after attention back to his Dark Whisperer.

Letting the indigenous creaks and cracks, slithers and whispers surround him, he played the words over in his mind.

'Welcome to The Dark Realm'.

***

The dead village of Marston, the slowly consuming quietus and the Burning Bluffs posed no problem for Garrick, Baylin and Mythos. It was not in their manifesto to be scared and even if they were, it would never be mentioned; it was a moot point … to emote.

They trailed relentlessly, ignoring the lifelessness after the eating plague, ignoring the grisly apparitions of the Bluffs.

The sun had risen while they were part way through and they exited to discover the charcoal remains of a fire from the party's camp.

"Do you know where they've headed, Mythos?" Garrick turned to his academic companion.

"I do."

"Would you care to enlighten us non-magic types, then?" Smiling, Garrick was taken blissfully by surprise. Mythos wasn't normally one to hold back information.

"Have you ever heard of Verilis?"

"As in Verilis, The Dark Realm?"

"How did you know it was called that?"

"Stories, I suppose," Garrick said.

Putting a stopper on the conversation, Mythos responded, "Then you have your answer."

Garrick stopped, looked to Baylin who shrugged, looked back to Mythos and then to the distant, horizonal cliffs, until finishing his gaze back on Mythos.

"Is everything all right?" It was uncaring and insincere. "You seem … bothered."

"Of course," he replied, remembering their manifesto. But he *was* scared; he had a history here. He knew the horrors of the past and he turned to the Bluffs in an almost commemorative manner. Mythos returned back and pacified; Garrick wasn't convinced; Baylin didn't care.

They continued.

***

In quick time they followed the scent of fear like a pack of wolves. It seeped off every one of the frontward nine. It was visible in every shaky footprint, stained on every atom of air.

The final leg of the journey slipped away like its predecessors and they worked through the giant fissure until ending in the giant basin. Every sound they made was taken, amplified and bounced around the crater.

With the out-of-place spire located, they headed without question. Yanking open the wooden door, it was left to smash into the side of the circular stone walls. The ease with which the door opened was a sure sign of previous activity and Garrick's nerves tingled.

The stories he had heard set him on fire, as he bathed in the excitement, letting it wash over him. Although he was sure most would cower at the magnificence of such a place, he would take the vanguard in its marvelling, and as he walked down the spiral stairs and into the azure underworld, he embraced it.

'Welcome to The Dark Realm' *for here, there will be death...*

Chapter XII
Hell's Here

Jerome's shoulder was feeling marginally better.

He'd implemented a simple exercise regime of circular motions, which agonised at first, but as time progressed and The Dark Realm deepened, the pain lessened.

However, the most unsettling thing was feeling the prying eyes of the party digging into him.

What were they thinking? What *must* they be thinking? What did *she* think? And it was while on that train of thought that he realised she *still* hadn't told him her name. *That must be a sign* ... and he sighed and carried on.

Keldor had made an early point of thanking her for saving him and then promptly apologising for awkwardly smothering her.

She responded gracefully, but was, principally, quiet. They were all lost in the matrices of their own heads. Who wouldn't be, enmeshed in such an abyss?

Spookiest of all were the little relics that had been left behind by the inhabitants, the little insights into people's lives. Etchings on the walls were the most provocative, and one such engraving, Jerome surveyed, told of two people: *'Tomas'* and *'Le—'*. It was worn and he couldn't quite read her name, but betwixt their carvings did an arrow forever impale a heart.

Keldor slowly jogged up beside him, breaking his silent touch of history. "Do you hear that?"

Jerome stopped. If their momentous introduction was anything to go by, then he was going to take Keldor's every warning with the utmost importance.

Quietly, they listened. The party behind were also stopped, caught up in the stillness.

"What are we listening for, Keldor?"

He was just about to spring away and become invisible, but the moment he started to bolt he was stopped by a figure stepping out of the sapphire shadows.

"Show yourself." Keldor had his bow drawn back, arrow aimed with deadly precision.

"Friend," the man appeased and he eased himself into full view.

Looking straight at him, Jerome could see him to be no older than he was. There was still a youthful glint in his eye. Rethinking, maybe he was more Peter's age. It was hard to tell: the murkiness was blinding; the blueness was stifling. But he couldn't be far wrong.

Carefully the man approached, hands up in supplication.

"I don't like this," Keldor whispered, his bow retracted.

"You think it's a trap?" Jerome copied his volume.

"I wouldn't doubt it."

Jerome heard the words, but was so stunned, so stressed by the events – by being 'leader' – that he was unable to make a decision, before being interrupted.

"I come in peace," the stranger said, his sword sheathed at his waist.

Apart from continuing to close the gap, he was showing no signs of aggression.

"Stop there," Keldor said.

Jerome was thankful that Keldor took a morsel of charge.

The man obeyed, quietly assessing them, just as they were assessing him. He had an air about him, not necessarily evil, but unsettling. His Dark Whisperer *certainly* didn't like him either, as it stood glaring at him, but he couldn't see why not.

"What's your name?" Jerome asked.

"Jason." His answer was quick.

"You live down here?" Without meaning it, Jerome had added a disparaging tone.

Jason didn't respond straight away, and his silence was a hushed reproach. Jerome felt his face flush red.

At last he addressed the party and said, "I saw you all, and thought maybe you were lost…" Then, as if little more than a threnody, he added, "It's easy to get lost down here…"

Jason was still speaking when Jerome caught a glimpse of his hands – in particular, his wrists. Present on each was a single scar than ran a solitary red route all the way round the circumference. They looked sore and angry and instantly got Jerome thinking about what could have caused them.

Perhaps it was just a reality of living in such a dangerous place. How long could you go without encountering something as severe as *their* welcoming party?

It was all a matter of time…

"I can help you," Jason persisted.

Right now, Jerome was keen to take any help. The trouble was, he still didn't know where he was going and as time fell, he was questioning whether his Dark Whisperer did, too.

"There are others," Jason continued. "Others who have come through here."

Jerome's mother came flooding to mind at the mention of 'others'. "How many others?"

"Lots."

"Where do they go?"

"I can show you."

Jerome took a half step forward but he felt Keldor grab his upper arm and give an *are-sure-you-know-what-you're-doing?* squeeze. They exchanged eye contact briefly before he let go.

The party followed, although Jerome's Dark Whisperer was not happy about it, as It slumped slowly behind.

For the first time, since leaving Alatacia, Jerome was not leading the group and it was like a huge weight had been lifted from his shoulders. He hadn't been aware of how much it had been getting him down, suffering in silence from the images of his Dark Whisperer – he was still wondering a name for It, but maybe that would make It too personal and he really wasn't sure if he wanted It to be *personal.*

Ignoring any directions his Dark Whisperer attempted to give, he followed Jason. It was a curiously stilted arrangement. After all, this was a highly surreal – *un*real – situation.

Here they were, in a sunken city, being led by a seeming resident with strange scars gift-wrapping his wrists.

His skin tone, also, was different. Jerome considered if it was just The Dark Realm's colourlessness, but as he looked to his own hands and the faces of his friends, there definitely *was* an added deficiency to Jason.

But there was clearly going to be some sort of deficiency, he concluded. Going without *any* sunlight was sure to have an impact.

Onwards they walked.

Time – usually a thing of great importance on the surface, now reduced to a mere word – passed.

"…Where do all the people go?" Jerome asked the very silent Jason.

Jason's lips didn't move.

Jerome waited, but was eager to learn. "…Do they ever come back?"

Just silence.

"Will *I* come back?"

Peering at Jerome through broken lenses, Jason simply said, "I'm sorry."

"Sorry?" said Jerome. "Sorry for—" And all too soon it hit him.

Scanning around and seeing the emergence of a number of unsavoury, evil-ridden figures, he wasn't apologising for not being able to give him an answer, not even for his unfortunate fate; he had led them deliberately into a trap.

Why did Keldor always have to be right?

He should have known better…

***

"This could be interesting," Garrick chanted under his breath.

He watched idly from a long distance, as the party were herded together, stripped of their armaments and marched forward.

He signalled to Baylin and Mythos to follow, and they crept out from behind the corner of the far back street and swiftly on to the next, which Garrick poked his head round to get another glimpse of where they were being taken.

Corner to corner and street to street they followed, far enough back to avoid detection, close enough, at least for Garrick, to imbibe their terror; for God only knows what would happen to them, but whatever He had planned, he wanted a front row in the stalls.

It was a dingy, well built-up district of the dead city, to which they were led. Garrick considered that it was probably a slum before it became a ghostly, *abandoned* slum. It drove him to thinking, wondering, that a city in this state, primarily from its disuse, why, if you're bent on living in such a place, pick a slum? It probably didn't work like that, but then, you can't change who you are. If you're gutter-trash, then gutter-trash you'll stay. And anyway, what did he care? If there was a morsel of something to feed his blood-hungry nihilism, then he didn't mind whether it was noble blood or whether it stood up for too long from the sewer. He tightened his grip on his sword, expelling some of the excitement...

***

The ramshackle buildings either side, burnished blank from the cobalt candescence, went hand in hand with the rotten detritus that littered every road to vivify the deathly existence.

This was a huge failure on Jerome's part and he took full responsibility.

However, what Jerome found curious was the way *Jason* was being treated, how he was being forced to march in similar fashion to how *they* were. It was as though he were as much a prisoner as them. But it didn't make him feel any less angry or any less betrayed though, even if he *was* being treated badly.

He deserved *it.*

And Jerome couldn't see it from a different angle ... yet.

At a particular point they veered off the street and into one of the tumbledown buildings. The interior matched the outside with ragged, cloth curtains filtering spectral blue twilight into the dishevelled room. That was another thing he'd noticed; it wasn't like Marston, which was a ghost village. Here, there were no cobwebs, no traces of *any* life. The stale food scraps remained un-rotten and maggot-free.

For evil to be so palpable that it would scare away even the creepy-crawlies sent a chilling shiver inside Jerome. It sat deep within him, and stayed.

It stayed with him, as they were led down a set of steps, through a stone corridor with a number of doors on either side, until stopping at one.

It had been hours since being out of the natural sunlight and their eyes had grown accustomed to the ethereal light offered by The Dark Realm, but down here it was lit by torches dotted down the stony hall.

The flickering flame next to the door caught Jerome's gaze, as he got lost in its capricious dance, thinking of the demise that he all but wanted to think about. The irony slapped him in the face, but it was the rattling keys of one of the guards unlocking the door that brought him back.

On the other side was another long, straight corridor, with another array of doors. And following the same procedure as before, they walked – walked for ages – and then stopped at another single door, one which was unlocked and then opened.

But on the other side of this door wasn't another corridor, it was a...

Jerome couldn't find the word. *Torture chamber* came to mind; he felt sick. In quick time, with fantastic clarity his mind ran riot over all the tortures he had heard about. Then the sick bile bubbling up backed down and was replaced by a weakness in his knees. He wanted to be strong; he wanted not to break, but it was so horrific. But he wasn't broken yet, and he showed himself to the party, and they showed their faces back to him, to each other. They were all together.

Besides, he *had* to stay alive, because he *still* didn't know *her* name...

The room was as good as square, with a number of racks, restraints included, next to each other circling a central table, which felt a complete manifestation of just how ominous the whole room seemed.

One by one they were forced down and manacled to the wooden racks. Jerome released a solitary whimper, as his still injured shoulder was forced up and over his head.

And after a while, trapped in this position – aside from the slight magic traces coming from the shackles – he felt his arms slowly go dead, while his locked shoulders solidified.

But he *still* didn't know *her* name…

The door creaked open and footsteps brought attention to a black-robed figure.

"What shall we do with Jason?" a dull voice asked.

"He did well, bringing in such a stock. Remove his hands again," – *What!* Jerome was shocked – "but be quick about it."

That was the reason for the scars around his wrists. He had to say something. He couldn't let such a thing happen without at least saying *something*. "Why?"

"Who would speak?" said the man who had just called for the amputation of Jason's hands.

That sick fear churning inside now aided him, and Jerome hoped it wasn't an acceptance of death, rather strength. "Me."

There was a pause, as the man considered Jerome. "…You would care for someone who has tricked and trapped you?"

"I would care for someone who was about to have his hands removed for—" But it was true, Jerome thought, halting mid-sentence.

Jason *had* led them to this place. Torture imminent, death likely and he here he was, locked down *because* of the man he was now defending. It was this internal conflict that stopped his words and continued the ebon-dressed man's.

"Is compassion something you show to everything?"

But. "If he did this for you, why punish him?" It made him feel better … defending.

"You didn't answer my question."

"You didn't answer mine!" Jerome thundered in response.

He shocked himself, shocked everyone.

There was another pause, another degree of consideration, but the shadowed man at last broke silence and said, "Certain undesirable qualities in his lineage that need to be – how do I put this? – trained out. Now we'll see about your compassion."

Jerome heard the crack of a smile forming at each side of his mouth, as though his smile lines were petrified still. "Would you take his place?"

The transmuted strength that gave Jerome a voice dribbled back into fear. He wondered if he could actually take his place, save his pain… "No," he said. It was quiet.

"What was that?" beckoned the shadowed man.

Riddled with torment and upset, he cried the word, "No!"

"Good. Either way, I have no interest in your compassion. It's what is deeper that I'm interested in. I want to discover the truth, to help *you* find the truth. But it's a hard journey and it's near the edge of the soul, somewhere between life, death … and madness."

Two cloaked figures had entered and moved into the middle of the room around the central table.

"Take *him*," – he pointed to Jerome – "to the 'chamber'."

What was that? He got a fetid reminder of his stomach contents again, as it touched the back of his throat.

So far, everyone had kept quiet, until now.

"No, take me!" Peter bellowed.

The two guards unshackling Jerome paused for a moment, awaiting further instruction. Jerome looked at the man and watched as he held his fate – bounced it about – inexorably in his hands.

"Take them both."

The guards did as ordered, removing the shackles, which had already started to chafe his wrists red, *nothing like that of Jason's though.*

The blood returning to his shoulders and arms, refreshing as it was, rapidly began the pins and needles. He contemplated struggling free, but there were too many barriers preventing him, the most powerful being Galliana, to whom he looked. She was scared; they all were, but they all looked like they were controlling it, grasping it.

***

Peter and Jerome were funnelled in silence down another few corridors. It was like a huge underground maze, a never-ending mass of tunnels.

Shoulders and arms recovered, they were shuffled through a door, Jerome in front, Peter behind. The door slammed shut behind. The two friends turned to each other, neither one sure what to say, and then they looked at the door. It was the most logical thing to do. Here they were, unguarded and ostensibly ... *free.*

Except they weren't, and when the realisation dawned on them that this door didn't even have a thing that might open it – no handle, no lock, no hole, nothing – they turned back to each other, grateful, at least, for the company.

"What do we do now?" Peter said and shrugged.

Jerome waited a moment, having had one more look at the door. "We're going to get out of here."

And Peter smiled.

***

The two cloaked figures returned to the room where the remaining party members were restrained.

They unshackled Misto who, when free, was flung against the far wall. His head, as always, was the first part to collide and his body squashed and scrunched together until falling to the floor.

There were rapid intakes of breath from most of the bound party, as they saw little Misto so badly treated. Just breaths for most, but not from Keldor, who used his to fuel his voice, and he shouted, "Hey!"

He shouted, even restrained and unable to make a *real* difference, he ripped his vocal chords *because* he couldn't move, like his voice was an extension of what his arms could – *would* – do, if ever they were given the chance to slaughter those who would be so cruel.

His voice didn't stop them, but it did get a reaction and the figure, with striking celerity, slipped a hidden knife from the pleats of his robe – a beautifully crafted, curved blade, which intimated an unspeakable horror, an older life, hailing from within the walls of the demented chirurgeon's chamber.

With the same swift manner, he zoomed to Keldor, holding the twisted edge firmly against his neck.

Go on then! Do it! Keldor silently coaxed, his dark eyes enticing, cajoling him, *willing* him to do it. It was just a show of power, and then the man who had introduced them to their fate, who was now standing, watching in the corner, extended a hand out of the shadows, demanding him to back off.

Shortly after, and definitely *not* quickly, the robed man retracted his knife and slowly himself, before returning the ornamental blade back into the dark furrows of his uniform.

They next approached Slayne. With violent disregard, they unlocked the manacles and pulled him to the table. He did little to resist. He knew the futility in it and instead, focused his efforts to try and remain in control.

After he had been secured to the table, hands and feet chained, one of the two robed men moved towards a winch system, which was inbuilt into the table. It had a handle poking out from the side, and he put his hands to it.

Then he started turning and, as he rotated the handle through the complete circle, it squeaked, squealed – sounded like the torment of a dying faerie … dying over, and over, *and over*.

Lowering down from above the table were two chains each with a manacle attached to the end. It moved so excruciatingly slowly, with only the piercing mechanical squeaks of the rotating handle breaking the silence.

Once the chains had been lowered to what was deemed a satisfying height Slayne's hands, one by one, were unchained and then re-chained to the manacles above his head. His feet were then freed and he was left to dangle in that position until the winch was turned in the reverse, raising him.

He moved his feet beneath to support him as he was lifted, and again the horrific squeal of the winch rattled through him.

Keldor had been watching with utter disbelief. He could shout again, but ultimately watching was the only power he or anyone had.

And what power was that?

Then, as Slayne was hoisted up, he could swear he caught a glimpse of Misto, flinching.

Rapidly, it came to him; he harkened back to when he and Jerome first saw Misto being flung out of the tent, headfirst into a tree.

That ogre was bound to be stronger than either of these robed figures. But was this one throw too many?

However, Keldor looked again at the felled goblin and this time he really *did* flinch.

***

As Jerome and Peter returned to the task at hand, they took the time to assess where they were and what this 'chamber' was all about. It was a massive place, not very wide, but almost end-less. The floor was beautifully detailed with ornate and elaborate designs. The walls were the same with exquisite markings, but on both sides of the room, they failed to join the floor, as a five-foot gap of depthless nothingness spanned from the walls to the central floor. The only way was forward.

On the surface, it looked like a harmless work of art. But they both knew – without knowing – that ticking beneath this opulent exterior was something far worse.

"What do you think?" Jerome asked.

"…I think *you* should take the first step."

Jerome turned to his friend. "Very funny."

Peter let out a little smirk, and then his face hardened. "I'm not joking."

"Fine."

Jerome was just about to put his foot down when he was stopped by Peter hurriedly sputtering, "Wait!"

His pause was so sudden that he wobbled and, for a brief second, nearly toppled over, but he found his stability, his foot held a mere an inch from the ground.

Balance found, Jerome asked, "What is it?"

"Move your foot back here, slowly."

He did as Peter said, gently reversing the half step he'd taken and putting it firmly on the ground behind. He pushed down a little with his foot, just to confirm that the ground behind was truly safe.

"Do you see that?" Peter pointed to a place on the decorated ground.

"I see lots of things; what do you want me to look at?"

"Very funny," repeated Peter. "Do you see that raised bit? That raised bit *you* were about to step on?" Peter avidly held him arm and finger out.

Jerome squinted to where Peter was pointing, but then, yes, he saw it. And then he turned back to Peter.

"Do you know something I don't?" Jerome asked, slightly ridiculing Peter's observation.

"No, but would you take the risk?"

"You seemed to want me to," returned Jerome, shaken.

After a slight hesitation, Peter pounded a magic bolt at it and it depressed, unclipping two catches on both walls, either side, releasing two immense wooden battering rams.

They smashed together no more than a foot ahead of them, the fury of it pulsing vibrations into the air.

Both were stunned silent and when the battering rams were almost completely stopped – no more than a tender wavering in suspension – they slowly wound back into the walls, the clinking of cogs and gears echoing through the 'chamber'.

They both caught their breath and let their hearts settle.

Peter looked at Jerome. "Glad?"

"Very."

They both exhaled.

***

Keldor watched intently and then abruptly lost all sight of the little green-skin. But a moment later, slowly and completely without sound, a green hand, armed with a small, bejewelled blade, slipped just beneath one of the robed figure's necks. The figure was primed and only milliseconds away from slicing into Slayne's leg.

Harshly, with lightning speed, Misto pressed in with the knife and drew back with his arm, the blade so horrendously sharp it sliced clean through the robed-man's neck. He fell to his knees, clutching at his half-decapitation, gurgling and choking, because everything he needed to survive – air, blood, all of it – was gushing out faster than he could plug the gap.

In quick succession, Misto turned to the other figure, who was only just realising – too late – that the lavish dagger he was trying to unsheathe was, in fact, heading for him in a little green hand. Misto ran straight into him and began mercilessly assassinating him.

Still stood in the corner, the man who had ordered Jerome and Peter be taken to the 'chamber' was visible only to the well-adjusted eye.

Under the highly skilled hand of Misto, the events had unfolded in a matter of moments and the shadowed man was just about to make his escape.

The little goblin had just finished massacring the man – who happened, also, to be the one who threw him against the wall – and he flicked his head up.

The shadowed man had his hand primed at the door handle and Misto threw the dagger, slicing through it.

He yelped, but with a shocking, and surprising, degree of brute force, he tugged down, the knife ripping through the remaining tendons and ligaments. He snarled and tucked his butchered hand into himself and finished his escape.

There was a silent period, just a moment, taken by all, to relish the triumph. But not Misto, who set to work, locating the keys and unshackling the remaining five. When he was free, Keldor shot over to the winch system and lowered Slayne.

"Weapons," Misto muttered. "We need weapons."

Using his foot against the door, Keldor jiggled and loosened the knife free and he thought. He had never, even after all these years, ever seen Misto fight. He'd had his suspicions since the ogre's death – the second time they were captured – but also, it explained *why* he had never seen him enter combat; he was a cloaked assassin. But more importantly, he certainly was a lifelong companion and good friend.

"We's two daggers," Misto continued. "Who's good with a dagger?"

The party was quiet, sifting through the previous events to the only obvious conclusion.

Galliana looked from the party down to Misto and said, "I think … *you* should have the daggers. Thank you for saving us."

Misto was so much shorter than everyone else, as they all looked down to the little goblin – like staring at something no bigger than a child – who was handed the second dagger by Keldor. He took it, sheathed them both and led the party out – *no messing*.

That, Keldor knew, was the outright mark of an assassin.

***

Jerome and Peter stood back and reassessed the room.

All those beautiful details and carvings weren't for aesthetics, but to disguise the verisimilitude of a death machine.

Since the sneering dissuasion at Jason, his Dark Whisperer had been quiet, but now, after some calibration, It resurfaced. In a strange way, Jerome was almost pleased, for the odd truth remained – this entity had done nothing but to keep him safe. He hoped that this was the reason for Its emergence out of hiding, and as Jerome looked at It, It looked back, regarding him. It was like a guardian angel. *His* guardian angel.

"Do you have an idea, Jerome?"

Jerome was silent, drawing knowledge from his guardian. Then he said, "Actually, I think I do."

"…Go on then, spill it."

"We go through the walls, the gaps that those two massive things came out of."

"I don't know, Jerome."

Peter was looking at the holes – where the holes *had been* – that the wooden battering rams came out of. There was probably some hatch that lifted or shifted to allow them in and out. Craning his neck and squinting his eyes, though, he could see the thin gaps above that must have accommodated the ropes holding aloft the huge wooden rams. But looking at the wall design beneath and seeing the *shape* of a hatch – within the artistry –, he wasn't convinced that there was room to admit the width of a human.

Peter turned and looked back to Jerome, saying, "Those gaps look small. Do you really think we can fit through?"

Jerome was also looking at the wall, but in response to Peter, he said, "I haven't noticed you get a paunch," smiling. "Is there something you're not telling me? How does Garveya feel—"

"Garveya has kept me in *good* shape, thank you."

Which shut Jerome up, *instantly,* and then he realised what he was missing, and it made his heart quail.

Peter was very aware of his friend's inexperience with women, though it hadn't been for lack of trying. Early on, Garveya had confirmed to him that Jerome was a handsome enough man – "No, not as handsome as *you,*" she'd always suffixed – and he had always sought Peter's counsel when it came to girls, but nothing had ever *happened.*

He and Garveya had talked about it, wondered mostly, and he appreciated how helpless, how *frustrated,* Jerome must feel. And not one part of his soul wanted that for him – not even in jokes (*especially* not in jokes) – and he rapidly tried thinking of ways to calm him. He thought of that girl, whom he clearly liked. Everyone could see it; amidst glances across the faces, he always looked a little longer at *her.*

She was his type and, judging by all the times he *had* talked about girls he'd wanted, she had all the features that he loved: brown (mousy brown) hair, green eyes … curvaceous.

Even he, whose tastes in woman differed massively, could see that she was attractive – *"No, not as attractive as* you,*"* he could imagine himself pretend-saying to Garveya.

Maybe *she could* be the one, but she wouldn't have been the first Peter had thought to be 'the one'. However, these were unique circumstances, and she *did* like him too. It was another truth that everyone was aware of, even if *they* weren't. Even considering Thermion – armed with an age that undoubtedly gave him experience with women, who seemed nice enough and was, by all accounts, a striking man – Peter had frequently watched her snatching glimpses at Jerome.

It was almost as if something, some secret phantasm, were drawing them together.

Peter was righter than he knew, but Jerome was still reeling as he said, "Anyway, joking aside, you're…" – he paused, as he searched for the right word – "smaller," – not the *best* word, he knew – "than me. You always have been."

And he always *had* been. Not by much, not in height anyway, just size, but from the looks of things – especially the gap Jerome was purporting would accommodate them – it didn't need to be much.

"We'll make it," Jerome assured, but he wondered in that instant if his Dark Whisperer would be so conscious at to account for his friend, or if it were just looking out for *him*. But he repeated, "We'll make it."

Convinced or not, Peter said, "If you're sure."

"…Well let's hope Garveya *has* kept you in good shape."

Peter stiffly baulked as Jerome said it. It returned to him his feelings of pity for his innocent friend. Nonetheless he rose above it and said, "But if I die, I'm coming back to haunt you."

"And it'll be my pleasure. Shall we?" Jerome proposed, an air of joviality, similar to the one Peter had employed all those years ago before that ill-fated *swordfight*.

Peter smiled and launched another bolt at the raised trap and, like before, the hatches opened, giving way to the two wooden rams. With the same killing power as the first time, they smashed together, the wind blasting dust particles towards them. With a few seconds accorded to them they clambered on – choosing the right – before it would start to wind back in.

Peter was first up, Jerome a little slower, and he made sure Jerome would be first to go through the gap.

With their legs hugging the massive, ligneous thumper, the mechanism began clinking, dragging it slowly back in.

Jerome had the fortune of knowing he'd fit through, but Peter didn't have the luxury of reassurance and, as the opening approached and the abyss of nothingness – which would be all that awaited him should he not fit – passed beneath, he wasn't feeling any more convinced about it.

Just before entering, Jerome straightened, tucking his arms down next to him and lifting his legs straight behind.

It took a degree of balancing, but he squeezed through cleanly, the top of the gap only scraping his smock a little.

Then it was Peter, Peter and his slightly thicker set than his younger, *slimmer* friend. Just as Jerome had, he put his arms by his side and his legs out behind. Turning his head to the side and holding his breath, trying his best to suck up as much muscle, he forced himself into the wood, and then unforced, thinking that the last thing he needed was tensed-up muscle.

The rough surface at the height of the break tugged hard at his ear, squashing and scrunching it up. It felt like it was being ripped off, but it passed through and then sprang back to shape.

Head safely through, it was just his upper back worrying him now. Just as he anticipated, his clothing was struggling to get through and began bunching and pulling at his neck. It choked him and he panicked, but he *was* fitting through. Then there was a rip, coming from the material over his throat, and it gave his smock that little extra slack needed to clump into his lower back.

It was a vicious scraping and his skin felt flayed, but he was through; *they* were through.

And then they realised they weren't alone.

Standing, as stunned as them, were two slight individuals, skin as pallid as Jason's.

Immediately they began scurrying to the door, a clear indication that they weren't inclined towards a fight.

Jerome hopped off first and made for the nearest figure, while Peter landed and pulled in some raw magical manna.

Tuning it into a concise and harsh current of air, he aimed it at the figure nearest the door, who was probably only a foot away from opening it. It hit him in the back and drove him that extra foot forward, knocking his head into the hard wooden panels and dropping him off into unconsciousness.

With his accomplice collapsed by the door, the other man turned to Jerome, putting his hands up into a meagre guard.

Slayne, the absolute taskmaster, had trained him rigorously in hand-to-hand combat. In fact, it was the *only* combat art that had seen Slayne physically beat him.

Jerome remembered returning to Elisa's with more black eyes, cracked ribs, bleeding lips and gums than a torture victim during the reign of the evil triumvirate.

She had tended to him then, as he had lain awake wishing for sleep, but the tuition had done its job. His nerves had been battered into submission, his body inculcated to fight, to win, and at the end of each convalescence there was less pain, less pain and more skill, more desire to *not* get hit ever, *ever* again.

And now it all came to call: every black eye, every cracked rib, every bleeding lip and gum. But he had his compassion, a creation of his years of solitude. Even for this man, Jerome felt no need to take it further than necessary.

He saw, from the stiffness in his shoulders, the immobility of his guard, that he was frightened, but moreover had no idea what he was doing.

The man hastily tried his luck with a left punch, something between a jab and a cross – his inexperience made clear. His wrist wasn't even straight, and it was slow.

Jerome promptly blocked it and put in a jab of his own – a fake, aimed for the side of his head. It did more than he had hoped, as the pale-skinned man shut his eyes while reflexively shifting both hands up to defend.

His head wide open, Jerome came in with a quick straight punch. The man swiftly joined his friend in unconsciousness. But before he fell, Jerome caught him under his arms and slowly lowered him to floor.

Silence was imperative.

Jerome turned to Peter, who was grinning. It made Jerome smile back, but after a few seconds of silent inanity – this mad grin stuck on Peter's face – Jerome's smile dropped and he frowned.

"*What?*" Jerome demanded. "What are you grinning at?"

"You," Peter responded.

Perhaps a little self-conscious, Jerome asked, "What *about* me?" not sure whether to feel honoured or affronted.

Grin still very much attached, Peter finally said, "You're far too good with those," nodding at Jerome's fists.

Honoured but confused, he said, "…It was just a punch. One punch," he reiterated.

"A block, a fake jab, a cross *and* an unconscious man in the space of a second."

"He wasn't very good," Jerome said, arguing his victory.

"And you really *are*… Anyway, I just hope I don't have to come up against that," Peter said, brushing the tiny splinters off his smock, admiring Jerome's pugilism and, then, he knew why he was so good. In conclusion to his earlier thoughts, he related it to the simple fact – he had had *nothing* else.

Compared to his own time in Alatacia, which had been a cushy, *work hard play hard* chapter in his life, Jerome's had been marked by violence and solitude – and no women. All the times they had not been together, Jerome had been fighting and training, training and fighting, getting beaten by his mentor, developing his thaumaturgy and … had just been on his own. It was the fighter who defined him now.

Peter hadn't been there for him enough before. It shouldn't just have always been Jerome seeking him out, asking for his advice – his help. *He* should have gone to Jerome, *been there* for him, like the friend he claimed to be, like the one that said he could be 'counted on'. No, he hadn't been there for Jerome enough before, but he would in the future – should they finish this alive – but for now, Peter felt only the pangs of sorrow.

While Jerome let the wave of acclaim stroke his soul. And then he also brushed himself down, before getting a good look at where they were.

The room was thin, much thinner than the battering ram was long, but it catered for it with a bay that probably went a further fifteen feet deep within the far wall.

But there was more. The precision engineering required to make such a *thing* was remarkable. Each cog worked in concinnity with the next; tiny contraptions, all linked by a complex network of chains and gears, whirred, purred and droned together like little conspirators in a clandestine underworld.

The two young men considered the unutterable waste of such genius, to build something designed for a purpose little beyond that of killing.

Reflection over, they designated their attention to getting out. Jerome moved the sleeping body away from the metal-braced, wooden door, while Peter flicked up the crossbar with a *click* – that *click* stilling every movement, as they tried to keep hold of their newly found hope of escape.

Slowly, with the utmost care and attention, Peter opened the door, so slowly that the creaks were reduced to a hum of sub-human capacity, but he felt the soft ticking, as it was unsealed from its architrave.

Trying to grasp a topographical map of the huge under-ground complex, they started working out where the 'chamber' may have been and then tried to retrace their steps back to where their friends were.

It was a loose and unlikely plan, but it was all they had and although neither needed to say it, they were both petrified. But then Jerome became aware of his Dark Whisperer again and he almost sighed with relief; he – if It had any gender at all – was sure to help them.

***

Leading the party out of the room, Misto followed the way he saw the guards take Jerome and Peter. Admittedly, he had only caught a hint from his periphery, but it would at least put them in the right direction and that would be enough, he hoped, he prayed, to find them.

Elisa and Slayne had both tried engaging their magical sensors, but although this realm was abounding with magic, it was as though there was so much that it became hard to decipher and navigate.

The string of torches lighting the corridor fluttered as they walked past each one. The stagnancy in the air was indicative of under-use, as each flame went from being unnaturally motionless to imitating the invisible gusts and whirlwinds created by each contact with the nanoscopic world.

***

With Peter furiously racking his memory, trying to retrace their steps and Jerome enjoying the ease of being led, they worked a familiar path through the maze.

On edge and close, they thought, to their friends, they heard something up ahead, a disturbance which could have been anything. A glance between the two and Jerome quickly ran to the nearest door and tried to open it – *locked.* Peter had run to the next door up and also tried his – *locked* – but as the lock clanked, denying entrance, a voice suddenly started up from the other side.

"*Nooo!*" it yelled, prolonged and pronounced. "*Nooo!* No, please!" They could barely differentiate the masculinity of the person it was coming from, as his voice was so high, and *so* pumped full of terror. "I'll tell you whatever you want! Please, please, please, *pleeeaaaase* let me go! I can't take anymore… No more, no more, no more…" The 'no more's continued on the wing of a diminuendo – the begging fading to whimpers, the whimpers dropping to an otherworldly chant.

Jerome was stopped briefly in his dash to the next door, stung hard by the horrid pleas, but it was only a momentary thing, as he tried the lock and, this time, it wasn't a clank; it was a *click* – a joyous, relieving *click* – and it opened, allowing them both the opportunity to scuttle in, which they did, before ducking down hinge-side.

The begging voice had simmered down to silence now, and it was just them and the golden proverbial – although there was nothing *golden* about it now. Conscious of only their sharp breathing, amidst the *haunting* silence – that seemed a righter characterisation –, the sound of a door slamming halted even that.

"Jerome, I know this is a bad time and a really odd request, but I don't know if we'll get another chance. If we get out of here, I want you to talk to that girl," Peter whispered.

"What are you talking about? Peter, this really *is* a bad time."

"I know, but promise me, yes?"

"Fine."

A little later, still crouched, they heard the rumblings of people. They were quiet, searching. *What were they looki—?*

Mid-thought, the door began screeching open and the two young men turned to each other and nodded, Peter preparing a magic attack and Jerome clenching his fists.

With the door now open, Peter was sandwiched between it and Jerome, and still the footsteps came nearer...

***

"Boys," Elisa gently whispered.

It was a leap of faith, because even at this close range she was still only aware of very faint familiar signatures. But it was the rumbling in the magical ether, a hallmark of a magical assault, coming from behind the door that made her speak out. She, an experienced magus, had the know-how to separate existences and identities and she could only guess at the fear her two boys were struggling with.

She poked her head round and, tucked behind the door, huddled up together in the shadows were Peter and Jerome.

Instantly she smiled and repeated, "Boys."

The magical friction lurking in Peter's fingers dissipated and the whites of Jerome's knuckles faded back to a healthy skin tone.

The relief became more overwhelming than the fear, as they saw Elisa, but they got up and shared some *stunning* silence; no words would have truly expressed the moment; only something quieter than silence would do.

Walking round the door, they all exchanged eye contact, but when Jerome flashed eye contact with Galliana, they both turned away and then he realised that one of them was missing.

"Where's Thermion?" Jerome said.

"He was right h—" Percy looked around, flicking over the heads of the party, but Jerome was right. Where was he?

Everyone had been knocked off guard and they all needed their own piece of mind to see he wasn't there. Just taking the word of another wasn't enough. And then everyone wondered at what point *had* he left? Jerome turned back to Galliana, to see her reaction at his vanishing and, oddly, she didn't seem as sad as he expected ... maybe even a little relieved?

It was curious, but not as curious as a voice that began to bounce inside his head. *"Jerome,"* it said.

"What?" he muttered.

The party looked at him, while he was still wondering who'd spoken. *"You need to listen and—"* it said.

But Jerome cut it off mid-speech, asking, "Who's saying that?"

All the party were curious, but it was Slayne who stated the fact. "No one's said anything." Which he quickly followed it up with, "Are you all right?"

All eyes were on him, expectantly. *"Say it's nothing and that you just heard something,"* the voice commanded.

Jerome was utterly speechless – probably for the better. Under the harsh scrutiny of the party, his fears about his sanity, and of being taken for *mad,* were rapidly coming true, so he tried it. He had nothing else to lose. "It's nothing. I just heard something."

Over the next moments he waited to see if they had taken the lie. Those few moments were excruciating, however, and mercifully, they returned a normal, unconcerned gaze. *Phew.*

"Now, don't say anything," the voice ordered, maybe with a hint of frustration.

It was hard to balance the voice with pretending to be *fine.*

"You don't need to say anything, you just need to listen to me and I will guide you out. You don't have much time ... so, say that you remember the way out."

Jerome just caught the tail end of someone asking, "Does anyone remember the way out?"

It was like coincidence and he said, "I do," throwing it out there.

"I do," Keldor offered, "but if you're sure?"

"Say you're sure," commanded the voice.

"I'm sure."

"Lead the way," Keldor said.

And the party split, letting him to the front, *again*.

Jerome began to take the directions, but he was worried about Thermion. Perhaps this voice in his head would know where he is. That must be the best decision. He would have liked to think that his party would be searching for him, but how was he going to get through to the voice?

Unprompted, the voice answered his question, *"Thermion isn't here."* Jerome wondered, *was it angry?*

Jerome carried on, not convinced of the route. Neither was Keldor, but the voice had told Jerome to say 'trust me', so he did; and so the party did.

Under the instructions of the voice, he was amazed that he was led to the room where their equipment was stored. They all, in particular Keldor, looked at him, stunned, but shook it off.

"It seems Thermion took his weapon before leaving," said Percy, ambivalence and indifference.

Little reaction was given to Percy's remark, before they all armed themselves and then continued under Jerome's – *the secret voice's* – flawless guidance.

It was impossible to deal with and he chuckled at the addition a new problem on top of his: conscience, bounty, Reformation, girl trouble, magical maladroitness, broken home, Dark Whisperer and – it's confirmed – *total* insanity.

"You're not mad; don't be so hard on yourself..." – the voice softened his worry – *"This door to your right,"* directed the voice, and Jerome followed.

"Easy for you to say," Jerome mentally responded.

"That's exactly what it is."

It seemed so familiar, the voice. The way it spoke, it was just like it had known him for years. But then, he supposed, of course it knew him. What delusion – a creation of the mind – wouldn't know the person whose mind had created it...?

Jerome opened the door and ahead was the set of steps that they had been marched down. The blue treacle shimmer of The Dark Realm oozed back in as they returned into the rundown, ramshackle building and finally out into the abandoned slums.

Chapter XIII
Leviathan, Part I

"Well done, Jerome," Keldor said, quick to compliment.

Now that they were out and the voice's instructions came to an end, Jerome felt on edge. What were they to do now?

He looked at the party and the voice gave its one final command, saying, *"Follow your Dark Whisperer."*

And this time, Jerome knew that it was gone.

Turning, he straightaway caught sight of his Dark Whisperer. Giving his mental go-ahead, It continued Its guidance...

***

The shadowed man had his bloody, mutilated hand tucked into the folds of his top garment.

Things had gone from bad to worse. People didn't escape – normally, *ever!* Now he had to explain what had happened... And what was he supposed to say? It could at least be said that he had already taken provisions to get them back or, if needs be, have them eliminated.

This, in some small way, could show signs of resourcefulness and an inclination towards proactivity. This may allow him some leeway, some leniency, some mercy.

Descending the steps to an even lower part of the lair, his heart began to pump harder and his breathing likewise. The increased surges of blood though, made his defaced hand throb at a varying rate, throwing his pain-control completely *out* of control. But he winced onwards, pushing ever deeper down the steps.

There was only one room at this level, *his* room, the room of his Lord ... and there it was, just visible past the final bend and the final step.

He didn't need to knock, he never had. He had no doubt that, even now, he didn't *need* to report to him. His Lord knew.

And the door slowly opened in that unsettling way that it always did.

He entered. "My Lord, there has been an escape."

The blackness gave no response.

He froze solid before the gloom.

"One day, Sahl, you will come to my chamber and not be the harbinger of bad news. I yearn for that day, as I believe you do, too."

"Yes, my Lord," he said, and quickly added, "I have sent out your overlords."

There was an eerie silence, but the Lord continued, "I do not envy you, Sahl. You have done excellent work for me, for *us*. And in time, you will possess the full truth of the world and of its future; I will *give* it you. For now, there will always be mercy for those who show dedication."

Sahl bowed his head, grateful for the leniency, the *mercy*.

His Lord continued, "I want *you* to lead my overlords. Do this for me, for *us!*"

Sahl said, "With honour, but…" and he pulled his hand out from the sopping-red material under his arm.

He found it hard to look at, but instantly the pain began to subside as he witnessed, from the inside out, the reparation of his hand.

The thin, snapped bones joined up, marrow first, reforming the basic structure. The snapped ligaments and ligatures were then recoupled, followed by the snipped strings and strands of lumbrical muscle, growing and weaving and wrapping around the skeletal base.

The completion of his hand was finalised by the flapping, blood-drenched skin strengthening and joining.

No scars, no pain.

The concept of healing was vital in this place, to heal the tortured, so they could survive, but it was never this simple. It required the power of far more than one magus and always took time. He looked again at his hand and struggled to locate where the damage had been done. His Lord was truly powerful and he looked to the depth to where he was, but saw only dark.

"Mercy, Sahl. Mercy... Now go."

***

The party had navigated for hours, voyaged over cavernous spaces and through and beneath tiny alcoves and caves. These strange creations, masterminded from the merger of a cadaverous metropolis beneath and a rocky, reversed mountainscape above, made the route as stunning as it was dangerous.

But their journey was ending. Jerome could feel it. It was only this last part of the city that needed crossing. But, the eyes of evil were spying down on them.

***

"Stop!" called a voice from behind. And the party were halted dead, just before taking the first few steps into the final part of the city.

One at a time, the weary eight turned.

It was the voice of the shadowed torturer and, once he had their attention, he continued, "So, where do we go from here? What choice do I have?"

The party raised no voice of response; they were all too busy masking their feelings of lethargy with a dauntless front.

"This is my territory, *my* dominion, *my* realm. How far did you think you'd get?"

Edging out of the indigo glooms emerged a number of haunting figures. A cursory count revealed thirteen, stopping slightly behind Sahl.

When no more came out, the shadowed speaker stepped back into the pitch. "End them."

Instantly, with faultless unanimity, each of their automaton stances thundered into life, booming around the sonorous city.

To the thirteen overlords, there was no battlefield etiquette. Their order was to lay waste and from the outset, that was what they were going to do; and, whether the party was ready or not, no amount of preparation would be bestowed.

They marched on, keeping an unswerving unison.

At the same moment, each of the overlords hurtled a magic bolt towards the weakened party. They were all so shattered from the gruelling endlessness that mounting a defence was all but impossible.

However, from out the corner of his eye, Jerome saw Elisa run out. She moved with the same graceful athleticism and celerity as when he first saw her.

Firmly in the field, she stopped and flung her arms up and out, holding up an intricate defensive structure. The magic bolts terrorised the void between them and her, as they neared with each cruel time slice.

Yet, as each spell collided, she was able to manipulate and shift the primary strength of the shield along its defensive wall and into the particular areas of contact – such was the complexity of her shield, the work of a fine magus.

Slayne was going to help – he'd decided – and he ran in, mesmerised by her, by her *and* her incredible control of magic.

Elisa felt the injection of his power pump into her shield, and she said, "Slayne, attack. I can hold them."

Order given, Slayne began his barrage of attacks. His first few strikes, coated in Elisa's aggressive shield, made contact and knocked the recipients back. But they returned to focus.

Peter and Jerome ran in and stopped the other side of Elisa. Jerome's magic was weak by comparison and so he chose to add power to Elisa's shield, placing his palms just behind it. He quickly felt Elisa drawing from him, and he focused.

Peter chose a different tack and, rather than shielding or attacking, he chose to aim his attacks to create a clear path for Slayne to strike. As his magic, Peter understood, was hundreds of years stronger.

With Elisa and Jerome at the centre, Slayne and Peter were able to dispense with two of the thirteen, but with their deaths, the others appeared to develop a resistance to the attacks. Even after the fall of the first, Slayne had to work three times harder to kill the second, and now that that one was dead, the others were virtually unaffected, invulnerable. He tried one more bolt, and he witnessed the target seemingly feed off it, like an elixir.

"Slayne, I can't hold..." Elisa was struggling to talk now. "I can't. Not much more. I'm ... sorry."

Peter was burnt out now and Slayne was near. Elisa took a sharp intake, as she disconnected from Jerome, and drained the last of her reserve power, but it was too little, too late, and the final attack shattered her shield into a million tiny fragments of magical dust.

The remaining eleven overlords may not have played to the rulebook of battle etiquette, but they paused for a moment and relished the defeat of their opponents.

***

"Damn!" The voice was back in Jerome's head.

He was about to open his mouth, but he stopped himself. There was something more, something about the voice that stopped it being just a voice; it was powerful, *really* powerful. It surrounded and shook the foundations on which everything was built. He looked to Elisa and Peter who looked like they both felt something, too.

Whatever this may be, it was magical, that much was clear, but even so, taken that his magical capacity was so much less than theirs, he was picking up on some very serious waves of might. Even Slayne, who was doing a rotten job of hiding his capitulation, also perked up at the disturbance in the magical flux.

And then it slammed down in front of them.

This invisible leviathan...

The ground shook and a deluge of death rattling towards them was suddenly stymied.

The party couldn't see what was doing this, but their aggressors seemed to be able to, as they turned to this invisible figure of massive power, and the battle began...

The eight could do little more than watch. Dwarfed by the greatest display of magical eminence ever witnessed, they watched as the eleven became ten, then nine, dropping to eight, their numbers soon halved, before dwindling ever lower.

Soon it was just one and astoundingly there was no retreat, not even a flicker of willingness to retire. The exchange continued, surging emissions rumbling back and forth between the invisible leviathan and the one, soon to become dead, single, remaining warrior.

As the altercation ended, so, too, did the presence of the mighty being. Was it dead? They all secretly hoped not. This was the first ally they had found in this place and they all hoped that it would remain that way.

***

Rest was a given, and Jerome was more than happy to allow a period of recovery, especially for Peter, Elisa, Slayne and himself. It was always a struggle to hold off his Dark Whisperer's will, but he would struggle, to supply an hour or two of rest.

***

Slayne, Keldor and Misto were not the sleeping types and, instead, decided to keep watch. Keldor and Misto had always been quiet together, but that was something that they knew, and could now respect, in each other. The uncomfortable hours and days of silence were over and, ironically, had become a point of conversation and humour for them both.

But sitting with Slayne was different. Little did Keldor and Misto know that Slayne was also a quiet type, and vice versa.

In the case of all the three of them, battle had become all they really knew. They were all masters in their own fields, veterans on the theatre of war and top of their game – and they all knew it.

"Keldor, that blade looks familiar," Slayne said.

Keldor looked at his sword and smiled, as though a secret joke he'd kept with the world had finally been discovered.

"People rarely notice," he said. "Its sister blade is just over there." And Keldor nodded to Jerome.

Understanding it and joining Keldor's secret joke, Slayne said, "Jerome's dirk."

And Keldor regaled him with the story. "The metal that both are forged from was once a longsword. Its name eludes me, but after a long lifetime of service it broke. Declared as worthless by its wielder, whose name *also* eludes me, it was sold as scrap metal to a blacksmith. Initially it was going to be smelted down, but my father saw it one day, heard of its history and commissioned the blacksmith to forge, from those two halves, two blades. The hilted half made this," – Keldor rotated the sword, its edge grazing the ground – "and the other smaller half made that dirk. My father bestowed the dirk to me before I became a Realm's Ranger, and the sword he presented me with when I was dubbed."

"…That's quite a story," Slayne remarked. "I could tell you some stories about this old girl," he said, lifting his own sword. "None as interesting as that, but she's no less precious to me."

"Ah, but it's not about the stories they've had; it's about the stories that are yet to be written."

"Well said; as *all* life should be. But listen," Slayne said breaking out of his *conversational* tone. "I have a bad feeling about what's up ahead."

Hearing his concern, Keldor said, "What do you suggest? A scout?"

Slayne nodded. "If you two have no objections, I'd like to run on ahead, make sure there's nothing undesirable. I'm concerned … for him." His voice was quiet as he gestured to Jerome, who was quietly catching some *haunted* sleep, head on his satchel.

"I agree." Keldor nodded, and then said, "Take care."

Slayne was as used to careful concern as Keldor was at giving it, but then he smiled and so did Keldor.

It was the start of another enduring friendship.

***

Jerome awoke, startled. He hadn't been dreaming of anything particular, just the usual horror of his Dark Whisperer, but something else had dredged him out of his soporific confines.

His head was still resting on his satchel when he saw Misto and Keldor sat together, quiet.

Slowly he turned over, un-sticking his face from his rough bag. He was just about to shut his eyes again when he noticed a white piece of material.

His eyes were still sleep-filled and his body was tired, but the compulsion to know what it was won out. Staying on his side, he reached his arm out and pulled himself those few inches further, until he could grab it.

It had a crisp texture, not what he was expecting and the little amount of energy he had expended in reaching it had shifted his mind to a more alert state.

Once he'd pulled it close and was readjusted on his back, he began to study it. He concluded that it was parchment, or near that, but it was stiffer – less clothy – than any parchment he'd felt before. He unfolded it, once, then twice, until it was open and he read the four words:

'Save Slayne, then yourself.'

He read it, and then re-read it. The handwriting looked slightly rushed and the strange parchment was still astounding him, but *was* Slayne in trouble? He didn't think so, unless he'd gone somewhere. *Why would he do that?* It hadn't really registered until now, but when it did, he bolted upright and immediately began scanning over the faces.

Elisa asleep; Galliana asleep; Peter asleep; Percy asleep; where's Thermion? Oh yes I remember; Keldor, Misto, they're awake; Slayne, not asleep, not awake. Where is he?

"Jerome, what is it?" Keldor said, having identified him the moment he sat up.

Ignoring his question, he said, "Where's Slayne?"

"He's just scouting the road ahead. Said something about having a bad feeling. Misto and I are keeping watch until he gets back. Jerome, *what's* wrong?" he said, reiterating his earlier question.

"He's not coming back." *Maybe a slight overstatement,* but Keldor didn't look like he was taking him seriously.

"Pardon?"

"Quickly, we have to wake everyone and find him."

"He'll be all right. He knows what he's—"

"Maybe the boy be right." Misto stopped his human friend. "He be gone some time now."

Keldor looked to his small companion who looked back, staring hard.

"Very well." Keldor honoured and respected the judgement of Misto.

As if given permission, Jerome immediately skipped from person to person, waking them all, except Galliana, who he woke, but only with a gentle shake before dashing away, trying to avoid any unprepared contact. There would be time to talk to her; maybe that's what the note meant: *'save yourself'. Or maybe I'm just crazy. Get a grip, Jerome!* He rebuked himself. This was no time for a crisis of character; Slayne may be in trouble.

A few minutes later, a few stretches on and everyone was in a suitable shape to continue.

"Keldor, do you think you can track where Slayne went?"

Keldor considered: tracking in the open wilds, where foot-prints – *any* kind of footprints (traces of life) – could be left, was one thing, but tracking in a city was entirely different. He gave the only answer he could. "I can try."

"Well if anyone can, *you* can," Jerome encouraged.

For the second time since the start of the journey, Jerome was no longer leading the party, although he didn't really count Jason's time as leader. So, in a way it felt like the first *proper* time. And he relished the moment, as Keldor was so much better at leading. He had the gait, the presence, of a lea-der and Jerome truly admired him.

***

This remote region on the farthest side of The Dark Realm was the darkest place so far, and the most untouched. Most of the structures were relatively unscathed, but even so, it still felt ruined and empty, like its soul had long since departed.

"Jerome," Elisa attracted his attention while taking place next to him, "I'm not sure about this. This – this isn't right. I don't know what it is, but I can sense something."

No doubt about it, he too felt the evil itching of something unstable. "Have you ever felt it before?"

"I can't say for sure; dark magus-like, maybe, but ... no. It's different. I know a dark magus and this just isn't—"

"Shh!" Keldor's piercing charisma – a perfect character of a leader – silenced and stopped everyone.

All eyes turned, mimicking to where Keldor was looking. With delicacy, they all caught sight of what had stopped them.

She was stood in the middle of the street and then Elisa, Jerome and Peter all understood that she was what they were sensing. *Magically speaking,* all she was, and could ever be, to Keldor was just a girl. However, he was an intelligent man and didn't need a magical perspective to tell him that she wasn't *just a girl.*

Lonely girl, strange underworld realm, skin ashen, *armed;* chances were that she was just as adverse as the other denizens of this godforsaken place.

And then her actions spoke louder, as she started running forwards, but as they watched, she wasn't just running, she was using some strange derivation of void travel, with the shadows. Fading into some and then exploding out of others, she covered massive distance and rapidly.

"Not a dark magus then," Elisa said, prepping herself.

Jerome drew his dirk and glanced around the rest of the party. Percy had taken place next to Galliana. Peter had his sword out, Keldor and Misto, too. He took another moment to try and locate Slayne, as was natural – he was still a member of the party – and then he remembered.

She moved with a frightening and ghostly incongruity. Her feet never appeared to touch the floor, yet she whispered through the space as if she were. Swaying to the thump of a spectral tempo, her gaze never shifted and, in a wash of smoke and mirrors, she dashed out from a patch of shade near Keldor and went in for the kill.

Keldor was quick and he blocked her attack, using her own momentum as a driving force. She carried on moving, landing and fading into another patch of shade.

As swiftly as she entered, she burst out of another, with the same haunting speed, the same thump of a spectral tempo.

She was heading directly for Peter, and Jerome's heart was pounding for the safety of his friend. She engaged and he held her off, and just as Jerome was turning to assist, she dematerialised, only to emerge out in front of Elisa.

Even before engaging Elisa had already readied a selection of prepared magics, and she released the quickest and simplest, which struck her, and promptly stunned her.

Peter, who was stood next to Elisa, was also ready (as they all were) and he turned and lunged, piercing this Dark Realm dweller's stomach. She screeched as the impaling dropped her out of her strange pattern of movement.

Frantically wriggling and writhing, she scrabbled around on the floor, hurriedly scurrying towards a shady area. But it was close though, as Peter was only moments from spearing her again. One hand in the shadow, like a pool of black ooze, she pulled the rest of her body in behind.

Now there was silence. Everyone was keeping their eyes on everyone else…

"Jerome, down!" shouted Percy.

Jerome instantly dropped his body weight and the second his hands hit the cold cobbled floor, he spun round, using his free hand to bolster himself. But the ground was uneven and while he rotated, he slipped and fell back.

Like she was eyeing a piece of weak and defenceless prey, her breath hissed as it left lungs, as she began to cut away the distance between them, the odd absurdities of her movement back as if she were unscathed.

She was so close that he could see the discolouration in her eyes. Then, Percy's giant shield, normally hitched to his back, was suddenly dropped over and in front of Jerome, dampening out most of the light, but the blueness was all encompassing.

The strange resonant atmosphere behind the tower shield was like being in a realm within a realm, with each collision upon the shield amplified. But it didn't last long before Percy rammed forward, spryly stepping over Jerome, relieving him of the haunting acoustics.

And the second he was over, Jerome got to his feet. Percy was still blocking his view and seconds before he could assist, the sound of her screech – a sound he very much equated with pain – stopped him.

A quick glance from over Percy's shoulder saw Slayne, standing behind her and then, as he moved to get a clearer picture, he saw his sword sticking out the other side of her. He had an arm round her neck, holding her still while the sword destroyed her insides, her grey, colourless pupils slowly draining of life.

Her last dying movements were her hands, clawing at her throat trying to pry Slayne's locked arm away, but he was too strong and Jerome could also see something else at work – something he had never seen from him before – *hate.*

The last droplets of her life were absorbed into the well of the dead and she stopped squirming. Once she slipped down from Slayne's loosened grip, Jerome officially – and silently to himself – announced Slayne saved: as dictated by the note's order. But, of course, it wasn't that simple – it never was.

Had he even been in trouble? He tapped the belt pouch in which he had stashed the note, and then considered its second instruction: *then yourself.*

He didn't need saving, not now at any rate, but more to the point, it implied that he had to save himself, and from what? And then he considered – was it even *him* that had actually saved *Slayne?* Or did Slayne save himself? This precipitated another question, was that note actually meant for him in the first place?

Was it even important?

Of course it's important! he snapped at himself.

If it transpired that the portent concerning Slayne was false then it might remove his own warning from the equation, that is, if the note *was* actually addressed to him. Who would have thought that four words could be so confusing?

He jumped back and forth from indecision to indecision, until finally landing on what actually mattered, whatever will happen will happen. He had enough to worry about, without worrying what else the future was going to throw at him. He just hoped that he would be able to *save himself* before it was too late.

Suddenly, billowing out of every shadow, between here and as far as the eye could see, were hundreds of those *things*. They all moved in the same bizarre, wraithlike manner, hop-ping in and out of the glooms – swimming pools of the umbra.

The party had huddled together, forming an outward facing circle. They all had their respective weapons out and ready, whether a fistful of magic or a firm hold on a blade, whether a sword, a knife or dirk.

Ready for war, the party watched frenziedly as every weird creature abruptly dipped and vanished into the shadows, leaving them all alone, stationary and facing out. Their breath cut the silence – the absolute ear-piercing calm.

Moments turned to seconds, just as their focus turned to confusion.

But what they hadn't considered was the area of deep shade created at the centre of them.

And unfortunately, it wasn't until these creatures suddenly began springing up and grabbing hold of them, that they realised the flaw.

As each of them became clamped under the grip of two *things,* they watched the mass emergence of the army of those creatures.

Shortly after, they were dragged down into the shadows beneath, into the umbra…

Chapter XIV
A Promise Made, A Promise Kept

It was like swirling around the veins of the world, where strands of memory joined to physical essences, both as real as the next. It was a big well of nothingness and as they traversed through, a bleak trace remained, leaving a permanent mark on the underlying paradigm of the world and then they materialised, and it left all eight of them dazed, weary and desperately trying to catch their breath.

It was not designed to be used by the ordinary mortal – it was not designed to be used at all. It was the matrix of the universe – the multiverse – where all the handwritten scripts of a superpower resided. It was a spooky truth, even spookier to have seen it and touched it, but now the physical world was returning to dulled senses.

Eyes slowly peeling open, they realised they were being studied. The room, in which they found themselves restrained, reflected the district above, pristine, but cold and soulless.

The floor shone like polished glass with each and every scrape and scratch completely unmissable against its glistening reflectivity. The walls, like the 'chamber', were an exhibition of a master craftsman, with every stone edge of every shaped glyph smooth. Even the graininess of the stone had been scrub-bed to a shine almost as reflective as the floor.

The ceiling, as seen through the reflection of the floor, was coated in a sea of fire, but the flamed peaks pointed against the accepted understanding, with gravity exerting itself through a different and somewhat inverted medium.

Jerome looked up and saw only shadows, dancing off each other, creating what he now knew to be little portals into the dimension of the umbra. The room showed no other function than as an antechamber between their world and the world above, and even that was buried beneath the sands of time.

"You are trespassers here," said a voice, in a melodious and soothing tone, even though the words were anything but.

The recuperating party looked up, drowsy, still stunned from the phantom journey. Standing, back to the ornate wall behind, was another of these creatures. Jerome wished he had more of a word by which to call them, but *creature* was all he could think of right now.

His skin, like the others, was ashen, his pupils slightly greyed, but it was his attire that distinguished him from the rest. Predominantly his loose fitting clothes were black, but specks of other dark colours garnished and added a definitive texture, even if consciously unaware of the extra chromaticity.

"That ... is m-my fault," Jerome carefully spoke out, but stuttered from the travel through the umbra. "I have been ... leading my—"

"Trespassing can be the sin of an honest person, as well as the deceitful," he said, his voice still melodious, "and forgiveness shall always be granted where there was no intent or ... naivety."

No one formed a response.

He continued, "But *that* is not why you are here. Your trespassing shall be forgiven; it is the blood that you have split that shall be not."

"It was ... n-not m-meant," Jerome whimpered, finding it hard to grasp a hold of any energy.

"We don't often get visitors down here, and crimes are few and far between. An apt punishment shall have to be decided."

"If anyone ... is to be punished," Slayne said, hastily, suffixing his sentence, "it should be me. I ... killed her."

"You will be punished. You will *all* be punished."

Elisa broke her silence and pleaded, "Please, have mercy. It was not meant."

"You expect so much when you show so little...?" The melody of his voice ached, as though a dirge. "Where was *your* mercy?"

With a dreamlike shift, he manifested into the reflection beneath and then proceeded to walk out of a door that, to everyone's ignorance until now, did not exist on *this* side of the mirror. Unlike every other one of these *creatures,* which moved with a strange disconnectedness, he was different. He was almost … human, but of course he wasn't.

The non-existent door closed, while fate rested and loomed just beyond.

There were so many things down here that defied all logical physics. This *place,* The Dark Realm, was like one giant mixing bowl of mistakes and rejections, all thrown together and left to rebuild itself into whatever abomination it chose, allowing only the limit of its horrific imagination.

Still restrained tight, two on one, they remained, unaware of time and mesmerised by the flame that didn't exist and the mirror that reflected only lies.

Minutes, *hours* may have passed while the umbral delirium worked through, and then the figure, the human-*creature* rejoined them, coming first through the door and then shifting back into their plane.

"I have spoken to my council and we have agreed … an eye for an eye – a life for a life."

Recovered, Slayne was quick to speak. "My life."

"No. That would not be a fair exchange of the *tooth.*"

He was met with silence; he hadn't finished talking.

"In fact, if we're being totally reciprocal, then it should be one of the young." He flicked out a finger, which he dubbed as his pointing tool. "You," he pointed to Elisa; "you," – Percy, his finger passing Galliana; "you," – Slayne; "you," – Keldor, skipping Jerome and Peter; "and as much I dislike green-skins, you," – Misto was the last to receive the *point.* "Take them to the edge of the city, if that is really where they want to go."

Shadows expanded and folded down from the ceiling, enveloping the selected five and fading them up, out and into the umbral plane.

Peter, Jerome and Galliana remained, and the room suddenly felt a lot darker. All three were still relatively young and, although they had learnt much, the adults that had accompanied them – that were now drifting back to the real world above – were more than just friends; they were their mentors, their guides, their life coaches and, without them and their unspoken support, it was like the safety net had been ripped out from beneath their feet.

Shadows returning to normal and silence growing louder by second, the man re-commissioned his pointing finger and, again, slowly started shifting between the three of them.

He was playing their heartbeats in time to an evil rhythm, like a conductor wooing the audience behind with his ultimate control of the orchestra. When his finger glided over each, their heartbeats became so explosive, and bashed so hard, that their insides almost ruptured. At least, that was how it felt, but as his finger stopped over Jerome, his pounding heart paused, while his mind prepared his body for the end.

"You," the pale man confirmed.

**

Shadows of an old, sparse wood on the remote edge of the city opened and the party, without the young three, materialised. Their captors released their grip and descended back into the rippling pools of the umbra.

The umbral fever was worse this time and they collapsed to the fossilised grassland floor. Minutes passing, they all tried to gather themselves, their thoughts and bodies until eventually, one at a time, they shifted to a sitting position.

With time passing in silence, they waited for their young companions to return; hopeful that they would – *all* of them – but doubt's unscrupulous hand was the puppeteer of a different outcome, an outcome they knew would be the epitome of tragedy.

The shadows slowly rippled open again and materialising slowly on their plane was Galliana. Able to get to their feet, Percy and Keldor sluggishly rushed over – as fast as they could in their delirious state – to her and helped her sit.

"Galliana," Percy muttered, resting her down.

She was conscious, but only just, and her eyes were faintly swollen and red from where tears had been.

She took her time to find her voice, but she spoke the moment she could. "Jerome."

"He's … gone?" Elisa took her turn to speak, but every word mustered felt as hard as running a marathon.

Galliana was about to open her mouth and speak again, but was disturbed by the expansion of another shadow near to where she had been deposited.

Lying down, a hand resting at the side – allowing room to pass through the shadow realm of the umbra – was one of the two boys. In a foetal position he was raised up from the pool of darkness and then left as the single figure touching him descended back down.

His side was moving up and down, under the motion of his breathing, and as Keldor approached, he was fully expecting to see Peter.

But instead, he discovered Jerome.

His eyes were closed and his face was bleeding from a number of lacerations and wounds. Not a novitiate of injury, Keldor could see that this was a severe beating. But something else then occurred to him, with double the speed of realisation, that if Jerome was here, then Peter was … *there.*

He hadn't thought. It was a split second discovery, expecting to see Peter and seeing Jerome instead, all the joy at seeing his young friend again flipped into reverse. His smile turned down at the edges and everyone could see.

"What is it, Keldor?" Slayne said, taking the conversation.

"Jerome is here."

"Here…? Then that means that…" Slayne's words turned to nothingness, his own realisation the stopper.

Those finishing few words didn't need to be audible to be known. Keldor looked down again to Jerome and his eyes were moving rapidly beneath closed eyelids.

***

He is pointing at me.

"You," he says and I can feel my heartbeat halt. Its earlier thuds denoting only the anticipation, but as his finger stops, leading my heart to stop with it, I prepare myself. It burns inside

and I want to cry, but something holds my tears back. Even the lump in the back of my throat begins to dissipate.

The man walks over to me. I can sense Peter and ... her – I still don't know her name – next to me. They are talking, shouting maybe, but I'm too focused and their words can't carry above that. He assesses me, looking me deep in the eye. I return his look and, although I'm trying to remain strong, I know that I am scared and I know, also, that he can tell. He holds my gaze for a moment longer and then, I don't know why, something changes. I can see some fear lingering in his eyes.

He steps back. He regards her, *but the same fear stays in his eyes. "Take her away, out of the city," he orders and she fades into the shadows.*

Peter and I stand together. I know something's changed, but can Peter also tell? I look at him and we share a glance. "Him." And his finger is on Peter.

He starts to take a step back, and my eye contact with Peter is broken by a sharp push jolting him forward. It suddenly kicks in, and I realise that it's not me being taken.

All my fear turns to anger. I don't take the time to fully understand it – I can't – but I feel cheated. It was going to be me. I had stared death in the face; I had accepted it, was ready for it. This is not right.

I try to release my hands from the figures behind me, but they are strong. I can also sense magic. It's weak, but yes, it's definitely there. Peter is the other side of the room now, near where the man originally melded into the reflection. I can't let them take him and I force the magic down my arms and into my hands and something explodes.

My arms are free and I run, charging to Peter, more importantly, to the two figures escorting him. With what little magic I can summon to my fists, I smash into the back of one of their heads.

He instantly releases Peter and then the creature *hits me.*

I'm still under the umbra's fever and my legs begin to quiver. My left leg collapses and my right leg bends, lowering me to a half-kneeling position. Powerless to do anything, I can see his hand clenching and he punches me on the cheek.

The hit is so hard that, rather than feeling pain, it squeezes the blood out from the pounded area, numbing it, but the blood rushes back, bringing with it the pain, which, in its time of postponement, has only increased.

My head throbs and I keel over. He begins to kick me, in the stomach, in the head and, with each blow, I start to become less aware of the pain.

"Stop," the voice orders and mercifully, the kicking stops, but unfortunately the hurt catches up with me – just like the original punch in the face – and my body is embroiled in an agonising web of spasm.

I open my eyes, desperate to catch sight of Peter. I can't see him at first, but then I do. He is already through the reflection and being led through that door. Peter looks back and I can see him saying something

I can't hear it, but it looks like, "I'm sorry I—" and I can't make out the rest. A chill runs over me. I can remember every event in our lives together, playing in super-quick time and perfect clarity, but why is he sorry? What is he sorry for?

And then he is gone.

The door shuts and that's it, but something tells me that's not the last time I'll see him. And I really want that to be true.

***

Drowsily, Jerome unstuck his eyelids from each other as he began to remove himself from his dream. He was on his back and kneeling over him was Elisa. She was the first person he saw as his eyes adjusted to remove the blur, but when he turned his head, he saw everyone else, everyone except Peter.

He was still trying to look for him, clinging to the hope that a dream was only ever a dream and not something des-tined for the light of life, but as he stirred and the bruises were revealed true, so, too, was revealed the Peter-sized hole that existed inside.

He tried to shuffle his body up on an angle and, in doing so, revived the agony, but he wouldn't let it stop him.

"Jerome, you need to rest," Elisa said, but he already had enough problems fighting the temptation of the pain, prompting him to give up at every corner, let alone being encouraged to lie down.

He stopped in some half-position between lying down and sitting up. It was painful, but it wasn't the pain that stopped him – he'd had worse from Slayne, whom he'd personally forgiven years ago for his harsh, and malice-free, training – it was the emotional pain, the cloying hopelessness of being without Peter. However, something changed when he felt Elisa's warm hand brace him and help him up.

He wasn't used to help, but with a wince he accepted it and he found some comfort in being sat up, able to join everyone else. "Thank you," he said.

Jerome looked around, thinking himself to be the worst affected by Peter's absence, but seeing everyone's faces, he saw that he had won their hearts, just as he had captured his.

They had successfully crossed The Dark Realm – well, as *successfully* as you can call it. They were two down and he had seen better days, but as they sat, surrounded by dead, petrified trees and other upper worldly features outside the city, as dictated by the antiquated, wooden city gates, adjoined either side by two ancient chunks of stone wall, it struck them. They *had* negotiated probably the most deadly of places in Aramyth.

And they sat in silence to consider this, and the silence was welcome, but not for all…

"I need to apologise," Slayne said breaking the moment.

With remembrance still upon them, Slayne's words only added confusion and they looked to him, but as he acquired their stares, they could see something genuine – regret?

"It should be *me* not sitting here," he remarked.

"You have nothing to apologise for," Keldor offered. "The choice was not ours."

Slayne took his words and said, "You don't understand."

Elisa had been listening intently and she encouraged her fellow magus. "Then explain. We will listen to you, Slayne."

The conversation had uncorked the bottle, in which a history of trouble had been locked up, and he was being wracked by blame and, its close colleague, guilt, but he found his first words.

"It happened a long time ago, back when I was young, when *Alatacia* was still young and growing and new magi from all over Aramyth found a home there. The thousands that live there now were just hundreds then. I was still in my *first life,*" – Slayne looked knowingly at his protégé and it touched Jerome deeply, seeing him like that, understanding that his teacher was once a pupil – "and had just finished under the *full* tutelage of my mentor, Mithra, and was enjoying my freedom as a blade magus.

"But they were saddened times back then and, with Aramyth under the heavy tyranny of King Vian, Queen Casadriel, King Morrowyn and their black guard, the people of the realm had no spirit, no identity. But the horror of the triumvirate was not the worst thing coming for the people. To the east, some-thing was stirring."

Slayne jiggled, his discomfit clear. "Like I said before, Alatacia was still in its infancy and, like everything young, we moved quickly, formed groups and councils. We were impetuous and we acted as such. But with all this power at our fingertips, we sensed this eastern uprising and we wanted to help. By then, the magi of Alatacia had naturally split into three divisions, all depending upon the varying interests and foci of magic. The groups, we all know to be, were the Blades, the Battles and the Pures. The Blade Magi, from their levelled capacity to understand both aspects of magic and weaponry, fell into the position of command and it was us who were elected… It was us who elected *ourselves.*

"It was a mismanaged and badly organised expedition, but we didn't consider that then, and a few days later we were in Marston, overlooking the Burning Bluffs. The oppression within the village was rife, but our presence gave some degree of hope and, in turn, sparked us on to continue. With no rest, no planning, we marched onwards and—" He stopped. He breathed. He looked around. The emotion surged through him with torrential desecration.

The blue tranquillity of The Dark Realm had settled around them, but with this hiatus it quickly grew unsavoury.

Slayne thankfully rediscovered his words and at last said, "It was a massacre. I don't know how many of us there were before we left – fifty, maybe less – but I was the only one to return, and it was in my *second life*. We all died, but I had that second chance… We call them dark ones.

"With the elimination of the Blade Magi and our leadership, Alatacia quickly fell into disarray, with power wars rising between the two remaining factions. Those power wars still go on to this day, and I was left as a grim relic of the ancient guild, but life went on. I carried on training, alone, waiting."

Jerome felt honoured to be privy to such knowledge, but…

"But how does that make you responsible for Peter?" Elisa was quick to vindicate Slayne from his turmoil. "She attacked us."

"No," Slayne amended, and it was a shamed correction. "I swore personal revenge for the death of all my kindred Blades, friends and mentor." His tone changed. "And then I sensed them here. It was the day I'd been waiting for, to exact revenge, to fulfil the vendetta that had been forged in blood over five hundred years ago… No, I attacked her first. I had a chance to—" And his tone fell back to shame. "But, I've only succeeded in creating more suffering and I need to apologise, because – because it should have been me."

He had spent most of his time talking looking at the ground, extracting the dark memories hidden deep in the remote boundaries of his mind, but now he stole himself away from that and deigned himself to the judgement of his friends.

"I know that I can never—"

"Wait," Jerome said, speaking against him. The lines that defined them as teacher and pupil blurred as he was silenced. Jerome tried to reason with what he had said, but with every passing moment he found it harder to associate with him. Was he angry? Yes, *furious*. His friend may still be here if it hadn't been for the rash actions of his mentor. He couldn't even keep eye contact with him and, ignoring how much it would hurt, he eased himself back to a lying position, and then rolled on to one side. Every movement was a painful reminder and it stung, not the wounds that were lavished across his body, but the shock that every stir was twinned with an emotional pang.

"I think we should all get some rest. It has been a tough day." Percy, being the oldest and most reasoned, took his status as the *old man,* and the party listened to him and they all retired.

***

"Jerome, I know this is a bad time and a really odd request, but I don't know if we'll get another chance. If we get out of here, I want you to talk to that girl," Peter whispers to me.

"What are you talking about?" I whisper back, surprised at his choice of words. "Peter, this really is *a bad time."* Why is he talking to me about this?

"I know, but promise me, yes?"

"Fine." I put an end to it and think no more about it.

***

"Peter!" Jerome sat up and the cold sweat that lined his face began to trickle down.

The promise, he remembered. He relaxed himself back down and then noticed the blanket that someone had put over him. He really was among friends, but then he began to remember and the anger he felt earlier crept back; it all did, but he was too preoccupied to be as angry as he was before; he had a promise to keep.

Of course, that meant actually talking to her, maybe even finally finding out her name. *But how can I talk to her now?* He rolled over and carried on thinking. *She'll be asleep, and I can't wake her just to satisfy my desire to find out her name...* He rolled over again. *But I promised him. Wouldn't be so bad if he was still ... but he's not, which makes this so much worse, because it's turned a whimsical promise into a last rite!* He repeated that line of thought then moved on. *Get up.* He didn't want to. *Open your eyes and get up!* He completed 'part one' of his personal command, and had even rolled uncomfortably up onto legs. He then underwent the rigmarole of bestirring himself to get fully up, and was just about to heave, when he felt a hand rest on his shoulder.

It startled him, but he didn't flinch.

"Shh," came the order of silence. It was a female and he had his suspicions but, equally, he didn't want to get his hopes up – he'd had enough of hope going bad and ending up false.

He turned and it was *her* looking at him. She had taken her coat off and her arms were bare, her skin was—

Nerves and impulse won out over control and composition and he said, "I was just about to find you."

"Really?" she spluttered.

He couldn't back down now. "Yes, I wanted to…" Maybe he *could* back down.

She waited for him to finish, but when she sensed his reticence, something he was not in short supply of, she helped him find his words. "What is it, Jerome?"

Just the great blue nothingness.

"Tell me," she begged.

He regarded her, and then, before he could stop himself, he found that he was outright staring at her, picking up on all the details he hadn't the courage to map before. Her hair, as tinted by the Dark Realm's natural colour, was a mirror of amethyst mines. Her eyes of green were the mesmeric lures onto which he was hooked. And he was *hooked. Bound by her…*

And now that he was, the thought of becoming *un*-hooked, *un*-bound by her, felt so far away from all possibility, would have been like spitting at the gates of heaven. Turning it down.

His body was a smouldering ember and the question he so longed to ask, which lingered so long in the well of his soul, came out not from choice, but because her will had swooped down and plucked it out. "What's your name?"

Unprompted, she beamed and went in to kiss him. It was soft and timeless, as it joined them into a single weft thread that endured through life's tapestry.

***

Galliana couldn't answer why she had kissed him.

It was something she had wanted to do since seeing him, since defining him as something beautiful, something folkloric, something that the stars might gift – but only if they were trying to impress.

She had been unable to keep away from him. All her dreams, of which there were many, seemed purpose built around him now. She felt she knew him, felt as close to him, as though they were crossed fingers, but the reality was that they were from different hands completely. That was why she went over to see him: to see her dream, to see the stars' gift.

She had seen him sit up onto his legs before trying to move further, like he was getting up, and she had rested a hand on his shoulder. She had done it because he looked in so much pain, and he had stopped upon her touch.

She had seen his back rise and expand, like he was going to speak, and she had asked for his silence with a 'shh'. She didn't want to wake anyone. She just wanted this to be him and her.

He had turned to look at her, as she had knelt. His face alone was enough to galvanise her, but then he'd said, "I was just about to find you."

And she was taken off guard – as if her thumping heart, pumping, pumping, *pumping* away inside her, wasn't already working hard enough to combat this nonesuch. She couldn't help but splutter a 'really?'

He had been so quiet. Apart from their brief time together, back in Marston, she had felt so separated from him. She felt like he had been avoiding her. Maybe he had, but *how* could he look at her like that?

He had spoken again, saying, "Yes, I wanted to…" But his words stopped.

"What is, Jerome?" she'd said, maybe begged.

Just the great blue nothingness.

He was *so* silent; she couldn't understand it. Even when he'd *talked* he'd seemed quiet, maybe shy, like his words were just *breaks in his silence,* as if his soul were too scared to come out, as if the injuries his body bore were a true depiction of the recesses of his heart. But once they had been attacked, she almost couldn't recognise him as the same man. She remembered Elisa saying that she had found him alone, looking for his mother. It pained her to think of him like that, because she could relate, but where was the real man now? Where was the man that was being masked by the fighter? What was *he* really like? She thought she'd seen traces of him, small amounts that had only driven her to higher tiers of curiosity.

She wanted to coax his soul out, to let it know that if it were to show to itself, it would not be ill-treated, that *she* could be trusted, that she would nurture and nurse it back to health.

But what did *he* want? "Tell me," she'd said, definitely begged. He may have wanted, but she *needed*.

And then he had asked her name – just that which he had wanted – but it was how he'd said it: as though he were asking her for something sacred – asking after some secret passage from an ancient volume of forgotten lore.

His eyes had been soul-searching her in a way that no others ever had, and her *impulsion* to kiss him was more like *his* will, winding up the spool of invisible thread between them. She leaned forward, rolling her hands out, taking the weight of her top half and putting her lips to his. If she were being honest, his unshaven face grated against her skin, but his touch was so tender – so innocently naïve and tender – she completely overlooked his rugged texture.

As they parted – as she walked her hands back, back to kneeling – and she saw him, frozen, bathed in the azure spring, she was suddenly struck with worry that she had gone too far, too early.

"Galliana," she quickly answered, hoping to free him from his motionless confines.

His eyes opened, but motionless he remained. Unable to keep his eye contact, she found herself looking at the dark impression inflaming around his right eye. *They had really hurt him,* she inwardly thought, wanting to kiss the pain away, but he was still unmoving.

So she quickly added, "But call me Ana." Which she thought *really* strange, because she hadn't divulged that to *any*one since – she'd not even *considered* uttering it since –

she'd heard her mother's voice, a whisper as it had been, but it projected the urgency of a roar – *'Ana, you have to go. Now! Get out, while there's still time. Run!'*

But he was still motionless.

Growing self-conscious at his wordlessness, and stillness, she swiftly apologised for kissing him.

As soon as she'd said it, Jerome couldn't free the 'no, no's from his mouth fast enough, but his legs were beginning to go sorely numb from where he was sat on them at a funny angle, and the kiss had only brought forth a new discomfit. "Please," he spluttered, as he agonisingly heaved himself onto his haunches, easing his weight down onto the backs of his feet, lowering into the prayer position. "Don't be," he said, half-apologising and wishing for another of her kisses, and half-praying that he hadn't blown it.

His blood was already charging around his body so fast that it was strumming the inner lining of veins, and now that she had kissed him, he was experiencing excitement on a whole new, ineffable level.

They were now both knelt, a perfect reflection of each other's posture, their eyes meeting, connecting in the void of the weary-eyed woods that *slept in the place beyond.*

"It was… I'm just…" he continued, speaking his simple two-word mumbles in such a way that he wanted her to understand, but it was tearing him apart: he was so thrilled and, yet, so laden with woe that his shoulders drooped; his head dipped forward; his eyes flitted left and right, as he delved into the wonder of what was the thicket floor – the hardened, yet cushiony, grassland bedding their knees and their curled-forward toes.

"I know." Her hands came up to his limp arms. "I'm sorry about…" she said, stopping, because no more needed saying.

Jerome brought his head up and nodded at her remark, relieved that she *did* understand, but it remained to bother him that this – this whole *thing* – was morbidly founded upon the last wish of his dead – *ouch* – friend. However, it was only until *after* he considered that, while he felt her hands soothing him, while he remembered the *kiss* – a first for him, as it was for her

– that he attempted a new train of thought: this was not a stoic effort made to appease his friend.

He was *honouring* his friend.

His shoulders lifted a degree and his face must have brightened, and she must have seen it, because she smiled and released him, softly, softly; but it rapidly dawned on him that there were things he wanted to know about her.

"You want to know about Thermion, don't you?" she said, as if she could read the question from the young lines on his face.

"Yes."

"I wish I *could* explain it. My – I don't know what It's called … vision?"

"Dark Whisperer," Jerome added, "or so I was told It to be." And in that moment, in a strange and somewhat purgative sense, it gave them both the freedom to know that what they had suffered was a shared suffering, a misery that they hadn't borne alone, something that had put them as partners in a single breath of life – whether hallowed or cursed… It didn't matter.

"I … don't know," she continued, "but It always tempted me away from him. It was like there was something wrong with him, but *I* could never see it."

Like him, she was also dealing with a huge amount of misdirection and misinformation, leaving her to feel just some poor wretch at the mercy of the gods' vagaries, a neglected doll played into the follies of a much bigger, theurgical revolution.

Now it was *her* shoulders that had slumped, and it was now *him* taking a grasp of her arms.

They felt cold against his rough hands and he softened his grip, applying a depth of tenderness he never knew he had, he'd never been *allowed* to have … until her – until she'd conquered him, him and his torpor soul.

But it was the touch alone that she so desperately desired, and it was every bit as she'd imagined: sating, yet deepening, her must-have; quenching, yet stoking, the fire that was her addiction; his body a flaming ember, her body one spark away from igniting perpetual burn.

"But with you," she said, uplifted by his first real reach out for her, "my ... Dark Whisperer has ... almost gone."

He had unconsciously straightened his body, forwarding his weight over his knees, and she had done the same.

Their chests virtually grazing, breathing heavy, trembling from their hearts palpitating together, body heat flooding warmth into the closing gap between, he said, "Ana," speaking her name, like it was the most natural thing, like it was the millionth time he'd said it, like he was seizing it from the pool of ceaseless dreams. "Is that why it's me?" he asked.

Had asked, not because he *wanted* it to be true, not through innocence or for understanding, to discern truth from illusion, to separate out the granules of falsity, but for the simple fact that—

"...It was always you," she whispered, holding his eyes' gaze – before one of them swelled shut – mirroring his ardour.

And he kissed her, and where their lips started their bodies followed, blending together with the same voracious obsession as the ethereal blue hands of The Dark Realm's light, clinging to every surface – hungry, starving, *famished*.

They kissed, under nightly blue dreams, among the echoes of dormancy, until they found each other...

Chapter XV
Conclusions, Part II

The morning – rather, the hour at which they all woke – came. Keldor and Misto had their usual morning wake-up competition, a contest that Misto would frequently win and, from most times before, in which Keldor had got used to wearing the loser's cap. But they were both miffed to discover that they had both lost to Percy, who was sat, perfectly, in his white surcoat, chainmail coif beneath hugging his head.

Slayne, armed with what felt like only a few minutes of sleep behind him, stirred and woke. *Today is going to be a tough day,* he thought, reprimanding himself for his actions again. But he dug deep.

Elisa roused and her first instinct was to look over to Jerome. She was taken by shock to see Galliana next to him, but supposed it to be the most logical conclusion – both young, both lonely and seeking company – no, that wasn't it; she saw the *spark* between them when they first set eyes on each other … everyone had. And the truth was: he was no longer a boy.

The pair of them also stirred, waking each other, but when they saw everyone else, rising and alert, it became awkward and Galliana tried to quietly hustle over to where she had been sleeping before.

They worked, mostly in silence, getting themselves together, rolling up the bedding. Jerome touched base with Keldor and Percy and sauntered over to Elisa, but he didn't dignify Slayne with a look. He was still angry, but when he crossed eyes with Galliana, the anger, for the most part, subsided. In fact, he smiled, and she smiled back, and this time it was *real.* Their smiles were real. And then he remembered Peter and thanked him for making him talk to her.

Elisa, taking his jaw with a strong hand and moving his head at a slight angle, interrupted his reverie. She made an empathetic wince and took a sharp intake of breath. "Ooh, that's really shone up."

He didn't know for sure what she was referring to, but he thought it might be his eye. The muscles around it twinged a little every time he blinked and all of a sudden he felt very self-conscious. A kick in the eye had been one of many places where he had been battered. His arms, legs, body, everywhere had taken some degree of scarification. But that was over now; he had to move on.

Dark Whisperer located, Jerome turned round for one final nod to his party before turning back round to face the grim apparitions.

"Wait!"

***

Waiting, hidden in the sapphire shadows, Garrick, Mythos and Baylin lurked. They had tracked delicately behind, biding their time for the perfect moment to strike, that moment evolving with every passing second. And now, with two members down, morale at an all time low and tensions running high, Garrick deemed that moment now.

"Wait!" he bellowed from behind the huge, ancient city gates.

More precisely, they were stationed behind the two solid remnants of city wall that jutted out either side of the gates, he and Mythos one side, Baylin the other. They folded out, facing the party for the first time since they had begun their hunt over three years ago. And it was so much more than just the boy he was interested in – so, *so* much more. But, he would give them the chance. That would be the fair thing to do...

***

The dwindling seven turned and watched the three figures stride out.

"Keldor," Garrick said, catching the ranger's eye.

"Garrick," Keldor said, noting his presence.

They know each other? Jerome thought – everyone thought. He looked at the scar filtering down above his left eye, which looked damaged. Here, in The Dark Realm's blue synonymy, eye colour was distorted, but he could see the malevolence twitching beneath. He was a dangerous man, an unpredictable man, and it made Jerome nervous just looking at him. How Keldor had the stomach to even talk to him made his insides turn to mush.

"Just want the boy, Keldor. Hand him over and no one needs to die."

No! Jerome pleaded voicelessly, *not this time. Please, Keldor, don't hand me over.* He couldn't help the feelings, even though he felt them to be selfish. It wasn't like before, anymore. He cared too much; he had things to live for, to fight for… to *die* for…

"Not sure who you mean. There's no boy here."

"Don't play games with me, Marder." *Marder? Was that his last name?* "…Him." The hand that was rested inches to the left of his buckle slowly moved and straightened towards Jerome.

Instinctively, everyone, even the party, looked at Jerome and his cheeks turned crimson. What made it worse was that, because he was stood at the back now, every head had to turn right round. It was a slow, uncomfortable period, but he braved it. Garrick's eyes delved deeper than anything he'd felt before, upturning all his secrets, uprooting his self-control, upsetting his self-esteem. He felt violated by the evil incarnate.

Garrick looked back to Keldor, and in a tone that was insincere he spoke the cliché. "Give him to me and no harm will befall any of you."

Please don't give me up, Jerome wished.

Now Keldor waited, weighing up his words. "We both know that's not true, Garrick."

Galliana peered over to Jerome who looked visibly calmed at Keldor's answer, as was she, for she would see him again.

Garrick paused and looked to his old acquaintance. *It wasn't going to be easy. Good.*

"You're right, old friend. Let's settle this, finish what we started all those years ago," Garrick said, suggesting a history.

Crossing his body with the sword from his left and dagger from the right, Garrick waited, poised, allowing every blood-hungry, nihilistically charged muscle time to contract and release. He was ready, and he exploded into a sprint.

Simultaneously, Keldor equally armed himself with sword and dagger. He knew Garrick's fighting style – knew it as well as his own.

***

Garrick's charge was the baptism of battle, with Baylin circling around to the left, opposing Percy, and Mythos to the right, facing Elisa.

Percy turned to Galliana, whose face was the epitome of worry. "Stay behind me."

She nodded, fully obedient to Percy, a man in whom she had complete trust. While turned, he unhitched the shield from his back, drew his sword and then turned back round. He bashed the cold steel of his sword against his reinforced shield, while Baylin sauntered forward with an air of arrogance. His movements were in full contradiction to Percy, whose were perfunctory and efficient, but when they clashed, everything was clean, crisp and deadly.

***

Being manipulators of magic, Elisa and Mythos were not limited by distance. Their battle began as soon as Garrick started his charge. And it was during that first friction of crackling magic that they recognised each other's signatures – and their unique methods of creating spells – and remembered their earlier encounter outside the Tenebrae. It was long ago, but it gave them both a subtle insight into each other's focus of magic.

Mythos charged the first attack. Elisa had the counter and met it – *firebomb!* – between them. Taking the position as the attacker, Elisa tapped in on another sheet of magic, which she moulded, carving it into a spearhead of fire, pulsing it forward.

Misto vanished. That was his personal trait. His capacity to become unseen in almost every environment was only seconded by the mythical ability of invisibility, something that had yet to be mastered, less, even achieved. He was a threat, even to the best magus.

***

Prior to the attack, Slayne had taken a forward position before starting on the final leg of the journey. He was eager to catch up and speak to his protégé, to try and put right previous events. He was not looking for it to be easy, but he was a big enough man to know when he'd wronged, and this was one *wrong* that needed a hefty *right*. That, and he was as much a friend and life-coach to Jerome as he was a mentor. However, when they turned, it put him only one step closer to the melee than Jerome – not close at all.

"Stay back," he ordered back to Jerome, his wrong-righting attempt put stringently on hold.

It was just as instinctive for Slayne to take the role of guardian as it was for Jerome to be guarded. His anger meant nothing now and he adhered to his command.

Slayne lunged forward, arming himself as he did. Surveying and processing the details, he reasoned that assisting Percy would be most beneficial and it was for him that he headed.

***

Keldor didn't get scared of combat anymore, nor did Garrick. They had both been in the game long enough to dispense with the fear and aim for understanding, but this was different. With someone you didn't know – or didn't comprehend – it served no purpose in being afraid. You aimed to garnish as much understanding as you could from what little you were given. However, Garrick was probably the only person Keldor feared, and vice versa. They both knew their capabilities ... and each other's. The contrasting factor was that Garrick fed off it. Keldor was afraid, but although it didn't line his insides as sustenance, it did act as an ingredient to grind and hone his stagecraft on the theatre of war.

***

Elisa and Mythos were streaming magic to a central, focal point between them. The magical arm-wrestle – as that was effectively what it was – was a relatively equalled match with only minor fluctuations, but Elisa was aware of a growing force pushing her way. To her, Mythos was either drawing on some highly sinister energy or someone was helping him. Under the opinion that magi didn't just suddenly become twice as good at drawing energy, she concluded that he was being helped and, as such, changed her method, bringing the fluid compression to an end by pumping a thwarting element through her stream. Once at the centre, it erupted, knocking her back and also Mythos.

The aftershock dissipated and Elisa constructed a very makeshift shield, just as a precaution. There was definitely someone else and she needed to reassess. She saw Mythos, but who was the other?

***

Jerome watched Slayne charge forward, watched as he took position next to Percy, but he wasn't sure if he should 'stay back', as he had been so ordered. He knew how to fight; he could be useful. But he had to make sure that, if he was going to enter the fray, it had to be for the right reasons – not to impress a girl or to be deliberately disobedient – as now wasn't the time for heroics or rebellion. Angry or not, Slayne knew what he was talking about. He decided to remain back, but he had his trusty dirk in hand and ready.

Satisfied that there was nothing he could – *should* – do, he looked to Galliana and recognised that she had also been told to 'stay back', or something similar. She looked across to him and, as he held her gaze, it felt amazing to not feel as though he needed to look away. And nor did he want to look away, but he couldn't help it, as something was moving in the shadows behind her. *Was that Thermion...?*

***

"I see you've not lost your touch, old friend," Garrick said, blocking a close attempt from Keldor.

Keldor was not in the talking mood as Garrick held the block, but replied nonetheless. "We stopped being friends long ago, Garrick."

"Pity you see it that way," and Garrick riposted Keldor's close attack with a lunge, shaving a sword-shaped wedge into his stubble. His body was Hell's receptor; his sword – its tool; his eyes – the projector.

It was a narrow miss, but considering Garrick didn't miss that often, it instilled a fleeting modicum of hope. With his dagger, Keldor bashed the sword from under chin away, knocking Garrick slightly off balance. That marked the bout's end, and they reorganised themselves for the next.

***

Baylin was keeping up. Though fighting both Percy, and now Slayne, he was managing to hold it together, granted, not so much from an offensive standpoint, but that wasn't important.

But what really put Slayne on the back foot was Baylin's apparent immunity to magic. He briefly recalled back to the ambush outside Gatelock and the Lyrian Warriors' immunity. He had never encountered or heard of anything like it before. Was this the doing of The Reformation?

However, the most repercussive effect of this was that he was a blade magus and, without his thaumaturgical ability, he was simply a swordsman; and every half decent swordsman knew how to fend off two attackers ... and this person seemed very much more than a 'half decent swordsman', to quote himself.

***

The shadowed man? The man who was going to watch them be tortured? Who had led the attack? *But his hand?* Elisa was shocked. Magic, as *she* understood it, could help close up a cut – maybe leave a scar – or lessen a bruise, but never perform complex anatomical structure reparation.

She needed help. Looking frantically across to Slayne and Percy and seeing them fighting two on one, she reminded herself that magic wasn't the same. Maybe she could hold up for a minute, but something would have to give to equal out the scales, or this would be a tale she wouldn't live to tell.

For now, she had a very jury-rigged shield to hide behind, and a tiny amount of time to make another that she had to get up and quick. The proceeding bolt hit and as good as crippled the weak configuration of magic particles. But she was still not ready to fire up the new defence and she could feel the attacks brewing. And then the help she so desperately needed came; came in the form of a little green goblin…

***

Thermion skulked in the shadows. The attack had drawn attention away and, as Jerome spied him creeping, he didn't resemble the Thermion that he had come to know. Something was definitely outside of the norm, darker, more sinister; and he was approaching Galliana; and she *still* hadn't noticed him.

For Percy and Slayne, they were finding it troublesome to locate an opening, a break in Baylin's security. His blocks were flawless, his footing, perfect, expertly stepping back to control and slow an attack and stepping forward, conducting their movements in time within his own orchestral combat. Not forgetting that, like his opponents, he, too, was looking for that elusive *opening.*

"Ana, lookout!" Jerome yelled.

Thermion's sudden clasp around her neck made Galliana cry out.

Slayne instantly shifted to become the sole attacker, as Percy removed himself to deal with what was happening – his promise to *always keep her safe* currently in jeopardy.

Thermion had her neck buried deep in the crook of his arm. Both her hands were grasping to try and loosen the chokehold. Menacingly hovering around her cheek and eye was a knife. What had suddenly changed in him?

***

The second round was differing little from the first. Keldor and Garrick were both managing to subdue and counter each other's attacks, but Garrick didn't draw upon the calm stability of reason.

Unlike Keldor, his vim was fuelled by the sordid details, usually best kept hidden. Keldor could see it rising up inside, the madness like a tidal ocean violently finding equilibrium just beneath, but never able to settle.

Keldor lunged forward, but with the turbulent wash ravaging Garrick's innards, his block had an unexpected force, knocking Keldor off balance for just long enough to receive a blow to the side of the face. That force, twinned with the block, made his knees buckle and, to stop him falling flat, he released his knife and used the free hand as a support. He returned focus on Garrick, who was coming in for a downward strike and Keldor was just able to thrust against it, with his sword at enough of an angle to bring Garrick's down to the hilt.

With Garrick off-guard, Keldor leant back a touch and levered his leg up, which he thrust into Garrick's abdomen. He bent forward and stepped back with a grunt.

Keldor took that period to get back up and compose himself, as did Garrick.

"That's more like it," Garrick said, coughing. "But where's the *real* Keldor? Where's the *angry* Keldor that gave me this?" He stroked down the scar running from the centre of his forehead to over his left eye.

Keldor felt the pang of an old memory returning. "He's gone now."

"How unfortunate."

***

The ground was moving in front of Jerome. Looking closer, he perceived it not to be the floor, but the shadows, and moving shadows were something he was hoping never to see again. His spinal column felt raised, the cold shiver stretching his skin taut. And then, to manifest his worst fear, an arm pushed out. Jerome remembered their name – dark ones – and the arm began pulling the weird, anomalous body out.

***

Misto attacked from one of the dead trees – to him, it was perfect as an assassin's playground. He slammed towards Sahl, disturbing his casting and allowing Elisa the time she needed to finish her shield. No sooner had Misto landed than he was already away. And that was his best weapon – *the* best weapon of a cloaked assassin – the element of surprise.

Misto was a firm student of the principle 'Where there's a will, there's a way', but he knew that he could only ever be a disruption in this fight, because these were magi, with advanced defence systems and no amount of *will* was going to pierce them. But going back to his original thought, he could definitely be a distraction, *definitely* pull their attention away for Elisa to make a kill. She was powerful and it would only be a matter of time…

***

This is better, Slayne thought, as he took position, solo, against Baylin. There was no one to be in the way now, one-on-one, just the way a fight ought to be. It may also mean that Baylin would cease to be as defensive and work, more fool him, along the aggressive slant.

Slayne deliberately waited, baiting Baylin on and then the first attacks came, and they came with vigour. *Perfect.* The back foot, on which Baylin had been put, had left him feeling hindered, but now that he was free, his attacks, although straight and true, came unaccompanied with reasoning.

However, the half decent swordsman, as Slayne had originally assumed him, appeared only a *half decent* way to describe him and now *he* was the one keeping up.

***

"I'm sorry I was never there for you…" Peter tried saying to his friend, whom he watched try and rescue him.

Garveya," he said, opening up a line of telepathy.

Peter, what is it?" Garveya instantly responded.

He didn't know what to say, but he chose, *"I love you."* But how did she know so quickly?

"Oh no you don't. You're not getting away with it that easily." Even mentally she could admonish him.

"Please, just tell me you love me."

"What trouble have you gone and got yourself into this time?"

"I can't explain, but…"

"Peter, what are you talking about? Tell me. You can always tell me anything, you know that." Her telepathic voice of reproach was bittersweet and he was happy that hers was the last voice he would hear.

He savoured it. *"I have to go and I don't know if I'm … coming back."*

"What do you mean?" Garveya quickly asked.

Then she ignored her own question; she didn't want to wait for an answer – the answer wasn't important.

"Whatever you've done," she continued, hurriedly, *"we can find a way out. We can fix it; it can always be fixed."*

"Not this time. I love you."

"Come back, Peter." Desperation her final attempt, *"Please. Ple—"*

He was immersed in the conversation, detached from the lair of the dark ones. Her final plea was the last transmitted half-word before the connection was broken. Something was inside him, spreading like a disease, defiling his essence, laying waste to every cell. He couldn't source the origins, but he was dying and then he was paralysed.

From a perspective outside of his own, the green pigment colouring his eyes faded to grey and his skin dulled to white, the blood sat motionless inside his veins and arteries. He was dead, but he was still there; he was still inside, without control of his body. His limbs moved with a mind of their own, but he knew that he *existed*. Everything went black.

***

Peter used his arm to heave himself out of the shadows. He couldn't be sure what he was doing; his body was no longer his own, but once out of the confines of the umbra, he reached out and grabbed the figure running past him.

***

"Unhand her," Percy said cleanly, unfazed.

"Be quiet, old man. I don't take orders from you."

"And you do from these people? The Reformation? For how long?"

"Let's just say *this*," – his *this* he indicated to be Galliana by shoving his nose into her cheek and maddeningly inhaling the Galliana-fragranced air – "has been a long-term project."

"Percy..." Galliana whispered, whimpered.

"Release her, Thermion!"

Whose snapped motions and excited mannerisms stopped as he considered the old man, but he kept her held, tight.

"Release her *now!*" he ordered, *fazed*. Very, *very* fazed.

He looked at Percy, sussing out his sincerity and when he was sure of it – absolutely sure – he tossed Galliana aside. She hit the floor and the floor hit her back twice as hard. She yelped, and Percy saw Thermion through a sheet of red. Two poles, repelling, were going to become one pole, comfortable.

***

Elisa and Misto worked as a great pair. She could really see why Keldor relished having him as a friend. He was effective, reliable ... deadly. And, of course, she had her specially constructed shield to counter anything that made it out of Mythos and Sahl. The battle was equal, but where Elisa and Misto were flawed was their communication. However, Misto's absence, as much as it made forming a battle plan impossible, was his weapon, was what was making this melee a fair fight.

***

"It was you, wasn't it?" Keldor asked, as they prepared for the fourth bout.

"Probably," Garrick said, jocularly taking responsibility for whatever blame Keldor would apportion.

"Do you even know?"

"That's the wrong question, Keldor... Do I even *care?* Tell you what, let me answer that for you."

Keldor ignored him. "All those deaths? The Duke's and King's Rangers? In the name of The Reformation?"

Garrick ever so slightly closed his eyes to slits while he reflected. He grinned with a mirthless humour. "...Probably."

And he fired into combat.

***

"Ana!"

Jerome ignored the moving shadow in front – and the arm – and headed straight for her. Percy had gained Thermion's attention, but it looked like she hit the floor hard.

He had just dodged and passed the shadow and was nearly with her when he felt something grab his clothes.

He turned and his body stiffened. He was unable to move as wild temperatures shocked through every nerve.

The shadow, the arm, the dark one – it was Peter. What sick, twisted perversion of reality was this?

"Peter," he attempted.

Nothing, just the face of someone who had no identity.

"Peter, don't you remember me?"

He even had the same sword, but he was like one of them now. He moved in that weird, incongruous way and it was more painful to see him like this than...

He couldn't think about it.

"Peter, please."

Peter's grey eyes stared back and his sword lifted.

Reticently, Jerome unsheathed his own. By instinct, and by years of repetition, he favoured his left hand – drawing it from the right of his body – but today his left arm was not in good condition; his hand, smashed from the earlier punishment, could barely grip the weapon. His right was just as bruised, but at least it was able to hold the dirk and he returned the action, holding it up against Peter's.

He was thinking about their *sword fight* years ago, but never once did it occur to him that life would have wrought such poetic fate...

***

Jerome? Peter thought similarly to his friend. It was all he could do, as he watched his arm lift up. Jerome was trying to talk to him, but he couldn't respond and then when he saw Jerome give up, he also raised his weapon. Peter knew that Jerome was better with a blade than him and he wondered if he could find some way of controlling his body.

Detached, his body made the first attack and things became truly odd for Peter. No longer the master of his faculties, his spectator view of the combat granted him a strange foresight into the following moves and, for the most part, his assumption was correct.

But now that his body had taken the lead of the attacks – and failed – it was Jerome who came off the defensive back-foot.

Jerome made his first attack and, in Peter's mind – as that was *all* he had –, he instinctively wanted to move his body to block and, strangely, his body did.

He felt his unbeating heart slam around inside and return an attack, which Jerome successfully blocked.

***

Slayne had tried his magic against Baylin. He had tried blending it to mind control, tried warping it into a missile, even tried moving something *real.* And nothing. The magic, the verve behind each spell, just seemed to dissipate, turn into something else. However, he didn't stop or bow down to this adversary.

And looking around to his friends: Elisa and the occasional flits of Misto, Keldor, Jerome and *Peter...?*

Baylin only needed a moment – in fact, it was a treat not having to wait for an opening – and that shock was just enough to take a risk and he drove his sword forward. Slayne roared.

***

"Fight me, Marder! Why are you holding back?" Garrick said, growing angry.

It was true. Keldor hadn't considered it, but he had not been returning by far as many attacks as he was receiving. Why? Maybe he just didn't have that bit inside him anymore? Although, they were older now. Maybe that was it. Maybe he was just *old* and decrepit?

No.

No!

He stoked the fire inside, as he began to fight back and he saw Garrick's face twitch with excitement.

***

Thermion made the first move. It was different to how it was before, Percy thought. Maybe everything had been a lie, not *just* his allegiances. He discounted the idea and considered that under his cloak of obfuscate his abilities had been repressed, but were still a product of the same central, vile machine that beat beneath his ribcage.

Yes, his attacks were harder from the exposure of his true self, but Percy's resolve was equally stronger, made firm by this betrayal – and how very *dare* he hurt Galliana?

He countered Thermion's assault and gave back his own.

***

For Jerome, it still hadn't properly sunk in that he was fighting his friend – this strange version of him, anyway. For Peter, he was working furiously to regain control of his body, but he was finding it harder than he would have liked. In his first attempts, he tried to control an arm. *An arm? My arm,* he told himself. His failure had moved him quickly onto smaller things, just his forearm, then his wrist. Now it was his fingers. He would never have thought that trying to wiggle his little finger would pose such a difficulty. But he had to continue. He had to find a way of helping his friend.

***

Baylin's blade had scratched the surface, but that, thankfully, was all. Slayne roared as he side-kicked his opponent. It was punishment for the poorly planned and executed attack. If you take risks like that, expect to get punished when things go wrong. Baylin lurched back. Lesson learnt.

***

Galliana drifted in and out of consciousness for a while. When she was in, she had a splitting headache; when she was out, she couldn't feel *anything*. She didn't know what she preferred, but then the headache, thrashing around inside, jolted her memory and she remembered: hitting the floor, the floor hitting back, a stray knife hovering at the side of her face, the *betrayal*. She knew something had been wrong with Thermion, if that was even his name. *That* was why her Dark Whisperer had tried keeping her away from him.

He had had her trust; even against her Dark Whisperer's recommendation, he had had that. But at least she had never given him anything else. She had not surrendered her body to slake his lust – for, knowing what she knew now, that was all it could ever have been. That part of her was for someone else now and her Dark Whisperer allowed it, and that meant he was good for her: an almost deific rite. But she didn't need It to say that he was hers, and she his... But it was nice to have though.

Head resting on the spiked cushion of calcified grass, she opened her eyes and focused. The clashing of weapons and other hallmarks of battle rattled her eardrums and lying on the floor was not the way she wanted to spend the remainder of this fight.

Percy blocked a downward assault from Thermion with his shield while slicing towards his stomach. Thermion adopted a bent forward pose, shifting his feet back, to avoid the blade cutting him open.

He found his balance again, as Percy took the front foot, leading an attack to the right. Balance maintained, Thermion matched – no, *exceeded* – the old man's strength, blocking his attack and edging him round. Now it was Percy off balance and, while he was, Thermion drove his leg out, punching the centre of the tower shield with his shoe, nearly knocking Percy off his feet. Thermion bellowed at the same time, using the exhalation to clench his stomach muscles and assist in driving his leg forward, harder.

***

Garrick lay into Keldor, throwing swing after swing after swing. Garrick was unrelenting and Keldor couldn't keep with the pace. Three, four, five heavy strikes to the same place had flipped Keldor's sword out of his hand. It clanged and Garrick smashed his sword-armed fist into Keldor's face, this time splitting his lip and loosening a couple of teeth. The blood leaked and he tasted its sweet, metallic flavour before churning it around and spitting it out.

"Your heart's not in it, Keldor!" Garrick's voice carried over the fight. "And I'm growing tired of this. Fight me!"

He didn't want to use anger to fight – not again. "No, Garrick."

Garrick's breathing was so violent that his exhale was chucking globules of spit. His eyes closed and he looked up and around. "You leave me no choice."

Garrick unclipped his crossbow from his belt and aimed. Keldor couldn't see where, but when he flicked back the trigger and the machine made its bold boom, it was the all too familiar yelp coming from the right that turned his head. His eyes, just a fraction behind his head's spin, caught sight and impaled to a tree was Misto. The bolt stuck in his chest.

"No," Keldor whispered.

"I've seen you with that ridiculous green-skin. Thought I'd put you out of your misery. And *his.*"

"No." Louder this time.

"You'll thank me later."

The fire in Keldor's stomach was burning the roof of his mouth. This kind of anger hadn't penetrated his soul for a very long time, but now that it was very much in the vicinity he was going to feed off it. And he picked up his sword.

"Now, Keldor, are we going to finish this?"

The ability to form words had escaped him. Either way, that language was now obsolete to him. Manipulating sounds from frictions and hollows between his tongue, teeth and lips became an ineffective method of communication. He needed something more physical and now he had his project – he was going to kill Garrick and, as the noise perpetrating through his head desisted, he took the first step to accomplishing that.

***

They all felt the arrow go through. It stuck as hard, and with as much force, in their chests as it did to pin Misto to that tree. Elisa couldn't be sure if he was dead, but now that she was back to square one, drastic measures had to be taken.

The most important rule of magic, for magi, was the ability to control emotion and, for Elisa, who was, and always had been, a very reserved individual – for the better part of all the time – this was a rule that never had its flexibility tested. Primarily, the necessity for such emotional inhibition was not only to protect the magus, but everyone else, as emotions for a source of energy were unstable and, most dangerously, incredibly powerful. But this time, all those rules, regulations and teachings fell by the wayside. Not forgotten, but she could feel her trained, natural instinct, which would normally subdue and suppress these emotions, push against that which she now sought. She wanted to nourish and nurture them. She switched her established, emotion-control-unit off and the sluice gates opened. Swirling around, smashing through her, the whirlwind of feelings flooded her. She wasn't used to it, but she let it encompass her and the rage swelled, her fingertips becoming the release valve, venting the unnecessary, magical build-up.

But now it was starting to affect her. She *really* wasn't used to the rush of impulsive grief and her eyes clouded in a sheet of moisture. Normally, she would take the bereavement, bottle it up and release it at a given time in the future, in a controlled environment, slowly. She understood, perhaps more than most, that grief – rather the ability to grieve – was an important part of life, but she felt the tears sting her eyes and she didn't want it to affect her.

She didn't want to be affected by it.

However, she couldn't want the secondary aspect of power that it supplied without the primary pangs of loss. It was painful and hurtful and all she wanted was to bring Misto back, but she couldn't. So, teary eyed and primed with a thick coating of loss, she drew in the purer *Dark Realm* essence and weaved a spell that would end all others...

***

Slayne, too, heard the yowl and, although it didn't initially strike him to his core, it began to. He remembered, the little, annoying – *that was unfair* – green-skin, his lifesaver from a torture unimaginable, was now dead and *damn it!* It stung – made him angry. No doubt Elisa was going through the motions of bottling up and controlling her grief for later, but he wouldn't. His death, of all possible events, was probably the most painful. He was a humble figure who had never acted out of order, even in the face of such adverse prejudice. He was a symbol of all that was good, what everyone fought for, and died for, all those years ago.

It was pointless to push the invective into incantation, for Baylin was immune, so he chose to use the rage to sharpen his human reflexes.

***

On the outside, Jerome, Misto's first advocate, without whom he would never have been accepted, not only heard his cry, but also saw it happen.

Peripherally, he saw Misto – rather, a flying, green, unmistakably goblin-like figure – attacking from a branch on one of the solemn trees, just begin his leap down and then get thrown back, his head, arms and legs snapping forward as the arrow shoved him back. His limbs drooped, but there were minimal flickers of life twitching through his arms, vain attempts at trying to make for the arrow, but failing.

Like Slayne, Elisa and Keldor it hurt Jerome and he also chose to channel it – channel the hurt into fury.

On the inside, Peter heard it, but unlike his friend, he couldn't see it and therefore it took him a moment longer to process what was happening – the party slowly being taken to pieces: first Thermion, then him, now Misto.

In his mind, though, he was no different to anyone else. He still *felt* and he could use it as such, and it was just what he needed. Even his heart, which he noticed had stopped ever since his technical demise, burst to life, driving and heating the stagnant, tepid blood back on route, and he was reminded, just briefly, what it was like to have his body by stealing back control of his sword arm and pinning it down.

It was what Slayne had trained Jerome to do for the last three years. He saw Peter's arm drop, didn't question it, and he thrust his dirk directly through his sternum.

Even as the blade pierced the hard, bone structure Jerome didn't realise. It was only after Peter's howl and consequent retreat that he was brought to understanding and the pain he suffered, from the loss of Misto, tripled, quadrupled, multi-plied to infinity.

Peter sank into the shadows and away and Jerome prayed that he was still alive. But not so alive ... that he would come back.

***

Percy heard the howl coming from behind, but kept his attention focused. He had the least affiliation with Misto and Peter, and any feeling he had now was bound by his contempt.

Thermion was tiring. He knew the signs. The first, always, was a sudden surge, or flurry in this case, of strikes and lunges, a last-ditch attempt to overpower an opponent. It wouldn't last, and suddenly it all fell into place, just like sparring again. Of course, Percy would never admit it, but getting tired was inevitable. However, even inevitabilities could be negotiated, his understanding of combat transcending that of most. It went above being plain *good* and instead almost completely circumvented it. Percy now had the upper hand and he was leading Thermion in this dance of death. All he had to do was hold off against this foray. He wouldn't be overpowered, not now.

From her prone outlook, Galliana watched. Head strum-med by the finger of pain, she saw her Percy, looking in his element. She had never seen him like that before. He was normally so kind. Where was that kind old man that she—?

***

"That is why you should always wear a helmet," said Percy quietly, disdain under his breath.

Thermion's legs trembled and gave way as he crumpled to the floor. Galliana saw him and saw him looking back. His gaze was penetrating, piercing, and she thought that he could see the world through her, if she were just a bubble, something to refract the light and then waver and deform to match the shape of the air currents, until riding the breeze out of the way, just an unmemorable disturbance.

But his weren't the eyes of the living anymore, and when she took a sharp breath from comprehension, shifting herself out of his line of sight, his scrutiny didn't follow hers or distinguish her – or anything. She was shocked, but he just looked distantly beyond. Her stare then became as piercing as his had been, as she traced the trickling river of red, leaking from his mouth up, up to his nose and then following the second stream of blood, winding round his lifeless eyes up, up his forehead to his fringe, clumping and matting the darkened fair hair up, up the blade of the sword that was embedded firmly in his skull.

***

The shock wave, residue from Elisa's *spell to end all others,* rippled out. First, blowing back Mythos and Sahl who were nearest the central boom, but as a secondary, also throwing her back, as well as morbidly shuddering Misto's limp body.

It expanded rapidly, its punch lost to the thick dimensions of the massive realm. By the time it reached Keldor and Gar-rick, the next recipients, it was little more than a tempestuous flutter and, further on from that, even Slayne with his tingling, thaumaturge muscles didn't feel the aftershock.

Jerome felt the tremors, the faint remnants of the blast, but what snapped him out of his own mental crisis was seeing Thermion gruesomely fall and Galliana's face spilling out all its colour.

He rushed over to her, taking her into him as much him into her. It was a different Percy standing next to them, he thought.

The merciless execution gave him a new insight, a reality check from his own perception of the world. But, of course, it wasn't a different Percy, and to think that he was just a peaceful old man with any less than the capability of killing was a childish view. More to the point, Thermion had betrayed him – them both, them *all* – and threatened Galliana. Would *he* have shown any more mercy?

***

It was like dusting his hands of something horrid. Percy saw Galliana, protected, and wiggled his sword clean of the skull. Wiping it on Thermion's cadaverous back, he gathered him-self. He did not revel in death or war, but couldn't refute that he felt drawn to it.

***

Keldor swam in the lake of fire, his memories clocking innumerable repetitions.

'You leave me no choice.' And he smashed his sword down on Garrick. It was blocked, but Keldor felt him strain beneath his ire.

Garrick unclips his crossbow from his belt and aims. These thoughts flowed with such ease as he struck down again.

The bolt impales Misto to a tree. 'I've seen you with that ridiculous green-skin. Thought I'd put you out of your misery...' Another strike and it was Garrick on the back foot, just as *he* had been before.

'You'll thank me later.' The next strike knocked Garrick down to his knees, his weight sitting on the backs of his feet.

'Now, Keldor, are we going to finish this?' Garrick asks.

"Yes," Keldor said, "yes, we are going to finish this..."

***

Sahl shook off the effects of the blast wave and tried to find Mythos. With no sign of him, he assessed the female. She, like

349

him, was also knocking away the subduing effects, but was also returning to focus.

He had been paying close attention to the environs and the second he heard the word 'Reformation' spill from Keldor's mouth, he became *very* interested. His master had often spoken of The Reformation, an elusive organisation that he sought to undo. Perhaps this was an opportunity.

But, he had to act fast; the man with whom he sought to speak was about to become two halves, *separate* halves.

He leapt to the side, opening the umbral realm as he did. It was a useful trick, to blend the shadows like his dark, brotherly diviners. He grabbed a hold of the man about to become another kill-notch on the blade of Keldor, and dragged him under, into the umbra.

***

Keldor saw the shadows splitting; he even saw the hands grabbing him, taking Garrick away from his rightful appointment with justice – *revenge.*

He couldn't have brought his sword down any faster, but even seeing that he would be moments too late, he continued to finish the movement, smashing it down, breaking the deadened grassland and shouting, roaring, thundering his rage out! One mouth wasn't enough. He needed more; he needed—

***

By no means did Slayne have the upper hand, but things had changed, *significantly.* With Garrick gone, Mythos absent and Thermion dead, Baylin had very few options left. Holding off two swordsman was possible, easy even, but as he watched the old man wiggle free the blade from his friend's head and watch Keldor pull his from the ground, and as both looked up at him, he decided that now was time to 'fight another day'.

***

Baylin's break from the combat was clean and well-planned. Knocking Slayne's sword down in a harsher, stronger way than a normal parry, he sprang back and sprinted away. How-ever, Slayne was still reeling from Misto's death and, in his need to vent, was damned if he was going to get off so lightly.

Instinctually, for ranged opponents, magic would always have been his first choice, but he knew – even though he still didn't fully understand why – Baylin's immunity, and so had to think up a new plan. He could try and run after him? But then he felt the weight of his sword and decided to try something different.

He harked back to his training, the hours of pain-stricken, physical exertion that he had applied to himself in an attempt to expiate the demons of his past, and in that was the key to his current dilemma. His ethic had always been to be prepared for every situation. He knew it wasn't a guarantee – not every situation could be accounted for – but this, of all of them, had been *one* of the remote possibilities. But a possibility nonetheless, and he had devoted *some* time to being prepared.

And watching the pathetic fleeing, he executed it. Throwing his sword marginally up, he reversed his grip from thumb nearest the cross-guard to thumb facing the pommel, like a javelin. And he used it as such, bringing his arm back, winding up the muscles like a spring and then releasing it.

Baylin's snappy and crisp arm movements, swinging in opposition to his legs, became an uncontrolled mess as the sword pierced his spine, severing control. He stumbled and tumbled over, unable to brace himself against the ground, scraping his face along the sharp flats, gouging out huge chunks of his chin and cheeks, leaving them in a bloody trail behind.

He died shortly after, alone, bettered, a coward.

***

Keldor wasn't allowed that satisfaction of release, but dwelling was not helping his internal struggle and then, as the shadows completely closed and stilled, the blue atmosphere chilled his core, reminding him… *Misto.*

Snapped out of anger, vengeance put well to the side, he ran over to his green-skin companion. His breath was minimal and jerky, as Keldor snapped the feathered end of the bolt. Making a concerted effort to cause as little discomfort to his friend as possible, he levered Misto off and down to the ground. He was so light, no heavier – or bigger – than a small child. The little goblin groaned as the wound was disturbed, extra globules of blood riding down his skinny abdomen, but he was soon freed from the arrow's clasp before being laid flat on the ground, feet and legs first, and then gently angled back. Keldor supported his head every inch of the way.

Close to expiration, Misto muttered a few sounds, his mouth trying to form words, but above the anguished splutters, not much else was audible.

"Shh, now. Don't try and speak," Keldor said, making every effort to calm him. "Elisa! Slayne!"

Slayne was still breathing in his victory when he heard Keldor's request. With immediate effect, he rushed over and was by Keldor's side, kneeling over the dying goblin. Elisa likewise, both magi called upon for their – any – healing skill.

"Can you help?" Keldor asked, his voice low and controlled, but the fear and upset as evident as his facade.

Elisa and Slayne rigorously ploughed through their brains, searching for any way to help cure Misto, but before they looked any further, something else was thwarting his chances. A surrounding field encompassed the goblin and then Slayne had an insight into Baylin's ostensible immunity. It wasn't *immunity,* but effectively a dispeller.

Slayne told Elisa and between the pair they began formulating theories. They referred back to the ambush between Gatelock and Marston, where some of the Lyrian Warriors had shown a similar immunity. They put together the facts and the common denominator was The Reformation.

The broken arrow embedded in the tree also exuded a similar field – not in such force – and they came to understand that the arrow must have been laced with the repellent – the repellent, they concluded, must have been some sort of liquid.

"I'm sorry, Keldor," Elisa began. "There's nothing we can do. Without any magic…"

The words ceased to contain meaning, as her voice trailed off.

Percy, Galliana and Jerome joined the congregation around the dying goblin. They were just in time to witness the last few exchanges between Misto and the departing world.

"I-I'm s-sorr…" Those final, almost incoherent, words he pushed out.

"Don't speak, friend," Keldor said. "You have nothing to be sorry about… It was an honour."

And Keldor meant it.

And Misto was gone.

They all felt it; he had a restorative spirit that, with his absence, accented the numbing truth of this pyrrhic victory.

Percy rested a hand on Keldor's shoulder. "Shall I say a few words?"

"No," he snapped, and everyone was taken by surprise. *No eulogy? Surely, out of anyone, it was Misto that deserved remembrance…*

Keldor continued, "We're not leaving him here. We're not burying him *here…* Not here… Save your words, Percy."

He held back the grief and the remaining five broke the circle to let him pass, to gather himself. Jerome suffered silently, but Galliana recognised it and took his hand. He was grateful and he luxuriated her feel, but Keldor was controlling the speed of the moment and he dictated otherwise.

"We should continue. The sooner we finish, the sooner we can leave this…" – they all had their own adjectival words for the realm. Keldor chose not to use his. Instead he let the death of his friend infuse the silence – "place."

Part III
The Answer

The deep canopy of The Dark Realm, which was pierced by the metropolis's buildings, began to dome down, forming a wall in the nearing distance. The trees and features of the consumed dead forest were sliced at arbitrary places marking the edge of the under-city. But central to where they were walking was a small cave entrance, which widened as they progressed through.

It was made all the more strange as tree branches and twigs poked out and, at the base, huge, gnarled root systems were visible, attesting to another old world buried deep within the walled jaws of The Dark Realm.

The tunnel itself sloped downhill at a shallow, but visible, gradient and twisted and turned until they were walking directly under the city and then, in the beyond, a grotto came into view, empty and solemn.

Jerome's Dark Whisperer faded and they were alone in the fathomless bowels, and without something to lead them, indeed without anywhere else to go, they sat.

Chapter XVI
Histories

"Garrick Tobranin," Keldor said, pronouncing his name before unravelling the history. Elisa had asked, where everyone had wondered. "Old acquaintance, genius marksman and ... ex-Realm's Ranger." Keldor sighed as he spilled the truth.

Listening, the silent five silenced further.

"We trained together, journeyed together. We had many phenomenal adventures all over the wilds of Aramyth. We were even dubbed Realm's Rangers together.

"But – and I will not speak of it – something happened. And he changed. It changed him... But, I don't know, perhaps that was nothing to do with it. Perhaps he was always like that, black-hearted and rotten to the core.

"What I find curious, though, is that he's been missing for years. Now, I can't begin to question what The Reformation has been doing, but something must have drawn attention to him... Maybe—"

"My father," Galliana interrupted. "He was an important figure involved in the Aramyth Concordia. Would—" she stumbled, "would his death have...?"

"Yes. That would have put the Realm's Rangers on high alert. That is *if* it was Garrick that... I'm sorry, Galliana. It seems it's not just my life he's bent on destroying."

"It's all of ours," Slayne interjected. "And if I ever see him again then—"

"Enough!" Percy let howl. "Revenge is *not* the way. Life is too short. If all you seek is death, then death is all you will find. It may even find you first. It probably *will.* Enough lives have already been destroyed. Put away your vendettas and seek life, for it *is too* short ... even for an immortal. And that's not just the old man in me talking."

Jerome had yet to confront Slayne, but the anger in which he was embroiled melted away.

"You're right ... *old man*," Slayne admitted, accepting the fortitude of Percy's words and mind.

Percy welcomed Slayne's jest with a smile.

This was a better way of living.

***

Time became bleak as they waited, somewhere between asleep and awake. At the far side of the grotto something was stirring and awake became the dominant state as they turned to see.

Delicately rising up from the ground was a podium. A soft, buzzing drone filled the spaces of the echoic cave. It was almost ominous, as glyphs began to glow, until it stopped, halting with a metallic lock.

The six approached, gradually becoming aware of other strange glyphs glowing through the surrounding rough walls. The quiet pit suddenly hummed with a creepy life. On the other side, about ten feet wide, was an abyss. It had gone unnoticed until now, but the blackness of it disguised it well within the dark environment.

The podium itself came up to waist-height with squared edges and was nearly all plain, except for some geometrically perfect shapes, the outlines only visible from the candescent glistening of the glyphic conformations.

Atop was also plain, but shortly after stopping, the metal plate began moving – becoming many plates – shifting in and out, under and over each other. It was an example of micro-precision that was so perfect, all they could do was stand and admire. Seconds later and the shuffling stopped. The final plate slid away, slower than the others, and beneath was a shallow, bowled depression with a still, liquid substance. It was almost imperceptible, but a shiver – whether from the machine itself or the slight motions of the party – caused a ripple.

The ripples stopped and, from the centre, a ray of light shot out; then another and another until the ceiling was speckled with a mass of tiny dots, almost like the night sky, the lights coming together, forming new and beautiful constellations.

The fluid grace with which the lights moved welcomed a solace inside the grounded onlookers. The lights continued to intertwine with each other, relating and moving with minds of their own.

The little constellations then began to bond together, bit by bit, building the foundations of letters, these clusters of letters then grouping, growing in size, first two, then three, then four, until the first word was inscribed, by the handwriting of light, upon the ceiling.

'Jerome'

This was its first word and even though it wasn't what Jerome had first expected, it was *exactly* what he had expected.

They then exploded back into a new starry sky, before regrouping, letters first, then a word...

'Galliana'

Galliana caught her breath, but like Jerome, expected it.

She looked around, at the people who did not know.

It seemed accepted that Jerome had been the focal point of this entire expedition.

"Galliana?" Elisa asked, puzzled.

Galliana meekly turned to her, somewhat ashamed by her silent deception, and then her name, as etched above, exploded and formed a new sky, full of shifting constellations.

The explosion suddenly captured the attention of all and they watched.

As before, the dots of light began grouping again to an esoteric gravitational force.

Before long a single letter 'e' was fully formed.

And a new one was materializing.

It looked like it could have been an 'r', but...

...then it rotated and another appendage started growing.

It was a 'y'. They all began thinking, *'e' and 'y'. 'Slayne'* maybe?

"Percy?" Elisa found herself again being the voice of the party.

Percy glanced down from the ceiling, from where his name was written, and graced his companion's startled faces.

"I may not have been quite as honest as perhaps I should have been."

Percy expected questions but none came, even though they all sought an explanation.

And he explained, "This is my second time here. And it was a long, long time ago. I fought in the War of Unity and—"

"The War?" Slayne stopped him. "That was – let me think – fifty years ago."

"I was a boy."

Slayne was quiet for a moment as he recalled. "I remember that boy; *everyone* remembered that boy." His response was calmer. "That was *you?*"

"The arrows had just stopped and the charge was ordered."

And he remembered...

***

The voice from afar shouted the final command and each and every man caught within the mist's clasps broke free and began the final charge towards the enemy.

Energy levels on a par with an empty barrel, Percy trudged on as one of the weary defenders. All around was exhibited the unity that would become synonymous with this war, and they forwarded through the mist towards the demons.

Faint outlines crept and crawled. The shock of being saved was wearing off and as Percy's eyes began to feel heavy again, he became more positive that if the fatigue didn't kill him, then the beasts would. But he was starting not to care. The discomfort of mud-soaked trousers and smock was a discomfort that he was learning to accept. It was cold and he was actually weighing up dying over living one more minute like this.

"Chin up, boy. Stay with me." The words of the man next to him snapped him back.

The mist was lifting and the outlines of the shrouded beasts were beginning to fade. Something was wrong and Percy couldn't be sure what it was, but these monsters had been anything but fading. So, why now?

The rhythmic, marching thumps that battered the muddy ground became the drums that unified everyone. Percy let the turbulence stir his body, as he literally scraped the barrel for any and all drops of life, the dregs.

Ahead, the Burning Bluffs were now visible again, but that was all. No strange beasts. Not another living thing.

The marching that had become so vigorous emulated the bewilderment, as everyone looked to each other, as if for answers.

Shrugs of shoulders became gentle whispers and Percy could hear the 'Is that it?'s and 'Have we won?'s.

He was glad that the man next to him remained voiceless, a silent stalwart. However, something inside was telling him that this wasn't 'it'. How could it be?

And, as if answering his fatalistic question, the monsters came back, rolling forward, shaping their own insidious paths through time and space, towards them.

"Stay with me now. There's no need for you to be a hero. You've done enough."

"…What do you mean?" Percy said, confused.

"You don't know? All these people, they're all talking about you. You've given everyone hope."

Percy stole himself away from the terrifying onslaught and sneaked a glance across the faces, and with each one, they returned a nod, like they knew him. He had been accepted into this guild of arms under secrecy and silence.

Thrown back into the well of dismay, they marched on, bringing back the rousing drum beat, the floor becoming the resonating body – the skin of the drum – booming their desperate and final efforts for victory…

***

"…And?" Jerome said, bereft at Percy's discontinuing.

"I'm not really sure what happened next. I think … we all thought … we were … going—" He furtively looked at Slayne, held in the moment of being a boy and slightly ashamed at his choice of words. "*I* thought *I* was going to die. The beasts didn't show any signs of stopping, but then – I can't describe it – a light burst out behind The Bluffs and … started to eat away at the evil horde. Did I dream it…?"

"It's true… And, Percy, we *all* thought we were going to die," Slayne assured.

"My father fought in the war," Keldor declared.

"My husband, also," said Elisa.

"I didn't know you were married," Jerome said, jumping on it.

She looked pained by the nostalgic pangs, but Jerome asked before he thought; touches of youth still drove an impetuous character.

"He left – oh – almost twenty years ago, now. Valkyre Adin was his name, and I loved him more than anything. As it was, I was only young during the war, but after we met, when I was older and the war was over, he told me about the boy. *You,*" she said, glancing over to Percy.

He wasn't ready for such attention and beneath his white beard he felt his cheeks go quite red.

Jerome wondered if his father fought in the war. He didn't know for sure and rather than wasting hours of time wondering, he concluded that if he was anything like the man his mother had made him out to be, he had. And he left it at that.

"So, you say you were here before." Keldor brought the party away from their reminiscence.

"Yes," Percy continued. "A couple of days after the war ended I began having visions." He looked to Galliana and Jerome. "I was confused about what It wanted, so I tried my best to ignore It.

"The man who saved me was a member of The Order, and he put my name forward. I was still too young to officially join, but my parents accepted my going to the city for preliminary training and… Anyway, in my twenties I'd learnt to keep the visions under control, but – and quite suddenly – they became so much worse. It forced my hand, and I felt I had little choice but to go, go on this journey of discovery, which It seemed so adamant for me to make. And It led me here…"

"…But you came back?" Galliana asked.

"I did," he said, hinting at a hidden pain.

Percy had become quite the focal point, and the group was still very intrigued – but silently so, as if anything other than delicacy might close the flower of his knowledge.

"…But why?" Galliana continued, her delicacy enough to keep the wisdom flower in blossom.

"I was," he said, looking down, "…too afraid."

Attempting further, she guessed, "That was why you didn't want me to go, wasn't it?"

His expressive eyes, framed by his expressionless face, told her.

"You knew I was … seeing It, and you—"

"Yes," he stated. "And … I believed – I *did* believe – I was protecting you, but … the truth is … I was only trying to protect myself… I thought that, if I could keep you away, then…"

"Percy," she said, stopping him from castigating himself. She wasn't angry with him. How could she be angry with him? His every action had been to keep her safe, and now she would be strong for him, as he had been for her.

"I'm so sorry," Percy whispered.

Galliana held his hand, for an apology that didn't need to be made – forgiven and forgotten.

"So…" Jerome said, his impetuousness making him the only one bold enough to break the moment. "You know what to do now?" he asked, attempting delicacy.

"Yes," Percy said, peering up at the podium.

The group were captivated.

"We have to jump in."

"…Into … *there?*" Jerome said, looking at the abyss. His Dark Whisperer returned and, for the first time, defied the rules of the physical world by hovering over the precipice. But against all the rules, It wasn't just Jerome he – if It was a he – was looking at, but Galliana *and* Percy. It was like where they were was a central point, a focus for all the Dark Whisperers – for it couldn't just be them who were afflicted.

The three of them broke away from Elisa, Slayne and Keldor and stood before the black depth.

"I could never do this before," Percy remarked, and then whispered, to Galliana, "Thank you."

"Do you think we will come back?" Galliana wondered aloud.

They stood in silence, unable to answer.

Until Elisa said, "We will wait for you."

They stood at the cusp of this infinite void, strangely, the darkness looking oddly tempting.

The Dark Whisperer beckoned them, changing into its most effulgent configuration yet. Minds anaesthetised by the splinter of dark magic, they dropped off the edge and fell into the shadows of the next dimension.

Jerome felt the surging adrenaline. The wind whooshing either side increased. His mind blanked, as the new world, fast approaching, etched itself into actuality.

He had arrived.

Chapter XVII
Land of the Gods, Part I

Jerome gazed around, mesmerised, as he saw endless, wind-whipped cascades of water thundering down from the boundless sky, tinted purple and green by the corrupt atmosphere.

Shattered walls stood twisted, cracked and ripped by some unimaginable violence and gusts of wind wound their way around the plates, howling through the gaps, singing with the voice of the banshee.

In the distance, huge enclosing peaks of black jagged rock had left scars on the land from where they jutted out; the unbalance of chaos played its presence like waves crashing on a forsaken shore.

There was no sun, no moon, only a haze of light that splashed across the dusty wastes. A pervasive smell, Jerome knew to be of dead and rotting flesh, filled his nostrils, the hard iron tang of blood, a counterpoint.

The floor was lined with an ochre dust, much of which seemed blighted by green fungal growth, but it was the sky above that left him reeling. Flickering bolts of lightning followed by waves of lost souls screeched in torment, knowledge of an eternal damnation, a torture beyond words.

Realisation broke with a stunning clarity; he was but a man trapped in a Land of the Gods.

So this is what loneliness really feels like, he thought. It seemed loneliness knew no bounds. The city of Arthak had taught him abandonment, but here, he learnt of its stronger more remorseless cousin – the stark plainness, demonstrating not a soul in sight for miles and miles.

Beneath his feet, he registered a circular platform. It was mostly black, with maybe some hints of dark blue, but with the addition of perhaps ten to fifteen fist-sized white circles lining the circumference; that was all. He stepped off and as soon as he did it disappeared, but not in the *normal sense* – if there was one. It didn't sink into the ground or slowly lose its visibility; it was like it had never existed. And then, when he referred back around to the other features, none of it was there. The desecrated constructs of the metropolis had gone and, now, it was just him and the Big Empty.

He checked his waist for his trusty dirk and it, also, wasn't there.

And then he realised that *none* of the physical damage he had sustained had come with him.

Afraid and alone, he walked.

***

Ana! Percy! He was shocked at how long it had taken him to consider his friends. He tried shouting their names, calling them. He tried once and nothing, not even an echo – an echo, to prove that he had a voice in this weird region. He tried again, and still nothing. He walked on, feeling the true irony of walking in the company of solitude. He shouted a third time, but the sound petered out. There was nothing here, no one.

He turned around to see if they might be behind him, but there was nothing.

Shadowed against the amaranthine desert, he began to re-member things that he swore hadn't happened. He remembered seeing something coming out of the sky – he couldn't describe it, but he was sure he'd seen it – and landing. The memory itself, he knew, wasn't real, but he saw it – could replay it, rewind it and pause it *exactly* as if it *were* real.

He closed his eyes and strained to clear up the shaky memory banks and, walking over the same barren landscape, he saw two figures. Jerome couldn't even be sure if they were male or female – they were so far away – but he thought he could just make out, whomever they were, one of them waving at him.

He unzipped his eyes in the hope that they were real, but there was nothing. However, the whole lot of *nothing* looked a whole lot different.

Gone was the plain horizon, replaced with a mountainous outline. The flat shell of the desert was now ridged and *gloriously* uneven and he realised he was heading for a rocky crag.

The sky had also deferred to a standard, with which he was familiar. The green tide of souls was now a blue backdrop with a white, textured blanket, swirling and wafting, canvassing the floor with its capricious darks.

With resilience, he ate up the distance, until he was within the stony cliffs. Regrettably, they had retained their ghostly physiognomies, the creepy stillness contrasting against the clarifying knocks of disrupted pebbles and shale rumbling down. And then he climbed the final step, and he saw it...

***

The goliath anthropoid stood crowned by the clouds in the sky. The motions of its head caused spirals and whirlwinds within the dense white mists, bordering the heavens.

The gargantuan was entrenched at the waist beneath the ochre wasteland and Jerome oversaw it from the height of a cliff edge.

It was indescribably huge. Jerome hadn't even considered God being this big – well, maybe God, but only just. Its stomach muscles were so scaled up, they were like mountains. It started to turn and Jerome felt the wind pick up, powered by the disturbance of such a mass stirring.

He could see the profiled facial elements and, as it rotated, exposing its frontward aspect, he could liken everything about it to an indistinguishable human, with no defining features and nothing to derive it to a male or a female. Its eyes were closed and yet it was facing him, looking at him, studying him, supplying Jerome with every ounce of its presence.

"You are here, now."

Jerome didn't see its mouth move, but he heard the words. Its speech was an amalgam of every kind of voice, from the deep, husky boom of the arrogant to the meek whimpers of the dying, from the seductive siren of the succubus to the hallowed chant of the cleric. It was the charge *and* the retreat, the divine *and* the demoniac.

"You are here, now," it repeated.

"Why am I here?" Jerome *spoke* his words. He didn't want to rely on thought alone.

"You asked for help."

The words reached him slowly, as though they were also massive objects, struggling to push against the air.

"And I want to help you, just like I helped you get here."

Jerome shuffled uncomfortably. "Help me? Help me how? When? With what?" He wondered: *his Dark Whisperer…*

"It is your *wish, Jerome. Do you not remember?"*

Jerome didn't know if he said 'no' or just thought it.

But it said, *"I shall* help *you to remember. The night you arrived home,"* – he saw it, was there, could remember – *"you knocked on the door and you realised your mother was gone. You knelt, looked up and your silent shout, your prayer, was unheard by everyone, but me. I heard your pain, your wish, and I answered it.*

"…But *what* did I wish for?"

Then, as if it didn't matter, the being said, *"Make a wish, then. You have my attention now, and I do* so *want to help you."* It was the seductive tones at the fore…

"What if I don't want anything?"

"We all *want something.* You *want something. I* know *you want something. It is inside you; it is tearing you apart; I can feel it. And although you can change what you want, you* cannot *change why you are here. What will happen will happen. Why suffer when you don't have to?"*

What did he want? It didn't seem like such a grand gesture when it was twinned with such an obvious threat. But what was the threat?

"I can see your mind working, Jerome. Make your wish."

"I … I—"

"Yes," the voice of *all* voices urged him.

He was harkened back to that night with Keldor, all those years ago, standing outside his house. He immersed himself in the shame and the disappointment. He owed it to her. He owed it to his mother, Driana.

"Very well…"

***

It had been a hard day's work, as he reclined on his bed, the rough, stone walls closing in. He blew out the waning candle and slept.

***

The floor is opening. I don't think I said anything, but the floor still opens and the giant looking at me, through closed eyes, turns his head up as if to ignore me and revolves away. The disruption in the air forces me to find my balance, but the hole before me is big now. It encompasses me and I tumble down, swallowed up by the darkness.

I am afraid.

I miss my friends.

I miss Ana.

I am awake in the strangest place I think I've ever been. I feel slightly queasy, because I can smell death – no, blood. It's too dark to see properly, but something is most definitely not right. Peripherally, I can make out movements and the room begins to brighten. Wait – it's just my eyes getting used to the dark. The ground feels like a bog, soft and squidgy. And sounds like it, too.

But now the room is beginning to get brighter and – oh!

The walls are ... living. They're made of body parts. It's vile. Limbs are sticking out, legs and arms. The fingers are clenching and unfurling. I look down and I can understand why I thought it was a bog. I don't recognise it, but they look like they belong on the inside.

All of a sudden, I am very aware of how much I weigh and how much pressure I'm applying to the floor and, in particular, if any of the organs are going to pop.

Eyes are following me and blinking – they look so much bigger when they're not inside.

I frantically look around to try and find an exit, but seeing none, I look up to where I think I've fallen from. More body parts and eyes greet me, and it really bothers me. With no escape in sight, I start to rush, my hurried response revving my heart rate, drawing my attention to other external hearts, trapped behind ribcages.

From in front of me, hundreds of tiny, fluorescent blue strands are growing, like ivy, towards me. It's quite stunning, but I'm not resisting it. And I can't decide if it's because I don't want to, or if I'm just too sure that it's going to get me anyway...

***

Jerome was working hard, mining. He was in a dark tunnel with a lantern precariously placed in a small, natural dugout. The dream was taking the majority of his thought, as he smashed the rock away with his pickaxe. He wasn't sure why, but he was awash with conflicting emotions. Part of him was adamant that this was his job; that *this* was what he should be doing. But another part felt missing, like there was something really important he should be doing. He felt like a captive in his own mind, like all of this wasn't real.

***

Galliana didn't know who she was anymore, as she chipped away at the wall. Every time even something vaguely familiar was on the tip her mind it was pushed further out of reach. She was effectively erasing her own identity and history by trying to recapture it, but her dream stayed. She had, at least, *something* to keep her occupied – the massive, anthropoid being bearing down, speaking to her, and then the floor opening and swallowing her into the walls of flesh, the blue tentacles extending and touching her, leaving her mind a prisoner, while her energy is feasted upon and devoured.

***

The floor is opening and I'm falling – I must be falling, as I can't feel the ground beneath my feet. I land and I look around.

It's dark, and it feels uncomfortable, but as the light begins to grow – or my eyes begin to adjust – I can see things moving, twitching ... blinking? It's alive.

***

Jerome was busy working in the mines again, his mind wrapped up in the dream. He still felt inundated with things he thought he needed to do, but couldn't remember. He couldn't remember *anything*. But it wasn't so bad as the day before, and he continued.

The hours trickled by with surprising speed. All day he had been focused on his work and hadn't taken even a second to consider anyone else, if there was anyone else. However, he steeled himself and, feeling slightly disobedient, he looked around.

There *were* others and his gaze was immediately picked up on by another. He looked old, worn, but kindly. However, his stare was becoming uncomfortable and Jerome turned back to his work.

His cheeks reddened, as he grew aware that this man was approaching, but he pretended to ignore it and carry on.

"You look familiar," the man said, nearing Jerome.

Good point, Jerome wondered, but he didn't respond.

"Do you know how you got here?" continued the man.

Jerome hadn't thought about it, but now that attention had been drawn to it, he wondered, *how* did *I get here?*

"You can't remember. I also can't remember, but I have dreams."

Jerome was unsteady at this man's admissions. "Do I know you?"

The man ignored Jerome. "I dream that I'm standing on a cliff and I've made a wish."

"Why are you telling me this?" Jerome asked.

"Because ... I think ... you may understand."

"Who are you? And why do you think I'll understand?"

"Valkyre."

Where had he heard that name before?

369

"Valkyre Adin."

Adin – Elisa. "Elisa," he said, remembering the name, but not being able to put a face to it. He just knew it.

"Elisa? The name sounds … familiar, but … I don't … I don't remember."

"We have to get out of here," Jerome muttered, and then he turned to Valkyre. "How do we get out of here?"

"Your guess is as good as mine. I can't even remember how I got here, so getting out could pose a small problem."

Jerome was filled with urgency, as he tried of thinking of a solution. "You say you have dreams, I have dreams, I *also* dream that I'm on a cliff and this massive *thing* is looking at me, talking to me." He was speaking fast, trying to get it out, worried that he might forget. "It's talking about a wish, I think I wish for my mother to be safe and then I find myself in a room … made of…"

"…Living body parts, I know."

"You have the same dream?"

"Yes. I can't remember my wish, but I can see a city – I think it's Arthak – and it's being destroyed."

Arthak? He remembered Arthak and it *was* destroyed. It hadn't occurred to him that these wishes might actually be coming true, but what other power was – *could* possibly be – responsible for demolishing a city? The shock struck Jerome hard. "It was you?

"What do you mean?" Valkyre said, confused.

"Arthak's … dead."

"In my dreams, but not…?"

"Yes… I remember; the streets were empty. The buildings were… It was dead. Why?"

"I was…"

Jerome didn't catch the last words before the surroundings started flickering. The mine, Valkyre – it was all jumping back and forth between this and the abnormal, flesh-crafted room; the balance of each flicker bowing more and more towards the sinewy room, until it stopped, and he was back.

It was like waking up from a dream again, and he quickly refreshed himself by trawling over his experience in The Dark Realm, making sure that he *could* remember.

Everything as it should be, despite being in a room that blinked and twitched, he reflected on the mine and Valkyre. Maybe *that* was the reality and *this* the dream. He stroked his beard. He hadn't shaved for a while, but nonetheless, it didn't seem much longer. He guessed he'd been out for no more than a few hours.

Looking around for an exit, Jerome was reminded of his earlier failure. Dashing his head from wall to wall, he sighed, as an exit appeared to be as real at the dream. And now, the glowing, blue strands were developing again.

He was going to let them take him again, and they almost had, but suddenly he heard something snapping and crunching, coming from behind. He felt the soothing balm of the fluid, blue wires and, as tempting as it was to let them take him, he turned and saw the wall was dying – actually *dying.* The arms hung limply, the hearts that were powering that area stopped and then it crumbled away, forming a pile of grey dust on the floor.

"Come quickly."

He recognised the voice.

"It's Valkyre," – *from the mine?* – "now come on."

He leapt for the hole, making a near miss of falling victim to the blue fibres.

Valkyre's face was so muddied and his beard so long and straggly that it was hard to recognise him at first, but his eyes retained that kindness that he became so familiar with in the dream – or whatever it really was.

"How long have you been here?" Jerome asked.

"Too long. Now let's go."

"What about weapons?"

"Improvise." And Valkyre ripped one of the bones jutting out of the wall.

Chapter XVIII
Conclusions, Final Part

Rudimentarily armed, the pair crossed through the living rooms, Valkyre and Jerome mauling, bludgeoning and killing the vital organs.

***

Percy shook Galliana, but it wasn't working, and the blue strands only held her tighter. He moved to plan *B*, grabbing her by the shoulders and yanking her away. The fluorescent fibres snapped, fizzing as they did, but almost straight after, more began to grow, eager to reclaim what they had been gorging on.

Galliana's eyes crept open. "Percy?"

"Yes, it's me. Can you walk?"

"I just need a minute. Am I still in the mines?"

"We don't have a minute. Come on."

Still dazed, legs barely moving, Galliana was hoisted up and Percy pulled her arm over his shoulder, so that he could support her as he kicked and bashed a way through the sentient walls. It was only his breath she heard. He hadn't the energy to roar; everything was channelled into his legs, as they kicked and kicked and kicked the walls to death.

However, their disruption was not unnoticed and, as they swept from one room to the next, the obsidian evil of the living constructions peeled away and began reforming into vile abominations.

***

With the fear running riot through his body, Jerome followed Valkyre. He felt ridiculous holding onto a bone as a weapon, but it at least gave him something to squeeze while he contemplated what fate – more specifically, his – had in store.

He lost count of how many rooms they had been through; to be truthful, he hadn't been counting them at all, but a heavy number of notional fingers down and something was different.

They crawled through the final hole into what looked like a huge atrium. After a superficial scan, it looked like they had emerged from just one of many flesh and bone annexes that were organised into rows and columns. The walls were lined with finely faceted black gems. And if it weren't for the twinkling of light splashing and dashing, blazing about, it would have appeared no different to a bland stone hall.

Central and conjoining with the ceiling was a giant, black formation. While it had statue-like features – rough features, smooth features, chiselled features, features that stuck out like grotesque limbs and others that gracefully adorned – it also seemed to be an integral part of the structure.

Valkyre looked at it, as mind-blown as Jerome. "How's your climbing?"

It had been a few years since Jerome had climbed a tree, and he couldn't remember ever having scaled a rock face. But he said, "I think we're about to find out."

Valkyre looked at Jerome and, through this entire ordeal, it was a ridiculous line of humour that connected them.

However, Valkyre caught sight of something and the smile in his eyes relinquished to fear.

"Jerome, get climbing. I can hold these off."

Did I tell him my name? "How do *you* know my name?" For everyone seemed to know it…

He smashed his bone down onto the hard ground and it split, creating two sharp, jagged points. "Never mind that. We haven't time, give me that." He indicated the bone in Jerome's hand. "Let's just say that I'm repaying the favour."

Confused, Jerome asked the only question he could. "What favour?" And then said, "Listen, we can both take these."

"No, Jerome," he ordered, snatching the complete bone out of Jerome's hand and discarding the shorter of his two broken halves of pointed bone.

"What about Elisa?" Jerome said.

Valkyre's battle stance suddenly fell, his arms resting by his side, as he turned to Jerome. "Tell her – tell her … don't tell her anything. She will be better off not wasting any more time over an old ghost like me."

As if to try one last attempt to get him to come with him, Jerome offered him back his identity. "Valkyre?"

Valkyre stood, firmly poised with his blunt and sharp dual-wield stance. "Go, now!"

***

"With me," Percy commanded.

She was stable on her feet now. She had been as they crossed the last few rooms and into the oppressive atrium. Percy scanned around and headed straight for the central statue, which he began to climb. When he had enough grip with one hand he lowered his other down to Galliana. She took hold and, with a foot on a lip of the huge sculpture, he pulled her up.

"We're heading up *there*." He indicated above, to where sky was visible.

"I can't make it, Percy."

"You are *going* to make it. Do you hear me?"

***

With his hand, Jerome explored the surface of the statue until getting a firm grip on a nubbin and then wrenching himself up. Progress was slow, but with enormous effort, he slowly crawled up the statue, sometimes finding only very minimal purchase, but always keeping just enough.

A few metres up and he couldn't resist the temptation to look down. Seeping mindlessly towards Valkyre was the horde of abominations, the most revolting and loathsome creatures he had ever seen. Valkyre's defensive manoeuvres were quick and he dispatched with the first, sparse line-up with ease. Jerome knew, just as much as Valkyre, that this was suicide. He would only grow more tired, compared to a growing and overwhelming enemy. He couldn't watch anymore and he returned back to his aching hands and arms.

Above, separated by four beams, were four openings and the blue sky was looking bluer than ever. This central structure was becoming easier to negotiate the higher up he went and Jerome made light work of the final metres.

***

Clutching with burning hands onto one of the beams, he hauled himself up, resting his stomach across it and praying that he'd made it. But as he dismounted onto the dusty wastes, aching from more than just physical exhaustion, he craned his head to the right and, to his alarm, realised that he was being shadowed by the colossal entity. It looked even bigger, and so much more frightening, now that he was so much closer. But it was made all the more worse, as when he looked behind to see the ledge, on which he was earlier stood and judged, it was virtually completely paled by the distance…

***

Percy and Galliana were halfway up when the creatures began swarming around the base. As the first wave centred, they only watched, but as more started assembling, they piled on top of each other and worse, they began forming different amalgams. And they were rising.

"Keep moving," said Percy. "Don't stop. Don't stop for me. Don't stop because it hurts. Don't stop for *anything!*"

"Where are you going?" Galliana exclaimed, seeing Percy moving down.

"Don't stop I said!"

It hurt her ears, but she didn't want to argue. With her fingers absolutely devoid of any feeling, she struggled up farther, rising above the sound of Percy roaring.

***

With surprise under control and clear-headedness back in the main seat, Jerome scanned his surroundings. He was shocked to see that the hole he'd emerged from was just one of many hundreds, probably thousands, maybe millions.

Moments later, he saw an arm poke up through one of the holes. It wasn't far off, and this sign of life – *any* sign of life – got him moving, and he ran. Beside him, the God – as he believed it – was turning and, because he was so much closer, that gentle wind he felt atop the cliff was a hurricane. Sparks of sand and dust, which were picked up by the violence, followed the various flows of the squall, bringing to life the unseen currents and airstreams. The sand-infused air pricked at his skin and the visibility was minimal, but he was near, his instinct *told* him he was near.

Recognising a similar metal beam, onto which he had levered himself to escape, he got to his knees and began fumbling around the edge. Whenever he felt strong enough to brave the cutting sand, he opened his eyes, and when he had traced past the second beam, he caught sight.

The ground rumbled, as the colossus grinded against the walls of its halfway incarceration, continuing to twist and turn the atmosphere above into a maelstrom. He couldn't see it, but he could hear it.

Jerome could see two hands now, desperately holding on, but he could see the fingers losing grip.

"Hold on!" he shouted, battling the howling wind.

He didn't hear a response, but he pushed on, carefully balancing his body along, eager to make contact so that this person wouldn't let go.

He shimmied towards the centre and reached out. He was just able to make a connection, delicately scraping the finger on the nearest hand. He saw it twitch in response and then clamp up, as if given a new strain of hope. He sped up, until he could get a clean purchase.

Taking a look just before throwing down his hand, he was stunned at the sight of Galliana. Beneath her, he saw the weird atrocity creeping up the central statue, and he thought he could see Percy, but he didn't waste any more time before grabbing her elbow. She closed her hand around his and, very careful not to fall off the other side, he helped her on.

Talking was all but impossible, while in the throes of the sandstorm, but they were content just being in each other's touch.

With Jerome moving backwards, he led Galliana to the coarse, hard land. The monstrous thing stopped turning and instantly the tempest began to lessen, its energy killed. The air was still saturated with the desert's dusty surface, but it was settling and the beast was slowly becoming distinguishable through the sand clouds.

It was looking down at them, anger hissing off it, and then it began to tilt forward, bending at the ground level, but circling its shoulders over and stopping at an almost vertical angle above them.

Concluding, and ignoring, the futility to be somewhere between moving mountains and commanding oceans, Jerome moved to protect Galliana. It was going to have to go through him if it wanted to get to her.

Its mouth opened and it raged and roared, the sound another blend of the wicked and the weary. They both covered their ears, but the sound was outright pervasive, resounding *in* them as much as around them.

Unable to bear it anymore, they were floored, knees burrowing into the sand and hands pushed firmly over their ears. And then the noise stopped, but the beast stayed, and then it spoke.

"It is no matter that you have found a way of living. I have what I need."

The storm had calmed now and the massive creature lifted itself up and they began to be removed from this land. In the distance, Jerome tried to focus on the image of a woman, but everything turned dark and he could strain his eyes no more...

***

Jerome was perching on the edge of the precipice, the podium to his right slowly receding back into the floor. He was back, the strange blue fuzz of The Dark Realm hovering around him. In front of him were his friends, Elisa, Keldor and Slayne. He looked to his left and he saw Galliana, also completing her shift back into this world.

But as he looked to his right, there was a disturbance, a shivering in the foreground against the textured sheet of the background. It was human-sized and he thought he recognised it, but he wanted to deny it, fear and uncertainty so much so that he didn't want to find disappointment, but now the features were sharpening and he could discern the familiar qualities. His mother's face was there, and he almost couldn't look…

…*Almost*.

Smiling, he chanced his arm one last time, as he tried to locate his Dark Whisperer. He looked everywhere, between the faces of his friends, behind him over the precipice – where It was last seen – but could find no evidence of It.

With these things now in the reality, he turned to his thoughts. It still stung to think of Peter and Misto, and he was left empty when he considered where Percy might still be, for he hadn't returned with them.

But most of all, how had he come back? How had *they* come back? But he laid his thoughts to rest. It was a long path he had walked and, of the opinion that he had the rest of his life to make sense of it, he needed five minutes.

For now, it was the journey's end and so it was the waves of the tidal realm lapping over him, of friendships forged and forfeit, of beloved found. And yet, never before had he felt so enveloped in the warm embrace of life, while holding hands with death.

***

Garrick slowly came to, invited back to consciousness by a flickering flame. The yellow glow of the candle was a shimmering ripple within the blue profundity. He felt absolutely worn; as he struggled to keep his eyes open and stop the world from spinning.

"It's the umbral fever. It will pass soon," Sahl said.

Garrick listened; a response just yet required too much effort, but he did shift himself up and brace himself on his elbows.

"You work for The Reformation, yes?"

Garrick nodded.

"Good. Now where do your loyalties lie?"

That was a familiar question. It was as much a threat as it was an inquiry. However, as much as his loyalties lay with The Reformation, he felt his demeanour undergo a shift – at least enough to hear this man out. He struggled against the fever and found his voice.

"My loyalties," – he inhaled, still fighting for breath – "are like my interests." Sahl raised an eyebrow. Garrick exhaled. "Susceptible to bribery and/or persuasion."

Sahl twisted into the lambent burn of the candle. He also took a long, drawn-out breath. "I want your help."

"And I'm listening."

"I want to take over The Reformation."

"What makes you think I'd be interested in that?"

"Power, money."

Garrick remained silent.

"…Death?"

Interest piqued, loyalty bought, Garrick spoke. "Where do we begin?"

"All in good time. We have much work to do…"